The Darcy Connection

A NOVEL

ELIZABETH ASTON

A TOUCHSTONE BOOK
PUBLISHED BY SIMON & SCHUSTER
New York London Toronto Sydney

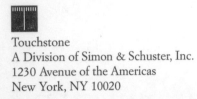

Touchstone
A Division of Simon & Schuster, Inc.
1230 Avenue of the Americas
New York, NY 10020

This book is a work of fiction. Names, characters, places, and incidents either are products of the author's imagination or are used fictitiously. Any resemblance to actual events or locales or persons, living or dead, is entirely coincidental.

First Touchstone trade paperback edition March 2008

TOUCHSTONE and colophon are registered trademarks of Simon & Schuster, Inc.

For information about special discounts for bulk purchases, please contact Simon & Schuster Special Sales at 1-800-456-6798 or business@simonandschuster.com.

Manufactured in the United States of America

10 9 8 7 6 5 4 3 2 1

Library of Congress Control Number: 2007039278

ISBN-13: 978-1-4165-4725-9
ISBN-10: 1-4165-4725-8

For Naomi Harries
Thank you!

Chapter One

"They cannot marry! It is impossible. Out of the question. I will not have it."

The bishop, for once shocked into silence by the vehemence of Squire Diggory's words, stared at his neighbour, his mind divided into alarm at the prospect of losing the goodwill of a man of consequence and influence, and displeasure at the folly of his younger daughter.

Sir Roger Diggory and his neighbour the Bishop of Ripon were sitting in deep leather armchairs in the library of Diggory Hall, a rambling mansion dating from the days of Queen Elizabeth, which had been shaped into some semblance of modernity by the addition of a noble classical façade and here in the library, by a remodelling in the style of Adam.

It was Sir Roger's mother and the present Lady Diggory who were responsible for these improvements; for himself, the squire was perfectly content to have his house and possessions just as they had been for generations of former Diggorys, who now lay in seemly ranks in the Diggory vaults of the nearby church.

A church that would not, Sir Roger insisted, thumping his fists on the arms of his chair, ever celebrate the nuptials of his son and Bishop Collins's daughter.

The bishop found his voice at last. "No, no, it is not to be thought of." No such marriage could possibly be countenanced! Yet, was Sir Roger perhaps making too much of a mere friendship? Anthony Diggory and the bishop's daughter Eliza had known one another for several years, were accustomed to being in one another's company. For himself, he had no idea of anything stronger than a kind of brother and sister affection.

"That's because you're a fool, Bishop." Sir Roger had a reasonable respect for the cloth, but first things first, and his family and his ambitions for his children far outweighed any need for civility to a man simply because he wore gaiters and a bishop's apron. Clergyman or not, the man needed to be sharper than that. "Maybe Miss Eliza wasn't making sheep's eyes at Anthony when he went away to Oxford. That don't signify; it's what she's been up to since he got back that worries me. And his mother. And should worry you."

Bishop Collins squirmed in his seat, which creaked at the pressure, causing the dog lying before the fire to raise his head and look at him. A look that seemed to say, Take care, Bishop.

Sheep's eyes! What had Eliza been up to behind her parents' back? That he should live to hear a daughter of his described in such a fashion. "I have no wish to defend my daughter's behaviour, if it is as you say—"

"It is, or I would not have said it."

"However, Anthony cannot be entirely . . . He is older than she, and—"

"Pooh! Older by some eighteen months, what's that?"

"He has a wider experience of the world, and surely—"

"Are you suggesting that my son has wilfully set himself to win the affections of your daughter? Are you calling him a seducer, sir? A rake, perhaps?"

Sir Roger was a bulky man, and his normally florid face was assuming an even more alarming hue; he might be about to succumb to an apoplectic fit. The bishop was quick with his protestations that he meant nothing of the kind. "Eliza is young, and young for her years. She is inclined to be impulsive—"

"Any inclination to impulsiveness should have been whipped out of her when she was a child."

"What I am saying is that we should not mistake high spirits and innocence for anything worse."

Sir Roger glared at the bishop from beneath bristly eyebrows. "I am not in the habit of making mistakes. The mistakes, sir, lie with your daughter in presuming to lay out her lures for my son, and with you for not having seen what she was up to, and putting an immediate end to it."

"I will speak to her directly we are home. I assure you that she will feel the full weight of a father's anger and disappointment."

The squire grunted. "All very well, but what needs to be done is to separate them."

"You think Anthony should go away for a time?"

"Anthony? I do not. Why should he be driven from his home, just when I need him to learn about the estate? No, no, that's not what I mean at all. Eliza must go. Send her away. Send her to Derbyshire, to those grand connections of yours, send her to stay with the Darcys."

Send her to Pemberley? It was a tempting thought, an easy way out of a difficulty—only, how to justify such an action to his daughter, or his wife? Mr. Darcy's daughters were all away from there, all married—one way or the other—Mr. Collins made it his business to know all the secrets of the Darcy family. Mr. and Mrs. Darcy were not in Derbyshire at present, he recollected. They were abroad again, on government business, Austria once again. Eliza would not want to go to Derbyshire to stay with her two youngest cousins, that was certain.

Sir Roger rose, hitched his breeches up over his spreading waist, and kicked a log into the fire. "See to it, Bishop. Talk to your wife, she don't want for sense. And now we must join the others, or they'll begin to wonder what we're so busy about, here in the library. Ecclesiastical business, we shall tell them, that'll put a stop to any questions. Ha!"

It had been a large gathering for dinner at Diggory Hall, for Sir

Roger and his lady enjoyed entertaining and were on good terms with most of the inhabitants of houses within visiting distance. A full moon made driving easy, the Diggorys' cook was a master with the substantial viands that pleased Yorkshire people, and Sir Roger's cellar was famous; no one refused his invitations to dine.

The party from Ripon filled the bishop's carriage. Apart from Bishop Collins and Mrs. Collins, their two daughters accompanied them: Charlotte, who was twenty-one, and Eliza, who had just had her twentieth birthday. In addition, making rather a crush on the seat, was the formidable presence of Lady Grandpoint, Mrs. Collins's aunt, who was paying a visit after taking the waters at Harrogate. The bishop had set off in good spirits, feeling his consequence enhanced by a ladyship in the family; now, on the way home, he was silent and gloomy.

The carriage rattled through the stately gates and up the drive to halt with a flourish before the doors of the Palace. Usually, the bishop gave a sigh of contentment at this point. A man of little intellect and less understanding, he felt vastly satisfied with his lot. Advancement in the Church had been more rapid and taken him further than he could ever have hoped, and until this last week, he would have defied any churchman in the kingdom to be more pleased with his life.

Tonight there was no long exhalation of prelatical breath, no expansion of his chest, decked in purple, no gracious nod to the coachman or to the waiting butler.

"Old gas and gaiters is in a mood tonight," the coachman observed to the groom as he swung down from his perch.

The groom, who had swiftly and expertly removed the carriage horses from their traces, paused in his work of rubbing one of them down. "Dined up at Diggory Hall, didn't they? Squire's in a rare taking on account of Mr. Anthony being sweet on our Miss Eliza. I dare say they had words about it." He gave the horse a slap on its broad rump to emphasise his point.

"It'd be a good match for her, she'd be Lady Diggory one day."

"It won't come to that, her ladyship has other ideas for Mr. Anthony, you mark my words."

Neither of the girls paid any attention to their father's brooding mood. Had Eliza thought about it, she might have wondered why, after a convivial evening, with plentiful wine, her father should be so morose, why his heightened colour spoke of temper rather than joviality. As it was, she cared nothing for how anyone looked or felt, since she had no thoughts for anyone except Anthony.

She had looked forward to the dinner party with the keenest anticipation, revelling in the delight of the hours to be spent in Anthony's company. He would contrive it so that they would sit next to each other at dinner, and then later there might be dancing, Sir Roger loved to see young people enjoying themselves, and Maria Diggory's governess was a dab hand at playing waltzes and country dances upon the pianoforte.

Until she entered the great hall at Diggory Hall, where the company was assembled, it never occurred to her that Anthony might not be there. As she dropped her curtsy to Lady Diggory and greeted the numerous company, all known to her, her eyes scanned the room, as though Anthony could be lurking in the shadows.

He was not. Anthony, Sir Roger blandly informed Mrs. Collins in Eliza's hearing, had gone away for a few days, to Udall Farm, where a few matters needed attending to on his father's behalf. Too far for him to ride over for the dinner party, although he had been eager to do so.

"No, no, I told him. There's no one here this evening that he won't see again while the good weather holds, and he's not to be riding twenty miles each way for a party at his father's house. I dare say he'll have found some like-minded young men around there to pass a pleasant evening with, no need for a young man to sit alone when the day's work is done."

It was all said in a light-hearted tone, but Eliza knew that his beady eyes were regarding her with no great liking. She turned away to find Charlotte standing beside her.

"You were set for an evening's flirting," her sister said. "Instead, you look as though you couldn't find yourself in more disagreeable company."

It was amazing that Charlotte could be so blind. If Eliza didn't know her so well, she would have said Charlotte was being malicious, but Charlotte was never malicious. Eliza knew how little notice her sister took of other people, and she suspected that Charlotte, wrapped in her own remote world, cared too little about most of her fellow human beings ever to need or to want to be malicious. Charlotte clearly had no idea how things were between Eliza and Anthony; well, that was all to the good, otherwise she might feel obliged to mention it to Mama, and then there might be trouble. No, *would* be trouble, and Eliza and Anthony had been so careful, so circumspect, had made so much effort to keep secret their growing delight in one another's company, that it would be dreadful to have it come out in such a way.

From the moment, a mere few weeks ago, when she had laughed up at Anthony and said in her curiously husky voice, "You are grown mighty fine, Mr. Diggory, after your time at Oxford," and he, about to refute any such suggestion with vigour, had instead gazed at her for one long moment before folding her in his arms for a kiss that had nothing of the brotherly about it, Eliza's world had changed.

The sun rose in a glory she had never before noticed. The greening countryside, alive with the promise of spring, glowed with life. Her mother seemed all amiability, and she even felt tolerant towards her father, instead of daily reminding herself that she must accept him for what he was and telling herself it was not her place to be passing judgement on her papa.

The simmering resentment that had accompanied her growing out of childhood into adulthood, the resentment born of the knowledge that she was the favourite of neither of her parents, fell away, and like so many other small rubs and pricks dropped out of her consciousness altogether. Her older brother's prosy ways no longer irritated her, and she did her duties with a good grace, scattering the corn in the poultry yard and gathering eggs, laughing at the antics of birds as they clucked and fought and pushed against one another, spending quiet hours in the herb room and even making some efforts with her needlework, no longer a thankless task when she could think of Anthony while she set her stitches.

It was the first time she had been in love, if you didn't count an early and unaccountable passion for Prince Leopold, glimpsed at a distance on a childhood visit to London. And Anthony, too, told her that she was his first love, although Eliza's more rational self told her that after three years at the university, with trips to London whenever he could manage it, this was unlikely to be true.

"That's not the same," he protested when challenged. "I've never been in love, I've never felt like this before. Every day is dazzling to me, simply because you exist! I don't understand it at all. How have you grown so beautiful and so dear to me? How came I never to notice what you were like before?"

He must be in love to call her beautiful. Eliza had no illusions about her looks. Her face was well enough, and she had a good figure, but beside Charlotte, whose beauty grew more astonishing every day, she was a cipher.

"Charlotte doesn't have your lovely eyes," Anthony said, kissing her eyelids to make his point.

What nonsense; Charlotte's eyes were remarkable for their size and brilliance.

"A painter might like them," Anthony said. "I don't, they aren't sparkling like yours, and they don't crinkle up when she smiles. Not," he added, "that Charlotte does smile very much."

"Charlotte has a lovely smile."

"I suppose so, but has she any heart? Oh, well, she'll marry a rising clergyman and all that perfection will go to waste."

Which was probably true. Whom else could Charlotte marry? With a very modest fortune, and of no particular family, she would be lucky to catch the attention of any youngish clergyman and could not hope for a handsome one. With so few eligible young men in the neighbourhood, the outlook for her was not good. Nor was it for Eliza, and when she and her close friends talked over the talent of the neighbourhood, they were wont to sigh and declare that it was hopeless, that unless their various mamas took them to York or Harrogate to the assemblies, or, best of all, to London for a season, how were they ever to find good husbands?

There was no question of assembly balls and parties in York or Harrogate for Charlotte and Eliza. Mr. Collins didn't approve of frivolity in any of its guises, and although Eliza knew that her mother had tried to persuade him that the girls needed to spread their wings so that they might meet suitable young men, he had always disagreed. His girls would find husbands at home, here in Ripon, among the unmarried clergymen who visited, or were appointed to livings in the diocese.

And now this miracle had happened, and Eliza had fallen in love with Anthony, and he was head over ears in love with her. And Aunt Grandpoint had appeared, like the fairy godmother in the stories, wanting—no, demanding—that she take Charlotte to London. Eliza wished her sister well, she wished everyone well just now. Why should Charlotte not have a chance of finding the same happiness that she had found with Anthony?

Lady Grandpoint was by far the grandest member of her family. She was sister to Mrs. Collins's mother, Lady Lucas, and had been married young to a respectable man of no especial position or fortune. Later on, widowed, and grown into a remarkable beauty—"I was very much like Charlotte is when I was her age," she informed them with some complacency—she had made an excellent and unexpected second marriage, far better than she could have hoped for, when a distinguished nobleman had met her on a trip to Bath and fallen in love with her. They had had no children; the younger Charlotte was her goddaughter, and this chance trip to Yorkshire had brought to fruition a plan that had long lingered in Lady Grandpoint's mind.

"I wasn't sure whether it would be kind until I set eyes on Charlotte, now that she is grown up," she told Mrs. Collins. "For a girl who has nothing to recommend her, no family, no money, no looks, a London season is the cruellest thing. But heavens above, the girl is a diamond, an astonishing beauty! With looks like that, there's no knowing whose fancy she may not catch. And, moving in the first circles as we do, she will have every opportunity to shine in the best company."

Lady Grandpoint had reckoned without the bishop. He did not want his beloved Charlotte going off to London, where she might fall prey to all kind of adventurers.

"Adventurers? Not under my roof, Bishop, I assure you," said Lady Grandpoint, her eyebrows raised in a haughty stare.

Bishop Collins could not give his consent. His girls had been brought up to be sober, industrious creatures, who would make good wives to hard-working, respectable clergymen, just as their mother was. Charlotte was a serious girl, with a mind above dancing and parties and the foolishness of London, a dangerous place for any young woman. True, her portion was small, and therefore every effort should be made to find her a suitable husband, but once the estate at Longbourn was his, he would be much better able to provide for his daughters from the income it provided.

"As to that, Eliza may marry a hard-working clergyman, if one can be found to have her," said Lady Grandpoint. "I detect a pert quality to that girl, Bishop. But Charlotte's beauty is an opportunity, not only for herself but for the whole family."

Bishop Collins had begged to differ, he must be permitted to know what was best for the women in his family.

His son, Charles, was keen in his support. "There is the expense, madam," he said to his great-aunt. "A London season, on however small a scale, is not to be thought of for a girl in Charlotte's circumstances."

"Circumstances may change," said Lady Grandpoint, with chilly disdain.

Chapter Two

So the matter might have rested, had Bishop Collins not received alarming news from Longbourn. Not alarming news of a welcome kind, such as that Mr. Bennet, his cousin, whose entailed estate would pass to Mr. Collins on his death, had fallen into fits or met with an accident. No, this was news of quite a different kind. There was a widow lately come into the neighbourhood; she had taken a house near Meryton, and it was clear that she and Mr. Bennet were getting along famously. Rumour was rife, said Bishop Collins's correspondent; the bishop took good care to keep himself informed about every detail of his cousin's life.

"It could not be worse," he said, handing his wife the letter.

"I never heard of such a thing, my lord," cried Mrs. Collins. "What can the man be at? He is past sixty, a widower these ten years, far too old to be indulging such fancies."

"Men have married before in their sixties and even seventies."

"True, but she cannot be such a young woman. A widow, you say?"

"Read the letter through. You see her age is mentioned, Harold has taken the trouble to ascertain all the details. She is not above five-and-thirty."

"Five-and-thirty, he could be her father, it is disgraceful behaviour. She is childless, though," she said, turning the sheet. "There were no children of her first marriage."

"Yet it is often so, that a woman's second marriage proves more fruitful than the first, and five-and-thirty is not too old for child bearing."

"Although risky," said Mrs. Collins. "A first child at that age, well . . ."

Terrible visions of a healthy son, a boy who would cut off the entail and deprive the Collinses of the house and two thousand a year that was their rightful inheritance, didn't need to be spoken aloud.

Aunt Grandpoint was soon in possession of the contents of the letter, and she did not, as she announced in ringing tones, care for the news at all. "You may be sure this hussy will do all she can to ensnare Mr. Bennet, of course she will. No, unless Mr. Bennet should go to meet his maker in the very near future, I think you can say farewell to your two thousand a year."

Bishop Collins gave vent to some most un-Christian language, which went almost unnoticed by his wife and her aunt as they contemplated the end to these hopes which had burned so brightly for so many years.

"There is no point repining," said Lady Grandpoint with her accustomed briskness. "It isn't only the money, it is also a matter of position. A minor bishop with a good inherited estate stands quite differently in the eyes of the world and, I may say, in the eyes of those who hand out appointments, from one who has only the income from his bishopric and one or two livings. Ripon does not carry a large income, as we know. In which case, my dear Bishop, you must seek advancement and an increase of income in the only way left to you. You must obtain a better bishopric, one that provides a more substantial income. Salisbury, Wells, Gloucester, one of those."

Bishop Collins shut his eyes to conceal the expression of pain that crossed his features. Lady Grandpoint had touched a sensitive spot, for, happy as he was to be Bishop of Ripon, the comparatively small stipend had always been a drawback. Moreover, in his heart of hearts, he had a hope that, once in possession of the Longbourn estate, more of the good things that the Church had to offer might come his way. The senior bishoprics tended to go to men with great connections or a good income, so perhaps, in due course, he might find himself installed in the close of one of the great cathedrals.

His careful ways and Mrs. Collins's shrewd housekeeping had made a small income go a long way, and now that they were more comfortably off, he and his family lacked for little. But what was there in that to encourage the minds of those who had the high Church appointments in their hands to look in his direction? His talents alone would not recommend him, and although he was assiduous in cultivating anyone who might advance his clerical career, the truth was that he simply did not move in sufficiently high circles for this to be of much use. He had been lucky in his patrons, but their patronage had extended as far as it was going to.

He gave a kind of groan, and his wife patted him comfortingly on his arm, her eyes full of concern.

"Pull yourself together," said Lady Grandpoint. "This settles it, Bishop. Your only hope lies with Charlotte. If she can attach herself to a man in a good position, a man whose voice counts in the circles of the great, why, then there is hope for you. For her husband would obviously prefer that his father-in-law should be Bishop of Lincoln or Bath or Wells or some such diocese, and speak with authority in the Lords, than that he should be languishing in Yorkshire, with an insufficient income to be able to attend sessions in the House on a regular basis." She didn't add that she, too, would prefer for her niece's husband to be among the great and good of the land.

It was settled. Charlotte was to go to London. There had been a difficult moment, when Mrs. Collins had felt it was her duty to accompany her daughter, but this idea was quickly quashed by her aunt and her husband and son.

"It will be hard enough providing for Charlotte," Charles said with a heavy frown. "Were you to go, there must be clothes and so on for you—"

"As to that," said Lady Grandpoint, looking down her nose at Charles, who was, she thought, nearly as dull and pompous as his father, "as to that, I shall see to everything that is necessary for Charlotte. No, do not thank me, she is my goddaughter, and I want her to have this opportunity, which I am sure she will make good use of."

Charlotte, on hearing of her good fortune, had smiled with unusual animation, which gave her lovely face even more beauty; Lady Grandpoint nodded her head in approval. "Looking like that, my dear, and dressed fine, you will turn the head of any man."

Eliza was delighted for her sister. She was fond enough of Charlotte, although always wondering how anyone could go through life with such calmness, a calmness that might even be called passivity. But it was right that her beauty should be shown to the wider world. No, she assured her mother, she felt not the slightest jealousy at Charlotte's good fortune. No one would look twice at Eliza if she went to London, and besides, she was perfectly happy here in Yorkshire.

She spoke no more than the truth. The sisters, so close in age, had neither been close friends nor indulged in the spiteful hostility which can sometimes arise between sisters. They were so different in character, had so little in common beyond the circumstances of their family life, that it was not so very surprising. Eliza was quick: in apprehension, in wit, in movement. She loved to laugh and took a keen interest in her fellow creatures and in ideas and opinions from beyond her immediate circle. In contrast, Charlotte was self-contained, resolute, quiet in voice and manners. It was almost, Eliza sometimes felt, as though her sister were in a state of waiting—for what? A prince? A revelation? Her self-control and reserve irritated her livelier sister, who disliked all forms of priggishness.

Still, family bonds were a strong tie, and Eliza did truly rejoice for Charlotte, and she knew that if her attachment to Anthony had been acceptable to his parents, if they could have entered into an engagement with the approval of both families, then Charlotte would have been pleased for her, in her cool way.

"You are a good girl," said Mrs. Collins to Eliza. "And we must look about for a husband for you, although you are young yet, barely twenty. Why, I didn't marry until I was nearly thirty, there is plenty of time for you to find yourself a suitable husband. And when *your* godmother comes back to England, I am sure you can go and stay with her for a few weeks."

Mrs. Collins sometimes felt that it had been unwise to ask her dear friend Elizabeth, who had made such a brilliant match when she caught the fancy of and married the rich Mr. Darcy, to be her younger daughter's godmother. It was as though an impish fairy had crept into the child's cradle and blown some of the liveliness and high spirits of Elizabeth into her namesake, for certainly, from the time she opened her eyes and smiled, it was evident that Eliza took after neither her father nor her mother.

Not for the first time, Mrs. Collins felt uneasy about Eliza. There was a glow to her that she could not like, and she had been almost sweet-tempered these last few weeks, and Eliza had formerly always had a quick temper which she found hard to control. Well, she was growing up, leaving behind the fidgets and fancies of her girlhood. Had there been a young man in question—but, no, who was there? Eliza had made no new acquaintance in the neighbourhood, there was no one new to meet. She had none but the men she had known any time these five years. No, she must just feel relieved that her younger, troublesome daughter might be growing more sensible and calm.

"You are not to mention it, but Charlotte is even more fortunate than at first appears. Lord Grandpoint's money will of course go to his family, but my aunt has some money from her first husband, and her settlement, and she hints that she will leave it to Charlotte. Expectations, of even a modest kind, added to Charlotte's beauty make me very hopeful for a good match for her."

"Oh, a good match," said Eliza. "I care nothing for a good match, as the world calls it. I only hope that Charlotte will meet a man she can love."

Mrs. Collins gave her daughter a sharp look, but Eliza's head was bent dutifully over her sewing.

"I hope that Charlotte will love her husband, whoever he may be, just as she ought."

Eliza helped with the preparations for Charlotte's trip with a will. Lady Grandpoint announced her intention to extend her stay in Yorkshire, so that Charlotte might accompany her back to London. "I shall write to Grandpoint," she said, "and tell him not to expect me so soon as I had planned. There is no point of going to the cost of another carriage for Charlotte when she can travel with me. And there can be no question of her going anything other than post, such a beautiful young woman could not travel on the common stage."

Eliza, still unaware of the storm that had broken around her father's head, took herself to bed, consoled by the thought that Anthony could not need to spend long at Udall, that he might be back the very next day, and if she walked in the Western Woods, and he were to be riding there— She laughed at herself. If he were back, he would certainly be riding in the woods. They had a trysting spot, beneath an ancient oak, just off the bridle path, where they could sit on his cloak and talk and gaze into each other's eyes and steal kisses, while always on the alert for some other walker or rider or a woodsman taking that way home.

Upstairs, Bishop Collins, in his ponderous way, was telling the doleful news to a horrified Mrs. Collins, while in the adjoining bedchamber, Charlotte slept the deep sleep of one whose conscience was utterly clear, and whose behaviour had been rewarded by this unsought treat of a London season.

In Diggory Hall, Sir Roger was also talking to his wife. They had retired for the night to their panelled bedchamber, a room that he had refused to have redone in the modern style, and her ladyship's maid had been dismissed. Lady Diggory was already in their high fourposter bed, where generations of Diggorys had been begotten, born, and died. Sir Roger wrapped his voluminous nightgown around his still well-muscled legs, pulled his nightcap firmly on to his head, and climbed in beside his spouse.

"That's done," he said. "I put it to the bishop fair and square. We'll have no trouble from him, he knows which side his bread is buttered. I've told him he must send the girl away, she's to go to Derbyshire, I believe, to Pemberley."

Lady Diggory drew her mouth into a tight line. Derbyshire! That was not so very far away; a vigorous young man might think he could make the journey to Derbyshire. Cornwall would be better, or the far north of Scotland, a remote isle among the Hebrides, for example. "Isn't one of the Darcy daughters living in Rome? Perhaps a trip abroad? Indeed, a continent between Anthony and that young woman would be best of all."

Sir Roger snorted. "Bishop Collins would never allow that, his daughter among all the papists? No, Derbyshire is the best we can hope for, she can go and rusticate there and perhaps her rich cousins will find her a husband." He made the snorting, sighing noise that indicated he was about to settle himself to sleep. "She must be got rid of before Anthony returns. I'll send a note to Collins in the morning, telling him to be quick about sending her off."

"Mrs. Collins may not be happy for her to go to Derbyshire; you talk of husbands and she won't meet any likely young men at Pemberley with the family away."

"We don't know they're away."

"Mr. and Mrs. Darcy are abroad, for Mrs. Collins told me so last week. And she is right to be concerned, that girl needs a husband."

"Not Anthony."

"I hope he doesn't take it too hard," said Lady Diggory. "If he imagines himself in love . . ."

"Nonsense! Out of sight, out of mind. Boy and girl stuff, and he's too old for that."

"She's a taking creature, Miss Eliza."

"Eh?"

"A flirt, too. Men like her."

"Well, I don't," said Sir Roger, heaving himself over to blow out the candle.

Chapter Three

Maria Diggory clattered into the stables at the Bishop's Palace in a swirl of red skirts, causing the groom and coachman to exchange glances. She was Anthony's younger sister, and as a close friend of Eliza's, she was a familiar visitor to the Palace. She unhooked her leg from the pommel of her saddle and slid to the ground before the groom could help her to dismount.

"Look after Plum for me, I will be a while," she said, thrusting the reins into the groom's hands. She gathered up her riding habit and almost ran out of the yard.

"Wonder what she's up to?" said the groom, stroking the mare's nose. "She's been riding at a cracking pace; look at the lather on this horse."

"Out and about without a groom, too; her mother would be fair vexed if she knew."

Maria was a frequent visitor to the Palace and knew all the ins and outs of the venerable building. Eschewing the normal entrance through the front door, with the inevitable need for the butler to greet her and announce her, she slipped through a side door and up a small staircase that led to the room Charlotte and Eliza used as a sitting room. This was a lofty chamber on the second floor, panelled as so many of the rooms in the Palace were. Mullioned windows kept out much of the light, except on the sunniest of days, but shelves of books, an old spinet with piles of music, and a neat table for Charlotte's embroidery showed that the dimness didn't deter the sisters.

"Thank goodness you are here, and alone, Eliza," Maria cried as she rushed in through the door.

Eliza, sitting in the window embrasure with her knees drawn up and a book resting on them, looked up in surprise. "Why, Maria, how hot you look. Is something amiss? Why are you here?" And then, suddenly anxious: "Nothing has happened to Anthony?"

"No, no. Well, not exactly, but I am the bearer of ill news!"

Eliza was used to her friend's melodramatic way of speaking, culled from intensive reading of popular novels whose heroines were greatly admired by Maria.

"What ill news? Take off your hat, sit down, and I shall ring for lemonade for you."

"No, no, there is not a moment to lose! And no one must know that I am here."

"Since I see that you rode over and therefore your mare will be in the stables, your arrival can hardly be a secret," said Eliza, giving the frayed bell-pull a tug. "News flies from the stables to the kitchen faster than you can run." And as a maid put her head round the door with an enquiring look, she asked for a jug of lemonade.

"Yes, Miss, and I dare say Miss Diggory would like to freshen herself," said the maid, eyeing Maria's disordered hair, and sniffing ostentatiously, for Maria had brought a strong smell of horse into the room with her.

"Water and a towel, then," said Eliza, ignoring Maria's exasperated expression.

Cleaned and refreshed, even against her will, Maria finally was able to pour out her news. "It is the worst imaginable," she declared. "Father is determined to separate you and Anthony. He has noticed how fond you are of one another—"

"We have been so very careful!" cried Eliza, alarmed. "Anthony always said we must be circumspect, that his father would be won round in the end, and that your mother, who is so fond of Anthony, would be on our side . . ."

"Anthony was wrong, she is furious! It's because she dotes on him so that she's angry about you. She wants him to marry an heiress. Oh, I don't understand her! How can she care for money when a person's happiness is at stake?"

"She cares for Anthony."

"She cares for money in the bank, and money to do more horrid things to the house, and being able to lord it over her neighbours, saying what a good match her precious son has made."

"If that's what she wants, then she definitely won't approve of our marriage. I'm not a good match, no one could say I am. Yet, when we are so deeply attached, she may come to understand that Anthony can't be happy without me."

Even as Eliza spoke, she knew she was deceiving herself. She wasn't a romantically inclined sixteen-year-old, as Maria was, with everything clear-cut, believing that love conquered all, that love was all that mattered. Eliza had fallen for Anthony with no thought of worldly advantage. He was considered, by local standards at least, a very good catch, as the vulgar would put it, but that had nothing to do with her feelings for him. There had been no intent to attract him, no setting her cap at him, it had been a coup de foudre, a sudden strike at her heart that made her, who had always prided herself on being rational, and who had never felt more than a mild pleasure in her flirtatious interludes, realize how blind she had been, how unaware of just how powerful love could be.

Anthony was—well, inexpressibly dear to her. He filled her thoughts and her heart, and the happiness she felt in loving him and knowing that he loved her was greater than any she had felt in her life.

None of this would matter to Lady Diggory, who, while civil enough to Eliza, had not, Eliza knew, ever liked her very much. She was just the younger daughter of the bishop, a pretty figure at the table or in the country dances, but never, Eliza had to admit to herself, likely to be on the list of eligible brides for her beloved son.

"If only she could be persuaded. If Anthony could talk to her about how he feels," she said lamely.

"It is no good," said Maria. "Papa is adamant, and he is the most obstinate of men. I believe Mama has been watching you; if it is she who told him of what she suspected, she will have done so in such a way as to present you in the worst possible light. Papa thinks he rules the roost, but it is not so. Mama controls him, even though he does not acknowledge it. She is determined that you and Anthony must be separated."

"Is that why Anthony has gone away?" A sudden fear gripped Eliza. "Did he know? Did he go at his mother's command, does he agree to our being separated?"

"Of course not," cried Maria, her cheeks flushed again. "How can you say that? He was grumbling at having to go to Udall, he didn't want to go at all, only Papa insisted."

"He sent me no message, no note saying he was going to be absent from the party."

"He is not a great writer of notes or anything else. He asked me to tell you, but when you arrived, Mama had sent me upstairs to change, she said she didn't like my dress, Mama is so stuffy sometimes. By the time I rejoined the company, you had already discovered he wasn't to be there."

Eliza was looking at Maria with sharper eyes. "Maria, how come you to know all this, about what your parents think of our attachment?"

"I heard Papa and Mama discussing it."

"You have been eavesdropping again, they cannot have known you were within earshot."

"How could they, when I was on the other side of their bedroom door, which is made of oak? Fortunately, it has a large keyhole, and the key is missing. I could tell something was up, with Papa closeted with your father in the library all that while. Church business, indeed, I'm not so foolish as to believe that story. When Papa emerged with the bishop, he was making such faces at Mama! He has no discretion, he is a hopeless dissembler."

"Maria, you should not listen at doors." And I should not permit myself to hear what you overheard, she told herself, but curiosity and the desperation of her circumstances overcame her scruples.

"Do you want to know or not?" said Maria.

"Tell me, then."

"*You* are to be sent away, not Anthony. That is what Papa told Bishop Collins. He says that Anthony has been away long enough at university and so on, and now he is to be at home to help run the estate and learn the ropes. He told Mama that your father has agreed that you are to go away. Papa is writing to the bishop today, this morning, to say you have to go at once, that he wants you out of the county before Anthony returns from Udall."

"Dear God!" said Eliza. "Sent away? Where, pray, am I to be sent?"

"Derbyshire."

"Derbyshire! I might have known it. To Pemberley, of course."

"You have been before, and enjoyed your visits, but of course now, it is all different."

"Yes, for all my cousins except the two boys are in London or Paris or wherever, and Mr. and Mrs. Darcy are gone abroad."

"How old are the boys?"

"Oh, they are just boys, still at home with a governess or tutor or some such. I will not go. They can't drag me there."

Maria had a streak of practicality beneath her romantic fervour. "They can," she said. "Not exactly drag, but they can force you to do as they want. You know they can."

"And my father has agreed to this, I expect without an argument. I suppose he feels he must keep in Sir Roger's good books."

Eliza was bitter; she was well aware that her father would go out of his way not to offend anyone of rank or wealth or position. Sir Roger was influential in the county, was well regarded by the clerical hierarchy, a man Bishop Collins would be anxious not to offend. And yet you would think her father would welcome the match for his daughter. How could he not want to see her married to a man like Anthony?

Her heart melted even as she said his name to herself. How could she bear to be parted from him? "How long does it take to ride from here to Derbyshire?"

"Too long for Anthony to go there, if my father is keeping an eye on him and making sure he is always busy, which you may be sure he will. For a while at least, for both he and Mama are convinced it is no more than a passing fancy, that as soon as you are gone, Anthony will begin to forget you, and they will make every effort to cast other girls in his way, ones they approve of. There's Harriet Woolcombe, she has twenty-five thousand pounds and will inherit land as well."

"Harriet! Anthony couldn't marry Harriet."

"Oh, he would never look at her, she's a dab of a thing, with nothing but her fortune to recommend her."

"She will turn into just such a frump as her mother. Oh, what am I saying?"

Eliza realised that in her consternation she was even feeling a pang of jealousy over Harriet, of all people. Dull, plain Harriet. Anthony wasn't in love with Harriet, he was in love with her. Didn't she trust Anthony? Of course she did, and in that, she considered his parents knew him less well than she did. He was steadfast, and wouldn't be so easily detached from her. What was obstinacy in the father was honour and trustworthiness in the son.

"What am I to do if I'm to be sent away before he comes back? When is he due to return?"

"Ah, as to that, I have been busy on your behalf. I rode here this morning with the groom, but as soon as we were out of sight of the Hall, I sent him off to Udall with a note for Anthony, informing him of what Papa and Mama are up to, and telling him to meet you in the wood this afternoon."

"Maria, you didn't."

"I did."

"You rode here on your own?" Eliza knew that Lady Diggory had insisted that Maria, who was inclined to be a dashing rider, must always ride out with her groom in attendance. Maria had fought against this, but had had to agree, or be forbidden the stables. As it was, she often rid herself of her groom's company by a combination of charm and bribery; he was young and impressionable and thought highly of his intrepid young mistress.

"You will get him into trouble. If your mother or father discovers what he has been up to, he will be turned off."

"He will not mind so much. I shall give him a character, I can forge my father's signature very well, you know, and he wants to go and work in a London house in any case. He doesn't like being in the country." Maria poured herself out another glass of lemonade. "Where is Charlotte?"

"Practising the piano, you know she always does so at this time of the morning."

Maria pulled a face. "That is what Mama will say I should be doing, an hour at the piano, an hour with my Italian grammar—what is the point of learning Italian, when I shall never go there? Then there is needlework, and I can help her in the still-room. Charlotte practises of her own accord, I suppose."

"You know she does, and she doesn't need to study her Italian grammar, because she mastered the language with our governess."

"Oh, well, she will be off to London soon, with her accomplishments and beauty. Stay, do you think that if she makes a great match, my parents would look more kindly on your marrying Anthony?"

"Not unless the great match decides to give his sister-in-law a handsome dowry," said Eliza.

"It could happen. In *The Duke's Revenge,* do you remember, where Sophronia—"

"Between the marbled covers of a novel, it might happen, but not in real life, I assure you. And I don't want Charlotte to make a great match, and remember that although she is beautiful, she has no fortune. I want her to meet a man she cares for as I do for Anthony, and to be happy."

"She will never love any man the way you do Anthony," Maria said. "It isn't in her nature. I wonder if Papa's note has been delivered, I wonder if your parents are talking about you this very moment."

"Papa has a meeting with the archdeacon this morning, so he is talking about what is to be done with Canon Hawthorn, who intends to publish a tract about the Second Coming that amounts to heresy, so Papa says."

"Heresy! How exciting."

"Your mind runs on the terrors of the Spanish Inquisition, on dungeons and torture, but heretical views in the Church of England are not of that kind."

Eliza's mind wasn't on heresy, or Canon Hawthorn. It was entirely turned to her own predicament, and with the restless energy that so worried and disconcerted her parents, she began to pace up and down the room. How many hours must pass before she could see Anthony? She wished he were here, now, that she didn't have to possess her soul in patience.

The time needn't be spent uselessly. She could sound out her mother at least, as to whether what Maria said was true. Maria was given to exaggeration, and what she heard through a thick oak door might owe more to her imagination than she knew.

It was now past ten o'clock. Her mother, always an early riser, would long since have finished her household duties. She reserved an hour every day for her correspondence, she might well be in her room, at her desk. How to broach the matter? How not to alert her suspicions, not to reveal she knew what could only have been learned in some underhand way? She must go to her with a mind prepared . . .

Her thoughts were interrupted by the return of the maid. "Mrs. Collins wants to see you in the drawing room, directly," she announced. And then she added, in less important tones, "She's in there with Lady Grandpoint, and your sister, and they're all in a right state, best hurry down, if you want my advice!"

Chapter Four

Both household duties and letter writing had gone neglected that morning by Mrs. Collins. The previous evening, her husband had given her a blow-by-blow account of his conversation with Sir Roger in the form of a curtain lecture, a habit of her husband's which Mrs. Collins deplored. She longed to say, You are not in church, you do not need to preach a sermon at me, but it was in his nature to moralise in a ponderous way, and, as a dutiful wife, she had made it her business over the years to hold her tongue and hear his prosy diatribes out in silence.

In any case, he ignored any attempts at interruption, merely pausing and then picking up what he had to say a lengthy paragraph or two back from where he had stopped, thus making the whole affair drag out even longer. He pretty much told her the whole in the first ten minutes, and she let his peroration, with his solemn pronouncements as to the innate wickedness of young women when allowed to give rein to their feelings, wash over her while she tried to make sense of what Sir Roger was about.

Her feelings were a mixture of exultation and mortification. How could any mother not be pleased that her daughter had attracted the notice of a man such as Anthony Diggory, whom she liked for his own sake, let alone his position and future inheritance? How could any mother not be mortified to know that her daughter wasn't considered good enough for the man she loved, and that, regardless of whether her sentiments were returned or not, a match was out of the question?

Anger, too, at her husband for giving in to Sir Roger so meekly, for taking his side against Eliza.

"I knew how it would be," he was saying. "High spirits are all very well in a young girl such as Maria, although she is given too free a hand, in my opinion; however, she has a fortune, she has a name, the situation is quite different for Eliza, who must mind her manners and take great care not to give offence."

"I do not think falling in love with a handsome and rich young man can be called giving offence."

"When the liking has not been sanctioned by his or her parents, then it is wrong, and Sir Roger is right to feel aggrieved."

"Sir Roger! Aye, and Lady Diggory, too. She worships her son, no woman is good enough for her. I do not see why the young couple may not marry. Sir Roger mistakes the matter, Eliza is not a dairy-maid or a drudge, he has welcomed her to his house—"

"You do not understand these matters, my dear. Such things are best left to myself and Sir Roger. There can be no question of Sir Roger and Lady Diggory approving the match, so there can be no match. All that remains for us to do is to consider where best to send her. Pemberley is the obvious place—"

"What, with two boys and a governess to keep her company? What will she do there?"

"Apply herself to feminine tasks, read improving books, and indeed, if the governess is a sensible woman, she may instil some better sense of propriety in Eliza."

Mrs. Collins opened her mouth to protest, and then shut it again. If her husband couldn't see the folly of expecting a girl of twenty to submit to the attentions of a governess, or to agree to spend any time at all marooned in the country, in however much state, then nothing she could say would make him see sense.

The next morning she was up before him, too distracted to pay proper attention to any of her usual tasks, her mind searching for a solution. She snapped at her son, Charles, when he enquired if she were out of sorts, and let her husband go off to his cathedral meeting without making any of her usual wifely enquiries as to the time of his return or the likelihood of his staying on to dine with his colleagues.

Her aunt, sharp-eyed and curious, came late to the breakfast room and at once noticed Mrs. Collins had something on her mind. She took the first opportunity of whisking her into the sitting room, out of earshot of the servants, and worming it all out of her.

"It is what Sir Roger said about Eliza that so distresses me," said Mrs. Collins. "To assert that she set out to ensnare Anthony! I know she can be a little wild in her ways—although," she added with vigour, "not half so wild as Maria Diggory, I may say. It is true that Eliza is inclined to flirt, yet why should a pretty girl not do so?"

"If this were mere flirtation, then Sir Roger would not be in this state," Lady Grandpoint said. "It is clear that the attachment is mutual. In which case, it is a great pity that Sir Roger is so obdurate, for, as you say, it would be a good match for Eliza. Cannot Bishop Collins persuade Sir Roger to take a more favourable line?"

"The bishop will not go against Sir Roger's wishes, he will not attempt to argue or disagree with him, I am sure of that. Sir Roger believes that once Eliza is gone from the neighbourhood, Anthony will forget about her, Sir Roger considers it is all a mere passing fancy."

"If that is so, then Eliza is in danger, because, to speak frankly, passing fancies can lead to unfortunate circumstances. Young blood runs hot. What if their passion proves stronger than their virtue? This young Mr. Diggory would not be the first young man to ruin a neighbour's daughter."

"Ruin! Consider what you are saying."

"I am saying what you should be thinking as a mother, and what any woman of the world would think and say."

"It is most un-Christian to—"

"This has nothing to do with Christianity, it is a practical matter. Can the girl go to her Darcy connections in Derbyshire?"

"She can, but I do not see how it will serve. She would be so bored she might even run away, for how can I know that this governess will keep an eye on her?"

"Indeed, and why should she? Eliza is not her charge, and if she has two boys to look after, then she will have her hands full."

Lady Grandpoint took a turn around the room, twitching a cover into place as she went past a sofa, pausing by the window to watch a crow pecking at some creature in the grass, before turning again to her niece.

"Eliza had better come to London with Charlotte. No," and she raised a hand to prevent Mrs. Collins from speaking, an unnecessary gesture, for Mrs. Collins looked as though the power of speech had been removed from her. "It is not at all what I had planned. With neither beauty nor fortune to recommend her, a London season can do Eliza little good, other than perhaps to add some polish to her manners. However, we must consider our dear Charlotte. It will not help her chances if her sister is known to be in a scrape—or worse. And word gets around, such news will travel swiftly enough from Yorkshire to London, you may take my word for it."

Mrs. Collins was silent for a few minutes, considering her aunt's offer. "It is exceedingly good of you to suggest such a scheme. After all, no one will think it odd if Eliza goes with her sister to London, there can be no hint of her being packed off in disgrace if she goes to London. Only there is the expense, you are exceedingly kind to help Charlotte, but you cannot do the same for Eliza."

"You must persuade your husband to loosen his purse strings a little, as I judge he is well able to do. It is a trifling amount to pay to secure Charlotte's future and to remain on proper terms with Sir Roger, if the wretched man truly has the influence your husband ascribes to him. How I detest these country squires, who have everything their way, who rule their petty kingdoms and consider themselves of importance in the world, when it is not at all the case. Still, while Mr. Collins remains Bishop of Ripon, he cannot risk offending those around him. And the expense need not be so very great, there is no point in decking Eliza out in any particular finery, she will not be noticed however she looks, a respectable appearance so that she does not appear too out of place is all we need aim for. Let her pack up whichever of her gowns are the finest, and she can manage with those and perhaps a new bonnet or shawl to add a touch of fashion. No one will notice her, she will blend into the background, there are always a number of young women of much better family, who make no mark in London."

Mrs. Collins thought of Eliza with her lively ways, her rippling laughter, her voice, her mobile mouth with its quick smile, and the way that men's eyes followed her when she was dancing. She felt a shiver of apprehension; should she warn her aunt that the role of dowdy younger sister which she was assigning to Eliza might not be as suitable as she supposed?

No. She would have a serious talk with Eliza before she left, impress on her how she must behave just as she ought, and not in any way do anything that might hinder Charlotte's chances. And she would listen, would heed her mother's words; she was at heart a good girl, who cared for her sister's well-being.

What a pity that Mrs. Darcy was out of the country; why had Mr. Darcy become such a gadabout? Government business! What need had a man of Darcy's estate to go meddling in government business that was better left to men who had neither great houses nor huge incomes, let alone a family to look after? Mr. Darcy was possessed of a keen sense of duty, so Elizabeth said. Well, Bishop Collins had a keen sense of duty, and no one chose to send him off to all these strange places.

"I do not believe you are listening to a word of what I have to say," Lady Grandpoint said sharply. "I was talking about a maid. If both girls are to come to London, then they had better bring their own maid. There is a girl here who can be spared, I dare say?"

"Hislop can go, she is devoted to Charlotte. Oh, dear, I do not think Eliza will care to go. How are we to break it to her?"

"Break it? You will tell her that she is to go to London and there's an end of it. I trust you are not going to indulge in any weak sentiments on this. It would be inappropriate to show the girl any sympathy. Good heavens, most girls would jump at the opportunity to spend some weeks in London. And who knows, despite everything, we may be able to find her a husband while she is with us."

"Anthony may forget her," said Mrs. Collins, shaking her head, "but I fear Eliza is not so volatile. If her affections are truly engaged—"

"Fustian. She will do as she is told, and it will do her a world of good to be in wider company, to come to a sense of her unimportance and to realise that she cannot run on in the way she is allowed to do here."

"My dear aunt, it is not a matter of allowed," said Mrs. Collins, goaded into open disagreement, rare with her. "It is not for want of trying, she was born with a quick mind and a lively disposition, and I do not believe she will alter in her essential being, however lowly she may appear in London society. And I would not wish that she should, she is very like her godmother, and Elizabeth was always my dearest friend, you know. I hope and pray Eliza will find a husband who appreciates her for what she is, a man she can respect and look up to, a clever man."

Lady Grandpoint was looking at her with cold disapprobation. "Pull yourself together, really, you make a mountain out of a molehill. Eliza will be lucky to find herself any kind of a tolerable husband, and indeed, that is all any girl can wish for, without she is born into the highest ranks of society. And even there, let me tell you, a girl is rarely allowed simply to follow the dictates of her heart, and since the heart has little to do in the end with a successful marriage, it is right that it is so."

"There must be some affection."

"Nonsense. You yourself are a perfect example of how a good marriage can be made out of the most unpromising material. Do you think I am not aware that Mr. Collins would have remained a mere village clergyman if it were not for you? That is a duty well done, you have supported your spouse and taken him further in his profession than he could ever have gone by his own talents or efforts. Let Eliza do the same for her husband and she will lead a life as contented as any of us may expect."

"Duty," said Mrs. Collins, a hint of sadness in her voice. "I find it difficult to talk of Eliza and duty in the same breath, but, yes, she has to live the life that is possible for her. Dutifully." And she considered what her own life would have been, had she not married Mr. Collins. She would have become a drudge at Lucas Lodge, a spinster aunt, expected to help in the house and run about after nieces and nephews, instead of having her own establishment and as much control over her life as any woman had the right to expect. Eliza growing old as an impoverished spinster! It was not to be thought of, anything was better than that.

She had no such unhappy predictions for Charlotte. No young woman as beautiful as Charlotte would remain unmarried, no, not unless a new breed of the male half of humankind were to come into being, who cared little for a lovely face and a graceful form. Mrs. Collins's mood lightened at the mere thought of Charlotte, with her fine looks and good behaviour. Charlotte had never given her a moment's anxiety.

"Send for Eliza directly," said Lady Grandpoint, "so that we can inform her of her good fortune."

"I think we should discuss the matter with the bishop first, he may have some objection to Eliza's going to London."

"In which case, better that it is all settled before he returns. And what is there to object to, pray? His daughter is removed from the orbit of this young man, his neighbour can return to his rural, rustic pursuits with a calm mind, domestic tranquillity is restored, and all this for the very modest outlay of a trifling sum for a little finery for his younger daughter. He will be grateful enough."

Or if he is not, he will hardly dare to say so, said Mrs. Collins inwardly; Mr. Collins would have been in awe of her aunt's forceful personality even if she hadn't been in possession of a title and a handsome income.

Chapter Five

"You sent for me, Mama?" said Eliza. What were they up to, her mother and Lady Grandpoint? Were they going to try to talk her out of her feelings for Anthony? Or break the news that she was to go to Pemberley? Up went her chin, she would fight them every inch of the way.

"We have decided, your mama and I, that it will be best for you to accompany Charlotte to London."

Eliza couldn't believe her ears. London? What were they up to now? She dropped a curtsy. "Thank you, ma'am, for the invitation, but I do not want to go to London."

It was all in vain. She knew it, from the first, and despite her insistence that, no, she did not wish to go to London, that she would not go, she knew how it would end. Yet even as she argued, the idea came into her mind that if she had to be sent away, might not London be better than Derbyshire? Surely Anthony could find reasons to go to London. Of course, the squire would try to keep him at home, but a young man had friends, visits to be made, he could not rusticate in Yorkshire for ever.

And then Papa came home, to be told the news, and to be soothed and flattered by Mrs. Collins, and instructed as to common sense by her ladyship.

"It is all very well, but I do not know how it can be contrived.

Here is a note brought from Sir Roger, hinting in the strongest terms that Eliza must be sent off directly, and you"—bowing—"my dear Lady Grandpoint, are going to stay with us some days longer."

"It is quite unnecessary. Charlotte will have to bestir herself, and it may be for the best. For we shall need some time in London to see to dressmakers and so on, if Charlotte is to be rigged out in a style to do her credit. Let all her clothes be packed up, and then, once I am home, we may go through her wardrobe at leisure and decide what is needed. It can as well be done there as here."

And there was Charlotte, obedient as ever, and only, when Eliza was still within earshot, confiding to her mama that she wished Eliza weren't coming, for it would be a grave responsibility, attempting to make sure her sister went on as she should, in a way that would raise no eyebrows, cause no comment which might come to Lady Grandpoint's ears.

"My love, I am sure in London that Eliza will restrain herself, and behave just as she ought. She will know better than to continue with her free and easy ways, and besides, my aunt will be there to give her a proper direction. You are not to distress yourself, you are to enjoy your time there, and make the most of this opportunity. I am sorry it has turned out like this, however, there are reasons why it is imperative that Eliza goes with you. I think you should know . . ."

And Charlotte listened gravely, shaking her head over what her sister had been up to. "It is wrong of her, Mama, very wrong. Not that Anthony is not also at fault, but in such cases, the female ought always to display more caution, inasmuch as the blame will fall more upon her than the man."

Maria sprang up as Eliza came through the door of her room.

"Well? Am I not right?"

"You are right, as to my being sent away, but wrong as to the destination. I am not to go to Pemberley, but to London."

"London! Oh, how lucky you are. London, why—oh, you do not

look as thrilled as I would be, but of course, London is nothing when the price is being torn asunder from your beloved."

"Maria, do not talk in that absurd way."

"You could make a scene," suggested Maria, "throw a tantrum, drum your heels on the floor. That would give your aunt such a disgust of you that she might refuse to take you after all."

"And the consequence would be, after she had thrown a vase of water over me, that I should find myself at Pemberley after all. No, I thank you. What time is it?"

"After two."

"I am supposed to be looking out my clothes for London. Hislop is with Charlotte now, we are to be off first thing in the morning."

"What clothes? You will need everything new for London, not even your green dress, the one with the flounces, is half smart enough for London."

"Maybe not, but it will have to do. Besides, I only care for Anthony's opinion, and he likes me well enough in that dress."

Maria had a strong streak of sense beneath her romantic fancies. "That's what you say now, but when you are at a smart party, and wearing a gown at least three years behind the fashion, you will find you do mind."

"Then I shall have to mind, for I do not expect to have any new clothes."

"And Charlotte?"

"Hers is a different case." Eliza laughed as she caught sight of her gloomy expression in the mirror. "Charlotte goes to triumph, I go in disgrace. Now quick, help me sort out what I shall take, and then we shall have to slip out."

"Perhaps Anthony will know how to get you out of this fix," said Maria, following Eliza from the room. "He is very resourceful."

Anthony had no ideas at all. Dismayed by Maria's somewhat garbled note, and fatigued by the long ride, he was not in a good temper when he reached the woods. He dismounted and frowned at his sister. "You here as well? The devil with you, Maria, all those governesses, and you write a note so ill spelt, and with sentences so ill constructed, that I can hardly make sense of it. Sweetheart," he said to Eliza, sweeping her into his arms. "You can tell me what this is all about."

Eliza, trying to keep her voice level, unfolded the story, restraining Maria with fierce looks from her attempts to embellish the stark facts. "There. I have no hold on you, Anthony, you know that. Your parents are distressed that you should have any feelings for me . . ."

"Feelings? Is that what you call it when I am deeply in love? Shame on you."

"I do not wish to say uncharitable things about your parents, nor to criticise mine. They are doing what they think is in our best interests."

"My best interests, not yours," he shot back. "I know my parents too well. Listen, my dearest Eliza, I will go and talk to my mother. I am sure I can win her round. She only wishes for my happiness, and she must be made to see that without you, I can never be happy."

"You're deceiving yourself," Maria broke in. "She is convinced she knows what will make you happy, and it isn't Eliza. Try, it will make no difference."

"I fear that Maria is right," said Eliza. "I have been tried and found guilty, sentence has been pronounced, and I am to go." Her voice was unsteady. "And perhaps, dear heart, you will find they are right, that when I am gone—oh, that it will prove to have been a green love, a spring idyll, an insubstantial—"

He stopped her mouth with a kiss, breaking away to bid his sister take herself off. "Here, go and walk your mare, I want to speak to Eliza privately."

When she had removed herself to the other side of the path—"Further off, if you please; I know you and your long ears"—he turned back to Eliza, and then, in a swift movement, dropped to one knee and took her hand. "Eliza, I offer you my heart. Will you marry me?"

Eliza was overwhelmed. Her love for Anthony had been intoxicating, and she knew that there could be no greater happiness for her than to marry him. But how could they marry, with their families so set against it?

"If the worst comes to the worst, we shall have to make a bolt for the border," he said.

"No, not that. Listen, Anthony, let us be secretly engaged. I know it is wrong, very wrong, but in eleven months I shall be twenty-one, and will no longer need my father's permission. By then, your parents will have to accept that our affection is not a fleeting dalliance."

"Yes, they'll have to give in eventually." His eyes danced. Then he grew sombre. "I want there to be a solemn bond between us, Eliza. I don't want you to go away a free woman, and I don't want you to think I'm not bound to you by my word. Damn it, I have no ring . . . this is not how I want to ask you to be my wife."

Maria was beside them. "I hear someone coming this way," she said breathlessly. "I heard what you plan, it is wonderful. And I shall do everything I can to help you."

"You can help us by keeping out of this," said Anthony at once.

"Pooh, don't you be so high-and-mighty. How can you write to Eliza, or she to you, except through me?"

"Write! What is this about writing?"

"Yes, brother dear, write; you will have to take up your pen and write to Eliza. How else can you keep in touch with her, or she with you? She will write to you, and address the letter to me. And I shall send your letters back as though they came from me."

"If you think I want you to read what I and Eliza have to say to each other—"

"Don't you trust me? You may on this, upon my honour. Quick, or you will be discovered together. By the snorting sound I fear it is Papa, you know how that old hack of his makes a noise."

A last swift embrace, and Anthony swung into the saddle, wheeling his horse round to plunge into one of the byways of the forest that he knew so well. Almost at the same moment, Maria and Eliza vanished into the greenery, hiding themselves behind one of the huge oaks that abounded in this part of the forest.

"We could climb the tree," Maria whispered into Eliza's ear. "Like Charles the Second when he was escaping after the battle at Worcester. Oh, heavens, Father has that wretched dog with him, listen to her bark, she knows we are here, the silly creature."

The squire's voice could be heard chastising the dog, calling her a damned bitch, and then the hound was distracted by a bird starting up from the undergrowth, and Sir Roger was past, cantering on towards the village.

Eliza wrapped her cloak around her. "Where is your groom?" she said to Maria.

"He'll be waiting for me in the clearing by the old charcoal burner's place. No, there's no need to come with me, it is barely a hundred yards. You had better get back to your packing, before you are missed, and everyone is calling out as to where you may be."

Which they were, but Eliza had the good sense not to run, not to arrive back at the Palace hot and bothered. Instead, with the basket which she had had the foresight to bring with her on her arm, she said meekly that she had merely gone down to the herb garden, to gather some fresh lavender to lay in her trunks.

"You were not in the herb garden," Charlotte said. "I looked for you there." She was holding a velvet pelisse over her arm, and stroking it with her long, white fingers as she spoke. Eliza knew that Charlotte loved the sensuous feel of silken fabrics; no doubt she was looking forward to indulging this taste, since she was to have so many new clothes in London.

"Then how came I to have this lavender?" said Eliza, brandishing a sprig that she had snatched up on her way to meet Anthony. She broke away from her sister and ran up the steps, calling out to her mother that she was here, and, yes, she had sorted out her clothes, what was the fuss about.

Chapter Six

Eliza climbed into the carriage with a dull, aching sadness in her heart. Charlotte, as always, was calm, seemingly not at all excited by the adventure that lay ahead of her. The bishop fussed and fretted, wanting to check the harness of Lady Grandpoint's horses, which irritated Eliza, since her father knew nothing about horses. Lady Grandpoint, used to travelling, was making sure that her maid had packed everything properly and that what she needed for the journey: a wrap, a footstool, a book, were all to hand.

Charlotte and Lady Grandpoint travelled forward; Eliza sat opposite, with her back to the horses. Charlotte had said she would sit the other way at the first stop to change horses, but Eliza knew that she wouldn't, and indeed, it was better if she didn't, for Charlotte was prone to motion sickness, while travel in a swaying coach never affected Eliza in the least.

Since they were making the journey in Lady Grandpoint's travelling chaise, they were extremely comfortable. It was not an ostentatious vehicle, but had come from one of London's best coach builders, and was well-sprung and well-upholstered. The Grandpoint arms were emblazoned on the door, which gave Bishop Collins considerable satisfaction. He hoped people in the town would notice his daughters travelling in such an equipage as the carriage passed through the streets at the start of the long journey south.

They were to spend a mere two nights on the road. Lady Grandpoint, as vigorous as many women half her age, didn't care to spend a moment more in inns than she had to. Charlotte was alarmed at the pace and was apprehensive at how tired they would be at the end of the day. Eliza didn't care if they drove all night. Every yard took her further away from Anthony, so what did it matter if the ground were covered quickly or slowly?

Her spirits rose despite herself as the coach turned on to the main highway. It was the last day of April, and after a mild winter and an early spring, the countryside had the lush greenery of freshly opened leaves and new growth. As they travelled through the towns and villages, they could see people busy with preparations for May Day and sense the expectation of holiday in the air.

They slept that night at Stamford, at a well-appointed inn, used to supplying the wants of such demanding travellers as Lady Grandpoint. Eliza fell wearily into bed, grateful for the sense of physical tiredness that sent her at once into a profound slumber, rather than leaving her awake and restless and thinking of how much she hated being separated from Anthony.

The next day she could not help but feel more cheerful, as with the sun beaming from a cloudless sky, they saw morris dancers capering on village greens, maidens weaving ribbons round the maypoles, and, when the day drew to its end, couples stealing into the shadows for kisses and love.

"Rustics," said Lady Grandpoint, who was not a talkative companion. In fact, most of the journey passed in silence, Lady Grandpoint absorbed in her book, only raising her eyes from the page and holding her place with a long finger to announce that they were passing some place of historic interest, here the site of a battle, there a large house inhabited by a distant relation of the Grandpoints.

She seemed to have a great many connections, Eliza thought to herself. That was what a good marriage did for you. She compared Lady Grandpoint's numerous relations with her own connections. They amounted to, on her mother's side, her late grandfather, knighted for some obscure success in trade, and Lady Grandpoint herself. On her father's side, the grandest of her connections were the Darcy family, and the relationship could hardly be called a close one.

It was not in Eliza's nature to brood, and as the carriage approached London, with the towns and villages growing more numerous and populous, she leaned forward, eager to catch a first view of London. They approached the city by way of Hampstead, a charming village with its pond, where three cows stood up to their knees in water, idly chewing cud as they watched the carriage rattle by.

"The heath used to be a prime spot for highwaymen," Lady Grandpoint observed. "However, we live in safer times, although I always travel with an armed man, as you have noticed, it would be folly to do otherwise. Grandpoint insists upon it, and he makes very sure that the guns carried by the postilion are in excellent order, there is no point in a gun that cannot hit its target, as he so rightly says."

Eliza wondered what Lord Grandpoint would be like. She had never met him, and her mother had been vague: "My uncle is a formidable man, too clever for me, and a man of stern principles."

Stern principles. What did that mean? Did he go to church twice on Sundays, and sit with a solemn face, intent on every word? Would he, a childless man, disapprove of any signs of levity or liveliness in his wife's great-niece? No doubt Lady Grandpoint would tell him about Anthony—how would he take to that? She pictured a grim-visaged man, with an obstinate jaw and an unsmiling countenance, and her heart sank. No doubt he would be delighted with Charlotte, as older men so often were, and would praise her beauty and calmness.

Older men tended to treat Eliza rather differently, slipping an arm around her waist and leaning too close. At least the stern principles might prevent a Lord Grandpoint from fondling and squeezing her in any such disagreeable way.

Aubrey Square, where the Grandpoints had their London residence, was in the best part of town, so Lady Grandpoint informed them. The houses were handsome, dating from the second half of the last century, their red brick façades broken by white-painted window surrounds and elegant wrought-iron balconies overlooking the centre of the square.

Lord Grandpoint came out of the house as the carriage drew up, and he descended the shallow steps to help his wife out of the coach. He had an austere look to him; clever, but humourless, was Eliza's immediate judgement. She told herself she must not be so quick to form an impression, it was a fault of hers, she knew. However, his greeting to his wife was kind and affectionate, and his welcome to his great-nieces hardly less so. Kindness must always be considered a virtue.

"You are fatigued by your journey. Lady Grandpoint does like to travel fast, which can be wearing for her companions."

"Nonsense," said Lady Grandpoint, accepting the salutations of the impressive butler with a nod and telling her maid to make sure the case with her bottles was taken inside directly. "Charlotte and Eliza have all the advantage of youth; a good night's sleep, and they will be quite recovered from the journey."

An appetising supper was laid out for the travellers, although after a glass of wine and a wing of chicken, Eliza felt she would burst trying to restrain the yawns that threatened her, while Charlotte, whom Eliza knew was suffering from the headache, could barely swallow a mouthful.

"Tell your maid to make your sister a tisane for her head," Lady Grandpoint told Eliza, when she realised how Charlotte was suffering. "Is she prone to headaches?"

"Sometimes, especially when she is tired and has been in a coach for a long while. They last for a day or two and can be very severe."

"Then she shall have the bedchamber at the rear of the house. It is not so handsome as the other room, where I intended to put her, but you will not mind the noise, I dare say. Not that Aubrey Square is noisy, not at all, it is one of the quietest squares in London."

If Aubrey Square was quiet, Eliza shuddered to think what a noisy street must be like. She slept soundly, the sleep of exhaustion, but woke early, wondering if there were an affray, a riot, some public disturbance. Voices, street criers, calling out for people to buy oranges, pies, muffins, the raucous sound of an organ-grinder, horses' hooves, and the steady, never-ceasing rumble of traffic on the main thoroughfare beyond the square.

After the ancient silence of the mediaeval Bishop's Palace at Ripon, the noise was shocking. How could one ever grow accustomed to it? Eliza had found Harrogate and York noisy enough, but they were nothing in comparison.

She found, lying there, that she liked the noise. Silence had its merits, but there was vitality in these sounds of a great city coming to life. She had been to London only once before, as a girl, and they had stayed far from the centre, in a genteel suburb with a clerical friend of her parents. She could remember little about it, except for a rather dark house and long, boring days, enlivened only by demure walks in the park.

This was quite, quite different, and as for Lady Grandpoint's house, Eliza was amazed at the taste and style of even this room, a mere guest bedchamber. A handsome rug was on the polished floor, cream with a pattern of flowers around its border. The curtains were heavy and patterned with more crimson flowers set on a pale background. There was a writing desk, elegant on spindly legs, and two chairs set beside the fireplace, itself much bigger than the tiny grates she was used to at home. No ancient discomfort here, no draughts whistling down stone-paved passages, no cramped windows of great historic interest but exceeding impracticality. And, she was sure, no vast stone fireplaces downstairs belching smoke into the room every time the wind blew from the north-east, and likewise the kitchens were probably modern, rather than the cavernous affairs of the Palace, unchanged, Eliza suspected, since the Middle Ages.

Eliza jumped out of bed and went to the window. Across the square, a servant was scrubbing steps; a few yards further down, a porter rattled his boxes along the pavement, whistling loudly. A maid stood by the basement railings of another house, exchanging saucy quips with a coal merchant, a husky young man who heaved the sacks on to his broad shoulders as though they were full of feathers, before tumbling the contents down the chute into the cellar below.

Hislop's voice startled her out of her reverie.

"Miss! Standing there at the window in your shift for all the world to see."

"Nobody is looking at me. The world has better things to do." Eliza took the wrap Hislop was holding out for her. "How is Charlotte this morning?"

"She has the headache very badly, poor soul. I knew how it would be, travelling at that dreadful speed. Her nerves are all to pieces, although of course she never complains."

"Are you recovered from the journey?" Eliza asked, not wanting to hear Hislop on the subject of Charlotte's nerves. Hislop and Lady Grandpoint's maid had travelled with the luggage in a second chaise, not such a comfortable one. Nerves, indeed! Charlotte didn't have nerves, she merely had a headache, because the motion of the carriage didn't agree with her.

That earned her a sniff from the wiry, tireless woman. Eliza should have known better than to express interest or sympathy. In Hislop's eyes, Charlotte could do no wrong, and Eliza could do no right.

"Annie will come and help you dress," said Hislop. "She's a young girl just joined the household, I understand, a flighty number, but I'll have my hands full attending to Miss Collins, so her ladyship said it was best for this Annie to look after you while you are here."

Annie appeared at the door as soon as Hislop had left, a dark slip of a girl with a dimple and a merry look to her. "Good morning, Miss," she said, bobbing a curtsy.

I just hope, Eliza said to herself, that Hislop's duties for Charlotte keep her completely occupied, since Annie looked to be a much more agreeable person. And a chatty one, too; as she helped Eliza to dress, she talked about the household, and Eliza was surprised to learn how large an establishment it was. All those servants, for a childless couple.

"His lordship likes to have everything just so," Annie told her. "The house runs like clockwork, and if it doesn't, he has to know the reason why. Her ladyship is just the same, she has eyes in the back of her head, that one."

Annie held up the dress Eliza had said she would wear, and, turning round from the mirror, Eliza saw the expression on the maid's face.

"Whatever is the matter?"

"Miss, you can't wear this!"

"Why ever not?"

"With these sleeves? And it's sprigged, and the neckline . . ."

"You're saying it's unfashionable," Eliza said with a laugh. Of course the girl was right. The gowns Eliza wore at home were plain in cut and style. Her father declared that he liked simplicity in the clothes his womenfolk wore; she knew quite well that what he liked was to spend as little as possible on what he called the girls' finery. Their allowances were small, and Eliza, spending money on music and books, rarely had enough for more elegant clothes.

Charlotte was better off, since she was content with the music she had always played, never wanting anything different, and as she grew out of the awkward age and began to show signs of exceptional looks, her mother gave her extra money for her gowns—justifying this to Eliza by saying that Charlotte's beauty deserved to be shown off.

"Unfashionable? Downright dowdy, if you'll forgive me, Miss. Have you nothing else?"

A quick scurry through her clothes left Annie shaking her head, and Eliza feeling more unsure of herself than she would have believed possible.

"It is only a gown," she found herself saying. "And this one"—she made a dive for a particular favourite, the dress she had been wearing when Anthony first kissed her—"what is wrong with this?"

Annie wrinkled her nose. "It's hard to say what's right with it." She came to a decision. "Put on your wrap again, and have your chocolate in here, while I see what I can do with this one."

And before Eliza could protest, Annie had hurried out of the room, a muslin gown that Eliza had never liked clasped in her hands.

Eliza sipped the thick, delicious chocolate, a luxury unheard of at the Palace, and thought about her wardrobe. Annie's reaction was extreme, there must be plenty of simply dressed young women in London.

Then she looked around the room and, with a sinking heart, knew that Annie was right. In London, yes. In the quiet suburb she had stayed in as a child, her gowns might pass muster. In these surroundings she was going to appear ridiculous.

Well, that was how it would be. There was nothing she could do about it. Her mother had been insistent on that point. Her going to London was not in the nature of a treat. She had behaved badly, had been all too forward with a young man, and must be aware that in her father's eyes she had disgraced herself.

Disgraced, because she loved Anthony?

In particular, she must be a good girl, her mother had continued, and not expect the same treatment as would be granted to Charlotte. "It was never my aunt's intention that you should do a season in London, and you must accustom yourself to not leading quite the same life as Charlotte will. Of course, you will go to some parties and so on, I am sure, but you will not be invited to the dances and balls and assemblies that Lady Grandpoint will take Charlotte to."

"Don't you think people will find it strange, my sitting at home in the cinders?" Eliza had said. "At twenty, it will be hard to pretend I am still in the schoolroom, and not yet out."

"Cinders, indeed! You will find that the Grandpoints treat you very well, it is simply that we all have expectations for Charlotte, so beautiful as she is. And if she were to make a good match, then that must have advantages for you as well, remember that. She is lucky to have such a generous godmother."

"It is a shame my godmother has so many children of her own, in that case," said Eliza, laughing, for she far preferred her own sparkling godmother to Lady Grandpoint.

"There, now, you take everything as a cause for amusement. I warn you to watch your tongue, for these manners and habits of yours will not do in London at all!"

"It will not matter if they do or don't do, if I'm to live such a confined life as you suggest."

Well, shabby gowns or no shabby gowns, Eliza was determined she was going to make the most of what London had to offer. She hoped Annie was a walker, since she suspected she wouldn't be allowed out unaccompanied. She intended to explore the city and see all the marvels that she had only read about or heard described at second hand. The river, the Tower of London, the monuments, and pictures and famous buildings. Then there would be all the books she could possibly want to read. She was determined to pay for a subscription to one of London's famous circulating libraries.

Annie was back, the gown held high. Eliza blinked. What had the girl done to it? It was hard to tell exactly; the sleeves had been altered, the neckline was different, and, when she put it on, it fitted much better than before.

"You are a marvel with your needle, I find," she said.

Annie blushed. "I should be, Miss, for my mother is a seamstress, and she taught me well."

"Yet you work as a maid, wouldn't you rather be a seamstress?"

"Oh, no. It is hard work, you know, and I love living in this part of London and being in a household like this. I have two sisters, and they are going into the trade with my mother. She doesn't need any more help, and so I chose to go into service."

Annie tweaked the gown into place. "I understand that M. Gaspard, the dressmaker, is coming round today, perhaps you could ask her ladyship if she can make for you as well as for Miss Collins."

Eliza shook her head. "I doubt it. No, I must make do with what I have. Lady Grandpoint has said that she will buy me a new bonnet, and perhaps a shawl to make me more elegant."

"A bonnet? A shawl? Why, Miss—"

"That will do, Annie."

"Thank you for sending a maid to me, so that Hislop can look after Charlotte," Eliza said when she was downstairs with her aunt.

"It seems best. Apart from this tiresome headache—and I do hope your sister isn't going to be falling ill all the time, London is so strenuous—Charlotte's clothes and toilette will need a lot of attention if she is to appear at her best."

"As to that, Charlotte always looks her best."

"I dare say, but in London a young woman on the lookout for a husband needs polish. She cannot afford to look countrified, that would never do."

"Countrified is what we are, I suppose. Annie is very scathing about my clothes."

"Who is Annie? Oh, the maid. It is hardly her place to pass personal comments."

"I fear she is right."

"Well, it is of no matter. I know she has some skill with her needle, she can smarten you up, I am sure. Have you a pattern gown? Yes? Then you may buy some muslin and so on, and she can make you one or two gowns, in a more fashionable style than you have brought with you from Yorkshire. Your father gave you a sum of money, did he not?"

"No. He was too angry with me."

Eliza had no intention of telling Lady Grandpoint that she had some money of her own, apart from the two guineas that her mother had pressed into her hand as she stepped into the carriage in Ripon. Her great-aunt would want to know how she had such a sum set by, and the source of the money must certainly remain a secret.

Lady Grandpoint made a clicking noise with her tongue. "How like a man. Well, I shall give you a few guineas, and you must do the best you can with it, and let your maid look over such gowns as you brought with you."

"Thank you, ma'am, but in truth I do not need to dress any finer than I do already."

"It is a great pity you do not share your sister's beauty, for two of you would be even more striking. I speak bluntly, do you mind? Do you envy your sister her extraordinary degree of beauty?"

"No," said Eliza, and she spoke the truth. Charlotte's beauty had come as much as a surprise to her as it had to everyone else, for as a child, there had been nothing remarkable about her sister's looks. She had been inclined to chubbiness, with a bad skin, and her eyes, now so lustrous, had often been afflicted with the red eye, so that they were nearly always sore and inflamed. Then, over the space of a year or so, her complexion had cleared, her face fined down, revealing a rare perfection of feature, the infections to her eyes had gone away, her figure had grown pretty and graceful, and her formerly lank hair had become thick and lustrous.

"Such a beauty can benefit her entire family," said Lady Grandpoint. "It is a blessing that her temperament is a calm one, there is nothing impetuous about her, she is unlikely to let her feelings run away with her, I would judge."

Eliza smiled at this. "Charlotte has a very equable, tranquil nature."

Cold, it might be called, but it would be disloyal to say so. Whereas she, Eliza, was all too impetuous, tumbling into love with Anthony. Just to think his name was to cause a wave of happiness to flow through her.

"What are you thinking of, to look like that?" her great-aunt said sharply. "It is that young man, Anthony Diggory, I'll be bound. Well, I was young once, and inclined to imagine myself in love, and so I can tell you, that kind of fancy soon passes, quick to come, quick to go. Here in London you will meet a great many men, and I assure you, this Anthony will soon appear to you quite ordinary in comparison."

How could a woman have lived so long, and know so little?

"I am glad to see that you are not resentful of your sister's looks and prospects. This one mistake you have made will soon be forgotten, and I am sure you will make the most of your time in London to improve yourself. Shed your hoydenish ways, and learn to control your impulses, and you will grow into a much more contented person."

Contented, said Eliza inwardly. Like those cows in the pond at Hampstead. No, thank you.

Lady Grandpoint held up a card. "You see, here is an invitation from Lady Bellasby. I sent a note to her as soon as we arrived, to tell her that I had brought my goddaughter to London. She is giving a small dance, will be happy for me to bring Charlotte. You do not mind that you are not included in the invitation?"

"Not in the least," said Eliza, with perfect truth.

Lady Grandpoint rose, tapping the card against the palm of her hand. "You are a good-natured young woman, indeed. Now, I must leave you, I have a lot to attend to after my absence in Yorkshire. I am heartily glad to be back, the waters at Harrogate did not suit me at all, and I find the provinces bore me more and more. Country houses are one thing, but provincial life has nothing to recommend it."

Chapter Seven

The taller of the two fencers parried the thrust from his opponent, then found the tip of the other's sword held against his chest. He laughed, and held up his hand to acknowledge the hit.

"Enough, Bart," he said, putting his arm round the other's shoulders and walking with him across the *salle,* to where Henry Angelo had been watching them critically.

"Lord Rosely," Angelo said to the tall man, "you lay yourself open, you move quickly with the tierce, and then are too slow in the riposte." He bowed to Bartholomew Bruton. "I am pleased to welcome you back to these shores, Mr. Bruton. You took lessons in Paris from Manit, I believe?"

"I did indeed. How are you, Angelo? Any new tricks up your sleeve?"

"We shall have a bout the next time you come, and you may see for yourself," said the fencing master.

As the two men left the fencing salon and walked out in Haymarket, Freddie Rosely kept up a flow of inconsequential talk, which made Bartholomew smile. "I am very glad to see you again, Freddie," he said, when his companion finally paused for breath.

The best of friends as well as being cousins, the two men were quite unalike. Freddie was tall and fair, Bartholomew dark and half a head shorter with a proud nose and a keen-eyed, expressive face.

Their mothers were sisters, they had known each other from the cradle, and although they had grown up in rather different worlds, they had gone to Eton together and then on to Oxford, Freddie to Christ Church and Bartholomew to Magdalen.

"It is so good to see you, Moneybags," Freddie said, clapping a hand on Bartholomew's shoulder. The nickname had no malice in it, not from Freddie, although at school it had been flung at Bartholomew as a term of abuse and contempt. The scion of one of England's great banking families might be going to inherit a fortune beyond the dreams of most men, and have a Lady Sarah for a mother, but to the sprigs of the aristocracy at Eton, he was tainted with trade.

Freddie had come to his cousin's rescue the first time he had flung himself at his taunter, but he soon realised that Bartholomew was well able to fight his own corner. Pretty soon, both his contemporaries and older boys took care what they said to him, for he fought without quarter and was so quick on his feet and so swift to sense and make use of a weakness that it was generally considered best not to annoy or argue with him.

Bartholomew knew the remarks and abuse still went on behind his back, they always would, and the idiots couldn't see that he was far more proud of his Huguenot goldsmith and banking ancestors than they could ever be of their dull forebears, whose titles had, as often as not, been earned in highly dubious ways.

"Do any shooting practise while you were away?" Freddie enquired as they walked down Bond Street.

Bartholomew laughed. A brilliant swordsman, and a tough man with his fists, he was a hopeless shot. He called his long-sightedness "farsightedness" and pointed out that the time he saved not going in pursuit of various forms of game could well be spent on more interesting pursuits.

"Such as going to the opera," he said to Freddie. "Do you care to come tomorrow? Angelini sings, I believe."

Freddie pulled a face. "Is she the stout party who sings so high you'd think someone had trod on her foot?" Freddie wasn't musical. "No, I thank you, I'll pass on that."

"Perhaps you're right. Last time I heard her sing, she was not in good voice."

"Then, if you have no other engagements, you can come with me to Lady Grandpoint's soirée."

"Good God, are you out of your mind?"

"I see your propensity to shun elegant social gatherings hasn't undergone a change while you've been making merry in Paris. Listen, Bart, you have to come. Well, the truth of it is that Lady Grandpoint has someone staying with her. My God, not just 'someone,' " Freddie burst out, stopping in his enthusiasm, then grasping his friend by the arm to reinforce his point. "Bart, the most beautiful creature I've ever set eyes on. Such eyes, such a face, such grace."

Bartholomew sighed. He knew Freddie's enthusiasms, which usually ran to ripe and luscious ladies of easy virtue. However, Lady Grandpoint would be most unlikely to have a woman of that sort staying with her.

"Who is this paragon?"

"Her name is Charlotte," said Freddie, lingering on the syllables of the name. "Miss Collins. She's a bishop's daughter, from somewhere in the north, so don't look like that, she's utterly respectable."

"And rich, by any chance?"

Freddie frowned. "What does that matter?"

"I can see trouble ahead if she isn't. Has your mother met this new beauty?"

"No, no, she hasn't, not yet. She'll be enchanted by Miss Collins, can't help but be."

Bartholomew doubted that, unless the bishop turned out to be a rich and well-connected prelate.

"My mother will be there tomorrow," said Freddie. "So she can meet Miss Collins."

"I suppose that means my mama will be also be there," said Bartholomew resignedly. "At least in company she can't ring another peal over me. I've been avoiding her ever since I got back."

"Why, what have you done?"

"There was a girl in Paris, the prettiest, liveliest creature you ever saw. We spent a good deal of time together, and word got back to England about her. That's the trouble with having relations all over Europe, all of them with their spies and sending letters flying to and fro."

"Bart, is this serious? Don't tell me you've lost your heart to a Frenchwoman? What about Jane Grainger?"

"You know me, coz. I've no intention of losing my heart to anyone."

"There's always the latest heiress. She's a face like a lemon, but is the toast of the town—or was, until Miss Collins made her appearance. It's astonishing what money does to you, eh, Bartholomew?"

"That will be Celia Chetwynd, I expect," said Bartholomew.

"It is, do you know her?"

"No, but I, too, have my spies. Perhaps they'll marry her off to Lord Montblaine."

"What, the Marble Marquis? He never comes to London these days, and I'm sure he isn't hanging out for a wife."

"That's not what I hear." Bartholomew touched his hat yet again to an acquaintance who was bowing to him across the street.

"Let's dine at Pinks tonight," Freddie said.

"Yes, I long for a slice of mutton; French food is all very well, but they don't know how to serve meat."

They crossed Piccadilly and turned down St. James's Street to their club. Two whores, sitting at the window of Mother Elkins's establishment opposite the club, leant out over the street, calling down to the men. "More fun over here, dearie," said one, and the other winked at Bartholomew. "I hear the money clinking in your pockets, darling, why not come and spend it on us?"

Freddie gave them a jovial wave and ran up the club steps after his friend, who was greeted by the doorman with a smile and a quiet "Good to have you back, sir."

"I see Snipe," Bartholomew hissed at Freddie, as he saw an all-too-familiar figure lurking within. "Quickly, into the dining room before he spots us."

Too late. The dandified man had seen them and came strutting over. "My dear Bruton, what a pleasure."

Snipe was a few years older than Bartholomew and had been one of his worst tormentors at Eton. Even had that not been the case, Bartholomew would never have liked him, and he resigned himself to a quarter of an hour of gossip as Snipe launched into enquiries as to the well-being of their families and expressed insincere pleasure at Bartholomew's return. "I am sure your father has missed you, busy days at the bank, I am sure, busy days."

"Money is always hard work," Bartholomew said, well aware that the courtesy accorded to him by Snipe these days was entirely due to the vast profits made by Bruton's bank over the last few years of the war and in the subsequent years of peace and all the opportunities that brought.

Snipe angled for news and dropped little bits of information of his own. He mostly talked about people who, although known to Bartholomew, were of no interest to him. Mercifully, Freddie, who was feeling peckish, cut the man off rather abruptly, saying they must get on or they would lose their table.

"Of course," said Snipe, with his mirthless smile. "And I fancy I shall have the honour of seeing you later on, at Lady Grandpoint's." He bowed and slid away to greet another member who had just come into the club.

"Good Lord, there's a reason for not going," said Bartholomew. "Do we have a table?"

"No, but we shall have in about ten seconds. That corner one will do nicely. Waiter!"

Chapter Eight

It was usual in the Grandpoints' house in Aubrey Square for Lady Grandpoint to receive the post in the morning, and that day she was in an upstairs parlour with Eliza and Charlotte when the butler brought in the post on a silver tray.

Charlotte's head was bent over a piece of exquisite embroidery, a design of birds and flowers that she was working as a present for their hostess. Eliza was at the window, watching life go by, a novel on her lap.

"Here is a letter for you, Eliza, I do not recognise the hand. It is not from your mama, in any case."

At Lady Grandpoint's words, Charlotte lifted her head, giving Eliza a long, considering look before she threaded a needle with a new colour silk and returned to her stitchery. Eliza sprang up, then restrained herself; she must not appear too eager.

Lady Grandpoint still had the letter in her hand and was examining it closely. "Whoever your correspondent is, she has not got a frank, she has paid sixpence for the letter."

"May I have it?" Eliza didn't want to seem impatient, but surely the letter had to be from Maria, which meant—

"Your correspondent writes an elegant hand," said Lady Grandpoint, as she reluctantly let Eliza have the letter.

"It is from Maria Diggory," Eliza said, looking at the direction, keeping her voice steady, although she longed to tear it open, devour the words, which must be from Anthony.

Another long look from Charlotte.

"Miss Diggory?" said Lady Grandpoint. "Why should she write to you, pray?"

"She is a great letter writer. She promised she would write frequently, so that I may have all the news from Yorkshire."

"I assume your mama will write to you, although I dare say she has not the time for idle girl's gossip. You may open your letter here."

"Thank you, ma'am, but I shall read it later, when I go upstairs. I have my writing things there, and I shall like to answer it at once."

Eliza slipped the letter into her book, ignoring the frown on her great-aunt's face.

Charlotte came to her sister's rescue. "Maria and Eliza always correspond when they are apart. Although Maria is younger than Eliza, they are good friends, and Maria is an amusing correspondent."

"I hope the letter is not full of news of young Diggory," Lady Grandpoint said tartly.

"I hope that she will tell me about all my friends," Eliza began in a defiant tone.

Charlotte gave her a quelling look. "If I know anything of Maria's tastes, the letter will be full of the latest novel she has read, together with requests for exciting new titles that Eliza has come across in London. Maria is a great reader."

"Reading novels is a perfectly respectable way for a young woman to pass her time, once, of course, all her other duties have been completed," said Lady Grandpoint magisterially. "I do not hold, as some people do, that they are a wickedness, or do any harm. A mother will always be quick to notice if her daughter's head is becoming full of unsuitable ideas, of whimsical notions, and will then step in to prevent her reading unsuitable books, but, on the whole, reading of any kind is to be encouraged."

Eliza had noticed that Lady Grandpoint was a keen reader, with not only a subscription to the library, but also several shelves of handsome three-volume novels which she had bought as soon as they came out; Eliza could see she would be spending many happy hours with those.

Which was just as well, given that she was excluded from most of the social events which Lady Grandpoint was at pains to arrange for Charlotte. "To be foisting two unmarried girls on society at once is not wise," she said to Eliza as she accepted yet another invitation for herself and Charlotte.

"Of course not," said Eliza promptly. While she loved a party and loved to dance, she had a notion that these parties would be dull affairs, with correct behaviour and little fun or flirting involved, probably not half so agreeable as the impromptu dances in Yorkshire—for although her father thought it unnecessary for his daughters to go further afield to York or Harrogate, he had no objection to their attending all the local balls and dances.

"Not to do so would appear singular to our neighbours," he explained to his wife.

"Indeed, we do not want to figure as a pair of killjoys," she had observed. "That would be neither kind nor Christian."

"As to kindness, that is women's business, and as to Christianity, you may leave it to me to decide what is or is not Christian, I believe!"

Lady Grandpoint became absorbed in her own correspondence, and Eliza took the opportunity to slip from the room. She bounded up the stairs and, once in her bedchamber, sank into a chair and slit open her letter.

The opening dismayed her; it began, in Maria's best copperplate, *My dearest Eliza.*

It was not from Anthony at all! Bitter disappointment flared up inside her, then she saw that halfway down the page the writing changed and became the scrawl that she knew for Anthony's hand.

She rose and carried the letter over to the window, trying to make sense of Anthony's words. He began, *Sweetheart*—that she could make out—but what did the rest of the squiggles mean?

It took a good deal of guesswork and puzzling over the words to make any kind of sense of what he had written. Its gist was that he missed her, that he had had capital days out with his gun, that his bitch had not yet whelped, and that, ah, this was important, Sir Roger had got himself back into a good temper, and so, when the time was ripe, he would attempt to convince him of the strength of his feelings for Eliza.

Which was all very well in theory, Eliza said inwardly, pressing the letter to her lips, as though she could absorb Anthony's presence from the paper that he had held, from the words he had written with his own hand. In practise, he would find Sir Roger wasn't interested in feelings, it would take more than a good mood and a talk to make him change his mind. No, Anthony had better work on his mother. Lady Diggory might not care much for Eliza, but was that not often the case with mothers who doted on their sons? No woman was ever good enough for their male offspring. Might that not be the situation here, rather than a particular antipathy towards Eliza?

Of course, Lady Diggory was keen for Anthony to make a good match, a good match in the eyes of the world, that was, to choose a wife who brought money and connections, but surely a mother as fond as Lady Diggory would in the end care most for her son's happiness? If Anthony could persuade her that he could only be happy with Eliza, that their affection was more than a springtime flirtation, then she must in the end come round and abandon her dislike of the match.

Eliza sighed as she folded the letter, but two minutes later she had it smoothed out again, to read over the few words of affection, to summon up Anthony's voice, his features, the reality of his presence. He was so dear to her that this small token, this single sheet of paper covered in handwriting, was enough to fill her with joy—joy mingled with anger that she could not be with him. Two hundred and fifty miles separated them, a distance indeed.

She had missed something in her pleasure at deciphering Anthony's words—yes, Maria had added some lines at the end. *Do not be afraid that I have read what Anthony has penned above. Indeed, I could not do so, for he writes a vile hand, and I only hope that your*

Eyes of Love will be able to penetrate the meaning of what he writes. However, this is to assure you always, that I am your most affectionate Maria, and that I rack my brains daily to come up with a scheme to bring you and Anthony together again. But no more on that for the moment, for I have to close if this is to be taken to the post today. Do write soon, or Anthony will grow troubled. Address it to me, and I shall not read a single word of what you have to say to my brother, for what you write shall remain private between you.

And then the letter was signed with a flourish of a *Maria;* her friend had once seen the signature of Mary, Queen of Scots, one of her heroines, and had taken care to copy the dramatic lines, against all the remonstrances of her shocked governess.

Where to put the letter? She must keep it safe, she would want to read it again and again—although, her reason suddenly asserted itself, what was there in guns and dogs to set her heart beating in such a way? How absurd, and yet she could not but be glad that the letter had come, had she not been waiting every day to hear from Anthony?

She would send a reply at once. She sat down at the writing table and, after nibbling for a few moments at her pen, began to write, the nib moving swiftly across the cream paper, while she tried to keep her writing as small as possible. She could cross the letter, but she had an idea that Anthony would not make the effort to read anything that was not immediately clear.

A knock on the door, and there was Charlotte, looking solemn.

"Eliza, that letter you received, was it indeed from Maria? I didn't want to say anything that might arouse Lady Grandpoint's suspicions, and I am sure you would never be so unwise—that is, there can be no question of Anthony writing to you? Where there is no engagement—"

Eliza wouldn't let her finish, but broke in with some irritation, "Where there is no engagement, any correspondence between a single man and a single woman would be most improper. I know the rules as well as you, Charlotte. Maria always writes to me, you know she does. She recommends a new novel by Miss Griffin that is just published, she asks if I will buy it, and if so, whether I will send it to her. She has heard it is a thrilling story. Of course, I have to tell her that I have not the means to buy novels, priced at three guineas the set, how can she imagine such a thing? But I will request it at Hookham's, and if it is worth reading, then I shall tell her so and she can find it in Harrogate, at the library there."

She was talking too much, she must hold her tongue, or Charlotte would know that she was not comfortable with her half lie.

All Charlotte said, however, was that she was glad to hear that the letter was from Maria. "Pray convey my regards to her, I see you are replying to her directly."

"Yes, there is so much to tell her, apart from novels, all about London, and the noise and bustle and what the Tower of London is like, you know how Maria loves a good dungeon."

Charlotte smiled, and Eliza gave an inward sigh of relief as her sister changed the subject, asking her what she would wear that evening.

The Grandpoints were holding a soirée, a large number of guests were expected, and as a guest in the house, Eliza would be among the company.

"My green organdie, what else?"

"It is a shame we are not more of a size," said Charlotte. "It is kind of Lady Grandpoint to provide so many clothes for me, only I do wish she would help you to refurbish your wardrobe."

Charlotte was taller and built on much more generous lines than Eliza. Eliza shook her head. "I am perfectly content with what I have brought with me, it would be ridiculous for me to try and cut a fashionable dash, and besides, there is no need, for whatever I wore, I would be eclipsed by your beauty. It is not of the least consequence; as you know, I am one of your keenest admirers, and so take great pleasure in seeing you look so well turned out."

"Soft words, Eliza, and I am sure no one could doubt your sisterly affection," Charlotte said in her primmest way. "And soft words are all very well, but to return to what we were talking of earlier, I should like to assure myself, before I leave you, that your letter from

Maria contains nothing which you would be reluctant to show to me, or our great-aunt, or indeed to Mama or Papa."

"Stuff," said Eliza, flushing with sudden colour. "Don't be such a prig, Charlotte. What is in my letter is my concern and no one else's. Pray, do you think you should read it?"

Charlotte had on her gravest face. "Why, yes, I do. If there is nothing in it of which you could be ashamed, or which you know to be wrong, then let me see the letter. I shall be interested to read what Maria has to say."

Eliza snatched up her letter and held it to her bosom.

"Read my letter? No, you shall not. Not this letter, nor any other one which I may receive. That is outside of enough, Charlotte. Who are you to be setting up as my moral mentor?"

"Mama and Papa both placed upon me the obligation to see that you behaved in London, under Lady Grandpoint's roof, just as you ought. Don't flash angry eyes at me. You know your behaviour in Yorkshire with regard to Anthony was not acceptable, and when a person has made one false step, it must be that those near and dear to her are obliged to make sure this one wrongdoing is not followed by another, more serious, perhaps."

"Go away, Charlotte. I'll tear my letter up and swallow the pieces before I let you read it, and I would do the same with a note from a mantua maker informing me a gown was ready sooner than let you fancy you have any right to pry into my affairs."

"It is not prying, it is for your own good."

That was the universal statement of the interfering kind of person, and although Eliza was not exactly surprised to hear such sentiments expressed by Charlotte, they nonetheless annoyed her extremely.

"It is my duty," said Charlotte, her face a serene contrast to Eliza's furious countenance, "to inform Lady Grandpoint of my suspicions. If I do, she will doubtless take it upon her to read any letters that arrive in her house for you, yes, and to see what you send in the post."

With which words, she was out of the room, and "Just in time,"

Eliza said to the closed door, "for I should have said something unforgivable had you remained another minute."

The door opened, and Charlotte's head came round. "I recommend that you take a rest this afternoon. You do not want to be presenting a cross face to our great-aunt's guests."

Chapter Nine

Rest! Eliza said to herself as the door closed for a second time behind her sister. Rest, indeed, I never had more energy in my life. I would be a poor creature if I needed to rest to get through two or three tedious hours in a crowded room. Lord, dozens of people I neither wish to meet nor to converse with, and I may be very sure that they have not the slightest desire to talk to me.

Eliza's temper was always swift to come and swift to go, and it was not many minutes before her irritation—for really, Charlotte was vexing, no more—had subsided.

Practical matters first. She must hide the letter. What if Charlotte did convey her suspicions to Lady Grandpoint? Would her hostess demand that she give up the letter or have a servant search her room? No, Charlotte was a great one for threats, but family loyalty would take precedence over her desire for Eliza not to stray from the path of rectitude. She would consider that the threat was enough to deter Eliza from any clandestine correspondence, and surely she did not actually believe that she had received a letter from Anthony?

No, what she thought was that Maria's letter was full of talk of Anthony, and words of encouragement and support for their friendship. That was wrong enough in Charlotte's eyes; what must it be like to have no imagination? Eliza asked herself.

Her thoughts turned to the evening. She hoped that Lord Rosely would be among the guests, he was exactly the kind of man that Charlotte might be happy with, handsome and with the ease and humour that would balance Charlotte's more serious nature. Eliza had met him only the once, at a dinner party she had attended soon after their arrival in London. The host was a distant cousin of her mother's, which made it a family affair, as Lady Grandpoint said, and thus Eliza had been included in the invitation.

It was evident that Lord Rosely admired Charlotte exceedingly, and indeed, who could not? Charlotte had never been in better looks than since she came to London, and that, coupled with the elegance of her new gowns, was enough to capture at least the attention of most men.

Eliza knew, for Lady Grandpoint kept up a running commentary on the day following any party on every man who had spoken to Charlotte or danced with her, that Lord Rosely was not considered a suitable aspirant for Charlotte's hand. "He is perfectly well bred, of course, and an earldom is not to be sniffed at. Yet his father, dear Lord Desmond, is as hale and hearty a man as you may meet, and I dare say he will live a great many more years. Meanwhile, the family circumstances are not quite what they would wish, and Lady Desmond has her eye out for an heiress for Frederick. She will succeed, I feel sure, for he is an engaging young man. Miss Chetwynd would make him an admirable wife, and she has not a penny less than seven or eight thousand a year, her grandfather's fortune, you know."

Eliza listened to her with only half her attention. She cared nothing for the schemes of matchmaking mamas, keen for their sons to marry heiresses, she knew all about that, thank you. She had not met this Miss Chetwynd, but she doubted if she could hold a candle to Charlotte in looks; indeed, she knew from her great-aunt, and Lord Grandpoint, neither of whom were given to exaggeration, that Charlotte outshone all the other beauties currently on parade in London.

By chance, almost the first person she encountered at the soirée that evening was Miss Chetwynd. Down at a dutifully early hour—staying in the Grandpoints' house, it would have been unmannerly not to be downstairs in good time, before guests began to arrive—

Eliza had been sent back upstairs for her maid to arrange her hair in a more becoming style. It was her own fault, for dressing in haste. Absorbed in the novel by Miss Griffin which Maria had enquired about, she had lost track of the late hour and had only had time to scramble into her gown and run a comb through her hair.

With the protests of her maid sounding in her ears, she hurried downstairs, pleased that after all she was not late, but Lady Grandpoint had taken one look and expressed her strong displeasure at her appearance. "Lord, have you done it deliberately? Do you want our friends to see you as a poor sister, a Cinderella, obliged to spend her time scrubbing floors? Upstairs this instant, and if your maid cannot turn you out looking more presentable than this, she will be turned off without a character."

So when she descended again, some twenty minutes later, her hair dressed in a more flattering if not exactly fashionable style, she reached the hall just as Miss Chetwynd and her mother were being shown in.

What a plain girl, Eliza said to herself, and then when Lady Grandpoint glided forward to greet them, with a "Dear Mrs. Chetwynd, dear Miss Chetwynd," she could barely suppress a smile. Miss Chetwynd might be possessed of any number of admirable qualities apart from the substantial income, but she would not stand any kind of comparison with Charlotte.

Lady Grandpoint beckoned Eliza and Charlotte over to the other side of the room, where a man stood beside the fireplace, a man in his forties, of above-average height, with such coldness in his expression, such icy hauteur in his bearing, that Eliza felt the room would be improved by a few flames from a fire, May or no May.

"Charlotte, Eliza, may I present Lord Montblaine? Marquis, these are my nieces, Miss Collins, Miss Eliza Collins."

"Enchanted," he said in a voice that was as cold as everything else about him. His eyes swept over Eliza and rested on Charlotte for a long moment. "Enchanting," he murmured, and then, without endeavouring to make any conversation, he walked away to join Lord Grandpoint on the other side of the room.

Eliza was indignant. "How rude," she whispered to Charlotte, but Lady Grandpoint seemed to see nothing odd in his behaviour. "My dear," she said to Charlotte, "did you see how gracious he was?"

"Gracious!" cried Eliza. "I would not call that gracious."

Lady Grandpoint paid no attention. "He is the Marquis of Montblaine, you know. Rarely in town, but he has come up for the debate next week. He wields immense influence, although he does not often speak in the House. He is an old acquaintance of Grandpoint's, of course, and we are fortunate that he has put in an appearance tonight, he seldom goes about in society. He is enormously rich," she added, with a sigh of satisfaction. "Look, there is Mrs. Chetwynd trying to catch his eye, but she will not succeed; there, he has turned away."

Eliza was introduced to a succession of men and women in whom she did not have the slightest interest, and she retreated to a quiet corner of the room, hidden behind a large urn containing a feathery fern, where she could enjoy a glass of wine and not be obliged to smile and talk. How she wished Anthony were here. What joy it would be if he should walk into the room, catch her eye, hurry to her side; how differently she would feel then, the evening would no longer be an insipid gathering of uncongenial persons, and instead become a thoroughly entertaining party.

There was Lord Rosely, no sooner through the door and paying his respects to Lady Grandpoint than his eyes were searching the room, Eliza noticed with satisfaction. A moment later, he was at Charlotte's side, greeting her with smiles and a glowing look of pleasure. There was another man with him, a dark man with a good figure and a keen, intelligent face. However, he looked to be as uninterested in this soirée as she was; no doubt Lord Rosely had dragged him here against his will.

At that moment, Charlotte said something to Lord Rosely and nodded in Eliza's direction. He turned to look at her, and Charlotte beckoned to her. Reluctantly, Eliza emerged from cover.

"We meet again," said Lord Rosely, bowing over her hand. "Miss Eliza, may I have the honour to present Mr. Bruton? Miss Eliza Collins," he added, as his aloof companion looked at her without a flicker of interest, and bowed. Eliza gave him her hand and dropped a swift, slight curtsy, looking for a short moment into a pair of dark, disdainful eyes.

Eliza wasn't affronted by his indifference; instead, a smile flickered over her lips. So much male arrogance, such evident disinclination to meet her, and, sensing an enemy, such clear disapproval of the fascination Charlotte's beauty was exerting over his friend.

He looked away and laid a hand on Freddie's arm. He nodded to the other side of the large reception room. "Lady Desmond is trying to attract your attention."

"Damn it," said Freddie. "Lord, there she is with your mama, feathers shaking in their turbans. Forgive me," he said with a lingering look at Charlotte. "I must pay my compliments to my mother and aunt, I shall find you again."

The two men walked away; Charlotte was immediately surrounded by a little bevy of admirers, and Eliza, moving quickly back to her position behind the urn, was thus within earshot of the two men. To her pleasure, Lord Rosely was expressing his admiration for Charlotte. "There, you have to admit I didn't exaggerate when I spoke of her beauty. Did you ever see such perfection of feature, such a sweet expression, and yet so serious?"

"Quite," said Mr. Bruton, who had clearly not been bowled over by Charlotte's beauty.

"And her sister, Miss Eliza, a charming girl, with a merry smile."

"Provincial," said Bruton, with a shrug of his elegant shoulders.

Retreating further behind the urn, Eliza was distressed to feel a rising tide of embarrassment and, yes, mortification. Provincial, indeed. To be sure, she wasn't dressed in the silks or satins of other women, yet . . .

For the first time she looked, really looked, at the women in the room. Not at the older women, although some of them were startlingly elegant, but at those nearer to herself in age. Charlotte's dress, which had appeared so fine to her, would pass muster, but was not exceptional. Her eye was caught by the way Miss Chetwynd's dress hung, with a movement that made her look graceful, although Eliza was sure that she was not naturally so. That dark girl, standing beside Lord Rosely and Mr. Bruton, wore what was apparently a simple white dress, yet the cut emphasised her fine bosom, and the excellent fit showed off her figure to advantage.

Eliza looked down at her own dress. It was more than three years old, and its heavy flounces caught up in bunches of tiny roses looked to her now fussy and odd. She tugged at her neckline, low cut, but with a generous fichu for modesty. It gaped slightly, and she knew that the set of the sleeves was poor, making the gown pull slightly at the back.

Annie had noticed that at once, saying she could have the sleeves off in a trice and reset. "And also, Miss, appliqué flowers are not in fashion this year, overtrimming is quite passé."

Eliza could no longer tell herself she didn't care. Provincial? Yes, she was provincial, but here in London, however much she might tell herself she didn't care a jot for the company or what any of those in the room might think of her, she knew that she did care when that word was used to insult.

What if Anthony were to walk into this room? Would he notice that she was ill dressed? Perhaps not, yet she felt she looked untidy, dowdy in a way that wasn't asserting her low opinion of London and its ways, but instead spoke of a lack of taste and style.

She heard her name and spun round to find she had been addressed by a man she had met at the family dinner party. She held out her hand. "Mr. Portal, is it not?"

"Ah, you remember me." He was a large man, large in physique and personality, with such an agreeable, good-humoured face, that Eliza felt cheered just to see him.

"What are you doing, languishing here? If I knew you better, I would venture to suggest you were hiding behind that ridiculously large urn, but why should you wish to do that?"

"Because I know few people here, and to be honest, I have just heard myself described as 'provincial,' and I have come to the uncomfortable conclusion that it is so."

"Ha," he said. "Nonsense. You look very well. Allow me to present Mrs. Rowan. My dear," he said to the tall, dark-haired woman who had come up to stand at his side, "this is Miss Eliza Collins, sister to the beauty everyone raves about. She is feeling provincial."

"Your sister is astonishingly beautiful," Mrs. Rowan said with a smile. "Do you find it hard to bear?"

"Oh, no, not at all. It's a gift of God, and one I am glad not to have. It is very difficult for people to see beyond her beauty, you know."

"As to provincial," said Mrs. Rowan, looking across at Charlotte and then back at Eliza, "there is nothing provincial about her gown. From Madame Jeannette, if I'm not mistaken. How come you to be dressed so plainly?"

Eliza winced inwardly at the direct comment. "I came to London as an afterthought. I did not want to come. For Charlotte it is different. Lady Grandpoint is her godmother, and very fond of her, it is only right that she wished to treat Charlotte to a season. Our father is Bishop of Ripon, you see, and normally, there would be no question of a London season for either of us."

"But your parents, sensible creatures, I am sure, jumped at the chance for Charlotte to spread her wings. Well, it may serve, I hear she has some expectations from her godmother, and that, combined with her looks and good manners and a respectable background, should stand her in good stead. But you, my dear, are you to spend the next few weeks lurking behind plants, listening to men casting aspersions on you? Or was it a woman?"

Eliza said, in her laughing, husky voice, "Oh, how absurd you make it sound."

Her laugh was infectious, and several heads turned to see where the merriment was coming from.

Among them that of Mr. Bruton, who looked surprised.

Lady Desmond looked as well, then said to Lady Sarah, "Who is that girl talking to Pagoda Portal and Henrietta? I have never seen her before. What a very unbecoming dress, one would think she was the governess or some such thing."

"Mama!" said Freddie indignantly.

"I know who she is," said Lady Sarah. "The new beauty's sister. Their father is a bishop, a minor bishop, somewhere in the north. Perhaps she is into good works."

Thoughtless words, that were repeated to Eliza a little later on, when she found herself standing beside Miss Chetwynd and her mother at the supper table.

Good God, was there a plan afoot to make her think ill of herself? "Good works?" she said with a lifted eyebrow. "There are worse things in this spiteful world than good works."

Chapter Ten

"Damned Whig," Lord Grandpoint muttered.

The noble marquis looked around the room with indifferent eyes. "You mean young Rosely."

"I do, and I can't think why he's here."

"That is obvious enough," said Montblaine.

"Raking after Miss Collins, by God, her ladyship will put a stop to that."

"Perhaps Miss Collins finds Frederick of interest to her."

"She'll do as she's told. That's a connection that won't do, I tell you. What influence does Rosely have in the Church, pray, or Desmond, either?"

"None whatsoever, the whole family are irreligious like most of their fellow Whigs, and anticlerical to boot."

"Exactly."

"Tell me, why are you interested in the clergy?" Lord Grandpoint saw that although Montblaine was talking to him, his austere gaze was fastened on Charlotte.

"Miss Collins is the daughter of a bishop."

"A particular bishop? Does he sit in the Lords? I have not encountered a Bishop Collins, to the best of my knowledge."

"He is Bishop of Ripon."

"An impoverished see, I dare say the cost of coming to London is beyond him. Is he an able man? Your nephew, did I hear?"

"Nothing of the kind," said Grandpoint. "His wife is niece to my wife. Lady Grandpoint has a fondness for Charlotte, who is her goddaughter."

"And a great beauty, her ladyship is to be congratulated on her goddaughter's looks. She is in town to find a husband, I suppose. One with influence in the Church. Has she any fortune?"

"Some few thousand."

"A pity, for it will limit the field. However, with such an extraordinary degree of beauty, her face will be her fortune. Who is the dab of a girl in the green gown who was with her just now?"

"She is also my niece, Miss Eliza Collins."

"Really. I had taken her for a companion. She has neither face nor fortune, I take it, and so is not on the lookout for a rich and influential husband."

"To tell you the truth, there is some entanglement in Yorkshire, a squire's son, but the squire won't have it. Quite right, too, it's a tidy estate, and the young man is an only son, he can look higher for a daughter-in-law. So she is come to London to keep her out of mischief. We hope perhaps that she may find herself a more suitable husband among the clergy. She has been well brought up, knows how a parish is run—"

"A clergyman!" said the marquis, a chilly smile just touching his thin mouth. "Is her father a fool?"

"The bishop?" Truth struggled with family loyalty in Grandpoint's breast. "He is not perhaps a sensible man, rather a pompous prelate, you might say."

"Ah, then it is surprising he has not already advanced further, most of the bishops in the Lords are nonentities. However, they have votes, and stupid men can be persuaded to do as they ought. Clever bishops are like clever generals—dangerous."

Lady Grandpoint came up to them. "My dear," Lord Grandpoint said, "pray tell me why that young rakehell Rosely is here?"

"It is vexing, is it not? He came with his mother."

"And you felt obliged to ask Lady Desmond?" said the marquis, raising an eyebrow.

"Not obliged, but I wanted Lady Sarah to come."

"Lady Sarah Bruton, the banker's wife. Yes. I have a great admiration for Bruton. He has a grasp of financial affairs way beyond that of most of our bankers. We need him in the House, Grandpoint."

"If you came to London more often, you would know that is what we have been active about. However, he is a very independent-minded gentleman, he can't be bought or bribed, he's rich enough to buy up half the Lords and not notice."

"And no marriageable daughter he wants to see ennobled, which is a pity. Only the son, Bartholomew Bruton. I see him over there."

"He's going to be as obstinate as his father by the look of him. They say he's clever, very clever. Speaks several languages, just got back from Paris."

"I hear he is to be married."

"He is not yet engaged," said Lady Grandpoint. "However, it is understood that he is to marry Miss Grainger, who would bring both the aristocratic connection to please Lady Sarah, one of her own kind, you know, and an alliance to satisfy Mr. Bruton, for she will inherit from her grandfather."

"The great banking families like to intermarry," said Lord Grandpoint. "Or young Bruton may choose to look further afield, for a foreign wife. Now that the war is well behind us, these bankers are spreading their tentacles across the globe."

"Which is why such men are useful," the marquis said. "One should not underestimate the importance of the Brutons, father and son."

Lady Grandpoint wasn't listening. "Drat the man," she said. "It is too bad of Charlotte. I dare say young Rosely is a handsome fellow, but she must not encourage him, it will not do."

"I should not concern yourself, ma'am," said the marquis. "Miss Collins does not appear to regard him with any particular favour, and going together into the supper room hardly constitutes a declaration."

Lady Grandpoint shook her head. "You are quite right, however, one thing leads to another. And as to Charlotte's liking or not liking him, it would be a strange young woman not to be pleased to find herself in the company of so very handsome and dashing a young man. She is a reserved creature, it is impossible to know what she thinks or feels."

The marquis took Lady Grandpoint's hand and bowed over it. "Thank you for a most interesting evening, Lady Grandpoint, and now I must take my leave. I am sure I shall see more of you while I am in London. A word of advice, do not disregard the dowdy sister. You should keep an eye on her."

Lady Grandpoint looked at him in astonishment. "I do not know what you mean."

"Grandpoint has told me a little of her history."

"Oh, that. A boy-and-girl affair. Do you think she may go bolting back to Yorkshire? It is not very likely, she is a sensible girl, at heart."

"Sensible? My dear Lady Grandpoint, did you not hear her laugh? Take care, or she will set the town by the ears, and that, you know, would do Miss Collins's chances in the matrimonial line no good at all."

"Really," said Lady Grandpoint as the marquis exited the room, with not more than a slight bow, and a brief word to other acquaintances as he made his way through what was by now a very crowded room. "How tiresome he is with his enigmatic comments. Eliza set the town by the ears indeed. Look at her."

Grandpoint flipped open his snuffbox and took a pinch. "Did her wretched father give her any money?"

"I believe not, he was severely annoyed with her."

"Then I think we should fund her to the tune of a few guineas, my dear, so that she may get herself rigged out in somewhat better style."

"I have offered, indeed I have, but she says, perfectly politely, that she cares little for appearances, and is not in London to cut a dash."

"She does Charlotte's chances no good by appearing at such gatherings as this looking like the poorest of relations. She cannot stay locked away, she needs to make a good impression or she will harm Charlotte's chances. She is fond of her sister, is she not?"

"I believe so."

"Then put it to her that she must smarten herself up for Charlotte's sake, if not for her own."

Which was how it came about that Lady Grandpoint was in Eliza's bedchamber first thing the next morning, while Eliza was still drinking her chocolate and looking out of the window at the swooping swallows.

She rose at once as her great-aunt came into the room. "Good morning, ma'am."

"Sit down, Eliza. Now, we have to have a talk about your clothes."

Eliza had dark circles under her eyes, she had not slept well. She could not have imagined that she would find the casual judgements of others on her appearance so wounding, and her strong common sense told her that she could blame no one for the remarks that had been passed except herself. It was petty and wilful to behave in such a way, a kind of act of anger against her parents, and a foolish one. This was not her small country circle, where wearing the unsuitable clothes could be regarded as a prank; in Yorkshire she had often caused merriment among her friends by choosing an outrageous or nonsensical ornament to wear in her hair, or even, on one daring occasion, borrowing her brother's breeches, so that she might try riding astride—in that she had been aided and abetted by Maria, who thought it a great joke.

It was different here in London. And, as her great-aunt told her with some asperity what Lord Grandpoint had said, how she might injure Charlotte's chances by making herself noticeable in this way. "For you may think you are making yourself less noticeable by dressing so dowdy, but I assure you, in London, it is quite otherwise. You do not have to dress fine, you simply have to dress in such a way as you do not draw attention to yourself."

Eliza had to hide a laugh at the look of surprise on her great-aunt's face when she said, in the meekest tones, "You are quite right. It was kind of you to offer to pay for some clothes for me, and uncivil in me to refuse to accept the offer. I need not put you to any great expense, for I have some money put by. I shall ask Annie to make me one or two dresses."

"That is being sensible!" Lady Grandpoint hesitated before going on, "There is another matter that I wished to speak to you about. Charlotte spent quite some time yesterday evening with Lord Rosely. Perhaps you may hint to her that it will not do to take his attentions seriously."

"Not do? Is an earl's son looking too high for Charlotte?"

"He is a Whig, and a rake, and his parents want him to marry an heiress," said Lady Grandpoint. "And it is not for you to be questioning my judgement, you will agree that I know a great deal better than you what match might or might not be suitable for your sister."

"You had better mention it yourself, ma'am, for I am sure she will not listen to me. Besides, I like Lord Rosely."

"Whom or what you like is not an issue. Do not encourage your sister to think well of him, that is all. I tell you, it will not do."

Eliza let out her breath in a whistle as her aunt left, a vulgar and unfeminine habit she had acquired from a much younger Anthony. Warn Charlotte off Lord Rosely? She would do no such thing. Not, she had to admit to herself, merely because she liked him, but more because she knew that Charlotte would pay no attention to anything she said on such a subject.

Chapter Eleven

Annie was delighted. "Make up some dresses for you, Miss? I will indeed. I've had your pattern gown apart already, I can't think who made it up, it can never have fitted you."

"It is three years old."

"Three years old, good gracious. My mother says that the secret of being well-dressed is to have gowns that fit. She makes for Madam Lablanche, who has her own establishment in Bond Street, and dresses some of the finest ladies in London. Oh, I'll turn you out in prime style, don't you worry." She paused. "If you was to get dressed quickly now, you might like to go out and look for some dress lengths."

Eliza put down her dish of chocolate. Suddenly, to be out and about on this sunny day seemed an excellent notion. "Where do we go?"

Annie looked at her doubtfully. "There are the fashionable warehouses, but . . ."

"I have only a few guineas to spend, and I dare say my money will not go far there."

"No, so if you don't mind coming with me to another part of town, we can go to Spitalfields, where my mother knows all the merchants. We can find some bargains there, I promise you."

"Spitalfields! Where is that?"

"Oh, it's in the east of London, not the kind of place the gentry go, it is not genteel at all. It is where all the silk weavers set up shop, long ago, although now they are having a hard time of it, for French silk is smuggled in and it is cheaper and the women are all wild for the French patterns."

"I will be ready in a trice." Then, looking at Annie, Eliza asked, "Is there some difficulty, after all? Can you not be spared from your duties?"

"Oh, no, I'm done for this morning, except to wait on you, it is just that I wasn't thinking when I suggested we go to the warehouses I know. I'm sure her ladyship wouldn't like you to go to Spitalfields."

"Because it is not genteel?"

"It is not the kind of place a young lady goes to, and that's the truth. Perhaps you can trust me to buy for you . . ."

"No, that does not suit me at all. I shall like to choose for myself, and as for Lady Grandpoint not caring for me to go into such a part of London, why, I shall not tell her."

"She will want to know where you are going, she likes to know the movements of everyone in the house."

"Then I shall simply say I am going to warehouses to look at lengths for new gowns, which is true enough. She will assume I am going to some fashionable establishments and will be perfectly happy."

Lady Grandpoint approved Eliza's plan. "Go to Dodds and Minton and mention my name. Only plain materials, naturally, you are not to be looking at fine silks and satins, they would not be suitable at all. Annie will know what is best, I am sure."

Annie bobbed a curtsy. "Yes, my lady," she said demurely.

Before they went out of the house, Annie relieved Eliza of her purse. "Where we are going, with you so much the lady, you should not have this in your reticule."

"What, you think I will be robbed, in my shabby gown?"

"It isn't the gown, Miss, it's the look you have. Some skunker will have your reticule off your wrist or your purse out of it in a flash. Let me take it for you."

Eliza watched as Annie took her money and folded it into a little pouch attached to a drawstring on the inside of her dress. "There," she said. "It's how we all carry any coins we have, and beside, no one in Spitalfields will lay a finger on me. If they did, they'd know they'd have my pa to answer to, and he's a bruiser of a man, even if not so young as he was."

Lady Grandpoint, with great condescension, had offered the use of her carriage. "Charlotte may go with you," she suggested.

"Charlotte has letters to write," Eliza said quickly. It was probably true, Charlotte was an avid correspondent, sending long letters to her mother and to various friends; Eliza always marvelled at her letter writing, for her missives were as dull as they were long. "And we shall walk, it is not a great distance, and I shall benefit from the exercise."

"Very well," said Lady Grandpoint, "although I do not like to see you skipping about London too much. A walk in the park is one thing, striding about the streets quite another."

"Can we in fact walk all the way?" said Eliza as they set off from Aubrey Square. "Is it not quite a long way?"

"Much too far too walk, or too far for you, in those shoes. It will be best to take a hackney cab."

"Why, then, Fermer could have called one for us."

"Yes, but he'd have summoned one of his cronies, and wanted to know where we were going, and I could hardly say Spitalfields, could I? If we walk a little way, we shall find one standing at the rank in Godmer Street."

They duly took a hackney cab at Godmer Street, which threaded its way through the busy streets. As they left the fashionable quarter behind, Eliza was fascinated by the very different appearance of the city. "This must be where the bankers are, and the great merchants, this is where business is done," she said.

"Yes, but it isn't at all smart."

"I wish I had been born a man," said Eliza with a sigh. "How much I should like to be able to walk up and down freely and go where I wanted, and have a profession, like these men here."

"I expect they would envy you your life of leisure, Miss, and one has to be content with the station the Good Lord has set us in."

"You sound like my father in one of his sermons," said Eliza. "Don't you preach at me, Annie, or I'll get a fit of the dismals. As to a life of leisure, well, I doubt it. Oh, you see me leading an idle life here in London, but I assure you, my days are quite full in Yorkshire, with household duties and visiting the poor and needy. Not so hard as yours, of course, although I do believe there was not a harder-working woman in England than my mama when we were little, and Papa was rector of a large parish."

And that would be her lot, if she did what was expected of her by her father, and married a suitable clergyman. Life as Lady Diggory would be very different, busy, of course. How odd, she hadn't thought of Anthony for quite three hours, that was the effect the prospect of new clothes had on the female mind. She would tell him when she next wrote about this trip to Spitalfields. No, perhaps she wouldn't. He might not know where Spitalfields was, but if he did, he would probably disapprove, just as Lady Grandpoint and the butler would.

The streets had changed again, gone were the broad, prosperous streets of Holborn and the City; now the streets were narrower, the buildings on either side higher and gloomier. The children playing in the street looked hungry and ragged, and they went barefoot. "Here am I, going to spend money on finery," she exclaimed, "when only think what my guineas would do for those children!"

"Those children would never see a penny of the money were you to give them your purse. Some trembler would have it off them in a second, or it'd go back to a drunken mother or a feckless father who'd drink it away in a day. What keeps people respectable and off the streets is work, and you can spend your money in Spitalfields without fretting about it, for it all finds its way back in wages and keeping other folk in business. That's the way the world works, least it does where I come from. The market's just here."

Eliza looked out with interest as the cab turned the corner and came out into a bustling market. Stalls piled with vegetables and fruit lined the square and the streets all around, as far as the eye could see.

"Potatoes is what most of them sell," said Annie, which Eliza could see for herself; sacks of potatoes were stacked high on stalls, against walls, were loaded on to carts, and, set out loose on the stalls, were the subject of much brisk trade. "Greens and spuds," said Annie. "The market's really busy first thing in the morning, long before you're up. That's when the carts come in from the West End to take back all the fresh stuff there."

"Are the warehouses here?" asked Eliza, as the cab made its way at a snail's pace through the market area. Good heavens, if this was quiet, what must it be like at dawn?

Now they were away from the market. The houses here were not modern, but large and many of them very fine. "Built by the silk merchants, way back, like I told you," said Annie.

Eliza strived to remember the scraps of knowledge she had learned from her governess. "Was it not the Huguenots who came over from France and set up the silk industry in this part of London?"

"I believe it was. Frenchies, they were, there are still lots of churches here with French names from those days. Now these houses are mostly let out as apartments, the rich folk have moved west." She called up to the cab driver. "Draw up at the corner, if you please."

They climbed out, and Annie handed over a coin, after a spirited bout of haggling with the driver—"He knows the fare's a shilling, same as I do, does he take me for a country bumpkin, new to the town?"

Eliza had gone once with her mother to some of the warehouses in Leeds, but that was nothing in comparison to these. Behind long, polished wooden counters were stacked bolts and bolts of fabric, some in sombre hues, others in myriad shades from peacock blue to rich amber, from glowing crimson to lilac and silver.

A man dressed in a drab coat came hurrying forward to greet

them. "Good morning, Annie, what a pleasure to see you. Your ma was in here only yesterday, did she forget something?"

"No, I've come on my own account, or rather on behalf of my young lady here. Have you forgotten I live up west now, Mr. Jessamy? I'm in service in Aubrey Square, with Lady Grandpoint. This is Miss Eliza, who's her relative staying in the house, and we've come to look over what you've got, for she wants several dress lengths." Annie gave him a beaming smile. "Of course, I brought her here first off, Mr. Jessamy, knowing as how you'd give a fair price."

Eliza's taste was all for the rich colours, but she knew as well as Annie or her great-aunt that only the lightest colours would be considered suitable for a single young woman of twenty. Even so, the muslins made her stretch her eyes, silk muslins, figured muslins, and for evening dress, Annie said, "Netting is all the rage just now, see how pretty this is with the leaf pattern, in silver. Was you to have that made up over an underskirt in— Fetch that bolt there down for me, Mr. Jessamy. The shot silk, in the silver, if you please." And when it was brought down and the bolt unwound with astonishing speed, and the foamy material billowed over the counter, Eliza could only exclaim at how gorgeous it was.

"For my way of thinking, your colouring is good with white," said Annie. "Miss Charlotte now, being fair, those pale blues and oysters are all right, but for you, since you can't wear darker or more vivid colours, white and silvers are best. That one there, that muslin with the berry sprig, that would do well for a day dress. With Marie sleeves, and a ruff . . ."

Eliza was impressed by Annie's expertise. She could judge the weight and quality of material almost at a glance, and certainly after running it through her fingers. "I grew up with it, Miss," she said. "So it comes natural to me. And my sisters know far more than I do, let alone Ma."

Eliza had in mind perhaps two or three gowns, which, if Annie made over what she had brought with her, would do, surely, for the time she was in London.

"You will need a ball dress," Annie insisted. "That gauze would look well, although it depends on the trimming. A thick coil of braid around the foot of the dress, and lots of detail about the bodice. You need a good few yards for that, with the fullness there is at the back now, almost a train, you could say, coming out from a yoke." She fell into technical talk with Mr. Jessamy.

Eliza, revelling in the colours, and indeed in the smell of the silks and muslins and linens, had to make herself pay attention. "I don't need a ball dress, I am sure I shan't be going to any balls."

"You will, all the young ladies go to balls in the season, and once you have a dress, then her ladyship will be happy to take you. Besides," Annie said, with a quick, sideways look at her mistress, "haven't you got some fine relations of your own? I heard you was connected to the Darcys; well, Mrs. Wytton, Miss Camilla Darcy she was before she married, she's a fashionable lady who often gives balls."

"Mrs. Wytton is indeed my cousin, but she is away, she is visiting her sister in Italy."

"Yes, but she's due back next week."

"However do you know that?"

"I'm friends with one of the maids at the Wytton house," Annie said simply.

Eliza made her selection, although, as she noticed, it was rather more Annie's selection than her own, Annie firmly rejecting the purchase of a soft crape with a pattern that she rather liked, saying it was unbalanced and wouldn't make up well, and ignoring Eliza's continued assertion that money spent for a ball dress was money wasted.

The lengths were cut, the bill paid; now Eliza could see why Annie had been so insistent that she bring money with her. "Those warehouses my lady talks about, they'd send the stuff round and the bill with it, but it would cost you three times as much, they've got to cover themselves, and pay higher costs for rents and all that. Besides, nobs like to pay fancy prices for the most part. Here it's cash down, and far better quality and prices than the Pantheon, if it comes to that."

Outside the warehouse, blinking in the sunlight, Eliza bumped into an elderly man in a snuff coat. He stopped and apologised, his hand on her arm. Eliza smiled at him and was about to assure him that it was nothing, when she felt a tug at the strings of her reticule and Annie let out a wild screech.

Chapter Twelve

The next second another man, wearing a blue coat and not looking in the least like a humble tradesman, had seized Mr. Snuffcoat's arm and had him in a firm grasp.

"I've got the boy," said Annie, but at that moment, the thin lad she had grasped by his collar kicked her shins, she loosened her grasp, and he was gone in a flash.

The man who had bumped into Eliza was setting up a whining song of complaint. What had he done wrong? This lady here had come out of the door and gone straight into him.

"Be quiet," said his captor, and, to Eliza, "Are you all right?"

Eliza blinked, as she and the man recognised one another. "Why, beg pardon, I hardly expected, Miss Eliza Collins, is it not?"

"It is, Mr. Bruton," said Eliza, recognising him first with astonishment, and then with some dismay. "Why are you holding that man?" she said, more sharply than she intended.

Annie, her face bright with indignation, burst out, "Because he's a thief, Miss Eliza, an old trick, and I'm ashamed that I didn't see it coming!"

"The respectable-looking man jostles you, while his apprentice, one might call him, his young accomplice, steals your reticule or picks your pocket," said Mr. Bruton.

"You've got nothing on me," the man said. "You can't prove nothing."

"He's right," said Mr. Bruton. "Although I've a good mind to haul him up before a magistrate just so his face gets known." He shifted his grasp so that he was holding the man up by the edges of his coat, and looked him straight in the face. "Clear off. And take care not to cross my path again." With a final shake and shove he let him go, and the man vanished nearly as quickly as his assistant had done.

Mr. Bruton turned to Eliza and said sharply, "What are you doing in this part of town? This is no place for you."

"Being a mere *provincial,*" said Eliza with a cold smile, "I am come to do my shopping."

Mr. Bruton stepped back a pace, as though he had been slapped.

"Thank you for your assistance, sir. Annie, let us find a hackney cab."

Mr. Bruton had recovered his poise. "No, my carriage is nearby, you will permit me to drive you back to Aubrey Square."

Eliza opened her mouth to refuse, then saw how petty it would be to do so. "You must have business here," she said. "We do not need to trouble you, I and my maid came in a hackney cab, you know."

"It is not the least trouble in the world, I am finished here and intended to drive back in any case. My groom is walking my horses, so if you will wait here, I shall be back directly."

"What a fine gentleman," Annie whispered to Eliza while they waited, standing just inside the door of the warehouse, while a distressed Mr. Jessamy kept up a lament as to the wicked ways of thieves and his dismay that customers of his should be attacked like that.

Mr. Bruton's carriage drew up, an elegant curricle with two high-bred greys in the shaft. Mr. Bruton leapt down to help first Eliza and then Annie into the carriage, and then, instead of getting up into the driver's place, he got in beside Eliza.

"I fear we must be taking you out of your way," said Eliza, striving for a cool and polite tone.

"I am a neighbour of yours," said Mr. Bruton. "I live in Falconer Street, which is close to Aubrey Square."

"What brings you to Spitalfields?" she asked. "I cannot believe that you were buying vegetables or silks."

He gave her a swift glance. "My family owns properties in this part of London."

"There are some fine houses there, but it seems to have come down in the world."

"My family built one of those houses, Miss Eliza. Mine is a Huguenot family, although my family moved from that part of London two generations ago."

Eliza was puzzled by this information. His mother was a Lady Sarah, and he clearly moved in the best circles, was every inch the gentleman, and yet he spoke of having his origins in Spitalfields, which, despite the elegant houses, could never have been a fashionable part of the town.

Lady Grandpoint had noted the entrance of the carriage into the square from an upstairs window; when it drew up outside her house, she at once came downstairs to see why Eliza was returning in such state.

"It is you, Mr. Bruton," she said. "Pray, Eliza, what is all this?"

Before Mr. Bruton could betray her, before even he had a chance to open his mouth, Eliza shot him a warning glance and said smoothly, "Mr. Bruton was driving down Bond Street and chanced to see us. It was coming on to rain, so he very kindly stopped to take us up."

"Rain?" said Lady Grandpoint, looking up into a blue sky in which only the tiniest puffs of cloud were visible.

"A sudden short shower, ma'am," said Mr. Bruton promptly, his mouth twitching; do not laugh, Eliza begged him inwardly. "But Miss Eliza was ill shod in her sandals to walk on wet pavements."

Lady Grandpoint had a suspicious look on her face as she invited Mr. Bruton to come in and take some refreshment.

"I thank you, no, ma'am. I do not want to keep the horses waiting." He bowed to Eliza. "Good day, Miss Eliza."

She curtsied an acknowledgement and murmured a brief thanks

for his assistance. Although she had been impressed by his swift and ruthless apprehension of the thief, she had neither forgotten nor forgiven his remark.

Lady Grandpoint did not press her invitation, and he swung himself up to the driver's perch and took hold of the reins.

"He is, I am sure, an estimable young man," Lady Grandpoint said as she swept through the front door, "and quite one of the most eligible men in London, if you are prepared to overlook his parentage."

"What is wrong with his parentage?" said Eliza, following her into the house.

"His mother's family of course are irreproachable, none higher in the land. They say it was a love match, that Lady Sarah, who always was a strong-willed woman, fell in love with Mr. Bruton. Others say that her father, the late Lord Tenderton, a reprobate, I have to say, sold Lady Sarah to a besotted Mr. Bruton. Either way I suppose it has turned out as well as any marriage does. They have but the one child, this young man, not so young, either, he must be quite eight-and-twenty, now I come to think about it. We are all surprised he is not married; these bankers, you know, are very keen to secure the succession to their piles of money, and like to have a son to carry on the business in the family name."

"Perhaps he has not yet met a woman he wishes to marry."

"Oh, as to that, a man of that age must have met several women he would be happy to marry, and certainly there are plenty who would jump at him, with all that wealth! However, I do not altogether trust him. He has a kind of disdain for the social niceties, he is in society but not entirely of it."

"Men are luckier than women in that; they can choose their own pursuits and interests, they are not obliged to haunt drawing rooms and ballrooms."

"One expects them, however, to conform to the norms of the world in which we live. Apart from the social round, so important for people of our sort, one expects gentlemen to indulge in sports of all kinds, naturally. Or even gaming, although I am glad to say Lord

Grandpoint has never been addicted to the tables, no, nor to horses or all the other creatures and contests that men like to bet on. Mr. Bruton is neither a sportsman nor a gambler."

"If he's a banker, it's as well he has no inclination for gambling. And perhaps that fact that he is involved in business precludes him from spending much time on the hunting field or out with a gun."

"His father does not own a country seat, which is exceedingly odd, since he is rich enough to buy an abbey or two. Lady Sarah regrets it, apparently, but he says he has no great love of the country. She has her family seat, though, she is on excellent terms with her brother, and may go to Tenderton whenever she wishes. Mr. Bruton is a fine whip, I will grant you that." Lady Grandpoint paused, as though unable to put her finger on what precisely it was that troubled her about him.

"Yet there is that something, a kick in his gallop, one might say. I should not like to see you become too friendly with him. Indeed, there is little likelihood of that, for if he has shown no interest in the most dazzling debutantes of these last few seasons, why should he look at you?"

"Why, indeed, ma'am," said Eliza gaily. She was pleased with the quick way Mr. Bruton had grasped her predicament, and his tact in not mentioning Spitalfields, but beyond that, he was simply a man whose present courtesy hardly made up for his unflattering remark on making her acquaintance.

Chapter Thirteen

Eliza walked to the Wyttons' house in Harte Street, which wasn't far from Aubrey Square. Lady Grandpoint had told her that three o'clock was no time to be paying a call, but Eliza said Camilla wouldn't mind at all. "In her note she says to come as soon as I can, and it is not a formal call, you know. We are old friends, and cousins as well."

"It is all very well in Yorkshire to neglect the forms of polite life, I dare say in the north these niceties count for nothing. However, as a matter of principle, you must be attending to what is and is not done in London."

Eliza heard her out in silence, and then, knowing that her great-aunt always took a rest in the afternoon—at least, she said it was a rest; Eliza was of the opinion that it was more in the way of a strategic recovery time, mustering her plots and plans for the rest of the day—she chose a propitious moment to slip out of the house.

Fermer was also having an afternoon retreat in his room in the basement, Eliza judged, as a footman with an impassive face opened the door to let her out.

"Shall I say where you are gone, should her ladyship enquire, Miss?" he asked.

"Out," said Eliza briefly, and skipped down the steps. She could have brought Annie with her, but Annie would not want to be torn away from the delights of cutting and making, for the dress lengths they had bought in Spitalfields had been sent home only an hour after they had arrived back. That had elicited a further enquiry from Lady Grandpoint, as to the origin of the rather humble packages.

"A warehouse Annie knows, where the prices are more suited to my purse," Eliza replied, and since Lady Grandpoint was more interested in Charlotte's toilette for a grand affair that evening than in Eliza's frocks, she let the matter drop.

The Wyttons' butler did not seem at all surprised at Eliza's arrival at this unconventional hour, and in a few minutes Eliza was upstairs, being enfolded in a hug by Camilla.

Her cousin held her away and looked at her. "You look well, you have a bloom, but my dearest Eliza, what a shocking gown!"

"Do not feel you have to be polite, cousin," Eliza said. "You sound just like Lady Grandpoint, let me tell you."

"Ah, your great-aunt, how do you go on with her? Alexander has a great respect for Lord Grandpoint, says he has a shrewd head on his shoulders for a member of the House of Lords, but I find him lacking in humour. Does anyone ever laugh in that house?"

"No." Eliza looked around at the room they were in, the main drawing room. "What a delightful room, full of light and airiness."

"I hate clutter," said Camilla. "We have just had it done up, it had dark walls and hangings before. While you are here, you must see my dining room—well, you shall see it in any case, for you must dine often with us. Alexander desires his compliments to you, by the way, he looks forward to seeing you again. He is away at his club, he was wild to get together with his cronies and catch up on all the town gossip. We have been away for several months, and he feels quite out of things."

Eliza had only met Mr. Wytton once, soon after Camilla's wedding, when the newlyweds had been travelling in the north and had paid a call at the Palace in Ripon. The bishop, who disapproved of all the Darcy girls, had stigmatised them as a rackety pair; Mrs. Collins had simply said that Camilla was very much what her dear mother had been at her age, and privately to Eliza, that Mr. Wytton was just the right husband for her. Clever, and an unusual man, and witty with it. Camilla would never be happy with a fool for a husband.

"Now, tell me everything," said Camilla, when they had paid a visit to the nursery floor, for Eliza to pay her respects to the Wyttons' infant daughter. "How do you go on in London? And how is Charlotte? I hadn't been back in town five minutes before I was hearing of the latest beauty, and imagine my surprise when I heard who it was. Is she really grown so lovely? For when I last saw her, she was nothing out of the ordinary."

"She is a grubby caterpillar turned into a magnificent butterfly," said Eliza. "Only there is nothing of the butterfly in her temperament, of course. I am the butterfly as far as that goes. Or rather"—with a grimace as she looked down at her shabby gown—"a moth."

"All that must change, you must spend some of the money you have put by on clothes for yourself."

"That is just what I have been doing, this very morning."

Camilla was one of the few people who knew the origin of Eliza's funds, and she found it a great joke. "You must be sure that no word of your activities ever reaches Lady Grandpoint, for she would be scandalised."

"I am used to keeping secrets," said Eliza. "I hope you left Alethea and her husband well?"

"I did indeed, her husband is a delightful man, mercifully after that dreadful man she first married." Camilla looked serious for a moment and gave a shudder. "You will have read about the murder, the whole affair was quite shocking. The Italian life suits Alethea for the moment, although they will come back to England in due course, I dare say, for Titus has his house and estate to take care of. And I saw Georgina in Paris, very much the grande dame, I assure you, living in great style, Wytton and I were quite overawed. Belle is in the country, expecting a child, and you may see Letty, for she is coming to London next month. Mama and Papa are still in Vienna, and there, that is all the family news. Your papa and mama are quite well, I feel sure, I have come to the conclusion that it is an odd fact of life that men who wear bishop's gaiters and apron are among the happiest and most satisfied of the human race. Now, I want to hear what you have been up to since you came to town, every detail. Have you met any pleasant men? For surely Lady Grandpoint is scheming to marry you off."

Eliza laughed. "She hopes to find me a respectable clergyman. No, the trip to London is all on Charlotte's account. Besides—"

Camilla was at once alert. "Oh, there is a wealth of meaning in that 'besides.' Out with it, you have a young man in your eye. No, there is more to it than that, I sense a positive attachment. Who is the lucky fellow?"

Eliza told her.

"Anthony Diggory?" Camilla frowned. "I am sure I met a Sir Roger Diggory, while we were in Yorkshire."

"His father."

"The very model of an English squire, clearly a descendent of Squire Western! Tell me, is his son like him?"

"Oh, no, Anthony is tall and handsome. Fair, and—well, I hope you may meet him one day."

"If you are to marry him, I certainly shall, I must look him over, to see if he will do for you. No, I jest, I would not presume to question your choice. Only, you don't look so very happy, the word *marry* has made you thoughtful."

Eliza wished she could tell her the whole story of her engagement, but even so unconventional a person as Camilla would consider a secret engagement shocking. Besides, these things had a way of coming out, and here in London, with the gossip that she couldn't help hearing, she knew just how easily a woman's good name could be lost. The engagement had not seemed so wrong at the time, although she was beginning to feel they had been rather too precipitate, too rash.

"At present, his parents do not approve of his marrying me. They wish him to make a better match, better in the material sense, that is."

"And he stands by you? That is excellent. And you are sent to London to be out of his way, for I can see that your own parents would not want to offend Sir Roger, he is a potentate in those parts, is he not?"

Eliza told Camilla, a keenly interested listener, a little more about

Anthony's virtues, and then, for she found that talking about him made her melancholy, changed the subject. Were the Wyttons now settled in town for the season?

"Indeed we are, and I plan to enjoy myself a great deal. And we shall be entertaining, so you will come to all our parties. Charlotte, too, naturally. Or is she under Lady Grandpoint's thumb, does she get taken out to much statelier affairs? And does she have a young man in her eye? Does she have a troop of admirers?"

"There is a Lord Rosely, who is very smitten with her."

"Freddie? Oh, that is charming, he is a sad rake, but with such a lively disposition—I do not believe his nature truly vicious, I merely think he has sown his wild oats rather more vigorously than his family and well-wishers think quite right. I know that his mother, Lady Desmond, is eager for him to marry, but is he not hanging out for a girl of large fortune? Has Charlotte come into an inheritance that I have not heard of?"

"No. However, Lord Rosely is clearly head over ears in love with her, he cannot take his eyes off her, and resents every word she says to other men."

"You amaze me, unless Charlotte is grown much less serious than she was wont to be."

"Not at all, it is a case of opposites attracting, perhaps."

"I shall call upon her and Lady Grandpoint of course, and we shall find an opportunity to invite her here, and I will ask Freddie Rosely at the same time, so that I may judge for myself." Camilla paused. "I have heard there is a Miss Chetwynd making her come-out this season, and the old tabbies say that Lady Desmond would like her for Rosely."

"In comparison to Charlotte, I am afraid she does not shine."

"Yes, the Chetwynds are all pug-faced, it is fortunate for them they are also so very rich."

Time flew past, with Camilla's quick wit and lively exposition of how life was in London keeping Eliza better amused than she had been since coming to London. She exclaimed at the time. "I have stayed too long, you will be wishing me away."

"Not at all, I am blaming myself for not planning to invite you to stay with us this year, for I know Wytton would enjoy your company as much as I do. I shall send you and Charlotte a card for a small dance we are having next week. Have you met Mr. Portal? Or Mrs. Rowan, who is, you know, his constant companion? You have? I dare say you got on well with Pagoda, that is what we call him, you know, on account of his having been in India so very long. I shall invite them, and perhaps some other Darcy connections, we are a widespread family, you will find."

Lady Grandpoint had something to say on the subject of the Darcys when Eliza finally returned to Aubrey Square. "Cousin or no cousin, it is a shocking length of time for a call. Half an hour is the correct time, please remember that in future. She is sending you an invitation? Charlotte, too? Well, you can hardly refuse, for although the Wyttons are a strange pair, they are unquestionably well-bred, and rich, besides. I consider Camilla has made the best marriage of all those girls. Letitia threw herself away on that clergyman—not that there is anything wrong with a clergyman," she added, recollecting herself, "but when you have a fortune the size of the Darcy girls, it seems a pity to marry a Reverend Nobody. Then Alethea made that disastrous marriage, and plunged the whole family into scandal one way or another. Now she is married again, of course, but she and her husband can hardly expect to be received in the best houses when and if they ever return from abroad. Belle's husband is nothing special, and Georgina's marriage to Sir Joshua, although it was all hushed up, was another shocking business, although I gather they now live a perfectly respectable life—or what passes for one in Paris."

Wytton came home from his club in good spirits and swept Camilla into his arms, giving her a most affectionate kiss. Then, holding her hand, he went up to the nursery to see the infant Hermione, who had all her audacious grandmother's and namesake's character, even at her tender years.

"My word, she's going to grow up a tartar," said Alexander,

watching with alarm when his daughter's cherubic smiles vanished at the prospect of being carried off by her nurse to have her grosser needs attended to. "How does Nurse put up with that din? I declare, she already possesses a stronger pair of lungs than Alethea, and her voice is trained."

"And Hermione is not near so tuneful," said Camilla, who found her offspring highly amusing, even when she was in a temper.

They dined at home. "Let us make the most of a few peaceful moments together," Camilla told her husband when they were seated in the dining room. It was a striking chamber, with the walls decorated in Pompeian style, a dashing choice that divided those who dined there, some holding it was shocking and outrageous, with female forms clad in little but loose drapery, while others declared it to be enchanting.

Alexander Wytton had revisited the excavations at Herculaneum while they were in Italy, and he looked round the room with great satisfaction. "I suppose that means our friends and acquaintances will all know in a trice that we are back, and we shall have a stream of callers and more invitations than we know what to do with."

"Most of which you will no doubt refuse," said Camilla, who had no illusions about Alexander.

"Most of them are nothing but a damned bore. Do you go out tonight? You are dressed very fine. Don't expect me to escort you, however, you have not forgotten that I go to the Royal Society tonight, where Professor Savrier from Paris is giving what promises to be a most interesting lecture on the results of his excavation in Upper Egypt."

"I have not forgotten, but I am going to the Rutherfords'."

Wytton pulled a face. "Into that den of Whigs! Sooner you than me, the talk will all be of politics and the treaties and the financial crisis."

"Is there a financial crisis? What has brought that about?"

"I guess, merely; there is always a financial crisis of one kind or another."

Alexander was not a political man. He had no hankering for a seat in Parliament, although he could have sat in the House had he wished to. He was more interested in history and exploration and the world of the mind, and found the new knowledge coming from all parts of Europe and further afield infinitely more rewarding than anything that went on in Parliament or in the houses of the great in London.

"You will give my regards to Sholto, of course, and my love to Octavia, if you manage to get a word with her. I dare say it will be a dreadful crush. And then once you have met all your friends again, the knocker will never be still, I shall have to flee the house."

"Which you do in any case. I had a caller today, my cousin Eliza. She is come to town with Charlotte."

"Now, that is not news to me."

"What, that Eliza visited me?"

"No, that they are come to town. They stay with Lady Grandpoint, who of course is related to Mrs. Collins, is that not so? Yes, and the club was abuzz with talk of Charlotte. Can it be true, that she is grown very beautiful? How came I not to notice that when we stayed at the Palace?"

"You would not have noticed if Venus herself had been in the next room, since all you did was complain mightily about the draughts and rage against the folly and pomposity of my cousin the bishop."

Wytton shuddered at the memory. "I expect the girls are very happy to be away from home. Nothing was said at the club about Eliza, so I assume she is not become a beauty. I remember her as hardly out of the schoolroom, all eyes and wild hair."

"She is not a beauty, no, but she has intelligence and wit and charm, which I don't think Charlotte ever had. What exactly are they saying at the club?"

"They are laying bets on whom Charlotte will marry. Rosely is crazy for her, and quite a few others are paying court to her. There are rumours that Montblaine is more than a little taken with her."

"Montblaine! You cannot be serious. The Marble Marquis!

Why, he is old enough to be her father, and besides, he hates women, everyone knows that."

"He was married for many years, so that can't be altogether true."

"And his wife was the strangest woman, completely silent and never came to town. All she cared about was her gardens, and wasn't that what killed her? A scratch from a rose that festered. But he has been a widower for many years, I do not think he would marry again."

"I would, if I were in his shoes, if only to cut George Warren out."

"Warren?"

"George's father is the heir presumptive and so he will inherit the title, if Montblaine has no legitimate son. Thus, in due course, the marquisate would come to Warren."

"Well, I do not think Montblaine would do for Charlotte, and I cannot believe she is high bred enough for him, he is a tremendous stickler, is he not?"

Wytton finished his slice of pineapple, sent up from his own succession house in the country, and wiped his mouth. Camilla had ordered a meal of all his favourite food; while he had cosmopolitan tastes, and when on an expedition or travelling to outlandish places, he ate whatever the locals did, he had a weakness for traditional English meats and game and pies.

"And no one in the club mentioned Eliza?"

"Not a word."

"I think Lady Grandpoint is keeping her in the background," said Camilla thoughtfully. "She has formed an attachment, you know, and has come to London to keep her away from the young man in question."

"Who is he? I should think she'd never meet anyone in that dismal Palace except some clergyman creeping along those endless stone passages, looking for a way out."

"Son of the local squire. We dined with him and his wife, Sir Roger Diggory."

"Sounds a suitable enough match, what's the problem? And how come London, I thought everyone in your family who was in disgrace got sent to Pemberley."

Camilla pursed her lips. "I imagine that if Eliza found herself at Pemberley, with no company, she would go mad with boredom, and would very likely run away."

"How old is she? Twenty? Then, if the young Diggory is truly fond of her, he has only to wait a few months, and she will be of age."

"I am not sure that Eliza is cut out to be a squire's wife."

"I'm very sure she won't make a good clergyman's wife, which is no doubt the alternative. She has no fortune, she is not blessed with exceptional looks, well, Lady G is probably wise to keep her hidden. Nothing more likely to spoil Charlotte's chances than a tribe of relatives hanging on her arm."

Camilla protested at that. "Eliza is hardly a tribe."

"You know very well what I mean. Indigent relatives are the devil. Pity the girl hasn't a talent. I suppose she can't paint, otherwise she could set herself up as Cassandra did."

"My dear man, can you imagine what her father would have to say about that?"

"I'd rather not." He stood up. "You take the carriage and you need not drop me off, I prefer to walk, after such an excellent dinner."

Camilla caught him just as he was leaving the house. "Alexander, just one thing."

"Yes?"

"What odds are they offering on Charlotte?"

"Don't ask me. Pretty long ones, I should say, on a match with the marquis. I can't see it, myself. Invite her soon, I want to see if she really is such a beauty."

Which left Camilla to reflect on how horrid men were, betting on a girl's matrimonial chances, just as though she had been a horse.

Chapter Fourteen

Had Camilla seen Charlotte that evening, as she came downstairs dressed for the Foleys' ball, she would have guessed that the odds might be going to shorten on a brilliant match, for Charlotte, dressed in a gown of silvery satin, with puffed sleeves and a plaited flounce round the deep hem of her dress, was a picture to take any man's breath away. She moved with grace, and her eyes, Eliza said to herself, had never looked more glowing and beautiful.

Lord Grandpoint, waiting for his wife, himself soberly attired in a black coat and satin breeches, ran his eye over Charlotte, before giving her an approving smile.

Eliza would have leapt forward to give her sister a hug, but Charlotte put out a restraining hand. "Do not come too near, Eliza, or you will crush my dress."

"You are in great beauty tonight," pronounced Lady Grandpoint. "Eliza, my dear, I hope you will not feel too lonely tonight. Do not wait up for your sister, we shall be back very late."

"I have some letters to write," Eliza said. Untruthfully, for as soon as the door closed behind the three of them, she turned and ran lightly up the stairs to fetch pen and paper. She would have the drawing room with its comfortable desk all to herself, and what she planned to write was not a letter, but a short piece on London life, as requested by the editor of the Leeds *Gazette*.

Eliza's writing was a secret known only to three other people: her friend in Leeds, who was sister to the editor of the *Gazette;* her one-time nurse; and Camilla, who had discovered her authorial activities when Eliza was spending some weeks at Pemberley. The publication of her satirical sketches had happened by chance, when she was staying in Leeds and had written some pieces to amuse her friend, who was recovering from an illness. The friend's brother had read them, and at once wanted to print them. His sister would not reveal Eliza's name, and since the question of payment had been solved by the guineas being remitted to Eliza's nurse, who was now Mrs. Palmer, that was the name the editor knew her by. The articles were, of course, printed anonymously.

"Any impressions of fashionable life would be more than acceptable," the editor now wrote, via her nurse, "with details of clothes and so on. Such articles are always eagerly read by the ladies, while your character sketches, even if not about the clergy, will, I am sure, be well received by the readers who so much enjoy your portraits of clerical life."

Eliza set to with a will, the words flowing easily as she penned concise and witty vignettes of those who had attended her aunt's party the night before. None of them would be recognisable, she had too much sense to risk that. She chose the subjects for her pen from appearances and scraps of overheard conversation and gossip, which she could portray as types, a pair of dowagers here, a statesman there, and circling around them, young misses on the hunt for husbands and mothers with watchful eyes and wagging tongues.

She had barely finished when Annie appeared, a gown draped over her arm and a determined look on her face.

"You need to try this on, for the fit, Miss. And I was wondering about your hair."

Eliza put a hand up to her head. Her hair had an uncontrollable tendency to fly about in all directions, however firmly she tried to anchor it, and it was cut in no particular style. Charlotte's shining locks had been given a smart cut, but Charlotte's hair was not at all wild;

sleek and easy to dress, it hardly need the attentions of the fashionable coiffeur who had been called in to wield his scissors.

"I am afraid there is little that can be done with my hair," she said gaily. "It is a great nuisance, I know."

"Her ladyship's maid, Miss Pringle, is very deft with the scissors, Miss, and she has offered to give your hair something more of a fashionable style, if you are willing for her to do so."

Eliza had no wish to have her hair cut or shaped, by Miss Pringle or anyone else. He hair was a lost cause, and she told Annie so. To her surprise, Annie took this refusal in good part. "As you say, Miss. Can I ask you to slip the pattern gown on for a moment?"

So Eliza went up to her room, her head still full of the piece that she had been writing. She wondered if Anthony would care to hear about London if she wrote to him in the same vein; she rather thought not. Maria would, but then of course there was the danger that Maria, an avid reader of all the newspapers and magazines she could lay her hands on, might recognise the literary style and put two and two together. It was better not to risk it. She would write instead of how much she was missing him, and remind him of the happy hours they had spent together, before the interference of their elders had torn them apart.

"Stand up straight, Miss," said Annie through a mouthful of pins. Glancing in the cheval mirror, Eliza was startled to see herself. "Good heavens, I look quite different. How have you achieved such an effect?"

"I would swear your pattern dress was made up for quite another person, had you not told me it was yours," said Annie. "If it fitted you anywhere, then it must have been by chance."

Eliza was full of admiration for Annie's clever fingers. "You are wasted, waiting upon me," she said with a sigh.

"They would not let me near Miss Collins," Annie said bluntly. "Besides, you pay for dressing."

Meaning, Eliza supposed, that Charlotte set off whatever she wore, whereas her own, not very distinctive looks could only be enhanced by good dressing. Eliza's mind flitted to her sister; she hoped

Charlotte was having a wonderful time at the ball, and making a great hit. Charlotte danced with lightness and elegance, and that was one thing which Eliza did envy her sister: the opportunity to dance, for she herself loved the activity.

Charlotte was wont to say that Eliza liked it too much, that there was a thin divide between dancing with zest and turning the dance into a romp. Charlotte would never be guilty of romping. What if she had to dance the quadrille? Would she remember all the intricacies of the steps? Lady Grandpoint had had a dancing master in to make sure Charlotte knew all the movements, and Eliza had played the piano for her and her teacher as they went through the patterns of the dance. No, Charlotte would do herself credit, she would sail through the steps.

Eliza wished that she could expect to hear all about it, that Charlotte would eagerly recount every dance, every introduction, every dish served at supper, the merits and demerits of every partner—only that wasn't Charlotte's way. Eliza would hear more about the ball from her great-aunt than from Charlotte's lips, although surely Charlotte would feel some excitement at attending her first big ball, one of the grandest of the London season, Lady Grandpoint had said with some satisfaction.

Eliza could only imagine it, the light from hundreds of candles, the clothes, the rustle of fans and trains, the glances between men and women, the heightened feelings aroused by a warm evening, by music; couples tenderly flirting in alcoves or together in the garden, jealous glances, hopes raised and dashed, the whole armoury of attraction and rejection.

She came back to her bedroom with a bump, as Annie gave her sleeve a brisk tug before inserting another pin and saying that was it, and now she would set about finishing the rest of the gowns. "For I hear Mrs. Wytton is giving a party, and they always dance there, you will want an evening dress for that. And as for your hair—"

Eliza wasn't sure how it was that she found herself seated at the mirror of her dressing table, with the hatchet-faced Miss Pringle, every inch the great lady's maid, setting about her thick curls with a pair of scissors as sharp as the expression on her face.

Snip, snip, snip, and what seemed to Eliza to be handfuls of hair fell in dark rings to the floor. "I shall be bald, I shall look like a boy," she cried out, putting her hands up to her hair.

"If you will put your hand down," said Miss Pringle, beginning another round of her relentless cutting. And, Eliza had to admit, as her face gazed back at her from the mirror, it did look far, far better. There was a lightness to her hair, which matched the upward tilt of her mouth and eyebrows.

Annie was pleased with Miss Pringle's achievement and thanked her warmly. "I hope Lady Grandpoint doesn't disapprove," she added, as Miss Pringle put away her scissors.

"Her ladyship is not in the habit of disapproving of my actions," said Miss Pringle with superb hauteur. "And she was saying only this evening as how she wished something could be done about Miss Eliza's hair; she was even thinking of asking Monsieur Gaston to do what he could, and you see I've saved her the trouble and expense."

"And no Frenchie could have done half so well as you have," said Annie. "We'll have you looking a picture tomorrow evening, mark my words, Miss."

Lady Grandpoint noticed Eliza's new style as soon as she saw her the next day. "Much better," she said. "Pringle told me she'd cut your hair. It was inclined to messiness before, and that will never do, not in London. Now, this evening, my dear, I want you to dine with us, put on the best of your gowns, for I dare say your new ones will not be ready. It is of no consequence, you do not need to look fine."

"I have been asked to Mr. and Mrs. Wytton's house for later this evening, I mentioned it to you, ma'am. They are giving a party and have invited Charlotte and me."

"Charlotte! I am not sure. I had planned for her to have a quiet evening, but one must not neglect one's relatives. It will be not quite what Charlotte has grown used to, there is nothing formal or ceremonious about the Wyttons, one might almost call them an eccentric young couple; however, family is family. Nonetheless, you can dine before you go."

It was Charlotte who enlightened Eliza as to why her presence was required at dinner. Sitting at the dressing table in her bedchamber, attired in a pretty peignoir and looking, Eliza thought, quite ravishing, Charlotte stifled a yawn—for the ball had gone on well into the early hours—and informed Eliza that Mr. Pyke had been among those present. "I am sure you remember him, for he visited us in Yorkshire. He is a cousin of the Marquis of Montblaine, it turns out, and Lady Grandpoint, who is acquainted with his mother, has asked him to dine."

The name rang a faint bell in Eliza's head, and then a somewhat louder one. How could she not remember Mr. Pyke? "The tall clergyman, with hot eyes, who is the most complete bore?"

"Eliza, you are not to say such things! He is a most estimable man, with a serious turn of mind. You are wrong to value nothing but levity, Mr. Pyke has many interesting things to say, he is widely travelled and has interesting opinions upon a variety of subjects. And as for hot eyes, I do not know what you mean."

"Then I hope you sit next to him at dinner, for if I am subjected to one of his interminable monologues on some perfectly uninteresting topic, while he looks at me in such a way, I shall disgrace myself. And moreover . . ."

"Moreover what?" said Charlotte.

"Nothing, nothing at all."

Eliza bit her tongue and beat a hasty retreat from Charlotte's chamber, aware that she had just been going to say, Moreover, he is one of my best clerical characters. Her portrait of him had drawn especial praise from the editor of the *Gazette*.

Chapter Fifteen

Charlotte was in her best looks, but it was Eliza who caused her host and hostess to raise their eyebrows when she made her appearance downstairs. "Upon my word," said her great-aunt. "I never thought you could look so well. Where had you that gown, pray? Did Annie make it? I had no idea she had such skill, I am astonished with what she has achieved."

The dress was white, with a net overskirt adorned with tiny red leaves, and Eliza had herself been amazed to see how fine she looked in it.

"And your hair, properly dressed like that, is a great improvement," went on Lady Grandpoint. "Unruly hair can never be acceptable in polite circles, it gives a very off appearance. Pringle has an excellent sense of style," she added with satisfaction.

The guests began to arrive, and despite her best efforts to avoid Mr. Pyke, Eliza was no match for the forceful tactics of her great-aunt, who cut across a conversation she was having with Miss Chetwynd—not an interesting conversation, she had to admit, but anything was better than Mr. Pyke—to say with a sharp smile that the young ladies must not be talking among themselves, and here was Mr. Pyke, whom she knew Eliza had met in Yorkshire, who wished to have the honour of renewing the acquaintance.

Eliza's eyes glazed over as Mr. Pyke, after saying that he had ascertained from Miss Collins that her estimable parents, Bishop and Mrs. Collins, were in good health, decided to recall, in painful detail, his impressions of his visit to the Palace in Ripon. He seemed to have the history of the building at his fingertips, an inexhaustible stream of dates and builders and bishops poured from him in an uninteresting monotone, until, when he said that he would venture to say that she would find the incumbency of an Anglo-Saxon bishop, one Adlebert, of exceptional interest, she almost had the inclination to go into a swoon, anything to stop the flow of words and the devouring look in his eyes.

She must contrive not to be seated next to him at dinner. Judging by the approving looks Lady Grandpoint was casting in their direction, Mr. Pyke was in her eye a suitable prospect for Eliza; well, if her great-aunt thought this bore with his lascivious eyes would make the slightest dent on her heart, or cause her to forget Anthony, then she was quite mistaken.

The hour when they would go down to the dining room was drawing near, the wretched man was still at her elbow, a faint smile on his rather full mouth. He was fit for nothing but the Church, Eliza could not imagine him for a moment upon a battlefield or on the hustings or galloping after a fox, or indeed engaged in any kind of manly pursuit. He was suited for nothing but a pulpit, addressing a congregation of doubtless adoring women, which was how, after their previous meeting, she had described him with her sharp pen.

Rather to her surprise, Mr. Portal was among those present, and she found he was making his way towards her. "My dear Miss Eliza," he said, imposing his bulky form between her and Mr. Pyke; it was done with such adroitness, such a courteous bow, that Eliza suspected Mr. Pyke would not be aware of how ruthlessly he had been thrust aside. Miss Chetwynd caught Mr. Pyke's eye and smiled at him, his attention was distracted, and with relief, Eliza found herself being guided away by Mr. Portal.

"You have saved my life," she declared.

"Prosy fellow, isn't he? How could I not respond to such a cry for help?"

"Cry for help?"

"Words are not necessary in such a case, you were looking around with such an air of desperation that my heart was quite wrung. Now, there is Lady Grandpoint trying to catch my eye, she wishes me to take that dowager in a turban into dinner, however, I am not on for that, that is Lady Gregory, whom I can't abide. We were in India together, and she will bore me with reminiscences about a very dull set of persons whom neither of us has seen for many years."

"And I am destined to endure more of Mr. Pyke's history lessons," said Eliza.

"Not at all," he said, hooking his arm for her to lay her hand on. "I shall take you in to dinner. I am so rich, you see, that even Lady Grandpoint, who is no respecter of persons, will not dare to gainsay me. How beautiful your sister looks tonight."

Mr. Portal's urbane assurance carried the day. Mr. Pyke escorted Miss Chetwynd into the dining room, and Eliza was thankful to find that on her other side was Mr. Philpott, a middle-aged MP, who was interested only in his dinner.

"I should not have thought this was your kind of company," she ventured to say to Mr. Portal as the soup was handing round.

"You are quite right. However, I had some business with Lord Grandpoint, and it would have been churlish to refuse his invitation to dine."

Eliza sighed. "Even you are constrained by good manners, I see."

"They are the oil of life, Miss Eliza, and not to be despised. What I am able to do, and what you may learn to do as you grow older, is to avoid what does not give one pleasure without giving any offence. And I am rewarded this evening by your company, and indeed, I think I shall see more of you later on. Do you not go to the Wytons?"

"Shall you be there?"

"Indeed I shall. And in addition, as a further blessing, I shall enjoy a good dinner beforehand, for Grandpoint has an excellent chef." He nodded down the table to where Mr. Pyke was talking at length upon some subject or other; Eliza could not catch the words, and had no interest in doing so. "Is that unappealing young man supposed by Lady Grandpoint to be suitable husband fodder?"

Eliza laughed. "You are very blunt, sir. I believe he is. He is a clergyman, you see, and I am a clergyman's daughter. And he is well connected, a relation of Lord Montblaine's, no less. No doubt he is supposed to be on the lookout for a wife who will be suitable for running the feminine side of whatever parish is unfortunate enough to have him as incumbent."

"I hate to cast a damper on your raptures, but I have to inform you, Miss Eliza, that you would not make him a suitable wife."

"Do you think not? Let me tell you that he would not make me a suitable husband. It is of no consequence, however, as to whether we are well suited or not, for I am not on the lookout for a husband of a clerical or any other kind."

"Ah, then your affections are already engaged, and you have left behind a bereft swain in Yorkshire. I am right, you see how you colour up. Do you care to tell me about him? He is not a clergyman, I suppose."

"No. That is—"

"That is, you don't wish to say any more to a man with whom you are barely acquainted. Quite right, quite right. The first rule of London life is to reveal nothing, to be exceptionally cautious in what you say, in whatever company you may find yourself. If you wish to be rude about a person, you may be sure his sister will be standing behind you. If you have a secret, you have only to whisper it to your dearest friend with the strictest injunction that it will go no further, and within half a day the story is all over town, and when you do make what would seem to be a perfectly sensible remark or observation, you will find it reported in the most grotesque form, thus incurring no end of criticism to rebound upon you."

"You are very cynical."

"I am simply wise."

The dinner wound its way through the courses, until, finally, it was over, and Lady Grandpoint graciously accepted Mr. Portal's offer to take Eliza and Charlotte in his carriage to Harte Street.

Bartholomew Bruton had no intention of attending the Wyttons' party, although he had received a card. He was a good friend of Alexander Wytton's, and liked his wife; however, he was not in the mood for being sociable. "People saying what they said to one another last night and will repeat again when they meet tomorrow at some other rout or ball or card party," he said in response to Freddie's question as to whether he would be among those present.

They had met in the park, Freddie astride a rangy chestnut and Bartholomew mounted on the big black horse he had brought back with him from France. Freddie, after casting a knowledgeable eye over his friend's mount—"I like the way he carries his head"—turned his own horse round to ride alongside Bartholomew. "Although he is a trifle long in the back."

"He is not," said Bartholomew.

"Oh, you are in one of your blue moods, you have a melancholy fit. That's what happens when you have your head buried in money all day long, all this finance is damned dangerous for a man's intellects, if you ask me."

"In which case, you should take up banking at once, Freddie, secure in the knowledge that you are unlikely to be harmed by it."

"Meaning I have no intellects, I suppose," said Rosely with a grin. "You can't get that past me, I'm not such a fool as you think. Come on, Moneybags," he urged. "The Wyttons are not your ordinary hosts, it will be a lively gathering, there are bound to be several people there whom even you will want to talk to. You never know, you might venture on a dance, I know you can dance perfectly well when you want to. You may dance with Mrs. Wytton or one of her sisters if any chance to be there, and then you are in no danger of inspiring unseemly ambitions in any scheming mama's breast. Although I doubt if there will be so very many debutantes there, it will not be that sort of party."

"You reassure me. However, are not the Miss Collinses related to Mrs. Wytton? I am sure it is so. In which case, no doubt the divinely beautiful Miss Collins will be there."

Freddie cast his friend a suspicious look and tugged at his neck cloth. "What a fellow you are, Bartholomew. She is divinely beautiful, but I am sure I hear a note of irony in your voice."

"Come, Freddie, she is as beautiful as a Greek goddess carved in stone and as vacant. You might as well pay your addresses to a portrait. Or take a marble statue to bed."

"I have written a poem to her," said Freddie, ignoring his friend's words. "At least, I have the first line of a poem: *Charlotte, from whose radiant orbs . . .*" he intoned in a theatrical voice.

"Spare me, Freddie. Her eyes are not radiant orbs, they are houri's eyes, if I'm not much mistaken."

"Houri's eyes, whatever do you mean?"

"Think about it."

"You mean to be rude about her, and I do not want to hear you, nor think about what you are saying."

"And I dare say among the other debutantes who are supposedly not the guests whom the Wyttons invite, we may expect to see Miss Collins's shabbily dressed sister."

Freddie inspected his glossy pumps and flicked a speck of dust off the tip of his shoe with the edge of his handkerchief. "Charming girl," he said. "Unusual voice, I like listening to her talk and laugh. And she uses no arts to attract, which is refreshing."

"That is just as well, for I never saw anyone with less power to turn the head of a man."

Bartholomew was cross, and he was made more so by not being able to put a finger on why he was out of sorts. Certainly he had put in a hard day's work at the bank, but he was accustomed to that, and besides, he found his profession extremely interesting. Perhaps he was spoiled by Paris, had spent too many nights whiling away the hours in the glittering, elegant society of the French capital.

"You are become proud," Freddie told him. "Above your company. Now, at the Wyttons' you will certainly be taken down a peg or two, for there are bound to be some very learned fellows for you to talk to, there is really no need for you to dance or even speak to a woman once you have paid your compliments to Mrs. Wytton."

There was too much of a gleam in his friend's eye for Bartholomew's liking. He was used to Freddie's impassioned declarations of abiding devotion to this woman or that, but these so far had all been among that class of woman to whom affection was a currency, not a matter of the heart. It was a shame that the first time Freddie's fickle fancy fell upon a woman of his own world, it was that chilly bishop's daughter who was the recipient of his affections.

It would not do, of course it would not. Bartholomew was well aware of the Desmonds' financial situation. Freddie need not hang out for one of the great heiresses, but he must look for a tidy fortune, and to a wife who brought the right political connections. There was no way Miss Collins could be considered a suitable bride for Freddie, for all kinds of reasons. Very well, he would accompany his friend and keep an eye on him.

Then he was disgusted with himself at the thought. Am I my brother's keeper? Let Freddie make a mess of things, what right have I to interfere?

His mother had no doubts on that score when she had raised the matter that morning over breakfast. "You must tell Freddie it will not do, this dangling after that nobody from Yorkshire. Yes, she is undeniably lovely, but then there are very many pretty girls in London."

"I am not to be telling Freddie whom and whom not he may admire, Mama."

"No, for you men are very reticent in such matters, when a hint dropped in his ear— Is that such a lot to ask?"

"No, but I won't do it, Mama, as you know quite well. What, to be telling a friend whom he may or may not admire? I find it hard to praise Miss Collins, who is a lovely face and nothing more, but for me to say anything—why, Freddie would very likely call me out."

They were all making too much of it, Bartholomew told himself as his valet eased him into his coat that evening. Easy come, easy go, with the Freddies of this world. His fickle fancy would soon alight upon some other desirable creature, and there would be an end of it.

It was a dark claret coat, for in the summer Bartholomew didn't care to follow the inexorable rules laid down by Brummell as to the desirability of wearing nothing but black for evening dress. His man brushed away imaginary dust and creases from the perfectly fitting coat, and handed his master his hat and the silver-headed ebony sword-stick which he always carried in London at night.

No, he was out, Freddie was determined to make a fool of himself, for the first sight that met Bartholemew's eyes when he sauntered upstairs to the Wyttons' handsome drawing room was Freddie in close attention upon Miss Collins. There was an ardency in his friend's eyes that he didn't like at all. It wasn't only that any attachment between him and Miss Collins was impossible in a worldly sense, it was also that he didn't want his friend to suffer as he would if he truly fell in love with that woman, who seemed not to have an ounce of heart to her.

Mrs. Wytton greeted him with a smile, and he raised her hand to his lips with singular grace. He liked Mrs. Wytton, but had the uneasy notion that she could read his thoughts. "You are admiring my cousin, she casts all the season's beauties into the shade, do not you think? No, you do not agree. But you must agree you have rarely seen such perfection of feature, such an excellent complexion. Her bearing, and manners, too, must please everyone."

"She appears cold to me."

"Oh, Charlotte is reserved, she has always been so. Do not assume, however, that she has no feelings, that would be an irrational judgement, and I am sure you pride yourself on your rationality."

He smiled at that. "What makes you think so?"

"All men do these days. Unless they are of a highly romantic disposition, in which case they are just as proud of their corsair looks and determination to live at the extremes of love's shore."

Bartholomew, looking around the room, found his gaze arrested by a girl standing beside Pagoda Portal, talking with great vivacity to him and Henrietta Rowan. Charmingly dressed. Surely it wasn't—? No, it couldn't be!

The husky voice exclaimed in mock outrage, and there was the laugh, bubbling with amusement. Mrs. Wytton was watching him. "Are you acquainted with my younger cousin, Eliza? Shall I introduce you?"

"We've met," said Bartholomew abruptly, and then he pulled himself together as Wytton joined them, clapping him on the shoulder, and waving to a servant to bring a glass of champagne.

Bartholomew tried to concentrate on what Wytton was saying, and moved round so that his back was turned to Miss Eliza Collins. What had happened to effect such a transformation? He felt almost indignant about it, since his hostility towards Miss Collins was bolstered by his swiftly expressed dismissal of her sister as provincial. Freddie had cried out at that, yet it had been a fair comment, if not a kind or courteous one.

The elegant cream-panelled drawing room led into another large room, added by the previous owner of the house to make a small ballroom. Tonight it was decorated with flowers that filled the room with their fragrance and blended entrancingly with the painted panels and ceiling, which depicted various classical deities disporting themselves in a pastoral landscape.

Bartholomew could hear musicians tuning, and Mrs. Wytton said that the dancing would soon begin, might she find him a partner?

"No, no, I do not intend to dance," he said hastily.

"Why not? Have you injured yourself, have you fallen from your horse, or tripped going up those handsome steps into the bank?" said Camilla archly. "Otherwise I will accept no excuse, you are not to be numbered among those who are too middle-aged or learned to venture a waltz or a country dance. Let me see, yes, I know the very partner for you." Before he could protest further, she had swept him across the room to where Miss Eliza Collins, with an impish look on her face, was listening to a droll anecdote from Henrietta Rowan.

"Eliza," cried Mrs. Wytton. "Allow me to present Mr. Bruton to you as a very desirable partner."

Bartholomew, startled, held out his hand; the devil take Mrs. Wytton, forcing him into this, it would be shocking bad manners to draw back—but what was this? Miss Eliza Collins was stepping back, smiling and shaking her head. "No, Camilla, I shall dance later perhaps, but for the moment I am hearing all about Turkish customs from Mrs. Rowan, and you would not take me away from such a fascinating account of life there."

With which she bestowed a glittering smile on Bartholomew and turned back to Henrietta Rowan. "You were just about to tell me about the harem you visited in Istanbul."

Portal gave Bartholomew a knowing look, which made him even more annoyed. "Rolled up, my boy," Portal said genially. "I like a young lady to know her own mind."

Mrs. Wytton seemed vastly amused by her cousin's refusal to dance. "Have you offended her in some way?" she enquired, as she drew Mr. Bruton aside. "I think there is more to her disinclination to dance than an interest in Turkish customs. She had a dangerous look in her eye."

"Offended her! I barely know her." His eyes faltered under Mrs. Wytton's knowing gaze. Clearly Miss Eliza Collins had heard his description of her as "provincial" and had not forgotten nor forgiven. It had been a careless remark, and certainly not intended to reach the ears of the lady in question. Curse it. He couldn't apologise . . . and, no, why should he? She looked a great deal more the thing this evening, but she and her sister were provincials, and on the make, if he were any judge of women. Why else come to London? Well, if she thought her rejection of his invitation to dance had piqued him, she could think again. He was not the man to be impressed by such tactics. He drank the rest of his champagne rather more quickly than he had intended, and had to restrain a fit of coughing as a consequence.

"Come and meet Professor Savrier," Mr. Wytton was saying. "Were you able to see the new display of Egyptian antiquities while you were in Paris? That is his field, you know."

And with considerable relief, Bartholomew gathered his wits, addressing the professor in fluent French, and forcing himself not to listen to that wretched girl's distinctive voice.

Chapter Sixteen

Mrs. Rowan finished her anecdote about her visit to the harem in Istanbul with the ringing words that to be an odalisque in the court of the Ottomans must be the most tedious fate imaginable. Even were you to like the sultan in whose establishment you found yourself, you would be obliged to share his favours with perhaps as many as a dozen other females. One couldn't imagine any woman setting up such a system, no woman could be bothered to have a dozen men languishing around her house, waiting for night-time when . . .

"My dear," Mr. Portal interjected. "Perhaps this is neither the time nor the place. You will shock Miss Eliza with your outspoken comments."

"Which, judging by the look on her face, she well understands. I am sorry, Miss Eliza, I did indeed forget myself. And you a bishop's daughter, brought up to be prim and proper, I am sure. And therefore not to be offended, because you will have no idea of what I speak."

"Ignorance is not necessarily a consequence of a clerical upbringing," said Eliza. "My father's predecessor at the Palace was a notable scholar, who accumulated a remarkable library. He died while still in office, and it was part of a handsome bequest to the Church that his library should remain in Ripon, for the benefit of future bishops, and I made good use of it."

Her father rarely set foot in the library, and he would be scandalised if he knew just how many hours his younger daughter passed in there. Curled up in front of a meagre fire, lit at her mother's orders, she would become absorbed in a novel, stories of travel, histories of strange and fascinating countries.

"No good will come of it," Charlotte warned Eliza more than once. "Learning is not good for the female brain, you will overtax it, or, worse, you will end up a blue-stocking, and that will make it hard for you to find a husband."

"I shall find myself a husband who does not want an ignorant wife, that is all" had been Eliza's rejoinder. "And besides, a clever woman is well able to hide how much she knows."

In such company as Eliza now found herself, it was much harder for her to hide the results of her wide reading than it was in Yorkshire, when the conversation never strayed into topics such as the customs of exotic cultures.

"Then I shall change the subject," said Mrs. Rowan, "and ask an impertinent question. What has Mr. Bruton done for you to turn him down in such a very abrupt way, just now?"

"Was I abrupt? I did not mean to be. I spoke the truth, I would rather hear what you have to say about your travels and adventures than to dance with a man I barely know and who seems to have nothing to recommend him."

Pagoda Portal regarded her with raised brows. "He is very rich, do you not know this, perhaps? Young ladies, single young ladies, are not usually so indifferent to making the acquaintance of rich and eligible young men."

"Never mind his wealth," said Henrietta. "He is also handsome, which a man should be if he can manage it. He is clever, and conversable, a witty man."

"And one who is making great strides in his profession; he will overtake his father one of these days, and he is a man who towers above his generation. I am sure, were you to get to know Bartholomew Bruton, you would find him a very interesting man."

Eliza smiled. "It will not be put to the test, for I am very sure I never shall get to know him."

"So do you mean to turn down all requests for a dance?" said Henrietta Rowan, exchanging a swift smile with Mr. Portal. "Dear me, a young lady who does not care to dance . . ."

"Indeed, I do enjoy dancing. Only not with Mr. Bruton."

She was annoyed with herself, feeling that she appeared gauche. Since no one here knew the reason for her disinclination to dance with Mr. Bruton, her behaviour would seem odd, and even ill-mannered. Still, other potential partners were in the room, including an agreeable-looking man in a green coat who solicited an introduction and promptly asked her for the next dance. It was a country dance, and it was with a smile and a light step that she joined the set as it lined up.

As always, Eliza found not only pleasure but a kind of release in the movement and music of the dance. Her slight irritation fell away, her partner was droll, with a flirtatious eye, and Eliza settled down to enjoy herself. He was a relation of Mr. Wytton's and a good friend of Mr. and Mrs. Wytton's, and he knew everyone in the room. "Except I have not had the honour of making the acquaintance of the new beauty, there is no getting near her, I find."

"I am sure you know that she is my sister. I expect you hope I shall put in a good word for you."

"My dear Miss Eliza, how can you think so little of me? I could not be more delighted than I am with my present company."

Eliza laughed at him, not in the least bothered by his tactics. For a moment she wished she were again dancing with Anthony, then she told herself that in fact it was very agreeable to love and know oneself loved and therefore to be able to meet and dance with other men in a spirit of complete indifference.

"There is one thing about those who are invited to the Wyttons', they are none of them here merely because they are rich or important. We must all sing for our supper, this is quite unlike most parties in fashionable London, you will agree."

"I might, if I knew much about fashionable London. I have only attended one dinner party and one soirée, given by my great-aunt, and this evening I dined in company at her house. That is the extent of my mingling in society, so you see, I rely on you to tell me that this is an unusual gathering."

"Well, the agreeable-looking man over there, with the round face and the pretty wife, that is. He is an essayist, John Hopkirk, who is making quite a name for himself, and his wife is Mrs. Hopkirk, the flower-painter. Have you met Mrs. Horatio Darcy, who is another celebrated painter? Of course, I was forgetting, you are a Darcy yourself, are you not a cousin of Mrs. Wytton's?"

"I am, but on her mother's side. Mrs. Darcy is a painter? How extraordinary. In what sense is she a painter? Surely she cannot be a professional artist? It is impossible."

"She made her living by her portraits before she married. Now she works privately, and chooses her subjects. Her paintings are much admired."

"And Mrs. Hopkirk?"

"She is a professional; indeed, without what she earns from selling her paintings, they would be hard put to live any kind of a comfortable life."

"You astonish me, I had not thought it possible. Women writers, of course, I know of several of those, but a painter!"

They were separated by the dance, and when they came together again, Eliza asked him how he sang for his supper, as he put it.

"I am a poet," he replied. "Not of the fame nor standing of Lord Byron, who is, of course, the favourite of most young ladies, but still, a poet."

"A published poet?"

"A published poet," he said, with a shout of laughter. "How very suspicious you are, Miss Eliza."

"And now I shall discover that you are famous and I am the fool for not knowing your name. You will have to put it down to my Yorkshire life, it takes time for new writers to reach us in those northern parts."

The dance moved into another sequence, and Eliza found that her next steps brought her face-to-face with Mr. Bruton.

"I see that you do dance, after all," he said, twirling her round with some energy.

"Oh, yes, even we provincials do learn to dance," she said, and observed with some satisfaction that he was completely taken aback by this sally.

Before he could say any more, she was back with her partner, going down the line with an extra spring in her step.

The dance finished, and while the poet went to fetch Eliza a lemonade, she walked over to the window, fanning herself, for the evening was sultry. She was aware that Mr. Bruton was watching her. Surely he wasn't going to approach her after the snub she had delivered?

"Step out on to the balcony for a moment and refresh yourself," said Camilla. "People would tell you that is a mistake, that you will take cold, but that is all nonsense. I cannot abide a stuffy ballroom. You were enjoying Mr. Ketteridge's company, he is a lively, amusing man."

"I was ashamed that I did not recognise his name. Is he a noted poet?"

"He has had some success, and when his new work, an epic on King Arthur, is published later in the year, his friends and well-wishers feel it will establish him among the first rank of living poets. Now, as soon as you are recovered from your exertions, I shall take you around to meet some other of our friends."

Camilla looked across to the ballroom and exclaimed, "There is Charlotte dancing with Freddie Rosely, how well she moves, and how even more lovely she looks with the extra colour in her cheeks. What a handsome couple they make, to be sure."

Eliza craned her neck to see them. "I am so glad, for I am sure he is in love with her, and I do think he would suit her. I shall do everything in my power to encourage his suit, for I hate the thought of Charlotte being married off to a man she does not care for."

"In this day and age, any woman may choose not to marry a man she dislikes," said Camilla. "Your parents could not be so Gothic as to stand in the way of Charlotte's happiness, and Freddie, although not rich, comes of excellent family, and of course there is the title."

"Perhaps his family would not care for Charlotte, not for any faults in herself, but on account of our family not being of any great distinction or wealth."

"Freddie is of age, and while he should not marry to disoblige his family, he is surely man enough to decide for himself what kind of a woman will suit him."

"And that woman is Charlotte, I am certain of it," said Eliza, with fervour.

She did not notice Mr. Bruton, standing close to the other window, hearing every word she and Camilla said, nor did she see the tightening of his lips or hear his muttered words, "Freddie marry that icy piece of nature? Not if I can do anything to prevent it."

As they came back into the room, Mr. Bruton had moved away, was walking over to the other side of the room, looking so thunderous that Portal called out to him, "Someone trodden on your toes, Bruton? That's a very grim face, for such a cheerful party."

Bartholomew, his eyes on Charlotte and Freddie, forced his countenance into a more agreeable expression, cursing himself for displaying his fury so obviously, cursing Freddie for being such an idiot, cursing that damned Collins girl for presuming to imagine that a match between Rosely and her sister was not only possible but desirable. She was not only a provincial, but a scheming provincial.

He was still fuming as he walked back to Falconer Street, accompanied by Freddie, who was drunk on champagne and Charlotte, and inclined to burst into sentimental song. Bartholomew hauled him to his feet when he tripped on a paving stone, and dragged him out of the path of a wagon, lumbering its way to market with a top-heavy load of vegetables.

His anger wasn't directed at Freddie for his folly, nor against Charlotte for ensnaring him. How could any girl on the hunt for a husband do otherwise than smile and dance with a viscount who would one day be an earl, if a rather impoverished one?

No, his anger was directed at Eliza Collins. It was unreasonable, his rational mind told him. What was her fault, but to have put him in the wrong and make him seem guilty of ill breeding, and to foster hopes for a good match for her sister? He was too experienced not to know the cause of his anger, too disturbed to admit it to himself.

"Saw you looking at Miss Eliza," said Freddie, suddenly and irritatingly lucid. "Taking girl, now she's rigged herself out in a better style. Dare say if she weren't a clergyman's daughter, you'd be taking her home—well, not home, can't do that when you live with your parents, your father wouldn't like it, he frowns on anything in the petticoat line, so my mother says. Offer her a carte blanche, only she wouldn't accept it, too respectable. Needs a husband, not an establishment. Bewitching eyes, but not a goddess like her sister."

And he was off, weaving his way across the pavement and carolling in a loud and surprisingly tuneful tenor.

"The devil take you, Freddie," said Bartholomew, grasping him rather roughly by the arm.

"Hey, who are you tugging at? Mind what you're doing, or I'll call you out. You insulted Charlotte, you said she didn't have radiant orbs, damn me if I ever saw such—"

"Shut up, Freddie. Here, this is your front door, as I see you don't recognise it."

Freddie stood swaying on the steps to the house where he lodged, and turned a suspicious eye on Bartholomew.

"No, I don't recognise it. Sure you haven't brought me to old Mother Harley's place? Bring out the girls," he shouted.

The door opened, and there was Freddie's landlord, with Freddie's man standing beside him. They moved forward with practised ease and led Freddie inside.

"Thank you, Mr. Bruton," said Freddie's man.

"Put his head in a bucket of cold water," Bartholomew advised.

He walked on alone.

All right, he was attracted by her, he had to be honest about it. He thought of the way she looked when she went with such spirit and grace down the dance, her eyes glowing with the pleasure of it, and that slanting smile on her lips . . . And her laugh, her husky voice, that husky voice!

"Bishop's daughter. Bah," he said to himself, as he found his latchkey and let himself into the silent mansion where he had his own apartments. She had nothing to recommend her, she was pert and ill-mannered and wanted her sister to catch an earl's heir. It would not do. Even if she had not shown so clearly what her opinion was of him, there could be no future there for the son of an eminent banker.

In the carriage, Charlotte gave a hearty yawn, then lay back on the squabs, her eyes shut.

"You flirted shamelessly," she said to Eliza. "I cannot believe it of you, I thought you had more sense of propriety. This is not like being at home, among people who have known you for ever and therefore make allowances for your frivolous ways."

"I thought I was rather dull," said Eliza. "I didn't have Lord Rosely eating me up with his eyes, after all."

"I cannot help a gentleman's behaving improperly," said Charlotte primly. "And it is just a pose. He will grow tired of it, and find another creature to catch his fancy."

"Nonsense, he is in love with you."

Another yawn, barely smothered. "Lord, how tired I am. And what have you done to incur the enmity of Rosely's friend Mr. Bruton? He was looking daggers at you."

"At us both. I do not think he approves of Freddie's obvious admiration of you."

"It is none of his business. And if he had any sense, he would take no notice of what Lord Rosely does."

"Can you dismiss a man's affection so easily?"

"I do not care to see any man wearing his heart on his sleeve. He said how well you looked this evening, and that dress is becoming."

"Who said that?"

"Lord Rosely said it. He thinks you have bewitched Mr. Bruton, by the by. I told him it was all nonsense."

Bewitched? Eliza was startled out of her sleepiness. What an ass Freddie Rosely was!

Chapter Seventeen

George Warren arrived back in London as dusk fell, out of humour after a difficult journey from Paris. Rain in France had made the roads bad, and then he'd endured a blowy crossing with the wind coming from such a quarter as to make the journey drag out over all too many hours. The last part of the journey, by chaise from Dover to London, was accomplished without any problems, but by then the tedium of his mad dash from the Continent had put Warren into a state of considerable irritation. What the devil was Lady Warren about, why was his stepmother summoning him with such a peremptory message?

She had sent one of her own servants no less, insisting that he return to England immediately, there was a matter of the gravest concern that needed his instant attention. It was no good interrogating the man. No, his lordship enjoyed his customary good health—a faint hope that had risen in Warren's unfilial breast subsided—and her ladyship, too, was perfectly well. No, neither war nor revolution had taken hold in England, nor had the banks failed, or any heavenly bodies landed on the ancestral home.

As he replied to this last, sardonic enquiry, the manservant had cast an uneasy glance at Warren. He didn't like the sound of celestial bodies tumbling from the sky.

"You're a fool," said Warren. "I spoke figuratively. Oh, to hell with it, I suppose I shall have to go back to London." He knew his stepmother well enough to be sure that if none of the aforesaid possibilities were at the root of her summons, then it was something to do with money and his own interest, for Caroline Warren held nothing more important than the interests and advancement of her stepson.

Now here he was, at his lodgings, his landlord, a disagreeable fellow at the best of times, grumbling that he had no warning of Mr. Warren's return. And since Bootle, his valet, was always prostrated with seasickness if he ventured aboard any vessel, he had not taken him to France, and the man would have to be sent for. He had gone home to Warwickshire, the landlord thought, so some clumsy fellow would have to be found to wait upon Mr. Warren. No easy task, for Warren was something of a dandy, a fastidious dresser.

"Here is a note brought round from her ladyship," said the landlord. "Came not an hour ago. I was going to send it back, knowing you was abroad."

Warren tore it open. It contained the imperious demand that he wait upon her the moment he returned.

"I'll be damned if I do." He demanded paper and pen from the landlord, and cursing the man for having a pen with such a vile nib, he scrawled a note to his stepmother. If she wished to see him tonight, she must visit him, not another step would he take until he had sat down to a late supper. "And make it substantial," he instructed.

The note was despatched, and not an hour later, when Warren was just finishing the last remnants of a neat supper of beefsteak, sweetbreads, and asparagus, he heard the sound of a carriage drawing up outside the house. Minutes later, and the door opened to admit Lady Warren, full of her news.

George Warren listened with increasing incredulity. "Wants to marry again? To marry a bishop's daughter? You're losing your wits, Caroline, the Marble Marquis is far too high in the instep to contemplate any such marriage. Have you brought me over from France to fill me with this moonshine?"

"I don't deal in moonshine. Have you been to your club?"

"Dash it, I've barely been back an hour. I might look in later this evening."

"If you do so, ask what the odds are on Montblaine marrying Charlotte Collins. You will be surprised by what you hear."

"What, they're laying bets on it at the clubs?" said Warren, startled despite himself.

"Yes, and the odds are shortening daily."

"He ain't a churchy fellow, what's this with the clergyman's daughter? Is he one of your noble bishops? Younger son of a duke or an earl? The girl must have some connections."

"Oh, she has, but not the kind that would impress the marquis. She is a cousin of dear Elizabeth Darcy, if you please. Her mother, whom I had the misfortune to know during that awful few months we spent in Hertfordshire, at a dreary place called Meryton, is a nobody. She was, before her marriage, a Miss Lucas. Her father was a plebeian merchant who somehow achieved a knighthood, and ever after talked about the Court as though he belonged there. Miss Lucas, a plain woman with a small fortune who had no prospects of catching herself a decent husband, threw herself in the way of a pompous cleric, the same man who has now risen to fill a bishopric. One of the poor bishoprics, I hasten to add, I have it on good authority that his see is worth scarce twelve hundred a year, very likely less. It is he who is related to Elizabeth, they are cousins, you know what a horde of vulgar relations she has."

"All of which convinces me that it's nothing but a rumour, London is full of gossip and rumours at this time of year."

"At every time of year, but I would scarcely have sent for you as I did on account of a rumour. I believe Montblaine to be serious."

"What has she to recommend her? No family, or only a vulgar one, no wealth, what are you thinking of?"

"She is extraordinarily beautiful."

Warren whistled. His stepmother now had his full attention. "You don't mean blood runs in Montblaine's veins after all? I suppose he's come to that age when men run wild for a pretty face."

"She is not a pretty face. I have rarely seen such a beauty. No character, little charm, but so lovely that people stop in the street to stare at her. She has a horde of devoted admirers, and she cold-shoulders them all. That may be another reason for her attraction for Montblaine, she is as icy as he is."

"Who are the other suitors? Can't we encourage them?"

"Oh, I could name you a dozen. The keenest is probably young Rosely, who is making an exhibition of himself, mooning about town, proclaiming his love to anyone who will listen."

"Can we encourage his suit?"

"His mother certainly doesn't do so. She would be more than happy to see Miss Collins marry Montblaine, she does all she can to encourage his suit, inviting them both to dine and so on."

"These damn Darcys, how they thwart me at every possible opportunity."

"Thwart! To deprive you of a marquisate is rather more than thwarting."

"Well, she won't do it. Not if I have to hire a set of ruffians to attend to her beauty with a cudgel or two, or a knife; a sharp blade does wonders to the features."

"Take care," warned Lady Warren, seemingly not distressed by this vicious suggestion. "Your reputation is none too good, and the authorities are altogether too eager to uncover the instigator of such attacks where there is not an obvious motive, such as rape or robbery. It is a pity, now I come to think of it, that there is no likelihood of the young woman's being ravished, since one thing that would repel the marquis would be damaged goods."

"How old is she?" Warren demanded.

Lady Warren shrugged. "Twenty-one, twenty-two, I neither know nor care. Young enough to be his daughter. And of just the age for producing an heir. She isn't one of your frail women who'll not make it through a pregnancy, I regret to say that she appears depressingly healthy."

Warren filled her glass with more wine. He stood by the fireplace, tapping the fender with his foot and simultaneously drumming his fingers along the polished wooden shelf. "Well, I confess I was angry to be called back from Paris, where I was having a good time, let me tell you, but if what you say is right—"

"When have you ever known me wrong about such matters?"

That was true enough. Whatever Lady Warren's faults, she had the sharpest eye and nose in London for an affair, a tendresse, an amour, whether illicit or not.

"God, if Montblaine's in London, I'll have to call on him, can't be seen to fail in my duty. It will be an effort to do the civil, I have to say. What a bore! Forty-eight hours ago, I was attending the most delightful party in Paris, and here I am back in London, where nothing is as it should be."

"You've been casting yourself at the feet of Madame de Genlis, by what I hear," said Lady Warren.

"You hear a good deal too much. Very elegant feet she has, too. She wore the most elegant shoes, pink satin with a diamond buckle." His voice grew warm; George Warren loved a well-turned foot.

"This Charlotte creature has quite a pretty foot," said his stepmother thoughtfully. "I wonder—"

"Oh, no. Don't, please, suggest that I add my name to the list of her admirers."

"You could do worse. Of course, nothing serious, you could not possibly marry her, a penniless nobody. On the other hand, if you played your cards right, you might cause a scandal."

"Pay my addresses to this icicle you have described? Are you serious?"

"Or, another possibility—she has a sister."

"What, two beauties?"

"Not at all. Miss Eliza Collins is perfectly undistinguished in every way. It is all round town that Bartholomew Bruton called her a dowdy provincial, that did her credit no good, I can assure you. But plain Janes are more likely to succumb to the charms of a handsome man, a man of experience."

And she regarded her stepson with great complacency. To her eyes he was the handsomest of men, and indeed, many women found him so. Those whose taste ran to the Byronic found his dark, wavy hair, his haughty, disdainful expression, and good figure attractive. Why should not this sister be among their number?

"I suppose she is called Eliza after Mrs. Darcy, who is her godmother. In fact, she is not unlike what Elizabeth was at the same age, just as pert and forward and lacking in style or any distinction of feature. Yes, she might well have her head turned by such an one as you."

"I do not see the point of it. The marquis is not enamoured of the dull sister."

"No, but create a scandal about one sister, and he'll go off the other one quick enough," said Lady Warren. "Destroy the reputation of one, and you'll drag down the other."

Warren kicked at a log that had rolled from the grate. "Devilish dull work, seducing the ice block or the ugly sister. On balance, I'll go for the beauty, I believe."

"As you please, whatever will work best to put a spoke in the wheels of the Collins chit. I don't need to remind you what is at stake: there is a world of difference between a barony and a marquisate."

Chapter Eighteen

Charlotte was invited everywhere, with all the season's most vigorous and successful hostesses adding her name to their lists. Even the patronesses of Almacks hinted to Lady Grandpoint that if she cared to bring the girl to the balls, they would be happy to supply her with vouchers. No one wanted to slight a young woman if there were the slightest possibility of her becoming a marchioness, or even a countess.

"Should the season finish without the girl contracting a brilliant match, then they will be left looking foolish," said Lady Jarvie to Mrs. Naburn when they stood together at one of the season's most glittering assemblies.

"And, should she marry Montblaine, I dare say he will keep her in the country all year round, as he did poor Gertrude."

"Gertrude liked the country, you know how bucolic all the Rowlandsons are."

"Miss Collins will find she has bitten off more than she can chew if she lands Montblaine," said Mrs. Naburn in spiteful tones. "I dare say she would make an excellent clergyman's wife; however, she would find running a great house and all that entails quite a different matter. She would have no idea how to go on, I don't suppose she ever set foot in a nobleman's house before she came to London, and she will have no idea of what living in a great house in the country is like."

"Her father, the bishop"—and they both laughed. "Does he not live in a palace?"

"*Palace* is no more than a courtesy title, I believe the one in Ripon is positively mediaeval in every way, and the bishopric is so poor, the stipend the lowest of all the bishops', that there is no money for any of the comforts of life. Were she to set eyes on Montblaine House, she would faint from shock, and as to being its mistress—she will learn her lesson if that should ever come about."

"Why are not her parents in London?" enquired another ill-wisher. "The House is in session, half the bench of bishops are here, making a nuisance of themselves as usual, prating on upon matters about which they know nothing. Why is Bishop Collins not among the throng?"

"I hear he cannot afford to come to London. He is not rich, he has no private income. Moreover, since he has the reputation of being a far from sensible man, I dare say Mrs. Collins, who is supposedly a woman of more sense than her husband, thinks it wise to keep him in his northern fastness, where he can do nothing to harm his daughter's chances."

So Charlotte sallied forth each day, her life a round of social activity: in the evenings, routs and drums, visits to Ranelagh, balls, dances. In the daytime, she went for drives to Richmond Park, to Hampton Court, and at the fashionable hour of five o'clock, she would walk or drive in the park. Lady Grandpoint was pleased, but in no way triumphant; she was too shrewd to show anything other than well-bred, indifferent acceptance of the success that came to her goddaughter.

As for Charlotte, well, reflected Eliza, no one could say her head had been turned. She sailed through this exhausting schedule with the same calm aspect as she wore to church, or which, as Eliza knew, but fashionable London didn't, she had shown when her favourite dog was lost, or she had endured a painful session with the Harrogate dentist.

Whether because Lady Grandpoint subtly discouraged hostesses from including Eliza in their invitations, or because she chose to keep herself in the background, Eliza was not often included in these festivities. Yet, to her surprise, and almost without Lady Grandpoint noticing, she began to be asked out on her own account. This was largely due to Camilla, who enjoyed Eliza's company, and whose own wide social circle, quite different from the rarefied world in which Charlotte was moving, was much more to Eliza's taste.

Alexander Wytton, rich and well-born, could have moved in the highest circles with his wife, had he chosen to do so. He didn't; as his mother dispassionately said to Camilla, "Alexander is as eccentric as his father ever was, they are all the same, these Wyttons, there is no persuading them to do what they are not inclined to do."

Lady Hermione Wytton was, like her son, a great traveller and spent a large part of every year in Italy. At present, she was settled in her house in London for a few weeks, and was a welcome guest at Camilla's parties. She met and approved of Eliza, although, as she remarked to Camilla, "The girl has a secret, maybe more than one, and not just of the romantic kind; it's to be hoped she's not going to get herself into a scrape, for I cannot imagine her family would look kindly upon her if she did."

That evening, however, Eliza was at home. Charlotte was out at yet another ball; Lord Grandpoint was in the House, and would not be back until the early hours. Camilla was coming later for Eliza, to take her to the opera. Meanwhile, she enjoyed the luxury of having the handsome drawing room to herself. She sat at the writing desk, nibbling the end of her pen, then writing quick paragraphs.

Her funds were running low. Annie's clever fingers had done wonders with her wardrobe, but she found she needed more clothes than she had bargained for. It was not that she wasn't earning money. Her sketches of fashionable London life, with a gallery of memorable characters to rank with those she had incorporated into her clerical pieces, were much appreciated by the *Gazette,* and the half guineas or even guineas were mounting up.

No, the problem was laying hands on the money. When she was in Yorkshire, it was not so difficult. Her nurse had left domestic service when she married Mr. Palmer, who was a haberdasher in Harrogate.

Mrs. Palmer and her erstwhile charge had come to an agreement that Eliza's money could be paid to the Harrogate address, and on her infrequent trips to Harrogate, it was perfectly in order for Eliza to visit the shop, to buy what she needed, and to enquire after the well-being of Mrs. Palmer, of whom she had always been fond.

If getting to Harrogate from Ripon was not always easy, from London it was, of course, impossible. Camilla came to her rescue. "I will advance you the money," she said. "Write to Mrs. Palmer, and she will tell you how much she holds for you. Then I can give you that much, and we can settle up in some way later on; Alexander can collect the guineas when he next goes north, he will not mind."

Eliza was still extremely careful to disguise the models for her characters, and the talk and comments flowed rapidly from her pen. With that task completed, she reached into her reticule and took out the letter that had come from Maria that morning. Charlotte had not been down to breakfast, Lady Grandpoint had been distracted by a maid dropping a plate, and Eliza had whisked the letter away from the pile before anyone noticed.

She looked down at the letter in her hand. Maria's part of the letter was mostly about Sir Roger's testy temper. *Most likely he is going to be afflicted with the gout,* she wrote. *I have observed that he is often in a bad mood before it strikes. Anthony hardly speaks to him, and that also makes him bad-tempered. Your name is never mentioned, although Mama tries slyly to discover if Anthony still thinks of you; he is wise to that, and lets neither of them know that his affections remain unchanged.*

Then came the precious words written by Anthony himself. His favourite bitch had finally whelped: five puppies, and a runt that would not survive. Should she like one of the pups for her own? And then he went into a eulogy about a new horse he had bought, sixteen hands, a perfect goer, good strong hocks. The horse had been offered to his father, but was not up to his weight. Eliza knew that the squire rode at eighteen stone and needed the heaviest of hunters to carry him.

It was not yet dark, and stepping out on to the balcony overlooking Aubrey Square, Eliza watched the gentle glow of candles and oil lights spring up behind the windows. The trees and grass in the garden in the centre of the square were at their most lush after some rain. Eliza's mind was far away, seeing a more distant landscape, with hills and forests and moors, and a stone house with huge chimneys from the age of King James. Diggory Hall, set in formal gardens this side of the ha-ha, with a wilder landscape beyond, where woolly-coated sheep grazed.

Eliza had the sensation of being in two worlds, here in London, looking down into the formal square, with its enclosed, ordered greenery and, behind her, the fashionable drawing room with its sofa, tables, mirrors, marble fireplace, fine rugs; and that other place, more than two hundred miles away, remote now, green with the colours of late spring, the mediaeval palace that had been her home for five years, the dirty country lanes, the rustics in their carts and wagons.

Yes, a provincial world.

Chapter Nineteen

For the first time, as she slowly turned and came back inside, she considered the contrasting worlds. She had never given it a thought. London was alien, another world. A world in which she didn't belong, never could belong, and didn't want to belong. The air she breathed was the air of Yorkshire, the grey northern stones, not the red brick and railings of London.

And yet. She looked up at the portrait that hung above the fireplace. Unlike most of the family portraits in the house, this one belonged to her great-aunt. It was her great-great-grandfather, one Tobias Lucas, who had come to London to make a fortune, which he then gave away in philanthropic and scientific causes. "A merchant," Lady Grandpoint had said, the stain of trade quite removed by the generations that came between. "An admirable man in many ways."

Eliza could see nothing of herself in his heavily jowled face, the full-bottomed wig, the pose of stout prosperity. Even so, he was a Londoner, born and bred, had risen in this metropolitan world. She didn't want to admit that London was beginning to fascinate her, that the noise and bustle, the crowds, the smoke, the grime, the pace of life, which had at first repelled her, had some appeal.

Would she come to London with Anthony? The squire and his wife coming to town, a joke among fashionable circles. Bumpkins, slow and inclined to stand and gaze. Lacking the urbanity to form any part of London society, although the wealth and solid acres of a Yorkshire squire could mean an income equal to many of those darting from one fashionable drawing room to another.

There's always something going on in London, she said to herself. Never an idle or a dull moment. Even for a provincial, such as herself.

A servant came in to draw the curtains and light the candles. Her reflective mood was broken, and she didn't feel inclined, after all, to answer Maria's letter. She wasn't in the mood to write to Anthony. What was there to say? She had written a little of what she had seen and done in London, and in his last letter—or had she imagined it?—there was a slight note of rebuke, as if he did not expect Eliza to be happy in London, so far from him and the country and her familiar surroundings.

He was content with his dogs and horses and his daily country pursuits. London, of course, was frivolous; he had said jokingly she had supposed, *I hope you are not grown smart, or above yourself, for I love you just as you are.*

Later, sitting in the carriage with Camilla, the warm darkness making it easy to ask a question she might not have ventured in the full light of day, she said, "Camilla, tell me honestly, do you find me changed since I came to London?"

A moment's hesitation, and then her cousin replied, "London changes everyone. It is your first venture out into the wider world. We women change in any case, it is not simply a matter of being out, but we become a little wiser and more experienced, and gain a better sense of proportion, more understanding as to who we are, and where our place in the world is to be. Or rather, I should say, where we would like it to be, for unless a woman is remarkably lucky, so much of what determines her fate lies under the control of others, or happens at the whim of destiny."

Eliza had never been to the opera before, although she had attended a theatrical performance some nights previously. She loved the colour, the lights, the glitters and glint of jewels at the throats and necks and wrists of the women in the moving throng of the pit below them, and in the layers of boxes all around them. Even more magnificent were the jewels adorning the dazzlers who strolled along the gallery above.

Camilla herself was wearing a fine diamond necklace with a small diamond ornament in her hair. Eliza had borrowed her sister's single string of pearls, which Charlotte had inherited from her grandmother, for she had little jewellery of her own. Lady Grandpoint lent Charlotte such of her own jewels as were suitable for a young unmarried woman; she had no need of her pearls.

They were in a box by themselves. "Alexander said he might join us later, for he is fond of Mozart," Camilla said. "However, he is at the Royal Society yet again, some lecture on an obscure subject close to his heart, and he was keenly looking forward to it, since the member giving the lecture has, in Alexander's opinion, an entirely untenable theory as to the dating of some tombs in Egypt, and Alexander is longing to tell him so. I expect they will be discussing mummies and hieroglyphs late into the night. I fear long-dead Egyptian kings are a stronger attraction even than Mozart, strange as that seems to ordinary mortals such as you and me."

Eliza had read an account of the plot, and had indeed played and sung some of the music. It was sung in Italian, a language with which she had only a slight knowledge, but she found that even though she understood few of the words, it didn't matter a jot. The singers were expressive, Camilla whispered helpful details into her ear, and the music was so ravishing, she wouldn't have cared if they'd been singing in some unknown, outlandish tongue.

The curtain came sweeping down, for there was an interval, and Eliza let out a long exhalation, she felt as though she had been holding her breath during the entire first part.

"Alethea sang Cherubino once," Camilla said.

"In a private performance?"

"No, and this is to go no further, Eliza; no, she sang it in a public performance, in Venice. It is an amazing story, it was when she ran away from her husband, the one who was murdered, you remember that. She was stranded in Italy, and being possessed of such a fine voice, and trained, of course, she took on the role of Cherubino and sang for money. Is it not shocking?"

"Is her present husband aware of this?"

"My dear, he was there, at the opera."

"Was there not a great scandal?"

"No, for Titus hustled her away, and no one ever knew that the soloist had been Miss Alethea Darcy. My father never heard of it, or at least we believe he didn't, for he hasn't ever mentioned it; however, you can't be sure with him, he has a way of knowing what you think is perfectly private. He would have hated it, of course, if it had been all over town that Miss Alethea Darcy had appeared upon the public stage, and for money, but it was never generally known."

"What an adventure," said Eliza, a note of regret in her voice. "I should love to go to Italy."

"It was a difficult time for Alethea, and she got herself into quite a few scrapes, and was on more than one occasion in real danger. However, it was on her journey to Italy that she met Titus. So it all ended happy. You could ask your Anthony to take you to Italy for your honeymoon."

Eliza thought for a moment before saying, "I do not think he cares much to go abroad. He is very much an Englishman who likes to stay close to his roots. He would not understand Mr. Wytton, with his fine house and estate in the country, choosing to live most of the year in London, and to so often be off abroad. You have travelled a good deal with him, I envy you that."

Camilla had seen various acquaintances, and she was nodding to them while Eliza let her eyes wander over the glittering crowd, talking and laughing, and, in the galleries above, strolling.

"Those are the impures," said Camilla, following Eliza's gaze as it rested on a trio of extraordinarily pretty women, dressed all in white, with fine jewels. "The demi-mondaines," she added, seeing Eliza look puzzled. "Courtesans, my dear. Ladies of uncertain virtue, who put themselves under the protection of one gentleman or another. They all know one another, and sometimes group themselves together, they know what a striking picture they present. That one there is famous, that is Harriette Wilson, who has been mistress to half the gentlemen in London, from Lord Craven to the Duke of Wellington."

"Good heavens," said Eliza, eyeing this young woman with awe. "Yet she is not really so very lovely."

"She is fascinating, which, let me tell you, is a great deal more use to her in her profession than mere physical attributes. For such women have also to be entertaining companions, you know, there is more to their profession than what goes on on the couch or behind the bedroom door." Recollecting herself, Camilla laid a finger on her lips. "I should not be talking of this to you!"

Eliza laughed. "I am not so rustic and ignorant as that, and what, after all, is Mr. Mozart's opera about, if not very much this subject?"

"Ah, Mozart tells us about the human heart, about love, and the price it exacts. That is a different price from that paid to and by these ladies in white."

"Do they wear white to indicate purity, a false symbol?"

"They wear white because it is so expensive. White gowns have to be cleaned frequently, and wearing them shows they can afford the expense. It indicates that they charge a high price for their company."

Eliza laughed, as a thought struck her. "They do not look at all miserable."

"No, why should they?"

"They are fallen women, they are sinful, they should be creeping in corners in shame, not looking as if they enjoy life."

"That's your father speaking, and indeed most of England. The truth is that compared to the lives many of them would otherwise lead, it is not such a bad deal. Some of them, of course, succumb to drink or laudanum or disease, and there is the problem of child bearing; however, others, if they have been prudent—for they can amass great wealth, you know—can, as their attractions fade, set themselves up in business, or even set up their carriage and live in a good part of town. Some marry, and marry well; why, the wife of the late Mr. Fox was one of them. Although I think there is a recklessness about many of them that precludes any degree of prudence; I think the jewels, the carriages, the presents, that are showered upon them by their admirers too often end up pawned or sold, and they have little to show for their years of glory. Now, who have you seen that has arrested your attention?"

Camilla looked over the edge of the box. In a lower box, slightly to their right, a party was just taking their seats. A tall man with an austere face, a woman in a turban with a jewelled clip at the front; Eliza had seen her at Lady Grandpoint's party. With them was a younger woman, with brown hair, elegantly dressed. The fourth member of the party was Bartholomew Bruton.

"Ah, there is our friend Mr. Bruton," said Camilla. "With his parents, Mr. Bruton the banker, a fine-looking man, I think, although *un peu sévère.* The very model of probity and propriety, so Alexander tells me, he banks with Bruton's, you know. That is his wife, Lady Sarah, and the woman is Miss Grainger, Jane Grainger. She is related to the Duke of Ilminster on her father's side, and they say she and young Mr. Bruton are to marry."

"She does not look entirely amiable," said Eliza.

"She's wearing a vastly smart gown. She had that from Paris, all her clothes come from Paris. She is half French, although you would never know it. Her mother is the heiress of one of the big French banking houses, do not ask me the name of it. I thought she had been in Paris, I thought that was why Bartholomew Bruton spent so long in Paris."

"Perhaps he went to Paris to get away from her," said Eliza. "She looks very cross. Yes, I'm sure she will suit him. Although he dare not be rude to her, I suppose."

"He is not generally rude. I know you found him so, but any man may have a sour mood, may make remarks which later he wishes unsaid."

"I have no notion of his wishing his remark unsaid. He and I do not get on, that is all."

"*Not get on* is one of those phrases that can mean almost anything, from polite indifference to contempt to dislike, and even worse."

Eliza shrugged, and looked elsewhere. "It means nothing, I do not care for his company, but since we hardly move in the same circles, it is of no consequence."

I wonder, said Camilla to herself, with a quick, sly glance at her cousin. "He is a handsome man, however. A vigorous man, with a good air and a fine figure, and an expressive face, full of intelligence."

"Let us hope, then, that he makes Miss Grainger a good husband. Here come the musicians, the performance is about to recommence."

Chapter Twenty

Lord Rosely ran up the imposing marble steps of Bruton's bank, nodded carelessly at the porter who stepped forward to enquire his business, and with a wave of his hand said that he was there to see Mr. Bartholomew Bruton. No, he knew quite well where he would be hiding out, and would make his own way there.

Bartholomew was in the inner sanctum of the bank, which was a lofty, panelled room, overlooked by a huge portrait of Mr. Augustine Bruton, goldsmith and founder of the bank, dressed in the coat and wig of the late seventeenth century. This was the room where the partners, directors, and most senior officials of the bank kept the private ledgers. Bartholomew was standing at a desk, frowning as he read a letter, and then, consulting a sheaf of figures, jotted down some calculations.

He missed Freddie's entrance, only looking up when he heard Mr. Hetherington give a little tut of surprise; visitors to the bank were never shown in here. "My Lord," he began.

"Never look at me with that fidgety face, Mr. Hetherington. I'm not here to beg, borrow, or steal so much as a groat, so you can be at ease. And I've no interest in the arcane workings of the bank, no need to hide anything away because I am here, eh, Bartholomew?"

Mr. Hetherington attempted a smile, but he was clearly distressed by Freddie's levity; banking and money were not subjects for jesting. Bartholomew took his friend by the arm and led him out of the room, closing the door behind him.

"What brings you to this unfashionable part of London, Freddie? And at this hour, why it is barely past eleven, you are usually still lolling in your dressing gown long after we toilers are at our desks."

"That's because you are a clever, brisk fellow, and I am an idle good-for-nothing," responded Freddie. "Or so my mama would say. I have been up this age, I couldn't sleep, things are very bad, and I want to talk to a friend who has a clear head, who can talk sense about my situation, can advise me what to do."

"Freddie, if it is a matter of investments or mortgages, I'm your man. If you want advice for the lovesick, then go elsewhere, it is not my strong suit."

"No, you have a flinty heart, that is obvious. Not a stirring of the blood when you look at the most lovely woman in London, you are barely human."

Bartholomew guided Freddie through the great hall and to the entrance, saying to the porter that he would be back shortly, that Mr. Leverson would be coming at noon and to show him upstairs.

"I can give you half an hour, Freddie, and that's only because I'm in need of refreshment myself. We shall adjourn to a coffee-house, and then you can talk and I will listen, but not if you're going to spout bad poetry at me."

"Bad poetry? I am three lines into my sonnet, it goes on wonderfully well."

"I don't care if it's the finest verse since Ovid, I have no desire to hear it."

They walked a little way along the Strand, then turned into Joseph's coffee-house. It was quiet, this being a busy time of day for those who lived and worked in this part of London, and Joseph himself came out from the rear room to serve them with coffee.

Freddie for a moment forgot his own woes and gave Bartholomew a keen look. "Were you out late last night? Roistering? Were you foxed? That is not like you, you are an odiously sober fellow these days, although I remember—"

"There is nothing wrong with me, and since you ask, I escorted my parents and Miss Grainger to the opera last night."

"Oh, tol-lol, that's it, is it? When are you going to make the announcement, Bartholomew? Time you took the plunge, it's been understood that you're going to marry Jane these last three years or so. She is a charming girl, I dare say, I don't know her well, but it's all fixed, is it not?"

Fixed. Damn it, it wasn't fixed. His mother spoke of it as all arranged, his father took it for granted that the couple would soon be making their wedding plans.

"You'd think a man of eight-and-twenty could choose his own wife," he burst out, startling Freddie, who took too large a gulp of hot coffee and was seized with a fit of coughing.

"Bartholomew, dear fellow, you sound fretful, this isn't like you."

"We are hardly living in the Middle Ages, yet here is your mother determined that you shall marry Miss Chetwynd, and my parents are certain that Miss Grainger will make me a perfect wife—have we no say in the matter?"

"I do," said Freddie promptly. "Nothing would make me marry Miss Chetwynd. I'll abscond to America before I walk down the aisle with her, and my mama can hint and complain and appeal to my better feelings as much as she likes. I shan't do it. Even if I weren't in love with Miss Collins, even if I'd never met her, had never known the delight of her angelic presence—"

" 'Angelic presence,' " said Bartholomew in tones of repulsion. "Pull yourself together."

"Even then," Freddie continued, unabashed, "even then, I would sooner marry the boot-boy's widowed mother than Miss Chetwynd. And I told my mother so. She ain't speaking to me now."

"Well, I told my parents this morning that I didn't wish to offer for Miss Grainger."

"Did your mother shriek and your father look grave and disappointed? Or did he stamp and hurl china about while your mama wept and wailed? No, I don't suppose your parents go in for that kind of exhibition."

They did not, but even without histrionics, breakfast had been a most unpleasant meal. It was Bartholomew's custom to take breakfast with his father. It was usually an amiable session, where they could talk over any banking business and when, as often as not, Mr. Bruton would tell Bartholomew of some interesting astronomical observation or discovery.

For the banker was a keen and distinguished astronomer, a fellow of the Royal Society, and a man with discoveries of his own to his name. He had a friend with an excellent telescope who lived in Hampstead, and he would often ride out there on clear nights to star-gaze.

That morning his mind had not been on the rings of Saturn or the forthcoming eclipse of the moon.

"It's time you settled a date with Jane," he said bluntly. "You must call upon Lord Walter to make a formal application for her hand. An autumn wedding will be suitable, you can travel to France for your honeymoon, before the weather turns bad. I have been sent details of various houses which might suit you, for you to move into upon your return, when you start your married life together."

His mother intervened. "I still hold there is no reason why the young couple cannot stay here, there is plenty of room for them both to have a very good set of apartments."

Mr. Bruton shook his head. "No, my dear. I know we disagree on this, but you will allow me to have my way this once. It is better for a newly married couple to have their own establishment, and I am sure that Jane will prefer it, indeed she said as much to me last night."

Bartholomew had not said a word, by now he was white with anger. "You have been very busy about my business, the three of you. Not only am I not allowed to choose a wife for myself, but where I am to live has to be decided for me."

"Don't speak like that to your mother," said Mr. Bruton, pursing his lips. "You are getting heated about nothing. We are your parents, we know what is best for you, and best for Jane."

"What is best for me is not to marry, or at least not to marry Jane."

"Not marry Jane!" cried his mother. "How can you be so absurd, when it is all settled, has been this last twelvemonth. Nay, these last two or three years."

"I have not asked Miss Grainger to be my wife, nor do I intend to do so."

"Do not intend to do so?" said his father, displeased. "I cannot believe what you are saying."

"You are out of sorts," said his mother in what she meant to be a soothing voice, which only annoyed Bartholomew more. "I dare say it is your liver."

Liver, indeed. Why would they not listen? He took a deep breath. "I regret it exceedingly, that I should not be prepared to oblige you in this matter."

"Oblige! This matter! It is your marriage we are talking of," said Lady Sarah. "Not some banking deal, some money matter."

"Ah, but a money matter is exactly what it is, is it not?" said Bartholomew. "Jane will own her grandfather's bank one day, if she marries me, is that not the deal? And this would be greatly to Bruton's advantage, I know how much you want to have a strong French affiliate, Father, and this would be more than an affiliate, would it not?"

"Can you pretend that you do not care for Jane? How can this be? She is a charming girl, a fine young woman. Accomplished, handsome, obliging—"

"And a bore," finished Bartholomew. "We have nothing to say to one another, that is the problem."

That caused Mr. Bruton to raise a sceptical eyebrow. "Conversation with one's wife, while desirable, is not essential to a happy marriage. You are a hard-working banker, you travel and will have to travel more. You have your masculine pursuits, while she will have her own feminine occupations and amusements."

"You paint a bleak picture. It is not true of your and Mama's marriage, you have plenty to say to one another."

"We are middle-aged; fashionable young couples these days often lead quite separate lives. Jane will make a life for herself, she will be happy to live much of the year in the country, she says, and—"

"Oh, I am to bury myself in the country now, am I? I hate the country."

"It's time a Bruton had a country seat."

"Then you buy one. See how much time you would spend outside London, were you to purchase an estate; you would not be there from one year's end to the other. And how do you know that Jane plans a country life? Oh, more talk about her life as Mrs. Bartholomew Bruton, talk that goes on behind my back. It is too bad!"

"You are being petty," said his father. "Your language is extreme, and you are upsetting your mother, which I will not permit."

"I beg your pardon, ma'am," said Bartholomew. And with a flourish of a bow, he escaped from the room, closing his ears to his mother's demands that he stay and listen to sense, and his father's unflattering description of his foolhardiness. The last words he heard were his father saying, "It is all show, he wants to make a stand, to prove his independence. I rely on his good sense, he will come round, you will see that I am right."

Now, at the coffee-house, Bartholomew looked gloomily into the dregs of his coffee. "Damn it, why are they so eager to have one marry? Do they long for grandchildren so much?"

"Not in my case," said Freddie. "My mother can't stand children, not her own, nor anyone else's. I think she hardly knew who I was until I was out of petticoats, and I remember her saying to me, before I went off to school, that she was thankful that my childhood was behind me. It's not love of the infantry, I assure you. It's heirs, dear boy, heirs that they want. In my case to the earldom, in your case to the house of Bruton. Your father wants to see a troop of young Brutons being bred up to work in the bank, your mother wants the entrée into society for your nursery brood as they grow up."

"I dare say, but a man has the right to decide for himself whom he is to marry."

"No, he don't. Not when there's a pack of females: mothers, grandmothers, aunts, sisters, even the governess, I wouldn't be surprised, thinking they know better than he does who would suit him. Besides, it's not my mother I'm worried about right now, it's that scoundrel Warren."

"George Warren? What has he to do with anything?"

"He's back in England, swaggering about town, and paying his addresses to Miss Collins."

"So are half the single men in London, and probably some of the married ones as well. Although that is odd behaviour, Warren has always seemed anxious to escape the parson's noose."

"Warren's father is heir presumptive to the title, to Montblaine's title."

Bartholomew let out a whistle. "So he could be planning to cut his uncle out, could he? Sound move. Miss Collins marries Warren, she will be a marchioness in the end, and a baroness meanwhile—at least she will when that shocking old reprobate of a father hands in his pail and leaves the title to George—with all the advantages of a young and virile husband."

Freddie banged the table and was rising to his feet. "How dare you suggest that!"

Bartholomew put out a hand and pulled him down. "I'm not saying that's the truth, but it is a scenario, a possibility. Although it is all rather too obvious, and I wouldn't lend Warren money on the expectancy, for if the noble marquis is looking about him for another bride, then should Miss Collins be unavailable, there will be others only too keen to take on the role of Marchioness of Montblaine. There's not a mother in London with a marriageable daughter who wouldn't jump at such a match."

"George Warren is up to some deep game, I'm sure of it."

"George Warren is always up to some deep game," said Bartholomew. "What do you want me to do about it?"

"I want your opinion," said Freddie, scratching at a spot of wax with a long finger. "I value your judgement. You meet more rogues and tricksters in your line of business than I do."

"In my line of business! I'll have you know that we at Bruton's are not in the habit of accommodating rogues and scoundrels. Not knowingly, at any rate," Bartholomew added, thinking of various members of the nobility who banked with them.

"Yes, and that's because you bankers have an eye for wickedness, you have to sort the sheep from the goats, the wolves from the foxes—I might know a card-sharper when I meet one, but George Warren isn't a card-sharper." Freddie looked thoughtful. "That's to say I don't know that he is, never played cards with him, but he's such a scrub, he might be up to any kind of trick. However, it ain't cards or shady dealings on the exchange that bothers me, it's why he's bent on fixing his interest with Miss Collins."

"Really, Freddie, use your sense, form your own opinion, can't you? He may simply want to ingratiate himself with his uncle. Is the marquis aware that he forms one of Miss Collins's court?"

"No, that's one thing I have noticed. Warren takes good care not to hang around Miss Collins when his uncle is present. You'd think all the old tabbies would be quick to tell him that Warren is getting assiduous in his attentions, but of course, Montblaine won't listen to them. He doesn't move among ordinary mortals, and certainly never listens to gossip or chitchat."

Bartholomew rose, and placed his hat back on his head. "I have business to attend to. And next time I find myself in the company of Miss Collins and Warren, I shall observe them closely, I can't promise more than that."

"That's all I ask," said his lordship. He grasped his friend's hand. "Thank you, Bartholomew, I knew you wouldn't let a fellow down." With which confident words, he sauntered off down the Strand, leaving Bartholomew looking at his retreating back. He would keep to his word, but since he had no plans to attend any of the social events where he might meet any of the players in this drama, Freddie would have to solve his problems for himself. He didn't want to see his friend married to Miss Collins, but Lady Desmond would take care to thwart him in that, and the interfering, controlling Miss Eliza would find her efforts to promote the match would count for nothing against that foe.

Oh, to hell with Freddie and Miss Collins, and Warren and the whole crew; he wanted nothing to do with any of them. Nor did he want to spend any more tedious evenings having to be civil to Jane.

He was in a thoroughly bad temper by the time he got back to the bank, and gave Mr. Leverson such a hard time as to make that gentleman enquire of his acquaintances whether all was well with Bruton's bank, since young Mr. Bruton seemed so uncommonly severe and unsmiling.

Chapter Twenty-one

Lady Warren sent a note round to George, a triumphant note. She had for years cultivated Lord Montblaine, well aware that she stood to become a marchioness when he moved on to the next world—an event she eagerly awaited, although the man was odiously fit, never a cough leading on to an inflammation of the lungs, such as might carry the halest of men off, never a hint of gout or apoplexy.

His lordship treated her with the cold courtesy that was normal with him, but he did make use of her services on such occasions as he wanted to entertain a party at his country seat. She would act as hostess, revelling in every stone and silk hanging of the immense house that she hoped one day to be mistress of.

To be supplanted by a clergyman's daughter—a bishop was no more than that, after all—was not to be tolerated. So she received with pleasure Lord Montblaine's imperious command that she assemble a party for a long weekend at the end of the month, and her scheming mind at once set to work.

He appended a list of guests to be invited; she might also invite those of her acquaintance as she considered would be acceptable to those named.

"Naturally," she said to George, "that includes you. And this is your chance, there you will be, day and night in that pile, with all the corridors and hidden places. If you cannot take advantage of Miss

Collins, then I despair of you. She is attracted by you, I am sure of it, and you know, these reserved young women are often the very ones to abandon all sense of discretion when their fancy is finally caught. Her passions may well overcome her head, it is up to you that they do."

"I see Miss Eliza Collins's name is there," said George, putting up his quizzing glass and running an eye down the list. "I've only met her the once, and I didn't take to her, she fancies herself a wit, to make up for her lack of beauty, I suppose. And her ladyship, that is a great nuisance, the woman is an oppressive guardian."

"She will have her guard down there, we are not to be such a large party, I shall see to that. She loves to play at cards, I will draw her off, as the hunting men would say, to leave you with a clear field. As to the sister, she is of no consequence, she will find herself so overawed by her surroundings that she will probably retire with the headache."

"I see he asks you to invite his banker, Mr. Bruton," said George Warren. "Hardly a suitable guest for Montblaine, unless he comes in by the tradesman's entrance. And forsooth, Lady Sarah and that odious fellow Bartholomew Bruton as well, who needs taking down a peg or two if ever any man does."

Bartholomew Bruton had ruthlessly turned down Warren's application for a loan when he was in difficulties the year before, even though the king himself had requested that Bruton's help his crony. "We are not obliged to pander to kings," Bartholomew had said, and his father concurred. The king banked with Hoare's, and they, in Mr. Bruton's opinion, were welcome to him.

"Never forget," said Lady Warren, "that through Lady Sarah he is related to half the House of Lords, although not, thankfully, to us. Bartholomew Bruton is very well connected on that side of the family, and when he marries that Grainger girl—good heavens, to think of the wealth of that young couple. It makes me feel quite ill—then he will take a step further up in the world. I dare say his lordship has some business to conduct to do with the estate. When a man is as rich and grand as Montblaine, you know, he can be eccentric in his acquaintance."

"When I become Montblaine, I shall make sure no bankers cross the threshold of the abbey, you can take my word for that. Who else? Mr. and Mrs. Wytton." George let his glass drop and it dangled on its silk ribbon. "Damn me, my uncle must be serious about that wretched girl. I would hardly be surprised to see the bishop's name written here. His only reason for inviting the Wyttons must be the Darcy connection, since they are the only respectable family Miss Collins can boast of."

"If you can call any of those Darcy girls respectable, married women or not," Lady Warren said sourly. "There is no one on that list I would have chosen to invite, but you see he gives me carte blanche, apart from those, and so I can make sure that at least some of our particular friends are among the guests."

Alexander Wytton received Lord Montblaine's invitation with ill-concealed fury. "I will not accept, I will not go. What, spend four or five days in that monstrous house? I think not. We have a perfectly good abbey of our own to go home to, should we want to leave London. What the devil does he want to invite us for in any case? I hardly know the noble marquis, and what I do know of him hardly makes me want to further the acquaintance. No, no, write a civil reply to Lady Warren, what a dreadful woman she is, saying that we regret and so forth."

Camilla tucked her arm into his. "Consider, my love, we are being asked for a reason. Not so that you can discuss ancient Egyptian kings with Montblaine—although does he not have some fine antiquities?—but because Charlotte is our cousin."

"You are out there, surely," said Wytton. "It will come to nothing, mark my words. The odds are lengthening, now that George Warren is back in England."

"George Warren? What has he to do with it? Does he plan to murder his uncle or perhaps do away with Charlotte, in order to safeguard his inheritance?"

Wytton looked down at his wife, his face softening. "How extravagant you are in your suppositions; have you been reading another of Griffy's racy novels? The buzz at Pinks is that Miss Collins is inclined to enjoy George Warren's company rather more than is suitable for a young woman likely to embark on matrimony with the uncle."

"George Warren! You are joking, Charlotte cannot like him, it is all nonsense."

"Have you seen much of Charlotte recently?"

"No, for Lady Grandpoint moves in different circles, and although I have asked her here more than once since she first came, she is always otherwise engaged. Good heavens, what you tell me fills me with alarm. George Warren!"

"A dangerous man, as we know."

And he and Camilla exchanged a long, thoughtful look, for Warren had brought nothing but trouble to her family. The enmity was an old one; his stepmother had never forgiven Camilla's mother, the then Elizabeth Bennet, for marrying the rich and handsome Mr. Darcy of Pemberley, the more so since she, as Caroline Bingley, had had every intention of marrying him herself. That it had been a passionate love match mattered nothing to her, she wouldn't have cared if Mr. Darcy had had the temper of Poseidon and the morals of a Turk, she would have married him for his money, estate, and position. Her brother had at the same time married Elizabeth's sister, Jane Bennet, which tied up the bows of her hatred for the family.

"He cannot be carrying his vengeful spirit so far as to attack Charlotte merely because she is a cousin—and not a close cousin of yours, my love," Alexander finally said.

"That will be the cream on the dish, the extra piquancy; no, he is protecting his own interests here, I am sure of it. I think we must certainly go, for if what you say is true, we need to keep an eye on Warren, apart from lending our support to our cousin. I wonder that Eliza has not mentioned it to me."

"Eliza does not move in the same circles as Charlotte, and she may be unaware of Warren's friendship with her sister, she may not have heard the comments that have been made about it. Lady Grandpoint and the dreadful bishop were perhaps unwise to let Eliza come to London and then not permit her to share in the social delights laid out for Charlotte, for she is quick on the uptake and would soon have taken Warren's measure."

Eliza called upon Camilla that morning, and was delighted to find Henrietta Rowan and Mr. Portal sitting in her drawing room. Camilla greeted her cousin affectionately, and then, when Eliza was seated, asked some very direct questions.

"I do not scruple to speak in front of Pagoda and Mrs. Rowan, Eliza, for they are old friends, whose advice may be valuable, and I know they are both the soul of discretion. What I have to say relates to Charlotte: Alexander tells me that George Warren is paying her a lot of attention, and that she is inclined to favour him."

Eliza was so astonished she nearly dropped the glass of lemonade she was about to drink from. She put it down on the little table beside her and stared at Camilla. George Warren. She frowned. "I have met him but once, a dark, not unhandsome man, with a rather contemptuous air of being above his company—that was, me. He kept looking past me to see if there were someone more interesting to speak to, and we barely exchanged a dozen words. He danced with Charlotte, but she favour him? I do not think so."

"That's all very well, but you are not often in your sister's company at these parties and balls she attends, you have your own circle of friends, I believe," said Mrs. Rowan. "I have seen Miss Collins with Mr. Warren, and I would say he was strongly attracted to her, at least he gives the appearance of being attracted to her."

"That is nothing," said Eliza, "she has many admirers. If she favours any of them, I would say it was Lord Rosely, and there is no harm in that, in fact—"

"In fact, you would like to see her married to Rosely," said Pagoda. "Well, you know your sister best; I am not sure they would suit. However, the point is, what are Miss Collins's feelings towards

Warren? You are her sister, has she not spoken to you about him? When you are in your chambers, preparing for bed, do you not talk over the evening's events together?"

"No," said Eliza.

She had barely spoken to Charlotte these last two weeks or so. Her sister's life was so full, she came in so late, long after Eliza, yawning her head off, had retired, and Lady Grandpoint, careful to cherish her goddaughter's looks, insisted that she have breakfast in their room and rise late, to get the hours of sleep she needed.

"Charlotte is not the kind of person to open her heart to anyone, except perhaps my mother," said Eliza. "We are not close in that way. She seems happy, as far as I can tell."

She fell silent, thinking hard about Charlotte. Yes, she was happy. Within that calm exterior, there was a certain radiance to her, a serenity that had not been there before. Was she in love, or merely enjoying her successful London season? For herself, being in love made her happy and lively and overflowing with good-will; she could see nothing of that in Charlotte. "We are so different in temperament, that it is hard for me to say. Charlotte never has been in love, and so I cannot judge what her feelings are at present."

"I dislike and despise George Warren," said Camilla decidedly. "I would not trust him an inch. However, women, some women, do find him attractive."

"Good heavens, and you think Charlotte and this man have formed an attachment? You alarm me."

"There is the title to be considered," said Pagoda Portal bluntly. "He will inherit a barony, although I am not sure whether the estate will be encumbered with mortgages and so on. And then, his father is heir presumptive to Montblaine. Warren inherited a pretty little estate not long ago, but he has not the money to put that in order. I do not see why he should be hanging out for anything but a rich wife. I do not believe for a moment that he would let his feelings overcome his hard-headedness."

Eliza bit her lip. "I wish Charlotte would be more forthcoming, or, failing that, that she would accept the hand of Lord Rosely, who

I'm sure must have proposed to her by now. That would see off Mr. Warren."

"What of her even more noble and distinguished suitor?" enquired Mrs. Rowan.

Eliza looked puzzled for a moment. "You mean Lord Montblaine. Oh, Charlotte cannot care for him, he is too old, too austere, and I am quite sure we are not grand enough for him. I know Lady Grandpoint cherishes hopes of him, but I think she is out there, I think it is all pie in the sky."

"Has she not been invited to Montblaine for the forthcoming weekend?" asked Camilla. "For we received an invitation this morning, courtesy of Lady Warren, and have been racking our brains to decide why we should have been so favoured, not being at all well acquainted with Lord Montblaine, and certainly not on Lady Warren's usual guest list. We came to the conclusion we must have been asked on Charlotte's account, being her only close family in London apart from you and the Grandpoints."

"Invited to Montblaine? Lord Montblaine's house? I know nothing of it, and I am sure Lady Grandpoint would have mentioned it were it so."

"Have you seen her ladyship this morning?"

"No, I have not, for I rose early, and left the house before she was awake, I had to go . . . I had some errands to perform."

"Such as visiting the offices of Mr. Mostyn at the *London Magazine*?" said Pagoda Portal, quizzing her through his glass.

Eliza's lemonade this time did take a tumble. A maid was summoned, the spilt liquid mopped up, and there was Mr. Portal laughing at her discomfiture. "Your secret is safe with me," he said, becoming at once more serious when he saw her distress.

Eliza was aghast. She had gone alone, in a hackney cab, to call upon the editor of the *London Magazine,* and had taken the greatest care to be discreet, dressing plain and wearing a hat that shaded her face. How was it possible that she had been seen and recognised? And if by Mr. Portal, then by whom else?

"Do not look so alarmed. I had it from Mostyn himself. He finds it a good joke that the witty pieces which are amusing London so much at present were written by a dowdy young woman. I assure you that he does not know who you are, he knows you only as Mrs. Palmer, and he believes you to be a governess in a great household."

"Because I told him so," confessed Eliza. "I lied. When I discovered that the editor in Leeds, without a word to me, and without asking my permission, had passed my pieces on to the editor of the *London Magazine,* I was horrified."

"Flattered, too," said Portal.

"What?" said Henrietta. "Do you tell me you are the author of the sketches of fashionable London life? My dear, I congratulate you, they make me laugh out loud."

"Do not be dismayed, Miss Eliza, your anonymity is preserved. It was by the merest chance that I saw you leave the offices of the periodical. I had business there myself, and Mr. Mostyn mentioned to me what you had been there about. I understand you want him to cease publication, and he considers it all a matter of money, nothing that a few guineas can't settle."

"Of course, I shall do no more of them," said Eliza, aware that there were still several pieces that had appeared in the northern publication and which would doubtless find their way into the *London Magazine.* "It seems to me quite wrong that a writer has no control, no say in these matters."

"No, he, or in this case she, does not. You earn your half-guinea or guinea, and then your words belong to the press and not to you. Never fear, we shall keep your secret, but I must congratulate you on your skill with a pen. It is cleverly done, for you portray types, not individuals, one cannot say, oh, that is Lady X or Mr. Y, we have instead the perfect portrait of the London dowager, the blushing debutante, the bored father, the eager politician, the besotted lover, and so forth. Have you never considered turning your hand to a longer work?"

"I have not," cried Eliza. "And I never shall!"

How difficult life was, one thing after another. But the immediate alarm she had felt at the discovery that Mr. Portal and now Mrs.

Rowan knew about her writing faded into the background. She could trust them, if Camilla did. And, being of a practical disposition, she knew there was no point in fretting over what was done and could not be changed. Should the truth come to her father's attention, she would be in deep trouble, but that was a future worry, what mattered now was the much more important question of Charlotte.

"I think you will find, when you return to Aubrey Square, that Lady Grandpoint and Charlotte will have received an invitation from Lord Montblaine," said Camilla.

"We are to be there also," said Mr. Portal, drawing his brows together. "It is his custom to invite me at least once a year, we are distantly related, you know. And he invited Mrs. Rowan, for he knows I accept few invitations which do not include her."

"I like to think he invites me on my own account," said Mrs. Rowan with spirit. "I am one of the few women who find the Marble Marquis agreeable. He unbends with me, for he has spent time in Turkey, as I did when my late husband was alive, and we talk about the cities and customs and history of that interesting country."

"I am not going to think about it, or discuss what it might mean, until I find out if Charlotte has been invited," said Eliza. And then: "I know nothing about Lord Montblaine's house, is it a fine one?"

"Oh, good gracious," said Pagoda, "as to that, I would sooner call it a monstrosity! The late marquis was afflicted with a passion for the Gothic, and having an immense fortune to squander, set about turning a perfectly good house of the last century into a virtual mediaeval cathedral of a place. You never saw such towers and turrets and crenulations and pointed doors and windows in your life."

"Now, be fair," said Henrietta soothingly. "The house was originally an abbey. It came into his family at the Reformation," she said to Eliza, "as so many abbeys did."

"As Mr. Wytton's did," put in Camilla. "Only Sillingford Abbey has remained as it has been these last hundred years or so, it has not been turned into such a Gothic nightmare as Montblaine now is."

"I cannot see Charlotte in such a place," said Eliza. "It does not sound as though she would like it at all."

Chapter Twenty-two

Eliza peered out of the window as the carriage turned in through the enormous gates, supported on either side by tall pillars, on each of which perched a ferocious stone hawk, the symbol of the Montblaines.

Lady Grandpoint imparted this information, as she had kept them informed of every other item she considered of interest once they had reached the vast Montblaine estates. Whole villages, elegant houses, tidy thatched cottages, rolling acres of farmland and timber; all these, she said in tones of high satisfaction, belonged to the marquis's family.

At least the tenants' cottages seemed to be kept in good order, although Eliza knew that there might, off the highway, be villages where squalor prevailed. She could not say whether Montblaine was a man of appearance rather than of substance. Lady Grandpoint insisted that he was an excellent landlord. "And the churches, all these parishes, are livings within his gift," she said, nodding at Charlotte. "He is a man with strong influence in the Church, I assure you."

Charlotte looked back at her great-aunt with her usual clear, unreadable expression, as she murmured, "I am sure he is good to his tenants and to the deserving poor, as he ought to be," before lapsing back into silence.

Sometimes Eliza longed to shake her sister, to shake her until her teeth rattled, to demand to know what was going on in her mind. Charlotte was not just a pretty ninny-head, she had intelligence, she couldn't switch off her mind, how could any human being do that? No, thoughts, emotions, passions, must swirl inside that exquisite head, as with every other human being, but their nature remained known only to Charlotte.

The carriage came round a bend and turned into the main sweep to the house, which lay before them in all its glory. The immense outline of turrets, spires, towers, and crenellations was etched against the shadowy light of early evening, and the sight caused Eliza to let out a gasp of astonishment.

Nothing that Camilla or Mrs. Rowan or Pagoda Portal had said had prepared her for this. The building was dominated by a central spire, soaring high above the rest of the house. From this approach, Eliza could see a long wing, with a square tower and a small turreted place at the end. The carriage drew up before an immense portal, with great oak doors set in an ornate, high-pointed arch, and liveried servants came hurrying forward. As she stepped down from the carriage, Eliza caught a glimpse of still more turrets.

An imposing butler ushered them up the wide flight of stone steps and into a lofty panelled hall, festooned with coats of arms and set with banners. Beams were visible in the smoky heights above their heads, and two vast stone fireplaces were set opposite each other. Their footsteps echoed on great flagstones, which sent up a chill even on this warm evening.

Their footsteps echoed as they followed the butler on his stately way, through another set of doors, along an arched passage, and into a huge, octagonal saloon. Stone escutcheons hung above the panelled sections of the walls, lugubrious heraldic beasts which looked to Eliza like a series of figures from a nightmare.

There they were greeted by Lord Montblaine, who welcomed them with grave courtesy, and by Lady Warren, who greeted them with glacial smiles. Eliza recalled Camilla's words of warning: Be wary of Lady Warren, she is a veritable weasel in character, if not in appearance.

The company was assembling in the Grand Drawing Room, Lady Warren informed them. They would be shown to their rooms by the housekeeper or the groom of the chambers, and should then join the rest of the company.

"I am already lost," Eliza exclaimed to Lady Grandpoint, when they had climbed up several more staircases, walked along endless passages, and turned numerous corners. Charlotte's room was a large apartment in a solitary turret, Lady Grandpoint was in one of the state bedrooms in the north wing, while Eliza, now on her own, found herself shown into a smaller chamber, which overlooked a dark courtyard.

To her relief, Annie awaited her there, keen to help her out of her travelling clothes, on her mettle to turn out her mistress in what she called prime style. "Although I don't know why they've put you in here, Miss, it used to be the governess's room," she sniffed.

"As long as the bed is comfortable, and no ghosts come gliding through the wainscotting in the dark of the night, they can house me in the boot-boy's room," said Eliza.

"Ghosts! I don't hold with ghosts," said Annie. "One of the footmen here was trying to frighten me with tales of headless monks and wailing spirits. Sauce! Now, Miss, you'd best hurry, for apparently his lordship is a stickler for punctuality."

Annie had a good sense of direction and had taken the trouble to acquaint herself with the way to and from Eliza's room. "It's part of my duties," she said, when Eliza said how thankful she was not to spend the rest of the evening wandering around gloomy passages and ill-lit towers. So she was delivered safely to the entrance of the Grand Drawing Room, a room which, as she entered it, took her breath away. What an abundance of monumental statuary, heavy curtains, Siena tables, sofas which could accommodate an entire family! There were no fewer than three fireplaces, the largest of which could provide a lodging for the same family. The ceiling was covered in Gothic tracery, and any opening that could be crowned with a pointed arch was adorned in this fashion. The windows were tall and wide, and afforded a magnificent view across parkland, with a castle set on a hill in the distance looking as though it had been created to be observed from this window.

"That is Rosely Castle," said a voice in her ear, and she turned round to find Mr. Wytton standing there.

"What a relief to see a friendly face," she whispered.

"Do you like the house?"

Eliza looked around to see if they might be overheard, then said in a voice hardly above a whisper, "It is overwhelming, and in my opinion, quite hideous. I would not live here for anything." Which thought cheered her up, for surely Charlotte, were any notions of trying to foster an attachment between herself and Lord Monthlaine really under serious consideration, must be repelled by this house.

Camilla joined them, and Eliza, feeling more at her ease, looked about to see the rest of the company. Pagoda Portal had not yet arrived, he was driving down with Mrs. Rowan, Camilla told her. Otherwise, she must know most of those present, if only by sight. "That is George Warren, is it not?" she asked in a quiet voice.

"The dark-visaged man over there, in conversation with Miss Grainger, do you know her?"

"The one who is affianced to Mr. Bartholomew Bruton?"

"They are not formally engaged, although, as I told you, it is only a matter of time before it is announced. I am not sure why she is here, the Warrens do not get on with the Brutons."

"She is not yet engaged nor married, and she is a considerable heiress, perhaps Caroline Warren has hopes in that direction for her stepson," put in Mr. Wytton. "Let us see whether she has a neat and pretty foot, that will be the deciding factor."

Camilla tapped his arm with her fan, her eyes full of laughter. "For shame, Mr. Wytton."

Eliza looked enquiringly from one to the other of them. Camilla, she noticed, had a slight blush on her cheeks.

"I apologise for my husband. He is jesting, and perhaps you might not understand the point of the jest," she said. "It is just that Mr. Warren has a reputation for liking a pretty foot."

"It is so with some men," said Eliza matter-of-factly; she knew what Camilla meant. "There is a friend of my father's, a clergyman—well, I won't go into that."

She wasn't altogether happy with this information as to Warren's inclinations, for Charlotte had dainty feet, of which she was justly proud. Since coming to London, she had taken particular care over her footwear, indulging herself with pretty sandals and slippers and, for more grand occasions, had even bought a pair of shoes in the French style, ornamented with a pair of paste diamond buckles that twinkled in the light as she moved. Eliza thought them vulgar, but Lady Grandpoint had pronounced them perfectly acceptable, saying that they were all the crack, and Charlotte was lucky that her lovely face was set off by a slim, well-shaped ankle and an elegant foot.

The last of the party were coming into the drawing room now: Pagoda Portal and Mrs. Rowan, the latter strikingly dressed in a purple robe and a turban with a feather set in a dazzling jewel. On their heels came the Brutons, Mr. Bruton, handsome, dignified; Lady Sarah, full of smiles as she greeted friends; and Bartholomew Bruton, looking moody.

The group of people shifted, and to Eliza's dismay, she saw coming toward her the objectionable figure of the Reverend Mr. Pyke. "Oh, no, what is that man doing here?"

"He is Montblaine's cousin," Mr. Wytton reminded her.

And Camilla, with a suppressed laugh, said, "Ah, I think he has been invited here on your behalf. I fear there is a plot afoot, coz. Indeed, the more I think about it, the more obvious it becomes that more than one scheme is being hatched this weekend. What joy!"

Eliza couldn't agree. Charlotte's well-being was too important to be treated in this light-hearted way, and Camilla's words did little to soothe her concerns.

"If the marquis means to have Charlotte, and I do think the signs are pointing that way, and if, which is a bigger if, your sister is happy to have him, then there is nothing that you or I or anyone can do to prevent the match," said Camilla.

"Montblaine is testing her," said Wytton with certainty. "His mind is not made up, he is not ready to make a proposal, he wishes to see whether she would be capable of becoming mistress of this house, of all his houses, of taking on the degree of responsibility that being his marchioness would entail."

"I should run a mile from it," said Camilla frankly. "Even if I fell in love with the Marble Marquis, I could not endure such a life."

"Then it is as well that you fell in love with me," said Mr. Wytton, quizzing her. "With my much humbler abbey, and no great title."

"It all smacks too much of King Cophetua," said Eliza. "She would never have the advantage, it would be an unequal match in every way and would remain so, she would be miserable, indeed."

Camilla held out her hand to Mr. Pyke, who had made his way over to them and was smiling winningly at Eliza. "I believe you are acquainted with my cousin Miss Eliza Collins?"

Eliza touched the fingertips of the moist hand held out to her, and dropped a light curtsy. Could she get away from him, or would her efforts be to no purpose? She had an idea that in a place like this, where everything was done with such state and formality, it would not be left to guests to decide who was to go into dinner with whom.

She was right in her surmise. Dinner was announced, and she found herself obliged to lay her hand on the arm hooked for her by the suave, smiling Mr. Pyke, as the company trooped out of the Grand Drawing Room, through the Crimson Drawing Room, which was only slightly smaller, and into the Great Dining Room. To complete her discontent, she found that she had Mr. Bartholomew Bruton on her other side. She was doomed to an entire dinner having to converse with two men to whom she had nothing to say, and she was hard put to know which of them she more disliked. For at a meal as formal as this, conversation was restricted to one's immediate neighbours; had one wanted to break the rules and speak across the table, it would have been impossible, given the regiments of silver and gold epergnes, candelabra, and flowers that were ranged along the centre of the long mahogany table, thus obscuring those sitting opposite from view.

Eliza was startled by the number of footmen, one to each guest, and others moving around the table to deliver the numerous dishes that made up each course. She was hungry after the journey, it was true, but there was far more spread out before them than she could possibly sample.

To her right, Mr. Pyke was urging her to try this and that delicacy, and judging by the eagerness in his voice and his knowledge of what was in the dishes and how each one was prepared, Eliza decided he was a greedy man, a glutton. The glint in his eye as the cover was lifted on a dish of quails in a cream sauce made her want to laugh out loud. He had figured in her sketches of clerical life, but not as a gourmand; this would add an extra facet to his fictional counterpart when she wrote another piece. Which she had promised herself she would not do, she reminded herself. If only money did not slip through one's fingers so fast in London!

Mr. Pyke would no doubt call himself an epicure; well, even that was hardly suitable for a man of the cloth. He was lean now, how would he look in twenty years' time? He would spread as Squire Diggory had done, although she couldn't imagine he had ever been thin. Anthony, she thought with some complacency, carried not an ounce of superfluous flesh, he had an excellent figure.

Mercifully, Mr. Pyke's attention was claimed by the woman on his other side. On her left, Bartholomew Bruton was eating duck; on his other side sat Miss Chetwynd, and they did not appear to have much to say to each other. Good manners impelled Eliza to enter into conversation with him, therefore, and she made a trivial remark about the extraordinary ornamentation of the ceiling above them.

"I cannot conceive how anyone can live in such a house," he said in a low, angry voice. Then, more loudly: "It is considered very fine, I believe, a unique specimen of the work of the late Mr. Wyatt."

Eliza knew little of the work of this interesting architect, and if Montblaine were an example of his style, considered that she was happy to remain in a state of ignorance as to his other buildings, and made some polite remarks about turrets and views.

"Do you not care for the country?" he asked.

"I do, indeed. I live in Yorkshire, as you know, and the scenery of that part of the world, with our moors and hills, is considered very picturesque and dramatic."

"It rains in Yorkshire. All the time. I do not know how anyone can abide to live there."

"You prefer town, I find."

"I do," he said shortly.

What was the matter with him? She supposed he thought himself above his company, that he was annoyed to find himself seated next to her. She smiled.

"You find something amusing?" he said.

"Only in sympathy with you for having to sit here, obliged to talk to a rustic who can have nothing interesting to say."

"I am sure you have plenty to say, were you so inclined. Or to write, although that is an occupation you no doubt reserve for the privacy of your room." His lips twitched. "Have you gathered good material for your pen this evening?"

Eliza was so shocked, she couldn't say a word. She flushed a deep scarlet and found herself the object of a gibe from his other side, as Miss Chetwynd observed the colour flying into her cheeks and remarked that Mr. Bruton's conversation must be too hot for her. She finished this comment with a knowing look and a loud whoop of laughter.

"Vulgar woman," Eliza said under her breath; she was wild to ask Mr. Bruton what he meant, did he know about her writing? His comment was so specific, but the look that had accompanied it had been hard to fathom. She had a suspicion there was amusement there; could it be that he was laughing at her?

Lady Warren was on her feet, and nodding at Eliza, who was the only person left seated. She jumped up, and followed the rest of the ladies out of the room, casting a last look of desperate appeal back at Bartholomew Bruton as she left the dining room.

Chapter Twenty-three

Bartholomew smiled as he sat down again and leaned back in his chair to allow the footman to pour him a glass of wine. Liberated from Miss Chetwynd, he moved away from the clerical gentleman to sit next to Pagoda Portal. Mr. Portal had banked with Bruton's for years and had known Bartholomew since he was in his cradle.

"You're up to some mischief," Pagoda said with a nod. "I can always tell. You were seated next to Miss Eliza, she has a witty way with her, was she making you smile?"

"She was, but I heard nothing of her witty tongue. I'm afraid I offended her the first time we met, and she has not forgiven me. And I was guilty of teasing her, I regret to say."

"Ah, it was what you said that caused her cheeks to be ablaze, was it?" Pagoda said jovially. "You should not tease her, I have a great liking for her. Her sister may be the toast of the town, and I will acknowledge her beauty, a ravishing woman, but for myself, I find Miss Eliza a great deal more taking."

Taking! It was a good thing Pagoda Portal could not see into his heart or his loins. What was it about Miss Eliza Collins that so stirred his blood? In a way that Jane Grainger never had done and never would. And Eliza's sister left him as cold as she was herself, he was unmoved by her beauty and couldn't understand Freddie's reckless and flamboyant pursuit of her.

"We'll have young Rosely riding over, no doubt," said Pagoda. "Perhaps he and Warren can fight a duel over Miss Collins's lustrous eyes. That would be a rare entertainment, quite out of the usual order of the day here at Montblaine. Have you been here before?"

"No," said Bruton.

"And you don't like it?"

"It would be impolite to express an opinion," said Bartholomew, with a swift glance at his host, who was, however, deep in conversation with Lord Langham, a lugubrious individual who lived, Pagoda told Bartholomew, in a house even more turreted and crenulated than Montblaine.

"Is that possible?"

"You prefer the classical style, I find."

"I prefer town. The country has its merits in the summer, fine views, open aspects, greenery, and so on, but that quickly palls, and in winter, with deep, muddy lanes and mist rising from the river and draughts from every window and opening . . ." Bartholomew shuddered. "Give me London or Paris, there a man can live life to the full, unoppressed by great belching fires, freezing passageways, and cows gazing at one from the other side of the ha-ha."

The ladies had retreated to the Crimson Drawing Room, and never had Eliza more eagerly waited the return of the gentlemen from the dining room to join them. Would they sit over their port and masculine conversations for ever?

Music was to be the entertainment for the evening, music and cards. Miss Chetwynd had brought her harp, the instrument had arrived in her mother's large travelling chaise and had been trundled into the room. Now she sat tuning it, interminable clinks and plonks, what an unappealing sound the harp made, would she never be done? There, she had finished, now she could be quiet and wait for the audience.

Miss Chetwynd seated herself more prettily, holding her arms in the approved manner, a smile pinned to her lips.

Lady Warren was bearing down on Charlotte, her glinting smile much in evidence. "I have not had the pleasure of hearing you play or sing, Miss Collins, have you brought your music with you?"

"Charlotte plays the pianoforte and also sings," said Lady Grandpoint. "I am sure she will be very happy to play for us."

"And Miss Grainger is a most accomplished performer upon the instrument; what a wealth of talent we have. I do not suppose—that is, does Miss Eliza care to play?"

"She sings," said Charlotte. "I shall accompany her."

Eliza was trying to catch her sister's eye; she did not in the least want to sing. Charlotte ignored her and resumed her conversation with Lady Langham, who was boring on about one Valeria Collins, a dreary woman by the sound of her, with whom she had been at school.

Which must have been a hundred years ago, Eliza said to herself. Mrs. Rowan came over to sit beside her. "Are you so eager to play? You seem full of suppressed energy, are you a keen musician?"

Eliza looked down at her hands and saw she had them clenched tight. "Keen? Oh, no, I am an indifferent musician. Charlotte is a fine pianist, whereas I am lazy, I have never practised as I should. Although even if I did, I would not come near to equalling her performance, she has talent and I do not."

"I can predict how the music will go," said Mrs. Rowan. "Miss Chetwynd will delight us with a long and dull sonata, played perfectly and quite without any expression or taste. Then, before the gentlemen start to long for their cards, Miss Grainger will take her place at the piano, and she will play an equally long and tedious sonata. By then, quite half the room will be asleep, or at least their eyelids will be drooping. So that by the time Charlotte comes to play, she will be wished at the devil. Lady Warren is no fool."

"In that case, Charlotte will wake everyone up again." Eliza lowered her voice. "You would expect Charlotte to play without passion and perfectly correctly, would you not?"

"I am afraid that is exactly what I would expect."

"And Lady Warren thinks just the same. It is not so. Charlotte's playing is quite out of the ordinary, she plays with vigour and real musicality. And she has excellent taste, she plays the most difficult pieces while making them sound effortless, so that even if one is not so musical, one is compelled to listen." Speaking almost to herself, she added, "It is the one passionate release that Charlotte's restrained nature has. It alarmed my parents, they never encouraged her music, but she had a good teacher, and such real understanding of music, that she improves even without instruction."

"Good heavens! Well, I look forward to that. And you will sing?"

"I may, or perhaps we will do a duet. My voice is not anything special, and it is not a drawing-room voice, it is too low."

Inwardly, Eliza was calculating how long these sonatas—for she feared Mrs. Rowan was probably quite right as to the programme—would take, how long it would be before she could speak to Mr. Bruton, to make him tell her what he meant, to find out how he knew, had he told anyone. If he had found out, could she trust him not to broadcast the story far and wide?

The gentlemen drifted in, took their seats, and there was Mr. Bartholomew Bruton on the other side of the room, ruthlessly annexed by Mrs. Grainger, obliged to sit between the daughter and the mother. More plonks and squeals from the harp, and Miss Chetwynd launched into a long sonata, which, as Mrs. Rowan had predicted, she played with technical proficiency and entirely without feeling; Eliza's dislike of the harp increased tenfold.

When finally it was over and people coughed, began to talk, yawned, looked hopefully towards the card tables, Lady Warren quashed their hopes by ushering Miss Grainger to the pianoforte. More tedium, every note lasting, to Eliza's mind, twice as long as it ought.

The yawns were ill-concealed, there was Mr. Bruton, senior, sitting bolt upright in his chair, asleep, until his wife gave him a sharp poke in the ribs with her fan, and he woke up with a start and a grunting sound. He was not the only one. The marquis sat aloof, his face giving nothing away; only Mrs. Grainger listened attentively, all smiles and encouraging nods.

Miss Grainger finished at last, and Charlotte made her way to the instrument with her usual grace, beckoning to Eliza to sit beside her on the piano stool. "They are bored," Charlotte said in her calm way. "I shall not play for long, and then we shall sing two duets, no more. Ballads, I think."

She rested her hands for a moment on the keys, and then, playing from memory, dashed into a sparkling composition by the late Mr. Handel.

She looked quite lovely sitting there, but as the music danced and spun about the room, it was as though the magical sounds were emerging from a statue; only those who knew her best could have seen a gleam in her eye or noticed the tension in her body as she played.

A burst of applause, a voice saying audibly, "Thank God for a short piece, let us hope that is not the prelude to another sonata in all too many movements."

The sisters sang, Eliza making herself concentrate on what she was about, she must not look at Bartholomew Bruton, she must relax her throat and breathe properly and sing as she had been taught.

"Charming, delightful, enchanting." The praise flowed over and around them as the audience, glad, Eliza suspected, that the music was finally over, rose, moved around, broke into a hubbub of conversation, settled itself at card tables. There was Mr. Bartholomew Bruton, sitting himself down at the other side of the room, a glass on the table beside him, cutting and shuffling the cards with quick, deft hands.

There could be no further chance for conversation this evening, she guessed. Tea would be brought in later, but the keen cardplayers might play on until the early hours, Mrs. Rowan informed her. "It is not like a London party, where carriages are called or when there is a natural end. At a country house, once the ritual of dinner is over, the men may stay up as late as they like."

"And tomorrow? I have never stayed in a house such as this. How do we go on?"

"Even at Montblaine, which keeps up some of the grandeur of

former times, the daytime is less formal. Until the company meets again for dinner tomorrow, everyone can do as he or she chooses. The men may take out a gun, or go for walks, or sit in the library for a chat or to read a book or peruse the newspapers, which will have been sent down from town. For us ladies, the day is likewise our own. Breakfast will be served in the morning parlour, I expect, should you wish for refreshment, and there will no doubt be a nuncheon later on. There is a billiards room, a music room, several saloons and parlours, extensive grounds to stroll in, archery, you can go to the butts if you are keen on that sport."

As Eliza took her candle and made her thanks and curtsies before retiring upstairs, she shot a glance at Bartholomew, a glance fraught with anxiety and an earnest appeal. If he read the message there, he showed no sign of it, merely giving her a polite smile.

He might be out all day tomorrow, and then they would meet only in company again in the evening, with once more no chance of a private word.

Chapter Twenty-four

Henrietta Rowan was right in her predictions as to how the day at Montblaine would be spent by the guests. Informality was the order of the day, but how hard it was to be informal in such an overpowering house! The very rooms demanded a kind of behaviour that took away any semblance of freedom or relaxation.

Eliza had a light breakfast, choosing from the extraordinary array of dishes set out in the Crimson Breakfast Parlour, before setting off to find the library, where, Annie had told her, such of the gentlemen who would not be out walking, fishing, or shooting would be likely to spend the morning. The immense room stretched away into the gloom, its severe shelves filled with large tomes that looked as though they might have been there since the days of the original monastery. Busts of Roman-nosed classical worthies stared haughtily down at her from their lofty positions atop pillars set between the ranks of shelves.

There were chairs, but not of a kind to invite any comfortable reading or cosy chats. These were upright seats, covered in stiff leather, set in rigid positions against the tables or against those same pillars. Had any hapless reader, deep—Eliza peered at a nearby volume—in *The Confessions of St. Augustine,* ever been crushed by a piece of toppling statuary? A large sofa at the end of the room was the sole invitation to ease, but since that, too, was covered in solid leather, she had no desire to sit on it and lose herself in a book.

Moreover, since most of the tomes seemed to be written in one or other of the ancient tongues, there was in any case little possibility of her finding a book she could read. She suspected she would look in vain for any of her favourite novels, let alone any of the newest offerings from the Minerva Press.

As she walked through the library, she came upon Mr. Wytton, who was standing on some wooden steps and reaching up for a large, leatherbound volume. He took it down and laid it on the table with care before greeting her. Eliza liked Alexander Wytton, for his own sake, as well as because he was Camilla's husband, and she knew him for a kind and affectionate man. Nonetheless, she also respected his tongue; he didn't suffer fools gladly, and was often impatient with the ordinary tos-and-fros of conversation.

"This is a capital library," he said. "I envy Montblaine. His father was a noted scholar, but I believe the present marquis has added extensively to the collection." He opened the book. "I have ordered a copy of this for my own library, but I do not know when it will come."

"Good heavens," said Eliza, looking at the page of Egyptian hieroglyphs. "What are those?"

"It is the ancient Egyptian language, which we have not yet deciphered."

"Do these represent letters or words?" Eliza asked, tracing the figure of an alert-looking owl and then the figure of a man, sideways on.

"It is, we believe, a symbolic language, so we cannot say, this is the letter *A* or the letter *B.* One day you must travel to Egypt, and see the beauties and marvels of that country for yourself. There are astonishing paintings, and many interesting inscriptions. It is a very old civilisation, dating many centuries before Christian times, and predating the Greeks as well."

Travel to Egypt! What a wonderful idea, and of course, now that the war was over, quite possible; she knew that Camilla had accompanied Mr. Wytton there, and had, she said frankly, found it the most fascinating place on earth.

Would Anthony care to go to Egypt? No. There was no doubt in her mind as to that. Anthony had often told her that he had not the slightest desire to leave the country of his birth. A great-uncle of his had embarked in the last century on the grand tour, and had perished as a consequence in some foreign town. "Of some sudden illness?" Eliza had asked, but, no, his horse had bolted, taking fright when a bird flew up from under its hooves, causing Mr. Diggory to suffer a fall and a broken neck.

"That could have happened on the hunting field in England," she pointed out.

"In England he would have known what he was about," Sir Roger had said, frowning at Eliza's temerity in questioning the logic of this family legend.

"Egypt," Eliza said with a sigh. "I doubt if I shall ever travel so far even as Paris, and I confess, I should love to visit that city."

Mr. Wytton gave her a sardonic look. "One's life is not as fixed as one believes at the age of twenty. Surprises may lie in store for you, the unexpected often tends to happen, sometimes bringing in its train the most delightful change in one's life or circumstances."

He bent his head over the book, and Eliza, knowing that he would rather attend to his hieroglyphs than to talk to her, moved away.

"It is not all Latin and hieroglyphs," he called after her. "Upstairs you will find books in English."

The ascent to the upper gallery, at least from inside the library, appeared to be by means of a wooden staircase spiralling around a barleycorn central column. Eliza wound her way up, and a more pleasing scene met her eye. The gallery was six or seven feet wide, again lined with shelves, but here the books looked more promising, more modern, and at once her attention was caught by some old favourites: *Tom Jones, Roderick Random,* and *Clarissa*—although she was not in the mood for Mr. Richardson's tales of seduction and rape. Nor for Mr. Lewis's *The Monk,* not in these surroundings.

Here the furniture was more comfortable, small sofas and chairs set about as though people might sit in them and read a novel or have a conversation with a friend. It was, however, deserted, and as she walked all the way round to the other side, where she stood looking down on Mr. Wytton, absorbed in his hieroglyphs, she found she was the only other creature present.

So Mr. Bartholomew Bruton was not in the library. The chances were he had gone out with the other gentlemen, and would not return until the afternoon, then he would retreat to his chamber to change his clothes and might not reappear until the company assembled once again for dinner, when, she felt sure, it would again be impossible for her to have a private word with him.

Still, she would search every room that was accessible, which might, she judged, take some time. If Mr. Bartholomew Bruton were inside the building, she would find him, and meanwhile, it was as good a way to pass the time as any other.

Her steps took her from the library along another long, vaulted corridor, where ancient escutcheons loomed down at her, and the mullioned windows let in only a pale grey light. Even when the sun was shining, it could not be other than a gloomy place, and she didn't linger, passing on until she came to a small octagonal room. This was the foot of a tower, she could look up and see the light far above her. Like being in the bottom of a well, she said to herself, wondering which of the four large wooden doors that led from the tower she should try first.

One led to a short passage, with beyond it a flight of steps leading downwards. No, definitely not. For all she knew, the original dungeons were still in place. Dungeons? Her fancy was running away with her; why should a quondam monastery and abbey have had dungeons? No, that would be the way down to the cellarage, no doubt lined with dusty bottles and crusty vintages. The cellars held no appeal for her.

The next door was no more promising, since it led into another tower, empty except for a prie-dieu set against one wall. A huge leather Bible lay open upon it, a gold ribbon marking a passage.

Eliza retreated once more. This was better, this door led into another passage, one containing a long line of pictures. Faces must be of interest, and these were, she soon saw, all portraits. Presumably of the Montblaine ancestors; good heavens, what a fusty, dusty-looking lot. Time and again, the long nose and thin lips of the present Lord Montblaine were to be seen, in faces that hardly changed from generation to generation. Only the trappings showed the passing ages, as the subjects moved from velvet hats to full-bottomed wigs to the neat curls and queues of the last century. Were none of them stouter or more jowly than their ancestors? Apparently not; there, repeated in each canvas, was the lean Montblaine visage.

The women were a more varied bunch, although for the most part expressionless as they gazed out from among their noble spouses and fathers. Until, right at the end, she came upon a charming scene of a different kind. It was a painting by Mr. Gainsborough, of a man in a tricorn hat standing beside a tree, a sporting gun under his arm. Sitting beneath the tree, wearing the wide pannier skirts of an earlier age, was a pretty woman, with a lively smile on her face; on her lap reposed an infant, and to her side a solemn child, dressed in a blue suit, stared out at the world. In the distance was a house.

Eliza approached to have a closer look. It resembled Montblaine House, in some respects, but was much plainer, without the turrets and towers and spires.

"That," said a voice in her ear, "was Montblaine House before the late marquis had a rush of Gothic to the head."

Chapter Twenty-five

Eliza whirled round, to find herself face-to-face with Mr. Bartholomew Bruton. Colour flew to her cheeks; now that she was here, facing him, she hardly knew what to say, and besides, why was her heart thumping in that unruly fashion?

"You gave me a fright, creeping up on me in such a manner," she said indignantly.

"Did you take me for a monk engaged in a spot of haunting?"

"It is hardly polite not to announce yourself. A cough, a salutation from some feet away, would be courteous."

"Ah, but I am the discourteous Mr. Bruton, am I not?"

He was mocking her.

"Have you delighted in the splendours of the Montblaines long enough? Should you care to accompany me on a walk about the grounds? Or we can join your sister in the music room, or Mrs. Wytton and Mrs. Rowan in the Yellow Parlour, where they are playing cards and making extravagant bets."

"I do not play cards," she said.

"Then a walk will do you good."

He guided her back to the octagonal tower and opened the fourth door, which took them along a series of stone-flagged passages, through another hall, hung with tapestries, and out into what he told her was the Fountain Court. "So called, as you will have guessed, because of that."

In the centre of the court was a large marble fountain, with water splashing from a writhing collection of tritons, dolphins, and scantily clad nymphs.

"It was brought over from Italy by an earlier Montblaine and is considered very fine," he told her.

"You seem remarkably well acquainted with the abbey, do you often stay here?"

"I have never been here in my life before; however, some thoughtful person, perhaps a former guest, left a small and informative volume in my room, which is a guide to various of the great houses of this part of the world, and I made myself familiar with the chapter on this abbey before going to sleep last night."

Eliza took a deep breath. "Mr. Bruton, you made a remark at dinner last night, and I have been wanting to—"

"Ah, yes, your secret vice. For earning money with her pen must be accounted a vice in a young, single woman. The daughter of a bishop, I believe?"

"Why should not a woman write as well as a man?" she said hotly, distracted from her purpose by this observation. "If my brother had written those pieces—"

"Your father would be just as annoyed, and besides, from what I have heard about your brother, it is unlikely in the extreme that he could do any such thing. He is not, I think, possessed of a keen wit, nor indeed of any great sense of humour."

"Charles? But you do not know him, why are you saying such a thing?

"One hears gossip," said Bartholomew.

It sounded lame even to his ears. He couldn't say that he had made it his business to find out more about the Collins family. He had done it in order, he told himself, to find something that would convince Freddie to desist in his ardent pursuit of Miss Collins. He lied to himself, and knew that he did so. In fact, his investigations had been made from curiosity as to what kind of family could have bred a girl like Eliza.

“Tell me,” he said, “where had you your looks? You were contemplating the Montblaine portraits in the gallery just now, all very much of a likeness, don’t you think? Yet you do not resemble your sister in the least.”

“Neither of us takes after either of our parents,” said Eliza, too surprised at the turn the conversation was taking to speak any other than the truth.

“I can see that the young Lady Grandpoint must have had something of your sister’s beauty, but you—”

Where did she get that lively mouth, those up-tilted eyebrows, a face that altogether could belong to a Titania? “And your voice, it is an unusual voice.”

“My mama has a low voice,” Eliza said. “But, sir, can we return to the subject of our conversation?”

What made her so fascinating? She looked worried now, her expressive dark eyes showing her concern.

“Let me put your mind at rest. I found out about your literary endeavours by the merest chance, and I shall not impart that information to another soul, you have my word. We bankers, you know,” he said, smiling at her, “are famous for our discretion.”

“Then how ”

“I happened to step into the office of the *London Magazine,* I went in at my mother’s request, to place an advertisement offering a reward for the return of a dog she had lost. While doing so, I heard you speaking, you were in an inner room, in conversation with Mr. Mostyn. I recognised his voice, I am acquainted with him. And your voice, well, it is unmistakable.”

“The consequences of my authorship of those pieces becoming known would be terrible, please believe me.”

“Your family would not approve, I take it.”

“Not at all, and it would do Charlotte no good if the London articles were known to have been penned by her sister. It would be all over London in a trice, and when the news reached Yorkshire, my father would be horrified. It is not just the articles about London, you see; there are others I have written."

"Satirising clerical gentlemen. I have read them, and you will allow me to say how very accomplished they are, I can hardly believe they could have been written by someone as young as yourself."

"And female," she flashed back at him.

"No, I should have thought them the work of a gentleman's pen; however, my reason tells me that women have a sharp eye for the absurd and the ridiculous, and, in some cases, a good insight into the motives and manners of their fellow human beings." He paused. "Tell me, knowing that your father would so disapprove, indeed, that you could do harm to his standing in the Church if you became known as the author of those sketches, how came you to write them?"

He could see that had struck home. "They are trifles, they could not harm a man of my father's standing," she murmured. "It happened by chance, that the editor of the *Gazette* in Leeds read some pieces I had written. I did not write them for publication, but when he offered to pay me for them, I accepted, with the strict proviso that I remained anonymous. I needed the money," she added defiantly.

"My dear Miss Eliza, I know how much writing pays, or rather, how little. You can earn at most a few guineas from what you write. Was it worth the risk for such a small reward?" He disliked himself even as he spoke the words, he was causing her distress, and yet he wanted to hurt her, he wanted to understand why she had done such an unwise thing.

"I took great care that my identity would not be discovered. The editor in Leeds does not know who I am, for I swore his sister to secrecy. I had no idea the pieces would be published in London."

"Has no one brought them to your father's attention?"

"Oh, yes, all the clergymen read them." Her mouth lifted in that smile that made his heart stand still. "They huff and puff and say how foolish and ill-observed the sketches are, and then set to discussing whether the clerics I describe are among their acquaintance."

"And are they?"

"No, I portray a habit from here, a turn of phrase from there, a feature from one clergyman and another from another, and then I use aspects of other people who are not clergymen at all, and together all these parts make up one of fictional beings. And," she went on, with spirit, "a few guineas you say, with disbelief, scorn, even. A few guineas is wealth to me."

"My dear Miss Eliza, I did not mean—"

"Since you have been so forward as to scorn my earnings, let me tell you that my allowance from my father is twenty-four pounds."

"Well, that is not a great sum of money, but many a family has to live on a lot less than two hundred pounds or so a year."

"I mean twenty-four pounds annually, two pounds a month. And, yes, in comparison to needier creatures, it is a not inconsiderable sum. However, it has to cover all my clothes and so on, and a subscription to the library. It does not leave a surplus at the end of the month. You will know about surpluses, being a banker."

Now he was frowning. "That certainly does not seem a liberal allowance."

"My father's bishopric is one of the lowest stipends in the kingdom, and although he has other livings, he is careful with money. My writing allows me to indulge myself a little in the way of books, chiefly, and also—"

She wasn't going to say it, but he had a good idea where some of her money went; tightfisted clergymen like her father would not be inclined to give generously to the poor.

"So," she said, putting her chin up, and letting a gleam of what he feared was active hostility show in her eyes, "although my guineas and half guineas are trivial sums to you, Mr. Bruton, they make a good deal of difference to me. And, moreover, this money has an extra virtue, in that I earned it from the efforts of my own labour, and that, for a woman in my situation, is a hard thing to accomplish, and one I take pride in."

They stared at one another. The light of battle faded from Eliza's eyes, and faced with the intent look on Bartholomew Bruton's face, she dropped her gaze, noticing the zigzag pattern of the inlaid brick on the floor of the courtyard, feeling like some character in a fairy tale, rooted to the spot.

Bartholomew put out a hand, and lifted hers to his lips. "I admire you for it, pray forgive me for having caused you a moment's unease, it was wrong of me to taunt you last night. It was—I confess I do not know why I did it."

She tried to take her hand away, but he held on to it. "Because," she said, with a quick, sudden smile, "I think you like to taunt and tease, to get a reaction from your fellow beings, to catch them off-balance. It is not a kind quality, but it is not uncommon."

"Kind! No, I was not feeling kind, not at all. I wanted to persuade— No, do not move away. Eliza, I . . . That is, oh, how can I say what I want to say?"

His heart was in his mouth. He had never felt for any woman what he felt for this one. He wanted to spend hours in her company, and long nights in her arms; in short, he wanted to make her his wife. He astonished himself as he made the acknowledgement. What, Bartholomew Bruton, the confirmed and convinced bachelor, wanting a wife?

"Whatever it is," said Eliza, "take a deep breath and the words will come, or, better, do not do so, because they might be words you would wish unspoken. As it is, the time is passing, and I think I will go and find Charlotte, so if you will excuse me—"

"I admire you more than I can say," he said, drawing her back. And then, ill at ease and thrown out of his usual poise, he blurted out, "Will you do me the honour of becoming my wife?"

Chapter Twenty-six

For a moment it was as though time had frozen. The water splashing in the fountain, the scudding shadows of a passing cloud on the paved ground, the sound of a bird singing in the distance; all these sensations came to Eliza as though in a dream where time and place had no substance and reality.

For a moment, she thought she was going to faint, but, no, she never fainted. She blinked, and gave her head a slight shake as though to restore her senses to reason. So sure was she that the words had not been spoken, that it had been her own mind playing a trick on her, that she could say nothing that would not be foolish. Now she succeeded in wrenching her hand away. "I must go, please do not attempt to detain me, Mr. Bruton."

She retreated, he stepped forward.

His voice was urgent, and loud, echoing off the walls of the Fountain Court. "Wait. You must give me the courtesy of an answer. I apologise, I was too sudden, too abrupt."

"You said nothing, Mr. Bruton."

"Damn it, I asked you to be my wife, to do me the honour of marrying me. Do you call that nothing? Are you so much in the habit of receiving proposals that you turn them aside with an idle word, brush them off as though they meant nothing?"

"Don't shout at me. You are jesting, joking, teasing me for some reason that is beyond my understanding."

"What do you want me to do? I will go down on my knees if you feel—no, I won't do that, you would take it as mockery." His voice was bitter. "What can I do to assure you I am serious?"

"Your wits have deserted you, either that or you drank brandy with your breakfast."

"Brandy! For God's sake, listen to what you're saying. Do you think I'm joking, could I joke or treat such a matter lightly? I love you, I have fallen deep in love with you, and I want you to be my wife. I want to spend the rest of my life with you."

"Sudden! Of course you are too sudden. You don't know what you are saying. You asked a question, why, I can't imagine, and you insist on an answer. Very well, I give you an answer. No. There, that is your answer."

"No?"

"No. Even if you were serious, which you are not, the answer must be no. As I said, you are not kind."

He looked furious. "Come, Miss Eliza. No man would mock a woman on such a serious matter. I am sorry, I was abrupt, I took you by surprise. But I did not speak in jest. This is not a seduction, a false promise to gain an unworthy end, what do you think of me?"

"I think you are mad. Even if I cared for you, it is impossible—Oh, do go away. Please, just go away."

Eliza's way to the door, and to her escape, was blocked by Bartholomew Bruton, but at these heartfelt words, he gave her one last look, his face suffused with an emotion she found it impossible to read, and he strode abruptly through the door, which banged shut behind him.

Eliza let out her breath, and took a gulp of air as though she had not breathed all this time. She was light-headed, and sat down abruptly on one of the stone benches which were set around the fountain. Overwhelmed by a flood of disturbing emotions, she stared into the placid streams of water. Bartholomew Bruton had asked her to marry him. Was he serious? Was he actually in love with her?

He couldn't be. Yet, as he said, why would a man propose if he did not mean it?

And why?— She did not want to let her thoughts go that way, but she took command of herself and straightened her shoulders. It had to be faced. She was nothing if not honest, and honesty compelled her to admit that there had been a moment, a wild, intoxicating moment, when she had looked at him and felt a tug of emotion more powerful than anything she had known before.

No. She was in love with Anthony Diggory. More than that, she was engaged to Anthony Diggory, promised to him, set to marry him when she came of age in a few short months. Anthony was sanguine. *We shall win them round,* he had written confidently in his last letter, in the few lines that were not full of looping handwriting about dogs and horses and wheat and rooks in the Eastern Woods. *There will be no need of an elopement, no hugger-mugger marriage. We shall walk arm in arm from the church here, joined in marriage and blessed by your father, with all our family and friends around us, wishing us joy.*

In her mind's eye, when she read these words, she had seen it all: herself walking from the church to Diggory Hall, on Anthony's arm, her newly-wed husband, with the soaring splendour of the hills behind them, and the local people, tenants and farmers and well-wishers, calling out their congratulations and hopes for the couple's happiness in the country way.

Now that picture appeared a false one, truly a figment of her imagination, a girl's midsummer dream. And the prospect of such a wedding day no longer gave her any thought of happiness, only alarm and uncertainty.

She was faithless and fickle. Nothing better than a flirt, just as Charlotte said. Her head had been turned by London, by the parties, the assemblies, the dances, the heady delights of town. When she went back north, that would be no more than a memory, a memory that would fade.

She couldn't deceive herself. Her feelings towards Anthony had altered. There, that was the stark truth of it. There had been a spark between herself and Mr. Bruton from the moment they set eyes on each other. Her anger at his casual, unkind remark had been out of proportion; her reaction to it, her determination to prove him wrong, should have given her an inkling; there was altogether too much feeling there.

Camilla had noticed it. She had given her a gentle warning—warning? No, merely a hint, that should have led Eliza to examine her feelings more closely.

Dear God, what was she to do?

In honesty, and not because of Mr. Bruton's abrupt and unexpected proposal, but because she no longer felt the same about Anthony, she must end their engagement. She would write to him that very day, now, this moment.

How could she? What she wrote must go via Maria, and while her friend promised she never read a word, was that to be believed, given Maria's delight in all the details of a clandestine love affair? Eliza was a trusting person, but no fool. Could she disguise her hand? Or, no, ask Mr. Wytton to address the letter for her?

He would disapprove. Eccentric he might be, yet Eliza knew he would not look kindly on a secret engagement, scandalous in anyone's book.

How could she have been so foolish? Headstrong, her mother called her, and it was a just description of her behaviour. She and Anthony could have parted as they were, their affection declared, but without any solemn commitment. Flirting, falling in love—that was all very well, but Eliza knew now, as she should have known then, that marriage was different. Marriage was more than an attachment between two people, it concerned both families, and, in the case of a man in Anthony's position, must involve lawyers. She had been deluding herself to think otherwise.

She was trying to justify, through her rational sense, what was largely a matter of feeling. Passionate about Anthony, she had consented to the engagement; now, after only a few short weeks apart from him, those feelings had diminished. Had been blown into little pieces from the moment of her first encounter with that wretched Mr. Bruton, if only she had been honest enough with herself to admit it.

And now the shock of his declaration, his insistence that he cared for her to such a degree as that! Eliza got to her feet and walked to and fro, thoughts whirling about in her head. She heard footsteps approaching, and alarmed, she shrank into a corner. Was he coming back? The door opened, and she slid behind a tree planted in a huge pot, a jasmine with white flowers heavy with scent, lush enough in its foliage to conceal her.

Chapter Twenty-seven

It wasn't Bartholomew Bruton returning, as she had half hoped, half feared. It was George Warren. Come out to take the air, no doubt, although it did not seem to her that he was a man to dwell on the beauties of nature, or on the charming tranquillity of this place.

He paced up and down, and she could see an air of expectancy about him. Suddenly Eliza knew why he was here. It was an assignation, he was waiting for someone. She felt all the awkwardness of her situation. How could she now declare her presence, how could she come out from behind her leafy hiding place and greet him without looking and feeling foolish?

More footsteps, lighter ones, and walking with less urgency than Mr. Warren. A woman's step. Oh, Lord, not a tryst! Miss Chetwynd? That horrid Miss Grainger?

To her deep astonishment, the young woman who came into the court was neither Miss Chetwynd nor Miss Grainger, but Charlotte! Eliza nearly let out an exclamation, she was so surprised, and had to clap her hand to her mouth to restrain herself. Charlotte! George Warren? Informality, the order of the day here at Montblaine House, was one thing, but Charlotte should not be here alone with Mr. Warren.

Charlotte was smiling at the man, with a warmth in her eyes that Eliza had never seen before. Charlotte could not be in love with Mr.

Warren. The man was up to mischief; Eliza might be naïve, an ignorant provincial, but she knew a dangerous man when she saw one, and Mr. Warren was dangerous.

It seemed as though he were looking in her direction, and Eliza shrank back against the wall, holding her breath, hoping that the slight breeze rippling the leaves would not part the branches and reveal her presence.

All trace of embarrassment had left her. To be a witness to a meeting between a man and a woman with whom she was unconnected could be awkward, but what was going on here must concern her closely. Whatever did Charlotte think she was up to? Gingerly, Eliza parted a few leaves, to allow her a better view. Charlotte was standing by the marble bowl of the fountain, dabbling her hands in the water. Mr. Warren stood close behind her, and then, sliding a hand around Charlotte's slender waist, he drew her round and into his arms. For a moment Charlotte looked up at him, and Eliza's blood ran cold.

It frightened her, the voluptuous sigh with which Charlotte melted into Warren's embrace, the eagerness with which she responded to his ardent kisses, the ecstasy in every line of her body as she tilted her head back, to let Warren's lips glide over her neck, her breast.

She had to put a stop to it. She and Anthony had never— The passion here went beyond anything Eliza had experienced, and it was a passion, her dazed wits told her, that Warren was going to carry to what the country folk called its right true end. Now was the time to act, never mind the fury that would doubtless be turned on her. She braced herself to jump out, even as Warren's hands loosened the tie around the bosom of Charlotte's dress.

Before she could let out the cry of indignation that was in her throat, the great door to the court swung open, and there was Bartholomew. The couple hadn't noticed him, but he gave a cough and said in a loud voice, "Miss Collins, your aunt is searching for you. I saw you coming this way, and told her that I believed you were in the Fountain Court. Hark, I hear her now."

Charlotte's face, always pale, was now chalky, as she tugged at the top of her dress. Warren, his face scarlet and suffused with rage, rounded on Bruton.

"What the devil do you think you're doing?"

"I could ask the same question of you," said Bruton coolly. "To be seducing your uncle's guest, in his house—Miss Collins, what are you thinking of? Have you lost all sense of propriety, do you not know what you are about?"

They all heard the unmistakable click-clack of Lady Grandpoint's heels coming nearer. Charlotte looked wildly around her, and then, with a convulsive start, she hurled herself behind the self-same plant that had sheltered Eliza. Bumping into her sister, she would have let out a cry, but Eliza promptly put a hand over her sister's mouth and told her to be quiet. "It's only me, no, be still, for heaven's sake, or you are undone."

Undone! A polite word for what had nearly happened to Charlotte. And here was Lady Grandpoint. "Good day, Mr. Warren, Mr. Bruton," she said, her eyes sweeping round the court. "Pray, what are you doing here? You look flushed and het up, I hope you have not been quarrelling, Lord Montblaine would not be pleased if his guests were to be at outs with one another."

Bartholomew Bruton forced a laugh. "No, ma'am, nothing more than a heated discussion. About politics," he added, hoping that a detail would add verisimilitude to his story, for Warren was glaring at him with such undisguised loathing that it would take more than a difference of political opinion to explain his hostility. "It was the question of the Reform Bill, ma'am, a subject on which we both feel very strongly."

"Oh, Reform! You had better take that up with Lord Grandpoint, his views on that subject are to be listened to, I believe, especially by men of your age, you have not the experience to understand the intricacies of politics. And you do not sit in the House, I believe, Mr. Warren. Nor you, Mr. Bruton. Of course, Mr. Warren will in due course succeed to his father's dignities and a seat in the Lords, although I imagine that it is a much better preparation for a young man to sit in the House of Commons rather than to go straight into the Lords. And you, Mr. Bruton, have you never thought of going into politics? I am sure with your mother's connections, and your father's influence"—she had been going to say wealth, but the severe look on Bartholomew's face made her think again—"a seat could be found for you."

"Thank you, Lady Grandpoint, for your interest in my career, but I find that banking takes up all my time and energies."

"Anyhow, I have not come here to talk of politics. I am looking for my goddaughter, Miss Collins, have you seen her? No? Perhaps she is with her sister, I have not seen Miss Eliza today."

With sudden presence of mind, Bartholomew Bruton came out with a swift lie. "I think I saw Miss Collins a little while ago, now you mention it. In the Yew Walk. With her sister."

"The Yew Walk? Very well, I shall go that way. And, Mr. Warren, your clothing is somewhat disarranged. You should tidy yourself up. Your uncle will not care to see you looking like that."

So forceful was her personality that Warren's gaze dropped, and muttering what sounded suspiciously like a curse, he strode out of the court.

"Your arm, if you please, Mr. Bruton," said Lady Grandpoint. "You may escort me to the place where you saw Miss Collins."

Bartholomew had no choice but to oblige, and with heartfelt relief Eliza peeped out and confirmed that the court was, at last, empty.

Charlotte didn't hesitate; without a word, she fled through the door, more distraught than Eliza had ever seen her, leaving her staring after her sister, her mind in complete turmoil.

She sat down hard on the nearest bench, trying to sort out her impressions of the scene she had witnessed. A rape? Nothing of the kind, Charlotte was welcoming, encouraging Warren's lascivious advances, and she shuddered to think what further liberties Warren might have taken had he not been interrupted.

His behaviour did not surprise her, he was a rakish kind of man, far more so in reality than Lord Rosely, who had a reputation for being a rake. It was Charlotte, remote, controlled Charlotte, whose reaction had been so astonishing! Who could have suspected for a moment that she was capable of such physical passion, that she would respond with such ardour to a man's embraces?

"This is the devil of a fix," exclaimed Mr. Bruton, coming back into the court, slightly out of breath.

He had ruthlessly handed over Lady Grandpoint to Miss Grainger, whom they met as they came out of the Great Hall. "Her ladyship wishes to go to the Yew Walk," he said, with a wave of his hand in the direction of what he hoped might be the Yew Walk. He had no idea of its exact location, had merely heard it mentioned by one of the other gentlemen at breakfast. Freed of her ladyship, he had hurried back to the Fountain Court.

"Where is your sister? Were you here all that time, while—?"

"Yes," Eliza said bluntly. "I hid behind that jasmine, like a character in a play, and watched a villainous man make advances upon a hapless maiden."

"Hapless? It appeared to me—"

"I know just how it appeared to you, and I beg that you will say no more about it, now or later."

"I told you I am discreet, Eliza, and I would not betray your sister for the world—but by God, what is she up to? Has she taken leave of her senses?"

"I can only conclude that she has fallen in love with Warren."

"Love! Well, that's a word for it, only your sister was venturing upon the wilder shores of love in this case. She should not do so, she should be more circumspect. Warren has a devilish bad reputation."

"I am sure that he has preyed on Charlotte's feelings, and that his intention was to ruin her."

"Ah," said Bartholomew. "Thus preventing any chance of his uncle marrying her."

"As to that, I do not care about it, I do not wish Charlotte to marry Lord Montblaine, they would not suit."

"Until I witnessed this incident today, I would have said they suited one another very well, two people with marble running in their veins. As to what passion the marquis might be capable of, I can't say, but your sister! Well, she surprised me."

"Surprised you? She has astonished me. What is to be done? Should I tell Lady Grandpoint? We should leave the house at once, she should not stay under the same roof as Warren."

"Tell Lady Grandpoint? On no account, that would be a disastrous move. In such cases as this, the fewer people who know what is going on, the better. What puzzles me is Warren's thinking. How can he benefit from seducing your sister? Does he intend to marry her? I doubt it, he, of all men, would never marry without personal gain, that is, he will want to marry a woman with a fortune."

"If any such could be persuaded to accept him."

"Women find him attractive, although he does have a bad reputation."

"I do not find him attractive in the least, and I cannot think why Charlotte, why my sister—"

"That is because it is not a question of thinking."

The colour had flown to her cheeks. "Ah," he said drily. "You do have a notion of what was happening there."

Stolen kisses with a young man in Yorkshire? Or warmer embraces in the secluded nooks and crannies of summer gardens, or those places off the ballroom, which experienced men and women could always find? A wave of jealousy surged through him, horrifying him by its intensity.

Because he had such strong feelings for her, and had imagined that she returned them, why should he assume that her heart was untouched, that she had not enjoyed at least some of the pleasures of love?

Were the two sisters not at all what they seemed, were they young women with the faces and manners of virtue and purity, hiding their likeness under the skin to the light-skirted women of the demimonde? He had known plenty of women like that, women whose virtue was simply another commodity to be exploited in the most favourable way.

Then he looked at Eliza, and his heart melted. So, she had been in love. How could such a lively, warm person not have fallen in love? Puppy love, the innocent tumbling into adoration and stolen kisses that was part of growing up, even for the most sheltered girls. For some, it was the drawing master at boarding school, for others a brother's friend, a neighbour; how could the round of courtship and launching on to the marriage market not have flirtations and experiments along the way?

Yet society was unforgiving to young women who strayed more than a few inches from the path of strict and apparent virtue. And Charlotte was heading for a precipice. Charlotte was what concerned Eliza now; she was deeply troubled, and he must find a way to help her.

"Surely," Eliza was saying, "if Warren ruins Charlotte, then his uncle—if he feels any affection for Charlotte, which I doubt—will be angry with Warren. Can he disinherit him?"

"No. Warren's father, Lord Warren, is the heir presumptive to the Montblaine title, and nothing can alter that. With the title go the landed estates and great wealth; those are inseparable from the title. The marquis does also have a large personal fortune, and, yes, he could choose to leave that elsewhere."

"Surely George Warren stands to lose more by his uncle marrying and having an heir than by displeasing him."

"It is odd, this affair of Montblaine and your sister. Since he was widowed, a good many years ago, he has existed as far as one knows without female company. He has no regular mistress, does not take those trips to Paris which men—"

"You travel to Paris frequently, do not you?"

He smiled at her. "You are a minx. I go to Paris on banking business, which is, let me tell you, quite a different thing. Let us keep this conversation to the subject of the marquis and your sister, and Warren, and what is to be done. Your sister knows that you saw her with Warren. You must go to her, talk to her, make her see that whatever her feelings for Warren, she is treading on treacherous ground."

"If she is in love with Warren, she will hear nothing against him, that is the way we women are."

"Lay it out for her, how her family will be affected, her own and your chances of a good marriage ruined if she takes this false step. If there is a genuine attachment between her and Warren, then let them become engaged, let them marry."

"She would be wretchedly unhappy with such a husband."

"Why has Warren not approached Lady Grandpoint, or written to her father, if his intentions are honourable? Ask her that."

"I will try," said Eliza with a sigh. "One never knows with Charlotte. There are aspects of her character I cannot fathom, even though I probably know her better than anyone else. Her reserve is strong and deep. Or I would have said it was, but then, seeing her with Warren . . ."

"There is a difference," Bartholomew said gently, "between an individual who has no strong feelings, and one who has a sensual nature kept under strict control."

"All the more reason for her to choose a man like Lord Rosely, who would allow her nature to become warmer."

"Rosely is not the man for her. I know him well, and it would be almost as unhappy a match as if she were to marry Warren."

In the distance a bell began to ring; it was time for the guests to go to their rooms and begin to dress for dinner. "Go to your sister," he said. "Reason with her, if you can."

Chapter Twenty-eight

How easy it had been to speak to Bartholomew Bruton. How suddenly the barriers between them had broken down. Yet there was a greater barrier between them than the one of their previous misunderstanding and incivility: his extraordinary proposal, his declaration of love, and—she cursed herself for it—her wholly inadequate response.

However, that was of no consequence just now. Of overwhelming importance at this moment was Charlotte and the fix she was in.

Did Charlotte regard herself as being in a fix? She must do; surely she would be in inner turmoil from the after-effects of that passionate encounter with Warren, and the discovery of them by Eliza and Bruton.

It seemed not. As Eliza entered Charlotte's chamber, her sister rose from the chair where she was sitting at a satinwood desk and said, in a perfectly calm voice, "Well, are you come to preach morality at me?"

Charlotte's bedchamber was an attractive room, with cherry-patterned curtains, a modern bed with curved walnut panels at head and foot, covered in a quilt of the same cherry pattern, and, dotted around the spacious chamber, soft chairs, tasselled cushions on a small sofa, and several pieces of light, modern furniture. The room and its furnishings seemed out of keeping with the rest of the abbey, and Eliza wondered who had been responsible for it. Perhaps the late marchioness had had different taste to her austere husband, or Lady Warren, who was so much at home here, had done the room over to please herself.

"You are very out of the way here," she said to Charlotte. "This is a secluded room."

Too private, to her way of thinking. Why had her sister been given this room? By whose orders? The housekeeper, working from a list of guests? Lady Warren? The marquis—no, surely he would not attend to the arrangements for his guests in that much detail. Were Charlotte to plan a meeting with her lover, were she so blind to all sense of restraint or indeed morality, then she would have every opportunity to entertain Warren here. Eliza blinked. What was she thinking?

"Charlotte," she said, her voice even huskier than usual, a sure sign of emotion with her, which Charlotte would recognise. "Charlotte, you have surely taken leave of your senses, you have forgotten what is due to yourself, to your family."

"Have I?" said Charlotte perfectly calmly. "That is for me to decide."

Eliza knew Charlotte in this mood, knew that there was no way to break through that wall of impassivity. How could this be the same person as the one who had embraced Warren with such voluptuous abandon? It was scarcely believable.

"Then I shall have to inform Lady Grandpoint of what happened in the Fountain Court just now."

"You are become a talebearer, is that it? Do so, and when you have finished, I shall go to her, and show her these."

Charlotte whisked some papers from her desk and flourished them under Eliza's nose.

Good God, what was this? Charlotte held each page out, not the slightest tremor in her steady hand. There was the last letter Eliza had had from Maria, with the page of Anthony's ill-formed writing, assuring her of the continuing warmth of his affection, reminding her of the last time he had held her in his arms, calling her his sweetheart.

That was bad enough, but the other paper was almost worse, for there, in her own hand, was the draft for one of her sketches of clerical life. On the other side of the sheet were scribbled notes for some of her observations on London society.

"You will go to my godmother with a story of my misconduct which I shall simply deny. Then I will produce this, no mere baseless accusation about this, here is evidence in writing for all to see. Whom will she believe, who will be packed off to Pemberley as soon as may be? Not I, Eliza, but you."

Eliza's mouth was dry, and for a moment she couldn't speak. Then her temper, which she rarely lost with Charlotte, burst out.

"Give those back to me, this instant! Those are my private papers."

"Did you think I didn't know that you were writing those pieces? I have held my tongue on that, although I disapproved, and had to wrestle with my conscience as to whether I should inform Mama and Papa."

"You knew! How did you know?"

"You neglected to hide what you were writing on one occasion when you were called away from our sitting room."

"And you read it. You are despicable, how can you stand there, looking so toplofty, and calmly admit to snooping among my papers?"

"A sheet of writing left lying around, why should I not read it? You should have nothing to hide from your sister, or from your mama if it comes to that. I doubt if I would read your journal if you kept one, although I would point out that any girl should expect to have no secrets from her parents; if you did keep a journal, they would be only doing their duty to read it. As to your correspondence with Anthony, you realise how shocking that is? For an unmarried girl to write to a single man is to act outside all the bounds of propriety. Without an engagement, it is a scandalous way to carry on, and if there is a secret engagement—well, that would be shocking beyond anything."

"You are threatening me," Eliza said at last. "It is blackmail."

"You threatened me first. Now, go away. I know what I am doing, so please do not try to interfere with me."

"How had you my letters?"

"Hislop found them for me. No, do not hold out your hand, do you think I will give them back? I am not so foolish."

"Hislop! Why, the traitor."

"She has my best interests at heart, that is all. Now, take yourself off. Go and splash cold water over your face; you will have to make an effort to compose yourself before we go down for dinner, you look positively demented, let me tell you, with your eyes flashing, and your colour high from indignation. Leave me to manage my own affairs, Eliza, you will find I do it very well. And I will not permit you or anyone else to come between George Warren and myself."

"High words," snapped back Eliza. "You are the fool, not I, not to know an insincere, scheming, wicked man when you see him."

She so far forgot herself as to slam the door behind her as she left, enjoying the sound that resonated all around the tower.

Back in her own room, she sank into a chair, her heart beating furiously. What had she achieved? Nothing. And now there was no one she could turn to for advice. Camilla? She knew about Eliza's writing and about her attachment to Anthony, but would surely disapprove of a secret engagement. She could tell her about Charlotte and Warren, but unless she had seen that passionate embrace for herself, she would merely suppose Charlotte was flirting with Warren. Which wouldn't be surprising, nor really scandalous.

Camilla might drop a hint in Charlotte's ear as to Warren's unsavoury reputation, and Charlotte would then rightly suspect that she, Eliza, had told their cousin—and perhaps, out would come the letters, the writing. Which would be disastrous for her, and do nothing to save Charlotte from a ruinous course.

Most of all, she found she wanted to confide in Bartholomew Bruton. What was it about him that inspired such confidence? Then, suddenly mistrustful of her own judgement, she chided herself. Two days ago, a day ago, she would have stigmatised Mr. Bruton as the most disagreeable man in England, and now she was *bouleversé,* the solid ground under her feet shifted into an unrecognisable landscape, the strength of her attachment to Anthony blown to pieces. It was all too much.

Annie came in, and Eliza spoke quite sharply to her. "It appears that my sister's maid, Hislop, has been into my chamber. Do you know of this?"

"Why, she told me that you had a jar of cream that was rightfully Miss Collins's, and that she would pop in to get it. Why, miss, whatever is the matter? What was the harm in that? Should I have stopped her? Indeed, I don't think I could, for she's a grim party when crossed, that Hislop."

Eliza smiled at Annie. "I am sorry to speak harshly. Hislop rummaged among my papers, that is all. It is not your fault."

Annie gave one of her expressive sniffs and, without a further word, set about laying out Eliza's clothes for the evening. Then, darting a quick look at Eliza, she said, "You look like you have the headache, Miss. Let me go down and make you a tisane."

"Thank you, Annie, but my headache is of the figurative kind." Seeing the puzzled look on Annie's face, she went on, "It is not a physical pain, it cannot be quelled by a tisane or drops. I have something on my mind, that is all."

Charlotte was dressed in more than good time for dinner, and, unusually restless for her, she decided to go downstairs, perhaps she would go to the library, where she might lose herself in a book. Charlotte was not a great reader, but she was familiar with the ability of a book to soothe a perplexed mind, for indeed, Charlotte was, beneath her composed exterior, more agitated than she cared for.

Warren had put her into this state, Warren, with his commanding presence, and with his power to make her feel as she had never done before. No, she would not think of Warren now, there was the whole long evening to go through, and then, he had promised in a note slid under her door to come to her room.

She was beyond propriety, beyond anything except the expectation of happiness, of delight in being in George's arms. It was wrong, in the eyes of the world, but she had lost her head and her reason, she was on the other side of the boundary of right and wrong, simply filled with a longing that could only be assuaged by Warren.

She entered the library through the gallery. It was deserted at that time of day, when all the guest and occupants of the house were preparing for dinner, the servants in the kitchens or dining room, the guests and their personal servants in their own chambers upstairs.

A book with plates in it would be agreeable, and less effort than reading words. She strolled along the shelves, looked for a likely volume. Then the sound of voices came up from below. Urgent voices, talking in whispers, who could it be?

With a thrill she recognised Warren's voice, as he exclaimed, in his normal way, "By God, you have a wicked mind."

Whom was he talking to? She should announce her presence, she was no Maria Diggory, famous for her eavesdropping habits, and yet, she lingered. She tiptoed closer to the edge of the gallery and strained her ears to hear what was being said.

"You will have to cover my back with the old man," Warren was saying. "I don't want to turn him against me."

"I will tell him that it was that girl's fault, that she led you on, threw herself into your way and begged you to run off with her. Good heavens, how she has played into your hands, I could never have believed she would turn out to be such a simpleton, nor that she would succumb so completely to your manly charms."

"Too easy a conquest, no sport in it at all," agreed Warren. "Such ardour quickly palls, I shall grow tired of her long before she has had enough of me."

"Where shall you take her?"

"Some inn, I think. Nowhere I'm known, don't want a scandal breaking out all over London, not this time. No, I'll keep her with me long enough to be sure of her ruin, then I'll return her to her godmother, by that time she won't have a shred of reputation, she'll be packed off back to Yorkshire, the family will try to hush it up.

Word will get about, it will be a two-day wonder, but she is a person of no consequence, a mere impoverished bishop's daughter, who in London will care? She will soon be forgotten by society."

"There is a brother, may he not call you out?"

"I doubt it, and if he does, I dare say I shall put a bullet through him. But it will not come to that, there is no section of English society quite so hypocritical as the clergy. They will pay some poor curate to take her off their hands, and she will languish away her life in some muddy parish, doing good works among the poor and for ever suspected by her husband of making eyes at the sexton or some other bumpkin."

Laughter; unkind, unpleasant, triumphant laughter.

The other person down there was Lady Warren, of course. Charlotte felt as though she had been struck a physical blow, that all the breath had been drawn out of her. She was clenching her hands so tightly that her nails were driving into her palms. She must stay in control, keep quiet, must not move a hair, must not let them become aware of her presence.

"Lord, look at the time," said Lady Warren. "I must make haste, how tedious it is here, always having to be punctual to the minute. How much better it will be when modern ways come to the abbey!"

Chapter Twenty-nine

Charlotte had never looked as lovely as she did that evening. Her complexion glowed, her expression held the serenity of a saint, as she sat in perfect tranquillity on a fat red sofa in the red drawing room, waiting for dinner to be announced.

"Montblaine cannot take his eyes off her," Camilla whispered to her husband. "I declare, the man is besotted."

Mr. Wytton was inclined to agree. "It is what happens when a middle-aged man falls for a young woman like Charlotte. Butter wouldn't melt in her mouth, but don't you wonder what is going on inside that beautiful head?"

"Nothing," said Camilla. "Charlotte has never been clever, and this late-developing beauty has taken over her life, in my opinion."

"And what ails Eliza? There, she is trying to smile, but she is anxious. See how she keeps looking at Charlotte, as though her sister were ill or about to make a dreadful faux pas."

"More interesting," said Camilla, her eyes sparkling, "is how Charlotte ignores Warren. She looked at him just now as though he were a cockroach."

"Odd that, for I held, you know, that she was more strongly attracted to him than might be suspected."

"Whatever attraction there may have been no longer exists," said

Camilla, speaking with utter certainty. "On the other hand, look at Bartholomew Bruton!"

Mr. Wytton observed him through drooping eyelids. "You have something there. Well, why not? Except that Eliza has no fortune, no banking connections, nothing to recommend her to Mr. Bruton and Lady Sarah, besides Bartholomew's being all but promised to Miss Grainger."

"Bartholomew's parents are looking at Eliza in no very friendly way," said Camilla. "They are not blind, they see what is happening there."

"While he is overflowing with admiration, can you say the same for her?"

Camilla frowned. "Ah, that is another matter. There are complications . . ."

Wytton smiled down at her with great fondness. "Don't tell me, I pray, I really would rather not know. While there should be no secrets between man and wife, I am more concerned that you honour your promises to your friends. Besides, I smell trouble, and I should prefer to keep well out of it. Heaven forbid we should have the bishop land on our doorstep!"

The dinner, and the long hours after it, were torture to Eliza. She did not know what to make of Charlotte, something had changed, had dramatically changed since their encounter, their quarrel, she must call it. Could her words have made any impression on her sister? She was very sure they had not.

She had little opportunity to be with Mr. Bruton, who was not tonight seated next to her. Instead, she found herself next to Mr. Portal, although still with the dreadful Mr. Pyke on her other side, and tired and dispirited, she found herself rather more cutting to the clergyman and rather more disjointed in her conversation with Mr. Portal than was quite right.

With huge relief, she finally went upstairs, and sat yawning at her dressing table while Annie put away her clothes. She jumped, mid-yawn, at a tap on the door, and then, without waiting for an answer, Charlotte entered the room.

"Charlotte! Whatever is the matter? Sit down, you are so pale. Annie, a glass of water, directly."

"Thank you." Charlotte's voice high and strained. "I intend to sleep in this room, tonight. Your maid can find me a nightgown."

"Charlotte, has something happened? Why do you look so strange, why are you here?"

"I shall tell you nothing, except that I do not care to sleep in that room tonight. It is too isolated. I am better here." And then, with an effort, she said, "I would like Annie to go there, directly, and to sleep in my room, if she would."

"I?" said Annie in astonishment. "Sleep in your room? Oh, Miss, I couldn't do that, I would be in such trouble for not keeping to my own place in the attics."

"If I ask you to, Annie?" said Eliza, whose quick apprehension had come to something near the truth of why Charlotte was here. "And if someone should attempt to enter the room, Annie, should come upon you while you were lying in bed . . ."

"I should scream the place down," said Annie frankly.

"That is just what you must do," said Eliza. "Now, why ever should Annie be in there, and not in her part of the house?" she said to Charlotte. "There must be a reason, and one that does not reflect badly on Annie."

"Well, Miss," said Annie, "suppose Miss Collins had asked for me to spend the night in there, since she felt unwell."

"Yes," said Eliza. "You have the headache, Charlotte, and I asked Annie to be there with you, for you know how ill you can become. Only, why should not Hislop be there?"

"Annie would be better," said Charlotte flatly. "Hislop will not come near me tonight, you will find."

"Bribed?" said Eliza, too low for Annie to hear.

"Drugged, I expect," said Charlotte, her voice sounding infinitely weary. "Lady Warren . . ." Her voice trailed into silence.

Eliza took her hand and pressed it. "I think you do have the headache, there will be no need for lies. Get into bed this instant,

Annie will see to you before she takes herself off. Annie, I sent you to my sister with some special—oh, special something!"

"Pastilles, Miss?" said Annie, holding up a small box.

"Yes, that will do. I desired you to stay there until she was asleep, and meanwhile, you fell asleep in the chair. She awoke, and suffering greatly, came to find me."

"No one who knew us would believe this touching story," said Charlotte from the bed, where she lay, her face pale and wan against the pillows, her hand pressed to her closed eyes.

Yet it was true, Eliza thought, as she laid a cold cloth on Charlotte's brow. She had come to Eliza for help. What had happened? She would probably never know, but it was enough that Charlotte had turned against Warren.

She sat at the desk and scribbled a note. "Annie, can you find out which room Mr. Bruton, the young Mr. Bruton, is in, and slip this under his door? I want no violence tonight, yes, I know you can defend yourself against anything from a headless monk to a prowling ravisher"—and how close to the truth that was—"yet I should prefer for there to be a gentleman within reach should there be any trouble."

Annie's eyes were full of conspiratorial zest. "Leave it to me, Miss Eliza. And if need be, I can set up a screeching to wake the whole castle, don't you worry!"

By the time the household had fallen quiet, Eliza had almost forgotten what might be going on in the turret room, for she was worried about Charlotte. Evidently in great pain, her sister was in considerable distress of mind as well as body, until Eliza crept out to find Lady Grandpoint to ask if she had any laudanum. No, there was no point in her coming to see Charlotte, she was sure the drops would lull her to sleep.

"She looked so well this evening," Lady Grandpoint said. "How can she be ill now? We have not been travelling, how do you account for it?"

How horrified she would be if Eliza told her the truth, but of course there was no question of that. Perhaps some food she had eaten at the light nuncheon which was served to the ladies of the house in the middle of the day, strawberries could sometimes have an ill effect on her system.

"Then she should know better than to eat them. However, I do not wish to be unsympathetic. Take the drops. Do not give her too many, fifteen is the proper dose."

Eliza had measured the fifteen drops into a glass of water, and then, looking at Charlotte, her face screwed up with pain, she added a few more, and had the satisfaction of seeing her, after a very few minutes, relax, and fall into a deep slumber.

Her visit to Lady Grandpoint and the request for laudanum, a perfectly genuine request for Charlotte's perfectly genuine indisposition, was no bad thing, she concluded; it added verisimilitude to her story. Would Warren venture to the turret room? Would the redoubtable Annie play her part?

The clock in the north tower struck the hour with two sonorous strokes. Outside the window an owl hooted, startling Eliza. She was wide-awake, ears straining for any sound that might come from Charlotte's room, although she knew she couldn't possibly hear anything at that distance.

Settling back in the chair by the window, listening to Charlotte's steady, even breathing, she wondered if she had been guilty of folly, letting Annie stay alone in that room. No, Warren was no violent rapist, keen on any prey. He was a seducer, intent on spending hours of darkness in the embraces of a woman who was passionate about him. Once he discovered Annie's identity, then what would he do but beat a quick retreat?

Yet might he not be so enraged by the failure of his scheme that he would lash out at the innocent Annie? He would know that to be discovered entering the bedchamber of a young lady, a guest of his uncle's, could only be interpreted in the worst possible way.

And now, as the moon rose above the grotesque outline of the abbey, sending its weird, draining light across the arches and spires, a flaw in the plan occurred to Eliza—why had she not thought of it? For if Warren were discovered in Charlotte's bedchamber, even though it was only inhabited by Annie, would not it naturally be assumed that he had expected to find Miss Collins there, and in that case, that she had invited him?

Annie must not scream. She must keep quiet, so that Warren could vanish as stealthily as he had come. Charlotte, in her desire to escape from Warren, had not considered this aspect of the matter.

With a final glance at Charlotte, Eliza took her candle, which was burning low, and glided out of the room. Her slippered feet made no sound on the stone floors, and yet she felt she could have clattered along in boots and spurs and no one would have noticed. It was not only that the household slept behind those solid wooden doors, but that the house itself was full of creaks and strange noises. Wind whistled in through ill-fitting window frames; where the stone flags gave way to wooden floors and stairs, they creaked and cracked as though an army were going up and down. There was a steady banging sound; it was ropes slapping against the flagpole, Eliza told herself, for Montblaine flew the family standard when he was in residence, a splendid affair of blue and gold, with a hawk emblazoned on it; the flag was raised each morning, and hauled down at dusk by a stout footman.

She concentrated on the known and rational, refusing to let herself be frightened by shadows in the moonlight, by the ancestral banners moving gently above her head, by the embers of a dying fire crackling into sudden life, by a log falling from a grate.

Her candle guttered and went out, and she caught her breath. Had she mistaken the way, was she in some other part of the house, far from Charlotte's lonely turret? Now the moonlight streaming through the mullioned windows, sending strange patterns across the floor, was her ally. She stood on tiptoe to look out. Yes, she recognised the yard below, she hadn't missed her way.

Here she was, finally, at the foot of the stone staircase that led to Charlotte's room. She ran up them, reached the landing at the top, and paused to get her breath back. In the corner, a shadow moved, and this time it was real, solid, not a figment of her imagination. She couldn't help herself, she opened her mouth to scream, and was silenced before so much as a gasp emerged, by a strong hand clamped over her mouth.

A voice whispered in her ear, "Be quiet, or we are lost."

She felt limp with relief. Even in the dark, even with just a whisper, she knew it was Mr. Bruton who had emerged from the shadows. There was a sound from inside Charlotte's room. Had they disturbed Annie? He pulled her back into the darkness of the corner. The door opened, and Annie appeared, a silhouette against the moonlight that flooded the room behind her.

At that moment another figure came bounding up the stairs. It was the figure of a man, his face quite clear in the moonlight. Warren. He leapt forward and swept Annie into his arms, showering her with kisses.

Annie rose superbly to her part. She delivered a ringing slap to Warren's swarthy face, and then, evidently possessed of excellent lungs, let out a stream of ungenteel screeches that echoed round the abbey.

Chapter Thirty

"Here you both are," said Mrs. Rowan, as she and Mr. Portal came into Camilla's drawing room. "The very people we wanted to talk to, and such a mercy, no other callers, so you can be as indiscreet as you like."

"Indiscreet?" said Camilla, raising her eyebrows. "Why, my dearest Henrietta, what can you be speaking of?"

"We want to hear the full account of the incident in the night at Montblaine," said Mrs. Rowan. "I have never been so vexed as when I woke from a soundless night's sleep to find my maid agog with such stories of nocturnal goings-on.

"And Lord Montblaine nowhere to be seen, and Caroline Warren and her wicked son bowling away down the drive, and the servants all in an uproar, and no sense to be got out of anyone. You and Mr. Wytton left before I could speak to you in private, for I was sure you must know what had happened, and poor Miss Collins with a dreadful headache, that terrible sort that makes you sick, I understand, and so you"—nodding at Eliza—"looking after her, as was only right, and Lady Grandpoint in such a bad mood, sitting and sighing and talking in that high-and-mighty way she has with Lady Sarah. Mr. Bartholomew Bruton had returned to London, Miss Grainger in a pout, and Mrs. and Miss Chetwynd twittering like a pair of dim-witted sparrows!"

"You may imagine our frustration," Mr. Portal said. "When we returned to London later in the day, we found the town already abuzz with rumours, all about Warren, although it is clear that Mr. Bruton is involved in some way. I feared for a moment that there might have been a run on the bank, and my fortune in danger; however, I realised it could not be so, Mr. Bruton himself would not be sitting there so complacently if that were the case."

"Complacently!" said Mrs. Rowan. "When he looked for all the world as though he had a bad smell under his nose?"

Camilla asked the butler to arrange for refreshments to be brought, and gave instructions that she was not at home, should there be any other callers.

"It is simple," she said. "George Warren assaulted Eliza's maid, there, that is the long and the short, the up and the down, the in and out of it."

"Assaulted your maid?" said Mr. Portal. "No, no, this will not do, there is more to the story than that."

Eliza by now had her story off pat, for she had had to explain to half the household why Annie was there in her sister's room, how she had ventured into the corridor, hearing a noise, and had there encountered Mr. Warren, clearly the worse for Lord Montblaine's excellent wine, there could be no other excuse for his behaviour.

"I cannot imagine how you failed to hear the noise," Camilla said to Mrs. Rowan.

"We were in the East Wing, you know, and the walls must be several feet thick. What was Annie doing there, is she not your maid, why was she not in her bed, in the attics with the other maids?"

Eliza explained, and if it seemed to her that there were gaps in the glib story of Charlotte's headache, the indisposition of her maid, the presence of Warren in that part of the house, neither Mr. Portal nor Mrs. Rowan noticed, although she did feel Pagoda's shrewd eyes on her with an appraising look in them.

"How is your sister now?" asked Mrs. Rowan.

"Oh, perfectly well. She woke the next morning, like you unaware of the fracas in the night, heavy-eyed, but with her headache gone. We returned to London at a gentle pace, I was afraid that the motion of the carriage might bring her headache on again, but it did not."

"Is she delicate?"

"Not at all. Some persons are subject to the headache, and she is one of them. In every other way, she is as healthy and strong as can be."

"Does anyone know what has become of Warren?"

"He is gone to France," said Camilla. "Mr. Wytton says the attempted rape of a servant is nothing for a man of his reputation, but it was under his uncle's roof, and the world is more censorious than it used to be on such matters."

"That is very true," cried Mr. Portal. "It is one of the few lasting benefits of the Revolution in France, that it made landowners in England aware that servants must have some rights, too, that if they could rise up and turn on their masters across the Channel, it could happen even here. So people of sense are taking a good deal more care about the well-being of those in their employ; Lord Montblaine has a good name as a landlord and master, and it will have annoyed him greatly that Annie should have been assaulted in this way."

"Beside, George Warren spends a good deal of time in Paris, does he not?" said Henrietta. "He came back in a great hurry when there were rumours as to his uncle enjoying the company of a beautiful young woman. Now he has had to scamper back with his tail between his legs, he will not be in a good temper."

"Nor will Lady Warren, it may be a long while before she acts as hostess for the marquis again," said Camilla. "Your sister had better have him, Eliza, it would be a great match for her, and then the abbey will have a mistress again."

"I cannot believe that Lord Montblaine has any serious intentions," said Eliza rather crossly. "There is no hint of a proposal, and I do not think it would be a good match for Charlotte at all, except in the eyes of the world. He is not the man to make her happy."

"George Warren seemed quite *épris* in that direction, did he not?" said Mr. Portal, at his driest. "There's one suitor seen off. Who else among the throng has serious intentions?"

"Lord Rosely," said Eliza, as she rose to her feet. "Dearest cousin, I must take my leave."

"Shall we see you at the Wintertons' dance this evening?" said Mrs. Rowan.

"Yes, I shall be there."

Much as Eliza liked to dance, and agreeable as she found the Wintertons, who were noted for the gaiety and mixed company of their parties, she knew that they weren't part of the core of fashionable London although they were well connected. "You can never be sure whom you are going to meet there," Lady Grandpoint had complained when the invitation arrived. "Last time there was the oddest Lithuanian, apparently a spy during the last war, and his wife, who came from Hungary, besides some strange, learned people from Germany and Holland, and a shockingly brazen woman from Spain who sang to the company."

Charlotte was indifferent, she would just as soon stay at home, but Lady Grandpoint had too much sense to allow that. "It will be a big affair," she said, "although there are those who will have nothing to do with them, many of our friends will be present. Besides, we have no other invitations for tonight, and it is essential that you are seen to be well and in your usual looks, Charlotte, for you may be sure all kinds of gossip is floating round about the affair at Montblaine."

As Eliza dressed, she found her thoughts wandering to Mr. Bruton. Would he be there? He was friendly with the Wintertons, but on the other hand she knew he disliked the social round of London. Still, she took particular care over her appearance; she had expended some more of her guineas on a length of silk muslin which Annie had made up with great panache in a floating, classical style.

Lady Grandpoint did not approve. "It is cut low for a girl of your age, and it is hardly in the normal mode."

"She looks like a dryad," said the taciturn Lord Grandpoint, who was, for once, accompanying his wife and guests, since there were to be some people at the ball whom he wished to see.

It was a hot, fine night, and the Wintertons had had the happy thought of extending their already large ballroom into the garden, by means of a large tent draped over a central pole, charmingly striped on the outside in a mediaeval style, and made into a bower of flowers inside. So although there were above three hundred guests present, it could not be called a crush, and it was possible to move from the warmth of the ballroom to the cooler area outside, where a slight breeze ruffled the trees beyond the entrances to the tent.

Charlotte soon had her usual throng of admirers about her, pressing her to grant them a dance. Eliza moved away, trying not to look as though she were looking for anyone, but hoping that she would see the elegant figure of Mr. Bartholomew Bruton.

He was there, he saw her, and he began to move through the crowd towards her, when a voice spoke her name. "Eliza!"

She was transfixed, she was hearing voices, it must be the heat. And then they were beside her, full of smiles and words of greeting, of explanation: Maria Diggory and Anthony.

Chapter Thirty-one

Eliza was too astonished to say anything, to do more than mechanically return Maria's kiss of greeting, or to shake Anthony's hand. He pressed hers warmly, and a feeling of guilt came over her, as she responded with no more than a light squeeze.

Nothing came to her lips but questions, what was Anthony doing in London, and with Maria, when did he arrive, why had they not let her know, where were they staying, how came they to be at the Wintertons' ball?

"It is all due to Sir Roger's gout," Anthony explained, never taking his eyes from her face. There was an intentness about him, he was holding something back, what?

"Not that I would wish the Guv'nor such an affliction," he went on, "only it was damn—very convenient."

"You have never seen a man in such agony," put in Maria heartlessly. "It was entirely his own fault, for he was warned not to drink port, and so what did he do but down several glasses of a new bottle, some crusty special vintage that had been sent to him by a friend. Mama told him not to, even threatened to take the bottle from him and pour it away, but by that time the damage was done. He sits in the library, his foot bound up, resting on a footstool, shouting at anyone and everyone."

"Well, I can see that can't have been very agreeable for the household, but did you need to come all the way to London to escape from his irritable mood?"

"No, that is not the reason," began Anthony. "Eliza, are you attending? You seem strange. This place is most dreadfully warm, the heat is affecting you."

"No, no, and of course I am delighted to see you. It is just that it is so unexpected." She could see Bartholomew Bruton out of the corner of her eye, looking at her intently. She tried to indicate with the tiniest movement of her head that he should not approach her.

"Why do you shake your head?" asked Maria. "Don't you believe us? Oh, I knew you would be in raptures at this happy turn of events. For Papa has a lawsuit going on, there are papers to be gone through, it is an urgent matter, it could not be put off. He was to come to London, you see, only with the gout it was impossible. So there was nothing for it but that Anthony had to come in his place, that or lose the lawsuit, and there is a great deal at stake. So we had everything settled in a trice, our bags were packed up, the chaise ordered, and here we are."

"But, Maria, you cannot be involved in a lawsuit?"

"Oh, I am here for another reason. Mr. Goshawk has offered for me!"

Eliza forgot all the turmoil of her mind at this astounding piece of news. "Harry Goshawk? Maria, you are out of your wits, you cannot marry Harry Goshawk. He is the most disagreeable man in all Yorkshire."

"Only very rich," said Maria with satisfaction.

Eliza looked at her friend, whose wilful face was brimming over with mischief. Harry Goshawk was known for his cruelty: to his animals, to his tenants, and he had come close to being taken up by the law for some of his practises. Not even the ambitious Diggorys could possibly consider him a suitable husband for their only daughter.

"No, you are quite right. His visit, to ask for my hand, put Papa into an even more shocking temper, I thought he was going to have a fit. And Mama was beside herself, wringing her hands, and lamenting—"

"No, Maria," Eliza said. "Not hand-wringing and lamentations, not Lady Diggory."

"Well, if she had an ounce of proper sensibility, she would have done so."

"The upshot was," said Anthony, before his sister could launch into another speech, "that my parents felt it would be wise for Maria to be out of the neighbourhood for a while. Goshawk is a vindictive man, and he did not take my father's refusal in good part. Mama wrote at once to her sister, and here we are."

Eliza's heart sank. This didn't sound like a fleeting visit. Yet, only a month ago, she would have been filled with delight at such news. "And the Wintertons?"

"Oh, Mrs. Winterton is an old friend of my aunt's, they were at the same seminary or some such thing. My uncle and aunt were coming to the ball, and so she whipped a note round, asking if we might come as well. I would not have had her do so, for it seems an intrusion, but now I see how many people are here, I realise one or two more or less cannot make any difference. And I hoped"—he lowered his voice, and looked straight at her—"dearest Eliza, that you might be here. For we have heard, even in Yorkshire, of what a success Charlotte is having in London, and of course, my aunt, who has a great interest in all that goes on in society, confirmed that it was so, and that Miss Collins would very likely be at this ball, and so might you. Which you are."

"And wearing a monstrous fine gown," said Maria, looking her up and down. "Where had you that, for I never saw it in Yorkshire?"

"I must say, you are dressed very fine," said Anthony, a slight frown on his forehead. "Oh, here are my aunt and uncle."

Sir Godfrey and Lady Hatchard seemed an amiable pair. Introductions were made, Lady Hatchard began to look about her for a suitable partner for Maria, and Anthony, telling his sister to take care how she went on, this was not a Yorkshire romp, took Eliza by the arm and led her on to the floor. "For we may talk while we dance, and to be sitting out behind one of those big palms, in close conversation, might be to attract attention."

"I don't think anyone would notice us, or care," said Eliza, who wanted nothing less than to dance with Anthony. How was it possible that in such a short time this man, whose mere name had been enough to set her heart thudding, seemed just like many other men, his evening clothes not as smart as many, his manners less polished than those of men accustomed to move in London society? Handsome enough to turn several female heads, though, she noticed, as they stood waiting for the music to strike up.

How could her feelings for him have undergone so complete a change? It was as though their brief courtship and furtive engagement had been a madness, from which she had now recovered.

He clasped her round the waist, and the waltz began. He waltzed well, despite being a tall man; sports at school and university had made him graceful, and she was the one who missed her steps, moved clumsily, trod on his feet.

"What is this, Eliza, I never knew you to dance so ill," he said into her ear. "I know how it is, you are all in a flutter at seeing me so unexpectedly. I did not write, we had so little time, and I wanted to surprise you."

"Surprise me? Oh, yes."

Was he going to stay by her side all evening? Hadn't his mother written to warn her sister about Miss Eliza Collins, with instructions that he should be discouraged from seeing her?

Apparently not. "You know how it is with Mama," he said with glee in his voice. "Once you had left Yorkshire, and I went on with my normal pursuits, and was clearly not going to throw myself into the river or fall into a melancholy—as if I should"—he laughed—"she put you out of her mind. Then news came through of how Charlotte had *taken*. Or isn't that the right word? We heard that she is to marry a marquis, I can hardly believe it, but my aunt assures me it is the buzz of the town."

"She is not engaged to Lord Montblaine, and I am sure never will be," Eliza said. "She has many admirers, and the marquis is a cold man, not the kind of man to fall in love with."

Anthony paused to look at her with astonishment. "What has

that to do with it? Of course, if he can be brought to the point, if he proposes, she will have him. And that, you see—"

His words were drowned in the music and the sudden flow of people twirling around them. Eliza looked at her feet, trying to mind her steps, vexed at her clumsiness, ashamed at her lack of enthusiasm for Anthony's arrival, in a quandary about what she should do. If only she had written to him, releasing him from the engagement, the minute she knew that her feelings towards him had undergone a change. Honesty demanded she tell Anthony the truth—yet what was the truth? She had met another man, whose proposal she had turned down with abruptness bordering on rudeness, who would probably never ask her again. Could she simply say that his parents were right, they should not suit, that they should part friends?

The ardent way in which Anthony was looking down at her had little of friendship in it and a good deal of the lover. Particular! Goodness, everyone in the room would guess how it was with him, and they would be quick enough to attribute reciprocal feelings to her. Anthony might not be in line for a seat in the Lords, nor heading for a successful career in Parliament or government, but word would fly around the ballroom that this handsome young man was heir to a very pretty estate, as well as the baronetcy, he would be considered eligible by most standards, and the gossips would say that Miss Eliza Collins might consider she was doing well for herself if it turned out he was in love with her.

It was with difficulty that she persuaded him that he must not stay at her side all the time. "Please fetch me a glass of lemonade," she said. "For I am very hot. I will give you another dance later, but for now I cannot be seen to be living in your pocket. Where is Maria?"

Anthony had flushed at being given his congé, but he accepted with more or less good grace, acknowledging the justice of her words, but extracting a promise that he might take her in to supper. "We have to talk," he added. "I have so much to tell you."

Maria was dancing with Lord Rosely, and they seemed to be sharing a joke. Eliza looked around for Charlotte, who was not dancing, but sitting talking to Lord Montblaine. She had seen Anthony, and she raised an enquiring eyebrow at her sister before turning back to his lordship; what did she find to talk to him about?

Mr. Portal walked in from outside, looking round in his genial way, and spied her.

"Forlorn, alone, no dancing partner?" he said. "Come, this will not do, you must let me find you a partner. I saw Mr. Bartholomew Bruton wandering around, not dancing, let me—"

There was a gleam of perception in his eye, which Eliza did not like, and she said quite sharply that she must not trouble him. "My partner is just fetching me a glass of lemonade," she went on.

"Ah, this handsome fellow forging a path towards us. From Yorkshire, perhaps?" And then, in a soft voice, before Anthony was near enough to hear, he added, "No, Miss Eliza, he will not do for you."

Eliza presented Anthony to Mr. Portal and they exchanged bows, smiles, polite remarks. "You are a stranger here, let me introduce you to some young ladies," Mr. Portal said. He looked about him, and his eye fell upon Miss Chetwynd, who was loitering behind a palm and looking at Anthony with undisguised interest. "Ah, Miss Chetwynd. Allow me to present Mr. Anthony Diggory to you as a desirable partner."

There was nothing Anthony could do but bow and submit, and take Miss Chetwynd off for the country dance that was forming on the floor.

"That's got rid of him for half an hour," said Mr. Portal with some satisfaction. "My dear Miss Eliza, it is none of my business, but you look somewhat fraught, and perhaps in need of advice. Mine is that it is best to be off with the old love before you are on with the new."

Eliza's eyes flashed. "You are making fun of me, Mr. Portal, and I do not care for it. Anthony is an old friend, that is all, you do not know what you are saying."

Mr. Portal took the rebuke with good humour. "I am right, however, and he looks like a young man who is inclined to be possessive. Take care, there, now that is excellent advice I am giving you: make sure you know what you are about with him, he is the type that will suddenly launch into some extravagant gesture, some excess of folly. Is that his sister, the pretty girl dancing with Rosely? She has a look of her brother. Perhaps she'll cut him out with your sister—no, don't flare up again. Your sister and Rosely would be at daggers drawn within six months of going to the altar, do not encourage that affair, if you have any feeling for your sister."

"While for my friend, it is not of any importance."

"I do not know your friend, so I can't say, yet by the look of her, she is just the kind of woman who might suit Lord Rosely. Time he settled down. Has she any money?"

"Enough."

"Ah, you are trying to crush me. It will not do, I shall know just how much she is worth within five minutes of leaving you. I think you should dance with Mr. Bartholomew Bruton. He is another man who should settle down. Although not, perhaps, with Miss Grainger," Mr. Portal added, looking towards where she was circling the room with Mr. Bruton's hand resting lightly on her waist. "I never saw such indifference."

That evening, Eliza was for the first time in her life grateful for the precepts and behaviour which her governess had instilled in her and Charlotte. The governess was a woman of modest accomplishments, and no intellectual pretension; she had taught them a little French, a little geography, and enough of the basics of arithmetic for the two girls to be able to cast a set of household accounts.

What she had most of all was a conviction that manners smoothed away all difficulties, that knowing how to behave in any situation was essential for even the most cloistered or countrified young women. She had been brought up as the poor relation of a great family who had seen to it that she had sufficient education to permit her to earn her living in a gentleman's family, and from them she had acquired her worldly knowledge of how a girl should "go on," as she put it, in society.

She had never succeeded in quelling Eliza's unruly tongue or temper, but had found Charlotte an apt pupil in whom to instil the virtues of self-control, patience, and a kind of polite stoicism. Whether you had the toothache at a dinner party or blistered feet and dancing were suggested, then you put your best face on it, you smiled, you did what was expected of you.

"Not to do so," she would say, "is to draw attention to yourself, and that is something that no young lady should ever do."

Miss Gibson had long since left the Palace for other employment, but now Eliza could see some sense in her tiresome precepts. She smiled, she danced, she even managed to flirt a little, and all the time she was thinking, What do I say to Anthony, when can I speak to him? and at the same time, Why does not Bartholomew Bruton come near me, why will he not dance with me?

Chapter Thirty-two

Had she but known it, Bartholomew was as much put out as she was. Who the devil was this Diggory character? What did he think he was doing, presuming on an old acquaintance to try to monopolise Eliza Collins? Henrietta Rowan remarked on his good looks and, with a quick glance at Bruton's set face, added that he seemed very taken with Eliza. "A beau, from her home country, I suppose," she said.

Yet Bartholomew could have sworn that Eliza was far from being delighted to see Anthony Diggory. He guessed at a boy-and-girl attachment, yet Diggory's proprietorial attitude to Eliza suggested a deeper liking, at least on his part.

Lady Sarah, who was sitting with the dowagers in a forest of turbans and feathers, was beckoning to him. "Who is the good-looking young man Miss Eliza is dancing with?"

"Anthony Diggory. He is from Yorkshire, I believe."

A jolly-looking matron with several chins, who was sitting next to Lady Sarah, broke into their conversation. "From Yorkshire? Tell Miss Eliza Collins to bring him over, Bartholomew, that is my home county, and I am sure I know his face. Let me see who he is, desire him to come over here."

Bartholomew could hardly bring himself to look at Eliza as he delivered his message. She had a taut look which was new with her, and her lovely slanting smile, the smile that had so bewitched him, was not much in evidence. She walked across the floor, her dress swishing about her ankles, to where Mrs. Darling was sitting. The chinful woman examined her from head to toe, then turned her beady gaze on Anthony and demanded his name.

"Aye, I thought so," she said. "As soon as I clapped eyes on you, I said to myself, that has to be a Diggory. You'll be Sir Roger's boy, you have a great look of him, you are the image of who he looked when he was a young man."

Eliza blinked, how could that be possible? Anthony was tall and handsome, with a clear complexion; Sir Roger could never have looked like that. Only . . . perhaps it was so. A heavier, ruddier Anthony some thirty years from now, perhaps even stricken with the gout; yes, he would be very like Sir Roger, how had she never seen it?

Mrs. Darling was talking about her girlhood in Yorkshire, remembering long-ago balls and picnics and parties. "Then I married a southerner, and came away. I fancied myself in love with your father when I was a girl, he was so dashing on the dance floor, he looked so splendid on horseback, all of us were wild for him. In the end he married Cecily, your mother, who was not the prettiest of us, not by a long chalk. Is that your sister? Yes, she is the image of her grandmother, and she, my mother told me, was considered very fast when she was young. Look at her bouncing down the dance there, casting saucy eyes at the young men, she will turn a few heads, I dare say."

Anthony did not seem at all pleased at this forthright speech, although courtesy demanded that he listen with an agreeable expression on his face. When Mrs. Darling turned to exchange another reminiscence with Lady Sarah, his eyes were on his sister, who was indeed in a high flow of spirits.

He finally escaped, taking Eliza with him, and as they moved away, she heard Lady Sarah say to her companion, "I am pleased to see Miss Eliza Collins with that young man, I think they are well suited, do not you?"

Eliza did not linger to catch Mrs. Darling's reply, a reply which wasn't at all what Lady Sarah wanted to hear. "I have no idea who she is, but with that voice and air, to marry a country squire? No, Sir Roger's son needs to marry a woman such as Cecily was, a practical, no-nonsense young woman, with a good fortune and no temperament, there is no room for temperament in a squire's wife."

By now, Lady Grandpoint had become aware of the young man's attentions to Eliza and, drawing Charlotte to one side, demanded to know who he was.

"He is Anthony Diggory, and his sister, Maria, is here also. I have no idea why they are here in London, and, no, ma'am, Eliza did not tell me they were coming to town. Indeed, I think she is surprised to see them."

"If you do not object, we shall leave early," said her godmother. "Really, it is more than I bargained for, having to keep an eye on Eliza. What is Sir Roger thinking of, to let his children come to London, when he was so eager for his son and Eliza to be kept apart? I must remember to make it clear to the servants that, should Mr. Diggory call, we are not at home, and that on no account is he to be admitted to see Eliza. I suppose, if they are to be fixed in town for a while, there will be nothing for it but to pack Eliza off back to Yorkshire. I do not scruple to say, my dear, that this visitation could not come at a more inconvenient time."

It didn't occur to Lady Grandpoint that Anthony might pay a call immediately after breakfast the next morning, before she herself was up, and before she had had the opportunity to issue instructions to her servants.

Eliza was up, and sitting in the morning parlour. Anthony was announced, and before she could deny him, he was in the room, striding across to her and taking both her hands in his. "My dearest Eliza, this is what I wanted, to find you alone."

She could tell that he wanted to take her into his arms, and she was determined he should not. She retreated, and backed behind a chair. "Remember where you are," she said in a firm voice. "Indeed,

Anthony, you should not be here, not at this hour, it is too early for calls, my great-aunt is still in her room, and Charlotte—"

"I have not come to see Charlotte nor Lady Grandpoint, although I am happy to seek an interview with her later today. Eliza, you must hear our wonderful news. My father has relented, and my mother, too, they have given their consent to our being engaged. And the instant they told me, I rode over to the Palace, to ask the bishop for your hand, and you have his consent and blessing."

Eliza came out from behind the chair and sat on it, staring at Anthony. She was imagining this, she was still asleep, it was nothing more than a tormenting dream.

"It isn't possible," she managed to say.

"Are you not overjoyed? It is all to do with Charlotte, you see. Now that she is to be a marchioness, well, it changes everything. Not for me, of course, I could not care whom Charlotte marries, so long as she is happy, but these things matter in the eyes of the world, and to my parents—and yours."

"It is all a mistake," cried Eliza. "Charlotte is not going to marry anyone, or at least, not Montblaine."

"Pooh, do not try to tell me that," he said, pacing up and down the room. "I saw her yesterday with his lordship—he is rather old, is he not? But that may suit Charlotte. My aunt pointed him out, and there he was, deep in conversation with Charlotte and taking her in to supper. My aunt says it is the talk of the town, that he is present at all the balls and assemblies where Charlotte is, for normally he doesn't stay in town for more than a few days together, and never goes out in society. I must say, she will make a very good marchioness."

"She is not—"

"I know there is no formal announcement, but it is only a matter of time, so my aunt says. As long as Charlotte behaves as she ought—and you, too, sweetheart, for my aunt says it would be a disaster if you were caught up in any scandal, everything has to be just so with his lordship, it seems." Anthony stopped pacing and pulled out a chair to sit close to her. "And that is why it is so good that we can now become engaged, for to tell you the truth, I didn't feel a secret engagement was quite right, and of course if that should come to his lordship's ears—well, he might not like it, he would certainly think it not at all the thing."

It was now or never. Eliza took a deep breath. "Anthony, you have been very busy on my behalf, however—"

Anthony paid no attention to what she was saying, as he searched in his waistcoat pocket. "I have here a letter from your father, and your mother has added some words to it, you will wish to read it—no, stay, this is not the letter, it is a farrier's bill. Ah, here it is." He thrust the letter into her hands.

Eliza let it flutter to the floor. "Anthony, listen to me. I cannot marry you."

"Not marry? Eliza, you do not understand. All the obstacles to our union are swept away. We can be married as soon as we like, I thought July."

"No, Anthony. We will not be married in July, or any other month. There is no way to soften what I have to say, so I shall say it directly, and you must believe me. I cannot marry you. I was in love with you, but that is no longer the case. We were guilty of folly, it was too quick an affection, and then, there, in Yorkshire, I felt—"

He was looming over her, his face reddening. "Eliza, you have taken leave of your senses. Of course we are to marry, of course you love me. We are engaged, we are betrothed, privately, and now it can be quite openly and properly announced."

"My sentiments towards you are not the same as they were when we parted," Eliza said bluntly. "And I am convinced that I would not make you a good wife, Anthony. Your parents were right, we should not be happy."

"Not be happy! When you fill my waking thoughts, aye, and I dream of you sometimes, and I am a sound sleeper, I am not given to dreaming."

At that moment, the door opened again, and in swept Lady Grandpoint, her nose in the air, the demeanour forbidding in the extreme, demanding an explanation for Anthony's presence, rebuking Eliza for receiving a young man alone, at this time of the morning.

Would it be better in the evening? Eliza said inwardly, as she watched Anthony try to quell the tide of Lady Grandpoint's indignation and manage to have his say before he was forcibly ejected.

"Ma'am," he cried. "Pray listen. I have a letter, from Mrs. Collins. I am permitted to pay my addresses to Eliza, to Miss Eliza Collins, indeed I have to inform you that I have asked Eliza to be my wife, and she has accepted my hand."

"No," began Eliza, desperate that this should go no further. "No, Anthony, no, your ladyship, it is not so, I am not going to marry Anthony."

With an audience, albeit one who was at that moment deep in the letter from Mrs. Collins, Anthony felt on surer ground. He grasped Eliza by the hand and drew her to his side.

"Our attachment is of long standing," he said, "and now we are engaged."

Long standing? A few weeks, that was all. Yet how long had she known Mr. Bruton, and if there was an attachment there, one strong enough for her to cast Anthony aside, then how could she say that those weeks with Anthony were not enough?

Lady Grandpoint looked from one to the other of them, sharply, appraisingly.

"I shall write to your mother, Eliza," she said finally. "Mr. Diggory, you are not to consider yourself engaged, or that Miss Eliza is in any way bound to you. I shall write to Bishop and Mrs. Collins at once, there are other considerations, important considerations, about which you know nothing. Meanwhile, pray do not call again. Miss Eliza will not be at home for the time being."

"With all respect, Lady Grandpoint, this is unfair, unreasonable. Eliza and I have been parted for several weeks, we surely are entitled to spend some time together."

"Entitled? There is no entitlement here. An engagement, even between a Miss Eliza Collins and a Mr. Diggory, is not to be undertaken lightly."

"Does Maria know of our parents' change of heart?" Eliza asked.

"She does not, for I wanted no one else to know before I could tell you. It was fortuitous that my father's attack of gout necessitated my trip to London, otherwise, I believe, your mother was going to write to you, to ask you to return to Yorkshire."

"As to that, I shall decide whether my great-niece remains in London or not," said her ladyship, pulling the bell tug. And, as her butler appeared: "Show Mr. Diggory out, if you please. Good day to you, Mr. Diggory."

Chapter Thirty-three

"Go to China?" said Bartholomew, looking at Freddie with exasperation as his friend burst into his sitting room with this dramatic proposal on his lips. "For God's sake, go and put your head under a pump. Why should you want to go to China?"

"Or the East Indies, or Chile, or anywhere on the other side of the world."

"Your geography is at fault, none of those places is on the other side of the world. I suppose you have asked Miss Collins to marry you, and she has refused you?"

"I offered her my hand and my heart," said Freddie, holding his hand against his chest in a dramatic gesture. "She turned me down. No drooping her head or blushes or beating about the bush, trying to do it prettily, leaving me a glimmer of hope. No. She looked at me straight in the eye and said no. She means to have Montblaine, I am certain of it. She is a heartless, scheming woman, but dear God, Bartholomew, she is so beautiful!"

"Have her portrait painted, and hang it on your wall, and make do with that," said Bartholomew. "She's not for you, Freddie, and you have to be fair, she's never shown any preference for you over all the other men who worship her beauty; her rejection of your proposal can't have been any surprise."

Freddie wasn't listening. "Montblaine! Why, the man's not made of flesh and blood. He's not won her heart, I don't believe she cares tuppence for him. She is simply dazzled by his rank and fortune."

"You were getting along famously with that dark, merry girl at the Wintertons' ball, what was her name? The sister to that disagreeable man who clumped around the ballroom after Miss Eliza Collins. Indulge yourself in a little flirtation there."

"Did you notice her? She is Maria Diggory, from the north, and, yes, she is full of fun. Her brother is in love with Eliza Collins, she told me that her father will not agree to their marrying, and so they will wait until she is of age. Miss Diggory says they will then marry even without their parents' blessing; she expects they will elope, at the dead of night. Why should an elopement not happen at a reasonable hour? I asked her, but she has a romantic nature, and insists that a daytime elopement would not be at all the same."

"I didn't think that Eliza Collins was as pleased to see Mr. Diggory as he was to see her."

"Now you mention it, Miss Diggory was annoyed with her friend's reception of her brother. Eliza was not half-pleased enough to see Mr. Diggory, she had no idea of his coming to town, apparently, but should at once have fallen into raptures or a swoon or cast herself into his embrace. I told her that in town young ladies behave with propriety and dignity, and do not fling themselves into the arms of their lovers when they arrive hotfoot from the wolds or whatever they have in Yorkshire. She is a romp, that girl, a rare handful, I dare say her brother will have his work cut out keeping her out of mischief."

Freddie's words were barbs in Bartholomew's soul and heart. That was why Eliza had refused his hand so abruptly, almost with terror. Why could she not have said, there is a former attachment, I hope to become the wife of another man?

He would not give way to the bitter swell of jealousy. That she had not spoken such words must give him some hope. And so must the fact that Eliza's welcome to Diggory was not as wholehearted as it might have been. He could not be entirely mistaken in her feeling towards him, and after all, there was no formal engagement, no reason for her to be bound to Mr. Diggory, if her feelings towards him had changed.

"Well, I suppose I'll end up married to the Chetwynd girl, with a nursery of bun-faced children," Freddie said mournfully. "What does it matter whom I marry, if Charlotte will not have me?" He kicked the fireguard with one immaculately polished boot, and stared into the empty grate.

Bartholomew's sitting room was a pleasant chamber overlooking the garden, which was kept in splendid order under the watchful eye of Lady Sarah, a keen horticulturalist and an expert rose grower.

"How your mother's roses flourish," said Freddie, looking out of the window. "Ours at Rosely are all afflicted with some bug, some insect that chews and chomps at the roots. They are all in a fret about it, there have been roses there for generations, of course, planted back in the time of one of those Plantagenet or Tudor kings on account of the family name. If they all have to be rooted up, I shall plant something dark and festering in their place, to mark a black day in the annals of our house."

"First China, and now weeds, do buck up, Freddie. I can't listen to your meanderings any more, I have to be on my way."

His valet came in at that moment, a coat laid with great care across his arm. He eased Bartholomew into it, and flicked an imaginary speck of dust from the lapel before smoothing a tiny wrinkle from the back.

"Nice cut," said Freddie. "Did Schweitzer make it for you?"

"He makes all my coats. Yes, what is it?" Bartholomew said to a footman who was hovering in the doorway.

"Her ladyship's compliments. And she wishes to see you before you leave. She is in the garden, in the rose arbour."

"It'll be an errand," Freddie said. "My mother is always sending me on errands, keeps a pack of servants in the house, but the minute I set foot in it, she's asking me to do this or that. If I lived on the premises, I wouldn't have a moment's peace. I don't know why you stay here, Bart, I really don't. Move out, and we'll find rooms to share."

Bartholomew had always been happy with the handsome apartments given to him in his parents' house. The location of the house was excellent, the rooms comfortable, and his parents had never interfered with his independence, he came and went just as he chose, and on the evenings when he was at home, he was glad to be able to talk about bank business with his father, over a glass of brandy in the handsome library.

Five minutes later, as the full blast of his mother's fury swept over him, he began to wish that he did indeed live elsewhere; he could understand the appeal that China had for Freddie.

Lady Sarah was dressed for the purpose in a wide straw hat tied under her chin with a ribbon, and a long, brown gardener's apron over her dress. She carried a shallow basket, in which reposed secateurs and twine and a little spray bottle.

Mr. Grainger had called on Mr. Bruton, Lady Sarah informed her son, and had delivered an ultimatum. Either the marriage so long planned between Bartholomew and Jane took place, with an immediate announcement of their engagement, or the proposals for the merger of the two banks would not happen. "You are dilatory," said Lady Sarah, snipping off a dead rose. "We long to have Jane for our daughter, it has been understood that you would marry, and you have shilly-shallied and delayed, all from some ridiculous idea that marriage would curtail your freedom—what, pray, does freedom have to do with a banker and matrimony?"

"It is not a matter of freedom," said Bartholomew, tugging at his neck cloth. "I do not care enough for Jane to marry her. I should make her a shockingly bad husband, we would be miserable. We have been through all this, and yet you keep thrusting her at me, as though I might suddenly change my mind. I am sorry about the deal, but I am not a pile of gold to be placed in the balance as part of the cost of the business."

"I know what it is. You fancy yourself in love with Miss Eliza Collins—no, do not deny it. I observed you closely when we were at

Montblaine, where you completely neglected poor Jane, and since you came back, all of London must have seen you wearing your heart on your sleeve!"

He was aghast. "Wearing my heart on my sleeve! I think not, ma'am."

"I am not stupid, nor blind." Snip, snap, went the secateurs. "It won't do, Bartholomew, and there's an end to it. There can be no comparison between this chit and Jane. Jane brings with her a great inheritance from her grandfather and blue blood from her father's family. Miss Eliza Collins can bring nothing but a lively nature and a clerical background. What use is that to a banker?"

"Jane is dull, and I do not love her."

"Miss Eliza Collins is a flirt, who does not love you. Did you not see her with that Mr. Diggory? There's talk about that, now, it's all over town. Not that she is a creature of the least importance, except for the reflected glory cast upon her by virtue of her sister having caught the eye of Montblaine. And that is all a hum, it will come to nothing, mark my words. If it were not for that, no one would notice or care that Mr. Diggory and Miss Eliza Collins have some kind of understanding."

"I would care. He may be in love with her, it means nothing."

"Does it not? And what if I tell you that the Grandpoints are determined she shall marry the Reverend Nathaniel Pyke."

Bartholomew's face darkened. "That lanky clergyman? Do you think I fear him as a rival?"

"It would be an entirely suitable match for her. I have told you, she has no position, no money, nothing in her favour."

"You do not know her, you should not speak of her in those terms. Not in any case, and certainly not when you know I am in love with her."

"You were in love with Clementine Joure in Paris, and we did not have all this nonsense then."

"Clementine Joure!" How had that affair come to his mother's ears? It had been a brief, passionate, delicious interlude, nothing more—nor less. "I was never in love with Clementine."

"In which case you should be ashamed of yourself, your attentions can have done nothing for her reputation."

Clementine's reputation was not such as would be in the least bit diminished by her affair with him, but he could scarcely say so to his mother. Not, his common sense told him, that she didn't know exactly what Clementine was like.

Now she was waving those damned secateurs in the air, to emphasise her point.

"Wild oats are all very well, but you are past that age now. What is youthful indiscretion in a younger man becomes pure folly in one of your age."

"I am not yet in my dotage, I believe."

"No." Lady Sarah bent over to sniff the scent of a glorious crimson rose. Then she frowned, and handed the secateurs to Bartholomew. "Hold these, while I use my little spray, there's greenfly on the buds here. Dreadful insects, I do not see why the Good Lord saw fit to create such nasty, useless things."

She finished her spraying and then gathered her skirts to walk to another bed of roses. Bartholomew's boots scrunched on the gravel as he kept pace with her, although he longed to turn on his heel and decamp from the garden and his mother's forceful presence.

"The choice is yours. You can continue in your wilful, self-indulgent refusal to marry Miss Grainger, which will bring inconvenience and considerable losses to the bank, and sorrow and grey hairs to your father and myself, or you can do your duty and propose, in proper style, and fix a day. One thing you will not do is marry a pert girl from Yorkshire, we will not under any circumstances allow that."

"I'm of age, I may marry whom I like," Bartholomew muttered mutinously to himself. It would not be pleasant to have a wife whom his parents disliked or despised, and, yes, there could be financial repercussions. As the only son, he stood to inherit the bank and a vast fortune, but his father, who had an obstinate streak, could well take it into his head to disinherit him and pass him over in favour of one of his cousins. The inheritance of Bruton's bank had not always passed in an unbroken line from father to son, it could happen.

He reached out for a fine bloom, a rich, deep claret colour, then swore as a vicious thorn dug itself into his finger. "We shall never agree on this. If you have no more to say to me, I have to attend at the bank."

Chapter Thirty-four

Eliza's mind and spirits were in turmoil. She was not inclined to introspection, preferring to direct her thoughts outward; in this case, she could not avoid a degree of self-examination. She was in no doubt as to her feelings. Those she had had for Anthony had undergone so radical a change as for there to be no question about her continuing with her engagement. And she had told him so, directly and forcefully.

She feared the message had not got through to him. He had left the house in Aubrey Square in high indignation, but not before pressing her hand, and whispering that he understood, that being in London had unsettled her, that Lady Grandpoint was offering her bad guidance, yet it would all come right in the end.

What about Mr. Bruton? There she was on less solid ground. Was she in love with him? Or was it desire, the same drive that had compelled Charlotte to behave so recklessly with Warren? Whatever she felt for him, it was different from her feelings for Anthony, when they had fallen into each other's arms and plighted their troth with such heedless abandon in the Yorkshire wood. That now seemed no more than a distant dream.

Yet she had been so sure of her attachment to Anthony, and here she was, out of love with him, and possibly tumbling into love with another man. Was she no more than a flighty young woman, attracted first by this man and then that? Would what she felt for Mr. Bruton vanish as swiftly as had her passion for Anthony? Perhaps she was a hopeless case, a hardened flirt, unable to take herself or the affections of any man seriously.

No, that was fancy, and self-indulgent fancy, too, she was not to be lashing herself in such a way. If she was to be the object of contempt and disdain, then let it come from others, not from herself. Lady Grandpoint, for instance, so unreasonably angry with her; she seemed to take Anthony's arrival almost as a personal affront.

"The letters must have crossed," Lady Grandpoint said in an annoyed voice. She had come into the sitting room unnoticed by Eliza, who had tucked herself away at the window in an effort to keep away from her great-aunt and her sister, and was startled by her arrival.

"What letters, ma'am?"

"We—I, that is, have written to the bishop, and I conclude that the letter regarding the Diggorys' change of heart must have been sent off from Yorkshire before your father heard from me. It is too bad, it complicates matters. I should never have thought he would be so fainthearted as to change his mind about your marrying Mr. Diggory."

Eliza could have pointed out that her father regularly changed his mind. Lady Grandpoint must surely know as well as she did that he would always take care to agree with Sir Roger; he had no opinions of his own to pit against those of any influential person. Although why Lady Grandpoint should be in such a fret about it, she couldn't imagine.

"What a tiresome young man he is, why could he not have stayed in Yorkshire where he belongs?" Lady Grandpoint complained. "I am pleased you have given him his congé, you did right there, my dear, he presumed too much, but I am afraid he did not believe you. That is what comes of encouraging the attentions of a man, you have not been as circumspect as you ought. Still, even Mr. Diggory will have to pay attention when—"

"When what?" said Eliza, who was retreating towards the door to make good her escape. Never had she less enjoyed her great-aunt's bracing company and conversation.

"Never mind. Do not disturb Charlotte, if you are going upstairs. I am anxious for her to have her sleep, for I want her in the best of looks tonight. You yourself rose too early by the look of you, you have dark rings beneath your eyes. I recommend an hour or so lying down on your bed this afternoon."

"I am not going out this evening, I can retire early."

"Not going out? Good gracious, do you not know that we give a party here this evening, and you must not look ill, you must be all smiles and on your best behaviour."

With which cryptic instruction, Lady Grandpoint swept past Eliza and out of the room.

If Eliza had been less caught up in her own predicament, she would have noticed the air of expectancy in the house in Aubrey Square. Servants bustled hither and thither, armfuls of flowers were brought in for the drawing rooms, and Lady Grandpoint and her butler were deep in conference as to the exact arrangement of the rooms, the table, the furniture.

"You will sit down twenty to dinner tonight," Annie informed Eliza, as she brushed out her hair that evening. She gave her mistress a sly glance. "They say his lordship, Lord Montblaine, that is, has proposed to Miss Collins, and it's to be announced tonight. I tell them it's no such thing, for wouldn't you know if your own sister had accepted a proposal of marriage?"

Eliza came out of her reverie. "Engagement? What nonsense. I hope you put a stop to that rumour, Annie."

"I said as how you hadn't mentioned it, but of course there's no reason why you should."

"No reason, because there's no truth in it. Is the marquis to be among the company tonight? I was not aware of it."

"Yes, he is, indeed, and your cousins Mr. and Mrs. Wytton and several other lord- and ladyships. Oh, and that Mr. Pyke."

"Good Lord, I hope not."

"Don't you like him, Miss?"

"Like him! Like that odious man? I do not."

"They say he's quite particular in his attentions."

"Who says so? Attentions to whom?"

"Why, to you, Miss."

"More nonsense. I wish you will not listen to this gossip, Annie."

"I think Mr. Pyke is a nasty piece of work," said Annie, bending down to retrieve the brooch that Eliza had let slip from her fingers. "Let me pin that on."

"Nasty? Annie, you hardly know him by sight."

"No, I don't know him, and I don't wish to, but I do know that he's the sort to brush up against one as he goes past, and he's rather too free with his hands."

"Annie, don't tell me so! I knew him for a disagreeable man, but I had not imagined him loose in his ways as that."

"He has a lickerish nature, for all he's a reverend. Sometimes they're the worst, with their pious faces and preachy ways, while all the time they're stuffed full of what they call sin in anyone else."

Eliza looked out of the window, where the late-afternoon light was beginning to cast shadows across the green of the square's garden. A man had been cutting the grass, and the sweet scent of it brought memories of country summer days, back in her other life. Engagement? Charlotte and Lord Montblaine? Surely, if he had proposed, and Charlotte had accepted him, her sister would have told her. Although things had been strained between them ever since they'd come back from the visit to Montblaine House. Charlotte had been even more reserved and imperturbable. It was as though the whole incident with Warren had never happened.

It would have been kind in Charlotte, given how Eliza had rallied round during that night at Montblaine, to have given Eliza back her letters and articles, but she had not done so. Thinking about it, Eliza realised that Charlotte had deliberately been avoiding her, taking care not to give her any opportunity for private conversation.

No, she could not possibly be engaged. Not after showing how she felt about Warren. Naturally, any connection with Warren was now out of the question, but the passionate nature of her encounters with the man couldn't so easily be forgotten. Eliza might chide herself for falling out of love with Anthony, but that had been gradual, whereas Charlotte would be going almost straight from the arms of a man for whom she had the most ardent feelings into matrimony with that cold fish of a man, the marquis. Not even Charlotte could behave like that.

Eliza was wrong. Summoned downstairs half an hour before the guests were due to arrive, she found Charlotte, with Lord and Lady Grandpoint, standing in the drawing room. Charlotte was wearing a new gown of silver gauze, with a bodice that sparkled as she moved. An ice queen, extraordinarily pale and beautiful and absolutely remote.

"Ah, there you are, Eliza," said Lady Grandpoint. "My dear, you must be among the first to know. Lord Montblaine has today done Charlotte the honour of asking her to become his wife, and she has accepted him."

"Charlotte, you can't!" The words burst from Eliza's lips before she could stop herself. Lord Grandpoint frowned, and Lady Grandpoint made a clicking noise with her tongue.

"Control yourself, Eliza," said Charlotte, still completely calm. "It isn't for you to say whom I can and cannot marry."

"Lord Montblaine has behaved just as he ought," said Lady Grandpoint. "He wrote to your father, to obtain his permission, although, of course, Charlotte is of age. However, it was right for him to do so."

"He didn't set off hotfoot for Yorkshire then?" Eliza wasn't able to keep the sarcasm from her voice.

"That would have been an unnecessary journey," Charlotte said. "Unfortunately, Papa cannot be spared from his duties just at present, so Lady Grandpoint is holding this dinner tonight to make the announcement. It will be in the *Gazette* in the morning."

Eliza was too stunned to say another word. She could not believe it of Charlotte. No, she was not going to let it rest. There were the sounds of a carriage drawing up outside, people were arriving, and as Lord and Lady Grandpoint made themselves ready to receive their guests, Eliza took the opportunity to seize Charlotte by the wrist and force her to listen.

"Why are you doing this? Are you so mad to be married? Do you think because it all went so wrong with Warren, it doesn't matter whom you marry? Charlotte, only consider, you will meet a man about whom you will feel what you did for Warren, only he will be a better man. Take Rosely, he will be a thousand times a better husband and lover than Montblaine."

"Let me go, if you please, you are hurting me. You are absurd. Marry Lord Rosely, indeed! I turned him down flat, we should not suit, which you would know if you had half the perception you pride yourself on. Lord Rosely is a frivolous man, volatile in his affections. His protestations of undying love are mere affectation. Montblaine and I will deal very well together."

"You are not in love with him."

"It is not for you to decide what I feel or don't feel towards any man."

The moment had passed, the door was open, and the butler was announcing names in a sonorous voice that drowned conversation.

And, to make Eliza's misery worse, among the first arrivals was Mr. Pyke, gleaming and spruce in his black evening clothes. Smirking at Charlotte, bowing to his cousin Montblaine, and then making his way over to Eliza, to greet her with unnecessary familiarity, presuming upon a connection that did not yet exist. "For I am soon to call you cousin," he said with satisfaction. "And, may I hope, perhaps . . ." He paused and gave her a meaningful look.

"Hope for whatever you want, Mr. Pyke. The connection between us is remote and will remain so."

Eliza turned a cold shoulder on him, but to no avail, he remained beside her, rubbing his hands together and praising Charlotte's beauty in terms that Eliza found altogether too warm. Thank goodness, here were Camilla and Mr. Wytton; they came across to where she was standing as soon as they had done the pretty to their host and hostess and had greeted Charlotte and the marquis, who was standing at Charlotte's side. Eliza forced herself to smile, to congratulate the marquis and to wish them both joy.

"My dear Eliza, you look as though you had been bitten by a snake," said Camilla, unusually serious. "You must not show a Friday face here, you know, however unhappy you are about Charlotte."

"Do I have a Friday face?" Eliza laughed. "I suppose I do. It is nothing to do with Charlotte, I cannot even begin to understand what she is doing, and what is the point of my being unhappy about it? Once Charlotte has made up her mind to do a thing, she will do it. There is nothing I nor anyone else can do that will cause her to change her mind, it is not in her nature. No, if I look severe, it is because I have been talking to Mr. Pyke, and that always puts me in a bad humour."

"I'm not surprised," said Camilla, frowning at the clergyman, who stood a little way apart from them, bowing as she looked at him.

"Why is he leering at Eliza like that?" said Mr. Wytton, flaring up in one of his sudden tempers. "I won't have the man looking at my cousin like that."

Camilla put a hand out to restrain him as he started towards Mr. Pyke, and Eliza begged him to pay no attention. "It is his way, it is his natural expression."

"Then it's a most inappropriate expression for any clergyman. Good God, does he lean out of the pulpit and smirk and grimace at his congregation like that? It's insupportable."

"I expect he does," said Camilla. "And his parishioners, his female parishioners, love it."

"Bunch of foolish women, why is it that churchgoers leave their common sense at the porch of the church, why can't they smell out a hypocrite as they would in their ordinary, day-to-day affairs?"

Eliza had no time to reply. Dinner was announced, the doors to the dining room were thrown open, and she was obliged by her great-aunt to go in yet again on the arm of Mr. Pyke.

Lady Grandpoint's housekeeper had excelled herself in the matter of snowy linen, acres of which seemed spread over the vast table, which tonight was extended to its fullest length, with all its leaves in place.

Charlotte was seated next to Montblaine. Eliza, ignoring the uninteresting conversation of Mr. Pyke, was watching her sister and her husband-to-be with close attention. The marquis, like Charlotte, was not a man to show any emotion, and yet there was a tender gleam in his eyes when they rested on Charlotte, and a softening of his implacable mouth as he watched her talk to her neighbour on the other side.

How much her father would have revelled in the company, Eliza thought with a pang. She didn't get on with her father, and yet she felt sorry for him, excluded as he was from this crowning moment when his eldest daughter was established in her alliance with a nobleman like Lord Montblaine. It was deliberate, she supposed; Lady Grandpoint would not have wanted to have the bishop in London on this occasion. Time enough for Montblaine to make the acquaintance of his new father-in-law once the engagement was formally announced, when there could be no drawing back.

Charlotte to be a marchioness! To be chatelaine of Montblaine House, of his numerous acres in Scotland, of his great London house. Mistress of dozens, no, hundreds of servants.

Mr. Pyke had his mouth unpleasantly close to her ear as he gave her to understand that he was to assist in the marriage ceremony. "Of course, your esteemed father, the bishop, will conduct the service, that goes without question. However, as his lordship's cousin, and, of course, being a man of the cloth, it is his earnest wish that I be present in an official capacity during the celebration of the nuptials."

He made the word sound like a caress, and a shiver of repulsion went up Eliza's spine.

"I hope that some day soon, I may be present at another marriage ceremony, only this time on the other side of the altar, ha ha."

He had an unpleasant laugh, and Eliza tried to lean further back in her chair to put more distance between them. He moved his chair closer to hers, and she felt his leg pressing against hers. That was too much, and jerking her leg away, she gave him a look so ferocious that he was stopped in mid-flow and his self-satisfied countenance took on a look of astonishment.

It didn't last; back came the smirk. "Do you not wish to know with whom I shall be joined in that holiest of unions, Miss Eliza?"

"Not in the slightest. That is your business, I have no interest in your affairs, Mr. Pyke."

Her neighbour just then turning towards her, she took the opportunity to talk to him; even a long and extremely boring conversation about a horse the man had just bought was preferable to any more of Mr. Pyke.

The evening was interminable. The betrothal was announced to the assembled company, none of whom was surprised. Congratulations and champagne flowed, and Eliza smiled and received her part of the well-wishing with outward good manners and pleasure which in no way echoed the fury she felt inside.

She found herself addressed by Lord Montblaine. Looking down from his great height, his face unreadable, he suggested they might withdraw for a moment. Eliza had no wish for any private conversation with his lordship, but he was resolute, and in a moment they were in the morning parlour. "You are to be my sister, you know," he said with a thin smile. "It is perfectly proper for us to have a private conversation."

Eliza nodded and waited, on her guard. What was this about?

"You do not like the engagement. Do not trouble to deny it. I am not a fool, Miss Eliza. I want to assure you that my feelings for your sister are such—" He gave a dry cough, and Eliza saw with astonishment that he was embarrassed. He was not accustomed to talking of feelings, anyone's feelings, let alone his own. She had to admit to a reluctant admiration for him; perhaps he was not quite such a cold fish as at first appeared.

"I shall do my utmost to make your sister happy."

"I hope so," Eliza said.

"And it is our dearest wish that you, too, should find a husband with whom you may live a happy and useful life. I believe you are acquainted with Mr. Pyke. He is my cousin, and admires you greatly, and I may tell you that it would give me great satisfaction to see you joined in matrimony."

All the good-will she had felt for Lord Montblaine evaporated. "I thank you, but I do not care for Mr. Pyke, nor could ever consider marrying him."

A frown crossed his lordship's brow. "You are too vehement. My dearest Charlotte said that it would be so, that you are often impulsive and headstrong in your likes and dislikes."

"I consider my dislike of Mr. Pyke to be neither impulsive nor headstrong, but perfectly rational. No sensible woman could want him for a husband."

"Your family would welcome such a match, do you not care for their opinion? They have your best interests at heart, as do I."

"I thank you again, however, I know best what kind of a man would suit me, and it is not Mr. Pyke! Now, if you will excuse me, I should like to return to the company." She gave him a very direct look. "I wish you and my sister every joy, Lord Montblaine, but I beg you will not try to interfere in my life."

Chapter Thirty-five

Eliza felt sure that she wouldn't sleep a wink that night. Charlotte had vanished into her bedchamber with a firm goodnight, clearly with no intention of there being any sisterly confidences or discussion.

She didn't understand Charlotte. Was there anything she could have done to remedy that? She prided herself on her insight into other human beings, yet her own sister remained an enigma.

She had said as much to Camilla, as they took tea at the end of the long evening, when her cousin had asked her if she thought Charlotte would be happy. And Camilla, to Eliza's surprise, had said that although there was a strong family bond between her and her four sisters, she had not truly felt close to any human being until she met and married Mr. Wytton.

"Letty, you know, is inclined to be censorious. The twins were, as I believe is often the case, so much a pair that they tended to exclude the rest of us. I suppose I am closest to Alethea, and yet her music set her apart in some way. Then she fell in love with a man who chose to marry another woman; that was a sad business. On the rebound from him, she married a man who—well, I still don't care to think about it. And all the while, she confided in no one. I still feel that I let her down, concerned as I was at that time with my own married life."

"Even so," said Eliza with a heavy sigh, "I wish it were otherwise between Charlotte and myself. And now that she is to be Lady Montblaine, I fear we shall see very little of one another, and move still further apart."

This conversation was in her head as she blew the candle out, but instead of lying fretful and awake, she fell asleep at once and did not stir until the sun was slanting through the shutters and Annie was standing beside the bed with her dish of chocolate.

The house was still in an uproar, Annie told her, with the door knocker never still. "For the notice was in the papers this morning, and all the old cats in London are keen to be in Miss Collins's good books now she's to be such a grand milady. And her ladyship, Lady Grandpoint that is, says you're to dress fine, on account of all the callers. So I've put out the new muslin with the russet flounce."

A good night's sleep had done much to restore Eliza's spirits, and left her with a more philosophical attitude to Charlotte's engagement. Hers wasn't a nature to dwell on might-have-beens. Charlotte had taken this step, knowingly and with her eyes wide-open. It was her decision, one that couldn't be undone, and so it was up to Eliza not to show by the least look or word that she was anything less than delighted by Charlotte's choice.

Hislop, with her face looking slightly less prunelike than usual, put her head round the door. "Her ladyship's compliments, and she wants Miss downstairs immediately. In the morning parlour, if you please."

It only occurred to Eliza as she turned the handle of the morning room that it was an odd place for Lady Grandpoint to be receiving morning callers, especially on a day like this, when the drawing room would be more usual.

No great-aunt, no cluster of callers awaited her.

Instead, there was Mr. Pyke, sleek and self-satisfied, coming forward to greet her with a warmth that set her teeth on edge and, with hardly a pause, launching into an unctuous, unwelcome, untimely proposal of marriage.

His words flowed around her, protestations of undying affection which were so patently insincere that she almost wanted to laugh.

He spoke of love, but Eliza knew better what kind of passion he felt for her, and she didn't care for it one bit. It was one thing to welcome the embraces of Anthony, when she had truly cared for him, it was another to imagine herself in Mr. Bruton's arms, which she could not always prevent herself from doing, but the mere thought of being kissed by this man made her want to slap his face and run from the room.

He had manoeuvred himself so that he stood between her and the door. She began to edge round towards it, even as she tried to stop his dreadfully fluent speeches, carefully rehearsed, meaningless.

"Do not say another word. I thank you, but I do not want to marry you, and, no, I will not ever want to receive such a proposal from you. I have never given you the slightest reason to think that I would welcome any attention from you, so please desist." A few more steps, and she would be able to escape.

He was not in the least disconcerted by her response, and stepped nimbly in her way, smiling down at her in a way that made her shudder. "Young women are not always at first aware of where their best interests lie."

"It is not a matter of interests."

"Oh, but I think it is. I have spoken of my ardent admiration and love for you, but if that does not reach your heart, then let me tell you that your family approve of my suit. I have obtained your father's consent; now what say you to that, do not pretend that such approval makes no difference?"

"My father's consent?" Now he was standing with his back to the door, quite blocking her way. Eliza retreated to stand behind an upright chair. Could she ring the bell, summon a servant, so that Mr. Pyke would be obliged to move away from the door? She could not believe her ears. This man had what, written to her father, asking permission to marry her, and her father, without consulting her, had given his consent? He must have taken leave of his senses, and besides, what of his permission for her to marry Anthony? Good heavens, what a tangle she was in.

"You see, it is the particular wish of my cousin Lord Montblaine that we should marry. He takes a keen interest in my career, and has expressed his conviction that as a married clergyman, I can expect a more rapid advancement in the Church. As it is, my position, as with a good parish, and my recent appointment as secretary to the archbishop—that is not yet widely known, so I must beg you, dearest Eliza, not to speak of it."

"Do not call me Eliza, and I am certainly not your dearest. I am hardly more than a stranger to Lord Montblaine. I know he is to become my brother, but I will thank him to keep out of my affairs, he has no right to interfere in my life."

Now he was frowning. "You speak without considering your words. What, are you to ignore what Lord Montblaine wants? I think not, I think a young woman in your position had better listen to the advice, no, the wishes of her elders. Lady Grandpoint encourages my suit, as well, I confided in her, and she welcomes such a match."

"It has no more to do with her than with the marquis." Eliza's temper was rising, and her hands were clasping the back of the chair so tightly that her knuckles were white. She must keep control of herself or, better still, remove herself as swiftly as possible from the presence of this dreadful man. She let go of the chair and dipped a slight curtsy. "Thank you for your offer, we should not suit. Now, if you will excuse me . . ."

To her dismay, as she moved forward, he grasped hold of her arm, restraining her, despite her best efforts to shake herself free.

"You shall hear me out, Miss Eliza," he said, the honey gone from his voice. "I am determined you will accept me. You have treated me discourteously, and I shall not forget that. Let me tell you why you will reconsider what you have said."

"Release me. You have nothing to say that I want to hear."

"Let us talk about those 'Sketches from Clerical Life.' Those satiric pieces which have annoyed far more clergymen than they have amused. Weak writing, a poor attempt at wit, I wonder they were ever published. However, they were, and because of that, your fate is sealed. I know you wrote them, no, do not attempt to deny it."

Eliza was aghast. How could he possibly know? The answer came to her in a flash. Charlotte! Charlotte, her own sister, must have betrayed her. How could she, how could she be so cruel? Had she talked to Montblaine about Mr. Pyke as a likely husband for Eliza? How could even Charlotte think for a single moment that Eliza could bear to marry a man like that? Bitterness welled up inside her, a rage at her sister's treachery swept over her. Charlotte was to live in the great house, and her sister was to be in the parsonage, safely and respectably married off, with no consideration as to how loathsome her prospective husband might be.

Good God, the man was still talking. Eliza, caught up in her angry thoughts, wasn't listening, but then, suddenly, she paid attention.

"So I made it my business to discover who was the author of those tawdry pieces, I had a notion that the information would be of use to me in some way. I paid a sum of money to a man at the office of the Leeds *Gazette,* who told me about the payments that were made to one Mrs. Palmer. I found she had been your nurse, and although the trail went cold there, for she was distinctly disobliging, it was of no matter, for I had better luck in London, where I was able to obtain a description of the woman who called in the office of the *London Magazine.* At that point the mystery was solved."

Relief swept over Eliza, and she shut her eyes, overjoyed that it wasn't Charlotte who had told Mr. Pyke that she was the author of those articles.

Mr. Pyke wasn't finished. "Your father, the bishop, is at the moment a happy man. He wants a better bishopric, and, indeed, Salisbury is likely to become vacant in the near future. Lord Montblaine has promised his influence, and I, having the ear of the archbishop, am quite willing to add my good services. Provided, that is, that you will promise to be mine."

Eliza didn't hesitate. "Then, unfortunately, my father will have to remain as Bishop of Ripon."

"My dear Miss Eliza, you are perhaps thinking of your young

neighbour, who has declared his affection for you to your father. I assure you, the bishop is quite prepared to agree that he should not have consented to Mr. Diggory's paying his addresses to you. Since there is no formal engagement, nothing need come of it, no obloquy will fall upon you with regard to that."

"You have indeed been busy on my behalf!"

"You do not quite understand your position, my dearest Eliza. If you will not accept my hand and heart, then I fear I must reveal to the archbishop that these sketches were penned by you. I shall say you wrote them with the full knowledge of your father, and I think you will find that Mr. Collins will end up as Bishop of Nowhere. Now, what do you say to that? No, do not give me an answer now. I have learned from dear Lady Grandpoint that you have a temper. I do not dislike spirit in a woman, although its expression should be reserved for private moments, when the right place and time render it more than acceptable. So I shall take my leave of you now, and will return this afternoon for what I know will be a favourable reply, to learn that you will make me the happiest of men. It cannot be otherwise, once you have thought it over, and realised where your duty lies."

"You threaten me, Mr. Pyke. There is an ugly word for what you are about, which is *blackmail.*"

He smiled. "That is a harsh word to fall from the lips of a lovely young woman. You will come to understand that my ardour is such that I will use any means to win your heart."

He grasped her hand as he spoke, and raised it to his lips. Then he let it go, and for a long moment, his eyes rested on her neck and bosom. She glared at him, feeling as though he were stripping her naked. He smiled, and ran his tongue over his already moist mouth. Then he slid out of the door before she could say another word, leaving her infuriated and hurling opprobrious epithets at the closed door.

Chapter Thirty-six

Bartholomew Bruton and Mr. Pyke passed in the hall. They greeted one another without enthusiasm; Mr. Pyke banked at Bruton's and so must be accorded the courtesy due to a client, and Mr. Pyke, for his part, didn't care for the young Mr. Bruton, who looked too much the gentleman in his well-cut green coat and, besides, had that sardonic glint in his eye. Why wasn't he sitting over some ledgers, what was he doing making calls in Aubrey Square at this time of the morning?

Mr. Pyke went on his way, and the footman attempted to usher Bartholomew up the stairs to where Lady Grandpoint was receiving callers in the drawing room.

Mr. Bruton had other ideas. "Just one moment," he said, and opened the door to the parlour in which Eliza was striding up and down, clearly in a great passion.

She whirled round as the door opened, her fists clenched, the fury draining from her face as she saw Mr. Bruton standing there.

"I am sorry if I intrude. I heard voices—" He looked questioningly around the room. "My apologies, you are alone. I thought there was some altercation, you sounded distressed."

"Angry, Mr. Bruton, angry rather than distressed. I lost my temper and was shouting at the door, which just closed behind the most obnoxious man in London."

Bartholomew came into the room. "Mr. Pyke," he said. He closed the door and took her hands in his. "My dear, what has happened? You look ill, you should sit down."

"Pray, do not speak so kindly to me, or I shall be overcome, and I hate a weeping female."

"My shoulder is at your disposal should you care to cry upon it." He watched her, his heart in his eyes, as she struggled to compose herself. "What has Mr. Pyke done or said to cause you such anguish?"

"He proposed to me."

Bartholomew raised his eyebrows. "Ah, and I know from my own experience that you do not care for proposals." He could not keep the dryness from his voice; was this how she felt when he had proposed to her?

The colour rushed back into Eliza's cheeks. "I did not mean— Oh, that was quite different."

"I trust you refused Mr. Pyke's offer? Rebuffed as I was, I should take it hard if Mr. Pyke were to have succeeded in gaining your affections where I was so abruptly rejected."

"Do not be absurd. Accept Mr. Pyke? I had sooner marry the linkboy out in the square there!"

"Well, Pyke proposed, and you refused him. I am glad to hear it, but what is there in that to make you so angry?" He drew up a chair for her. "Sit down, and you will feel better."

"No, I am too angry to sit still. It is not just the proposal, although his manner— Ugh, he is a veritable weasel, that man. No, it is that he threatened me, and . . . and"—her voice was suddenly forlorn—"I am in such a fix, and I can't see a way out of it. I cannot marry him, and if I do not agree to do so, he will ruin my father."

"Ruin your father?" Bartholomew was taken aback at this stark statement. "Forgive me, how is that possible?"

"I can tell you, since you already know my secret. It is those wretched articles. He has found out that I am the author, and he says that if I will not marry him, he will inform the archbishop and everyone else in London that I wrote them, and worse, that my father knew of it, and condoned my literary efforts."

"And, your father being a bishop, this would not be good for his prospects."

"Prospects! Mr. Pyke says he would have to resign, and I can believe it, for you may be sure he would slant it in such a way as to put the worst possible construction on everything. I do not know what to do."

"How did he find out that you were the author? I assure you, I have not breathed a word."

"No, I know you have not. Nor has Mr. Portal, and the only other people who know are my cousin and my sister. I confess, I did suspect for a moment that Charlotte—it seems dreadful to say so, and I was quite wrong. Only it appears that Lord Montblaine, who is to marry my sister, encourages Mr. Pyke in his intention to make me his wife."

"I have heard of the engagement, of course, and I have come to offer my felicitations to Miss Collins. My mama will be calling on Lady Grandpoint later on today, I came early so as to avoid—"

He hesitated, and Eliza looked at him with a quizzical expression. "Avoid?"

"My mother and I are somewhat at loggerheads just at the moment," he said stiffly. "It is a personal matter, however, I do not want to run into her just now."

"Well," said Eliza, attempting a smile, "you had best be off upstairs, to fulfil your social obligations."

"Oh, I don't give a fig for that," said Bartholomew. "Who, then, revealed your secret to the Reverend Mr. Pyke if it was not Miss Collins?"

"No one. He ferreted it out for himself, using bribery and wheedling his way into information that he had no right to. He is the most despicable creature alive!"

He was still holding her hands. Eliza knew she should withdraw them, but his clasp was strong and warm and gave her a kind of confidence. Now that she had given vent to her indignation at

Mr. Pyke and his perfidy, she became aware that her heart was thumping, and not from temper, but from the close presence of Mr. Bruton.

It was as though she were seeing him for the first time, and everything about him, the set of his shoulders, his firm mouth, the brilliance of his eyes, his air of vigour and assurance and intelligence, filled her with a sensation that she could not fathom.

Their eyes met, and she quickly looked away. There was a pause before he said, in a slightly unsteady voice, "So Mr. Pyke is a blackmailer. He has left you with an ultimatum, I assume."

"He has given me until this afternoon to consider what I am about; in other words, to see reason and accept his offer of marriage. His proposal," she said bitterly, "has the blessing not only of his cousin, the noble marquis, but also of my great-aunt. He even took it upon himself to write to my father, can you comprehend such behaviour? I am sure he held out the promise of great things to Papa, and he, not being always as . . . as sensible as he might be, no doubt believed every lying word Mr. Pyke wrote."

"So Mr. Pyke will be back later for an answer?"

"Yes, only I will not be here. I can see nothing for it but to return as fast as I can to Yorkshire, to attempt to explain everything to my father. Only—" Her voice faltered.

"Only your father will advise you to accept Mr. Pyke. A rising clergyman, with the archbishop's ear, a relation of your brother-in-law to be, it could seem a most suitable match to a man who did not know the individual in question."

"Exactly," she said, grateful for his quick understanding. "Perhaps I can make Mama understand how I feel about Mr. Pyke, but I am not sure that she will quite appreciate how disagreeable he is."

Not when Mrs. Collins had herself accepted her father purely for the sake of an establishment; Eliza had no illusions on that score. She didn't blame her mother for the decision she had made—what right had she to do so?—only she herself was not going to go down that path.

Mr. Bruton appeared lost in thought. "Do not return to Yorkshire. It would cause a deal of comment, just now, with Miss Collins's engagement and so forth, and I assume your parents will be coming to London in the near future."

"Not if Mr. Pyke carries out his threat."

"He won't," said Mr. Bruton with sudden assurance. "When you see him again, ask him what is in the black box he has lodged in Bruton's bank."

"Black box? What black box?"

"I can say nothing more. It may not work; on the other hand, it may mean that you are rid of the man for good."

Chapter Thirty-seven

Surely Mr. Bruton would be at the Wyttons'? As Eliza dressed for the evening, she sang to herself, causing Annie to comment on her high spirits, "It's a pleasure to hear you so chirpy, Miss."

Chirpy, what a word! Like a London sparrow, and, yes, she was happier than she had been for weeks. Now she longed to see Bartholomew Bruton again, to report on the success of his stratagem, to tease the truth out of him, and, yes, simply to be with him.

The carriage was brought round. Charlotte, who was calling in at the Wyttons' before going on to the theatre with Lord Montblaine, was already waiting in the hall, in great beauty, and wearing the sensational diamond necklace which the marquis had given her as an engagement present. Looking at her, Eliza felt a sudden pang, not of envy, but of a kind of sadness that Charlotte was moving away from her. Soon she would be the Marchioness of Montblaine, one of the highest-ranking peeresses in the kingdom, living a life which Eliza could hardly imagine.

Lady Grandpoint had gleefully spoken of how rich Charlotte would be, and gloated over the exceedingly generous settlements. Then there would be jewels, carriages, furs, a magnificent trousseau of silks and satins, of gowns from Paris. "What a change in station, what a difference from your life in Yorkshire it will be," she exclaimed.

Eliza thought all that rather vulgar, but refrained from saying so. She wished she could tell if Charlotte were happy; looking at her serene, remote face, it was impossible to judge what was going on beneath that impenetrable reserve, and Charlotte resolutely changed the subject if Eliza tried to talk about her engagement.

Charlotte's brief presence at the Wyttons' was little more than a courtesy. "She will soon be quite above our touch," Camilla whispered to Eliza after greeting her cousins and admiring Charlotte's diamonds. She clearly found the idea amusing, and Eliza knew that Camilla had no wish to move in the exalted circles where Charlotte would make her married life.

Charlotte went away after a little while, and the gathering of old friends grew noisier and livelier. Still no Bartholomew Bruton; Eliza had been so sure he would be present. She longed to ask Camilla if he were expected, but that would be too particular. Then, when she had almost given up hope, he entered the room, looking quickly round, looking for her, Eliza felt sure. She was talking to Pagoda Portal, but cast Mr. Bruton a swift, complicit smile, which caused Mr. Portal to raise his brows and, with exquisite tact, move away so that Mr. Bruton might approach.

They sat together on a sofa, the sounds and scents of London coming to them through the window, the perfume of the climbing rose in the Wyttons' garden mingling with the acrid smell of smoke and stable aromas from the mews behind. Here at the back of the house, the habitual town noise of wagons and carriages was muted, but voices hung on the air from other houses in the terrace. Swallows swooped in the twilight sky, and the raucous sounds of a couple of crossing sweepers arguing over a coin rent the still air.

Eliza kept her voice down, making it huskier than usual, and brimming over with laughter. "Mr. Pyke was rolled up, Mr. Bruton, you never saw anything like it. He went away with his tail between his legs, quite confounded and so anxious to be out of my presence! Pray, does discretion dictate that you cannot reveal to me the contents of his black box? I confess, I do long to know."

Bartholomew's mouth twitched, and he had answering laughter

in his voice as he told her, "Miss Eliza, I do not know! I have not been privy to that secret. For all I know, it contains a lock of his grandmother's hair and a pair of silver tongs!"

Eliza stared at him, then her laugh rang out, drawing all eyes to where they were sitting. "A joke, Miss Eliza?" said Mr. Portal in his genial way. "May we share it?"

"Oh dear, it is not a joke, just something so absurd!"

What an enchanted evening it had been, Eliza said to herself as she tumbled into bed hours later, radiant with happiness, knowing that Mr. Bruton was going to call upon her tomorrow, no, it was already today. He was going to renew his proposal, she was sure of it, and this time she would have no hesitation in accepting it, she could not imagine any greater joy than to be his wife.

Bartholomew was almost as exultant as he walked home from Harte Street. As he approached the front door, a figure came out of the shadows and greeted him with a whoop of delight. "Hoped I'd catch you, can I come in for a glass of wine with you?"

"Freddie, it's late."

"And you have to be at the bank tomorrow. I know, I know. You're getting staid, old fellow, is this the man who used to paint the town red with me?"

"Your memory is at fault. That was one of your more raffish friends, I dare say. Come in, then, or you'll wake the household, and I don't suppose you'll care to have a peal rung over you by my mother."

"Aunt Sarah? Good God, no," said Freddie, moderating his voice. "Saw her this evening, can't say she was awfully friendly. Deep in disapproving conversation with my mother, all because I danced two dances with Maria."

"Maria?"

Bartholomew opened the door into his sitting room and told his man to bring more candles and the decanter. "Then you can take yourself off to bed, I shan't need you again. Now, Freddie, who is this Maria?"

"Isn't it a wonderful name? There's only one Maria, it's Miss Diggory, of course. Did you ever see such sparkling eyes, such a glowing complexion?"

Bartholomew regarded his friend with a mixture of affection and exasperation. "Not again, Freddie. How fickle you are."

"Fickle!"

"It's only a week or so since you were languishing all over London, eating your heart out for Miss Collins."

"Miss Collins," said Freddie with disgust. "That was nothing, it was a madness. She's an icicle, and I wish Montblaine joy of her, it'll be like going to bed with something carved out of the icehouse, if you ask me."

"I think you do Miss Collins an injustice there," said Bartholomew, recalling that young lady's passionate embrace with Mr. Warren. "Anyhow, aren't you cradle snatching? How old is Miss Diggory?"

"She is sixteen," Freddie said with dignity. "And she is the greatest fun! She says the drollest things and is an accomplished mimic, I had to whisk her away before she started on my respected parent, who I must say sat there glaring at her with her most parrot-faced expression."

He tossed off his glass of wine and held it out for Bartholomew to refill.

"I must say, you're looking pretty lively yourself. Dined well, good company?"

"Yes," said Bartholomew abstractedly. "Yes, good company. I was at the Wyttons'."

"I suppose the Collins sisters were there. My word, they are a pair. Maria is a great friend of Miss Eliza's, you know, but she's in a mighty cross state with her, since she has written three notes to her, and never a reply. She thinks perhaps Lady Grandpoint made sure Eliza never saw them, which surprised me, until Maria explained that Miss Eliza and her brother, Anthony, have an understanding which her ladyship don't care for, and she doesn't want Miss Eliza to have any contact with the Diggorys. She warned them off, in fact, in the most high-handed manner. However, her ladyship is on a losing wicket there." Freddie sat up, looking solemn. "Bart, prepare to hear something shocking, for Maria told me—"

"Spare me the gossip, Freddie, I beg of you. I'm not interested in Miss Diggory's tittle-tattle."

"You should be, for it's scandalous, and if Miss Collins knew what her sister had been up to, she would have the vapours, I should think." Freddie's voice took on a confidential note. "It turns out that it's rather more than an understanding, that in fact, Miss Eliza and Mr. Diggory are actually engaged."

"What!"

Freddie nodded. "Yes, a secret engagement. Contracted before the Collinses left Yorkshire. It seems Diggory *père* and *mère* didn't approve of the connection, and that's why Miss Eliza came to London—originally, Lady Grandpoint had only invited Miss Collins to be her guest in town. She wants Eliza to marry that energetic clergyman who's such a bore. Only now Sir Roger and Lady Diggory have had a change of heart, so we may expect another announcement any day. There, I told you it was a shocking story. Ha, you are amazed."

Bartholomew said nothing, and Freddie, heedless of the stricken expression on his friend's face, rattled on, "Of course, you seemed rather taken with Miss Eliza at one time. My mother quizzed me about it, there's a bit of talk to that effect going about town. She asked me if you had serious intentions. I turned it off, well, I could hardly say that you would like to bed the wench, but social niceties being what they are, that wasn't possible. So I simply said that to my certain knowledge you didn't want to marry anyone."

"How dare you—"

Freddie wasn't listening. "Mind you, you'd better steer clear of Mr. Diggory, for he's got wind of it, Maria says, and is out for your blood."

Chapter Thirty-eight

Eliza waited all day. She rose early, and dressed with extra care, ate scarcely a morsel for breakfast, then prowled about her bedchamber until an appropriate time for her to be in the drawing room to receive any morning callers.

And there was a stream of them, still drawn by the excitement of Charlotte's engagement, the most brilliant match of the season, "Quite a Cinderella story," as one vicious dowager said, with a smile pinned to her lips and a glare at Eliza.

The hours passed. Every time the knocker sounded, Eliza caught her breath. This time, it must be him.

It never was. Not in the morning, nor after the nuncheon had been spread out in the dining room, and left untouched by Eliza. In the afternoon, Lady Grandpoint announced that she was going to Bond Street and to the circulating library. Eliza could accompany her.

Eliza stayed at home.

Wild, terrifying thoughts of accidents, street robbers, a fall from his carriage or horse, or a desperate financial crisis flitted through her mind.

Her reason told her that was nonsense, her anxious self sent Annie out to glean any news of any mishaps that might have assailed the heir to the house of Bruton.

No news, no gossip, no rumours.

No Mr. Bruton.

It was with anguish in her heart that Eliza sat down to dinner with Lord and Lady Grandpoint. Yes, she was a little unwell, she lied, in response to a tart query from Lady Grandpoint. She had the headache.

"I thought only Charlotte suffered from headaches."

"Perhaps it is the weather, it is very close today."

Lord Grandpoint looked at her in astonishment. "It is windy and unusually chilly for the time of year."

Mr. Bruton had arrived at the bank that morning in a terrible temper. Startled clerks and assistants took one look at his face and scurried to keep out of his way.

"Just like his grandfather," one of the oldest members of staff confided to a younger colleague. "I started in the bank when I was ten, and on days when old Mr. Bruton—of course, he wasn't old then—came in with a face like thunder, we all learned to keep out of his way. I've not seen Mr. Bartholomew in such a taking, though. I wonder what's happened to make him look like that."

Bartholomew put in a gruelling day's work, desperately trying to drive the deep sense of hurt and misery out of his mind. He was torn between a visceral jealousy of Anthony Diggory, and agony over Eliza's duplicity. Those sisters were two of a kind, deceitful, ambitious, secretive. He had helped her to get rid of Mr. Pyke, and this was his reward. Why could not she have been honest with him?

Yet if Eliza was ambitious, he, as a Bruton, had far more to offer than a Yorkshire squire's son, however many acres he might expect to inherit. She had a provincial soul, that was it; she preferred muddy northern acres to a civilised life in London. Let her waste her life away in the rural fastnesses of her rainy county, much he cared, he was never going to think of her again.

And he kept to that, for all of thirty seconds, and then he was off again, still smarting from Freddie's casual words, still aching with the joy he had felt when he saw her again at the Wyttons', when he had felt so sure that this time, she would welcome his addresses. He might as well marry Jane Grainger, or Jane anyone, what did it matter? Women were all the same, perfidious, sly, incapable of honesty.

By the end of the day, his mood was, if anything, worse than when he had arrived in the morning. He stormed out of the bank, hardly able to utter a civil word to any of the staff who were foolish enough to come within his range, only just stopping himself from snapping off the head of Mr. Hetherington, who cocked a knowing eye at him from between his grizzled brows, and said bluntly, "Don't fret, Mr. Bartholomew. It'll come right in the end."

"Useless, threadbare words," Bartholomew said savagely to the crossing sweeper, who took his penny and scarpered.

He was in a quandary. Short of throwing himself in the river, what was he to do, to escape the endless pain of losing Eliza? He couldn't mope at home, good God, his mother might even venture to his apartments, she was the last person he wanted to see. Nor would he welcome his father's company.

He would go out, find himself a wench, drown his sorrows in excess. Where was that tavern Freddie had taken to frequenting? It was in Covent Garden. Well, there would be some convivial souls there, nothing but men and whores, more honest in their dealings than any well-bred miss out to ensnare a husband.

A lively scene met his eyes as he entered the tavern. Freddie was there, greeting him with a shout of joy, ordering wine, saying they would share a chop later on. It was a cold night, in contrast to the blast of hot air, laden with the smell of ale and wine and sweat, which greeted Bartholomew as he entered the tavern. It would normally have repelled him, but tonight was a welcome contrast to the drawing rooms and ballrooms he had been frequenting ever since he had met Eliza.

That was over with. The bank and masculine pleasures were what he wanted. To hell with a wife and a house and all the trappings of domesticity.

Freddie must have had a bottle or two before Bartholomew got there, for he was growing slightly maudlin, cradling the bottle and crooning Maria's name to himself.

Bartholomew drank his share of wine, but it seemed to have no effect on him, he still felt stone-cold sober, damn it. A saucy girl, her fine bosom barely covered by her low-cut gown, was giving him the eye from another table. He had never felt less amorous in his life. He stared morosely into his wine, wishing that Freddie would change his tune, when he became aware of a large figure looming over their table.

"Maria?" the newcomer said belligerently. "Maria who?"

"Maria Diggory," said Freddie dreamily, not looking up to see who was addressing him.

The man gave a bellow and reached out for Freddie's collar, yanking him to his feet.

Anthony Diggory! Even drunker than Freddie, by the look of him, with a murderous eye. Bartholomew got to his feet. "Leave him alone, Diggory," he said wearily.

Bartholomew Bruton had a natural authority, and even there, in the raucous tavern, confronting an inebriated and infuriated Yorkshireman, his voice had its effect. Anthony let Freddie go and glared at Bartholomew. "You!" he said in a voice of loathing.

"Go away," said Bartholomew, sitting down again.

"I will not go away. I want a word with you. I've heard what people are saying about you. They're saying that you and Eliza—Miss Eliza Collins—that you've been forcing your attentions on her!"

"Get lost," said Bartholomew, hating himself for the stab of anguish caused by Eliza's name on Anthony's lips. How could she be in love with this man, how could she be intending to marry him, to live with him for the rest of her life?

Anthony didn't go away. His choler was up, and he stood there, panting slightly, his eyes fixed on Bartholomew's face. "Answer me, or by God, you'll regret it," he cried.

"I was not aware that you'd asked me a question," said Bartholomew in a perfectly calm voice.

Anthony was not alone in the tavern. Two other young men were with him, one with a violent shock of red hair and a Scottish accent, the other a dark, sturdy man, who now advanced on Anthony with a frown on his face. "Anthony, what are you up to? Come back to our table and calm down."

"Like hell I will. This is the man who's been making Eliza the talk of the town, he's been trying to win her away from me, playing fast and loose with her affections. Come on, answer me, what is Miss Eliza Collins to you?"

"If she meant anything to you, you would not bandy her name around in such a place as this," said Bartholomew, such venom in his voice that Freddie looked at him in astonishment.

"Bandy her name, is it? I'll have satisfaction of you for that."

"For what, precisely?"

"For that," said Anthony, snatching up a glass of wine and dashing its contents in Bartholomew's face.

Bartholomew stood up, and wiped his face with his handkerchief. "Freddie? You'll act for me?"

"For Christ's sake, Bartholomew, the fellow's drunk, you don't have to call him out."

"Freddie!"

"Oh, all right. Damn you, Diggory, for making such an ass of yourself. What will your sister say when she hears what you've been up to?"

"Are you insulting my sister?"

"Don't rip up at me, or you'll find yourself run through twice in the morning. Who are your seconds?"

Anthony looked at his two companions. "Aye, I'll do it," said the man with red hair. The dark man began to remonstrate with him and with Anthony. "A drunken row in a tavern, you aren't in Yorkshire now, Anthony." And, to Freddie: "You, sir, your name if you please."

"My name's Rosely. Here's my direction. Get your man out of here and put his head in a bucket of cold water. Maybe he'll see sense by the time the night's out."

"No," said Bartholomew. "I'm not crying off, and I'll accept no apology. We'll meet at dawn, Diggory, sword or pistols, I don't care which."

Freddie argued with Bartholomew all the way to Battersea Park, where the duel was to take place. In the subdued light of the false dawn Bartholomew's face appeared ashen, but his resolution was absolute.

"Pistols," groaned Freddie, not for the first tine. "Why ever did you agree to pistols? Swords, and you'd have scratched his arm before he'd moved an inch and there would be an end of it. But the mood he's in, he'll put a bullet through your heart. You know what these country gentlemen are like, they spend their lives shooting rabbits and rooks and God knows what else, they're practically born with shotguns in their hands."

"I don't suppose he'll be bringing a shotgun," said Bartholomew, with the first flash of humour he'd felt in the last twenty-four hours. He faced the prospect of a bullet with equanimity and a kind of fatalism. Why was he here, why was he doing this? He had never been a duelling man, he thought the whole business preposterous, a relic of past times, and yet here he was, as dawn broke, rattling over the river to kill or maim even as the morning swallows were swooping through the skies and London was waking to a glorious June day.

Freddie had summoned a cousin to act as Bartholomew's other second. "Let's try and keep this in the family. God knows what your father's going to say when he hears about this. I dare say it'll be all over London by ten o'clock, whatever happens."

"He'll disinherit me, probably, if I survive," said Bartholomew indifferently. "I've angered him by refusing to marry Jane Grainger, and this will put the lid on my misdeeds."

Anthony had brought the pistols, a matched pair of flintlocks. They lay gleaming in their mahogany box, with curved stocks and wickedly long barrels. Freddie and the dark man took them out and inspected them closely. Anthony, dressed in a dark coat, stood to one side, not looking at Bartholomew, who had taken his coat off. He handed it to the coachman, then began to remove his shirt.

"You'll never fight bare-chested," said Freddie, alarmed. "You're a perfect target."

"Yes, and if I'm in a coat and a bullet goes into me, the wound will fester. Give me the pistol."

The seconds paced out the distance, and the two men lined up, sideways on. Bartholomew balanced the weight of the gun in his hand, then looked at it, noticing in a curiously distant way the exquisite goldwork on the shaft, before he lowered the weapon to his side.

As Freddie's handkerchief dropped, the duellers took aim, and two shots rang out at exactly the same moment.

Bartholomew, his ears still ringing from the sound of the bullet that had shot past his head, saw Anthony twist round and slide to the ground.

The surgeon came across at a brisk trot from his carriage as the seconds ran to Anthony. Their voices came clearly across to Bartholomew on the still morning air, as they knelt beside the still figure. "He's done for."

"My God, and so are you," said Freddie to Bartholomew. His keen ears had caught the sound of a coach approaching at speed. "Word's got out, those are the magistrate's men. You must get away from here."

"Away?"

"Don't you understand? You've killed a man. There'll be the devil to pay for this. You fool, why didn't you delope?"

"I did," said Bartholomew. "At least, I didn't fire to hit him. I aimed at that tree, over there." He pointed to a plane tree some ten yards away from where Anthony had been standing.

"Curse you for a rotten shot," said Freddie. "Come on, coz, move!"

Chapter Thirty-nine

Eliza woke from a tormented, restless night and couldn't at first account for the sense of dreariness that overwhelmed her as she opened her eyes. Then she remembered, and, with a sigh, she pulled herself upright.

That was yesterday. Today was today. She had given way to doubts and depression; well, enough of that, it was a time for action. First and foremost, she was going to find out why Mr. Bruton had failed to appear. She could not write to him, how absurd were all these niceties, so how to go about it?

Lord Rosely. She could not send a message to him directly, but he might well be in the park that evening. He had taken to driving there in his elegant curricle at the fashionable hour of five o'clock, often taking Maria up beside him. Lord Grandpoint would lend her a horse from the stables, she would ride in the park and, if Rosely were there, question him about Mr. Bruton.

Meanwhile, she wasn't going to mope and sit around in misery. She would fill the day with activity, useful, interesting activity, she would not sit at home, hoping that Mr. Bruton would call and counting the hours until she might see his friend.

A knock on the door and Annie came in, clearly big with news. "Oh, Miss, I don't know how to tell you, what a to-do, there's been a duel and a man shot dead, and, oh, Miss, it's Mr. Diggory!"

"Anthony! Shot dead? What are you saying?"

"There's a note been brought round, it's from Miss Diggory, and the manservant who brought it told us all about it. Mr. Diggory fought a duel with Mr. Bruton, first thing this morning, and Mr. Bruton shot him, and has had to flee the country."

"Who has had to flee the country?" asked Eliza, bewildered by Annie's flow of words. "Are you telling me that Mr. Bruton shot Mr. Diggory?"

"Yes, Miss, that's it."

"Killed him?"

"He's been brought home, he was taken up for dead there in Battersea Park."

Eliza tore open the note and ran her eyes over the incoherent words. "I shall go to Maria at once. Annie, never mind the chocolate or anything else. Go downstairs and call me a hackney cab, I will be ready in five minutes."

Anthony shot, killed by Mr. Bruton. A duel! Dear God, what had they fought about? Surely not over her. And Mr. Bruton had to flee the country; of course, to kill a man in a duel these days counted as murder.

In less than five minutes she was downstairs, ignoring the protestations of the butler and Annie's pleas that she just pause to let her do her hair. "For you look positively wild, Miss, and your bonnet not straight, and your gown—"

She leant forward in the hackney cab, holding on to the leather strap as though her energy could urge the cab to go faster through the heavy London traffic. It was an eternity before it stopped outside the Hatchards' house. Eliza was out in a flash, pressing a shilling into the jarvie's hand and running up the steps to the front door. She lifted her hand to the knocker, and as she did so, a carriage drew up behind her. She turned to see a dapper man come briskly up the steps. He was carrying a black leather bag.

"It is Dr. Molloy, is it not?" she asked. He had attended her aunt when she was afflicted with sneezing fits, a consequence of the pollen in the air, he said.

He raised his hat, the door opened, and they stepped inside. Maria was there, distraught and with a tragic face. She leapt forward. "Dr. Molloy. Oh, pray come quickly, this way, he is up here."

Eliza's heart leapt as she took in the implications of his arrival and Maria's words. Physicians did not attend upon dead men. Anthony must still be alive. She followed the two of them up the stairs to where a door stood open on the landing. Dr. Molloy went inside and the door was firmly shut in Maria's and Eliza's faces.

"Well," said Maria, and then, in a violent storm of weeping, she fell on Eliza's neck.

Eliza did her best to soothe her hysterical friend, but seeing that words were of no use, she called down to the hall, where several interested servants were loitering, for one of them to bring a jug of water. It came, and she promptly flung the contents of the jug over Maria.

Who came to her senses, spluttering and gasping and full of indignation. "You are as cruel and heartless as Anthony said. I summoned you, for I knew if he regained his wits before he expired, he would want to see you one last time. It is noble of me, for it is all your fault, his end will be on your conscience for ever."

"How is he? Does he live?"

"He has been shot, there is blood everywhere, and he is at death's door. It was a duel, and they fought over you, that is what people are saying."

"What people?"

"Oh, we have already had callers, wretched nosey parkers, agog for terrible news, and full of tittle-tattle. Oh, how could he do it? And how could he miss, how came he not to put a bullet through Mr. Bruton's heart, you know what a fine shot he is!"

The door opened, and there was Dr. Molloy, regarding them with a pair of pale, cold eyes. "You are making a lot of noise out here. Pray request a servant to bring towels and water."

"Is he yet living?" breathed Maria.

"You are?"

"His sister."

"There is not the slightest cause for alarm, Miss Diggory. Your brother has received a trifling scalp wound, a nothing, not worth the time or expense of my visit. He will come to his senses shortly."

"A trifling wound," repeated Maria, and then sank to the ground in a swoon.

"Lord, these vaporous young women," said Dr. Molloy, his voice entirely without sympathy. "Call her maid and apply smelling salts. Good day to you, Miss Eliza Collins, is it not? If you know the whereabouts of Mr. Bruton, you may inform him that the magistrates may have him up for duelling in a public place, but that he is in no danger of standing his trial for murder."

With that the doctor went nimbly down the stairs and out of the door, leaving Eliza staring after him. Why had he given her that message?

This was no time to ponder the doctor's enigmatic words, however. Maria must be attended to—ah, here was her maid. "Betsy, you take her feet and I will lift her under her arms."

They carried her into the room and laid her on a sofa, across from her brother, who was clasping a bloodstained cloth to the side of his head and looking slightly dazed. "Eliza! You're here! What is the matter with Maria?"

"She fainted. She is perfectly all right, she is coming round this minute. Oh, Miss Chetwynd, what are you doing here?"

She had not noticed Miss Chetwynd advancing into the room—had she missed her knock? Her shrewlike countenance was alight with curiosity as she sent her eyes flicking from Anthony to Maria and back to Eliza.

"I was paying a morning call with my mother, and hearing that poor Maria was indisposed, Mama directed me to come upstairs to see if I could be of use. Oh, Mr. Diggory, pray do not get up. You are hurt." She darted over to his couch, and took up a clean piece of linen.

Eliza hesitated for a moment, then whisked herself out of the room. Minutes later, she was in another cab and bowling through the streets to Falconer Street. Dr. Molloy's words made sense, but how did he know that she would have any concern for Mr. Bruton? The duel, of course, the duel supposedly fought over her, doubtless word of that was all over town. How ridiculous men were, and what had Mr. Bruton been up to, neglecting her all day and then fighting at dawn?

Mr. Bruton and Lady Sarah were not at home. As the stately butler intoned the polite, meaningless phrase, a familiar figure came into the hall.

"Lord Rosely. Oh, Lord Rosely, do you know where Mr. Bartholomew Bruton is gone?"

"France," he said laconically. "Gone for good, too, just had it from his father. The law will be after him, he won't be able to set foot in England again. Don't know if he'll reach France," Freddie added gloomily. "The way he was driving, he won't get halfway to Dover without overturning or going into a ditch. He said he didn't care, it would save him blowing his brains out. Suicidal, Miss Eliza, that's what he is, suicidal. Far too nice in his conscience, that's the trouble with him, these things happen, you can't take them to heart."

He spoke these last words to the air, as Eliza was no longer there. Her skirts gathered up above her ankles, she ran down the street and cut through in the direction of Aubrey Square.

"Go by yourself, Miss?" said Annie, aghast. "You can't! It isn't seemly!"

"By myself," said Eliza firmly, tipping the contents of her purse on to the bed. "Go and do as I asked you, and hurry!"

She counted the coins, then went to a drawer and took out the rest of her money. It should be enough, surely. At least sufficient to get her to Dover, and then . . . She would worry about then later. Now all she wanted was to get to Dover, to find Mr. Bruton; what desperate mood must he be in, to drive off in such a way.

Eliza had never been south of London, but the journey, which might otherwise have proved full of interest, could have been through a deep forest in the dead of night for all the notice she took of the countryside the chaise passed through. The oast houses, with their quaint cones, the fields of hops, the fruitful orchards, might all have been on the moon as far as she was concerned. All she wanted was to reach Dover. Which way was the wind blowing? Was it not the case that on some days it was impossible to venture upon the Channel crossing? Might it be so today, might she find Mr. Bruton kicking his heels at some inn, instead of already halfway to France?

The coachman, who had regarded her with considerable disapproval throughout the journey, wanted to know where she was to be set down, at which inn she was staying.

"Whichever is the most important," she commanded, guessing that the rich Mr. Bruton would hardly stay in a lesser hostelry.

"That'll be the Ship, then," he said laconically, and a few minutes later, the coach turned into the yard at the Ship Inn. Eliza had caught glimpses of the sea as they came down into the town; did her eyes deceive her, or was the sea looking quite rough, with cresting white tips to the waves? Although that might simply mean a good wind to waft vessels across to the Continent, not that they were waiting in the harbour for more favourable conditions.

As she climbed down from the coach, stiff after the ride, a gust of salty wind struck her in the face, nearly ripping her hat off. The innyard was busy and noisy, coaches following one another in, ostlers leading horses into the stables, a wagon rumbling through the archway, piled high with luggage, passengers passing into the inn.

Once the chaise had been paid for, and a tip added for the long-faced coachman, Eliza took a deep breath, and told the boy who was hovering with her single small bag in his hand to lead her into the inn.

"If you're wanting a bedchamber, and ain't reserved one, you won't be staying here," he blithely informed her. "There won't be nothing sailing today, not with the wind as it is. They're making the crossing the other way in just a few hours, but none of the boats will put out from here until the wind's shifted into a better quarter."

Which must mean that Mr. Bruton was still in England! Her

heart lifted. She went into the inn, stepping into a panelled room, with worn, polished, creaking floorboards and nautical accessories hanging here and there from the immense beams.

A stout man appeared to be in charge. Eliza, ignoring the jostling throng of new arrivals and those anxiously making enquiries about the weather and sailing times, managed to push her way to the landlord and to ask, in a raised voice, whether a Mr. Bruton was staying at the inn.

The innkeeper, who was looking at her in no very friendly fashion, said that he was. "And," he added, "if you're wanting accommodation for yourself and your maid, we're full."

"Please send up to Mr. Bruton to tell him that Miss Eliza Collins is here."

The innkeeper ignored her request. "Not so high-and-mighty, if you please. Do you have a maid, a mother, a brother? Or are you travelling alone?"

"That is none of your business. Please convey my message to Mr. Bruton."

"We know your sort, and we'll have nothing of that kind here. Be off with you."

Eliza stared at him. Was the man mad? Good heavens, no, not mad at all. He had taken her for quite a different order of person.

To his evident astonishment, she let out a peal of laughter, and said, "Indeed, I am not what you think. I am . . . I am a relation of Mr. Bruton, and I have come from London with an urgent message."

She heard a sound and looked up. Bartholomew Bruton was standing at the head of the stairs, looking down at her.

This was no glad welcome, no joy sprang into his eyes. His face was set, cold, implacable. "What are you doing here?"

"I need to speak to you." Aware that the roomful of people had fallen silent and were watching and listening with intent interest, she made a pleading gesture with her hands.

He came down the stairs, slowly.

"Don't you be telling me this is your sister, Mr. Bruton, for I know as well as you do that you don't have a sister. I won't have my guests leading out a wench in my inn, and that's flat. If you want to get up to those sort of capers, you'll have to go elsewhere."

Mr. Bruton's eyes swept over him. "You forget yourself. A private parlour, if you please. My cousin is come from London upon family business."

The innkeeper, muttering to himself, told a waiter to take Mr. Bruton to the small back parlour. "Which I shall be letting out, sir, directly, so—"

"Thank you," said Mr. Bruton.

"Now," he said, shutting the door of the small, stuffy room, which smelt strongly of ale, "what the devil are you doing here?"

Eliza saw how it was. There was no affection in his eyes, no kindness, he had no pleasure in seeing her. What had she done, flying here from London? She had imagined a different welcome, not this wall of chilly hostility. To gain time to compose herself, she sat down on a worn settle and smoothed her skirts. Then she looked directly at Mr. Bruton and spoke in a surprisingly steady voice. "Anthony is not dead. He suffered nothing more than a trivial wound, and will make a complete recovery."

Was that relief in his face? He was standing in the far corner of the room, as far as possible from her, she suspected, and he was in shadow.

"I am glad to hear it, I did not intend to kill him," he said flatly.

A long silence. She would not speak another word, she would force him to say more than that. Finally, he spoke again. "Have you come all the way from London to tell me this?"

"It means that you no longer have to leave the country."

"I am leaving the country in any case. My father wishes me to spend some years in Paris, in our bank there. As soon as this damned wind turns, I shall be off."

What could she say? How could she get through to him? She took a deep breath. "Mr. Bruton, you are suffering from a misapprehension, regarding the relationship between Mr. Diggory and myself."

His eyes were even colder now. "I am not in the least interested in you or Mr. Diggory. Now that he is on the way to recovery, I shall not give him another thought. Nor you, Miss Eliza."

"No, you shall listen to me. I was secretly engaged to Mr. Diggory, in Yorkshire."

"So I was informed. I wish you every happiness for your future, and hope that a marriage that began in such a scandalous way will nonetheless bring you both whatever you desire from it."

"You sound like Mr. Pyke," flashed Eliza, thoroughly angry now. "Come down off your high horse, for goodness' sake. I was engaged. *Was,* Mr. Bruton, not am. As soon as Anthony arrived in London, I told him my sentiments had undergone such a change—in short, I no longer wanted to marry him, and I released him from the engagement, which we should never have entered into."

"In other words, you jilted him."

Eliza winced, but there was anger now in his voice and face, and that gave her hope, anything was better than cold indifference.

"Yes, and he was angry with me, and didn't want to believe that I was telling him the simple truth."

"What was the simple truth? That London had gone to your head, and you thought you could do better for yourself than the son of a Yorkshire baronet?"

"Of course, how could I think of Anthony when Mr. Pyke was offering for me?" she snapped back. "You are a fool, Mr. Bruton. I fell out of love with one man because I had fallen in love with another. An old story, and a common one."

He shrugged. "In due course, you will fall out of love and in love again."

"No. I made a mistake, that is all. I didn't understand what it means to love a man until I met you. And now, if you will excuse me, I have to find an inn for tonight, it is too late for me to go to London, and every room here is taken."

Her voice was so husky with emotion that she was barely audible, and when she finished, she was beyond words. It was as though her world had shrunk, leaving her nothing but this box of a room and a future which held certainly unhappiness and probably ruin. She lifted her hand and rubbed it over her eyes. There were no tears in her eyes, she was trying to wipe away an immense weariness.

Mr. Bruton took two steps towards her, banging at once into the end of the settle. With a curse he pushed it aside, and two seconds later, she was in his arms. Their eyes met for a long, still moment, then lips.

Rapt, lost in their passionate embrace, everything forgiven and forgotten, neither of them heard the door open. Then an all too familiar voice drawled, "Well, what have we here? The innkeeper told me you were in here with a lightskirt, and upon my word, I know the wench. None other than the sister-to-be of the noble marquis."

They fell apart, and Eliza blinked to see George Warren, triumph written all over him, standing in the doorway.

"Although this will put a stop to all your family's hopes and prospects. My uncle will not ally himself with a woman whose sister has been so comprehensively ruined. The rash deed of one must inevitably bring down the other. No maid, the innkeeper tells me, Miss Eliza. You came here alone in a hired chaise, you have no room booked—of course you have no need of one, since you can share Bruton's room. Oh, how ironic the situation is, how perfect my revenge! Usually, I find the morality of our world tiresome and irrational, but now, believe me, I most heartily endorse its ruthless code."

Ruined! The word rang in Eliza's ears. It was only a word, but what a world of dismay and disgrace it conjured up. And Warren meant what he said. This was no idle threat, and there was nothing that either she or Mr. Bruton could do to prevent his spreading this story all over London, a story so scandalous that it would pass from mouth to mouth, appear in the broadsheets, reach the outposts of the kingdom, even as far as Yorkshire.

How the populace, from Lady Thing in her gilded chamber to the potboy at the lowliest tavern, would lick their lips over the tale! A bishop's daughter, a single young woman, caught in flagrante with the scion of a notable banking family—for Eliza was not so naïve as to suppose that Mr. Warren would be content to leave the story at a kiss and the lack of a maid. A bishop's daughter, moreover, whose sister was betrothed to one of the highest in the land!

Mr. Bruton didn't stand and reflect. Instead, he launched himself at Warren, but that gentleman was too wily for that, and Mr. Bruton came smack up against a rapidly closed door. He flung it open and bounded out, scattering the two chambermaids and a waiter who were clustered at the door, all ears.

With a shout of fury, he went after Warren, who was beating a rapid retreat, but found his way blocked by a tall, dark, distinguished-looking man.

A shriek from behind him, and then Eliza's astonished, appalled voice: "Oh, good heavens, it is Mr. Darcy!"

Chapter Forty

Lady Sarah was in the drawing room, sitting upright on a sofa, while her husband prowled uncomfortably up and down. Bartholomew paused at the door, then took a breath and went in, crossing the large room to give his mother a kiss on the cheek. Then he said good morning to his father.

"Sit down," said Lady Sarah.

Bartholomew had not cared for the peremptory summons from his mother, which had been delivered to him by his wooden-faced valet. "I wouldn't dally if I were you, sir," he'd added.

Everyone in the house feared Lady Sarah when she was in one of her forceful moods, and Bartholomew had braced himself for a difficult interview; however, to his surprise, he saw that his mother had an unusually serene expression on her face.

"We have had a visitor today," she said.

"What, this time on a Sunday morning? Who was this uncivil person?"

"Mr. Darcy."

Bartholomew cleared his throat. "Ah. I don't think I need to ask which Mr. Darcy."

"You do not," said Mr. Bruton. "Your mother is speaking of Mr. Darcy of Pemberley."

"Ah," Bartholomew said again, uncertain what Mr. Darcy might have told his parents.

"Mr. Darcy came on something of a delicate mission," said Lady Sarah. "He is often stigmatised as proud, but once you become better acquainted with him, you find he is a warm, kind man. I have known him for a great many years, and I confess that I had a tendre for him in the days of my youth."

"What?" said Mr. Bruton.

"That was before I met you, my love. He was very handsome—he still is, I may say—and with a great air about him. However, he never looked in my direction; indeed, he never looked in anyone's direction after he met Elizabeth. Caroline Warren, Caroline Bingley as she was then, had set her heart on marrying him, although I think she cared more for his estate than for him as a person."

"Lady Warren?" said Bartholomew.

"Yes, Lady Warren. I mention it, because it explains something of what that wicked George Warren has been up to; he carries his stepmother's grudge further than she ever did, and hates all the Darcys."

They were coming to the nub of the matter, with mention of George Warren. "Mama," Bartholomew began.

"Let me finish. Mr. Darcy is cousin to Miss Eliza Collins, who came up to town with him and Elizabeth. They had been staying at Rosings. I had not known that the Darcys were back from abroad, but it seems they arrived late at Dover and posted straight on to Kent."

"Mama—"

"Don't interrupt your mother," said Mr. Bruton.

"Mr. Darcy came to talk to us about your marriage."

Bartholomew was growing warier by the moment. "You know that any marriage between me and Jane Grainger—"

"Is now out of the question," interrupted his father. "It is an astonishing fact that if one is out of London for even so short a period as twenty-four hours, some scandal will have broken while one is away. No sooner had the furore over your intemperate and foolish duel with Mr. Diggory died down than the news flew about town that Miss Grainger had eloped with her music master."

"Eloped with— I will be damned. No wonder she applied herself so diligently to her study of the pianoforte!"

"Bartholomew!"

"I beg pardon, Mama."

"Mr. Darcy came to talk to us about a marriage between you and his young cousin, that same Miss Eliza of whom we spoke a while ago. It is a match he approves of, and he believes that, in the circumstances, you have no choice but to make her your wife."

Circumstances? Just how much did they know about what had happened in Dover? His father's next words enlightened him.

"By whisking Miss Eliza off to Rosings, they seem to have spiked Warren's guns for the moment. Yet word will get out, rumours will spread, and so, for the sake of her good name and also, incidentally, for the sake of our good name, by which I mean the bank's, I propose that the notice of your engagement will appear in the *Gazette* as soon as may be."

Mr. Bruton finished this speech with a harrumph, and rattled the lid of the large silver coffeepot, which was on the table beside Lady Sarah. "This is quite cold," he said irritably.

"Then ring for some more," she said. "Bartholomew, Miss Eliza Collins is not the wife we would have chosen for you. However, the Darcy connection is not to be sneezed at, and of course she will be Montblaine's sister-in-law."

"I would remind you that Mr. Darcy is a valued client of the bank," said Mr. Bruton. "As were his father and his grandfather before him. I should not wish to offend such a man."

"Not the wife you would have chosen for me?" said Bartholomew impudently. "No, you'd have had me hitched to a wife who'd run off with her piano instructor as soon as my back was turned."

"You had better write to her father, to the bishop, today," said Mr. Bruton. "She is not of age, so you need his permission to marry her. And I think the less he knows about your and her journey to Dover, the better!"

"Write?" said Bartholomew. "I'll leave such distant courtesy to the marquis. I shall post up to Yorkshire this very day to ask the bishop for his consent!" And, he added under his breath as he left the drawing room, I shall take Eliza with me.

The ladies were at home. Mr. Bartholomew Bruton followed the footman up Lady Grandpoint's stairs and waited while he announced him.

His bow to Lady Grandpoint was mechanical, as was his handshake with Charlotte. His eyes were riveted on Eliza, who had been sitting at the window and now came dancing across the room, holding out her hands.

"Eliza!" said Lady Grandpoint.

"Ma'am, with your permission, I intend to abduct Miss Eliza."

"Abduct! What are you talking about?"

"I wish to escort her to Yorkshire, to her parents. I am on my way there to see the bishop."

"See the bishop! I know how everything is fixed up, and very havey-cavey it all is, too. I do not know for how long we can keep this from the ears of the marquis."

"He already knows it," said Charlotte primly. "I can have no secrets from the man who is to be my husband. He is of the opinion that the sooner my sister is married the better."

"Oh, I honour him for that," cried Eliza.

" 'Before you can get up to any further mischief' is what he said."

Eliza burst out laughing. "I do not know how I shall go on with such a brother," she said. "Ma'am, if I take Annie with me, may I go?"

"I suppose that if I said no, you would climb out of the window down a rope of knotted sheets and go just the same," said Lady Grandpoint waspishly. "Does Mr. Diggory go back to Yorkshire as well? To recuperate from his wounds?" This with a sharp look at Mr. Bruton.

"One wound only," he said. "I understand he chooses to stay in town, as does his sister."

"They say Lord Rosely is mad for Maria," Charlotte observed dispassionately. "And I expect Anthony will end up marrying Miss Chetwynd."

Eliza stared at her. "Miss Chetwynd? You can't be serious! Whatever put that idea into your head?"

"She was sitting with him when I called to ask how he did," said Mr. Bruton. "Reading to him out of some novel or other."

"She is not unlike Lady Diggory, now I come to think about it," said Eliza. She could see Anthony and Miss Chetwynd twenty years hence, Anthony stouter and developing a tendency to gout, and Miss Chetwynd just as brisk and efficient and hard-nosed as Lady Diggory was. "Do you know, they may suit very well."

Bartholomew took issue with her over that, as the coach rattled out of Aubrey Square. "It is beyond my understanding how any man could turn to Miss Chetwynd after he had been in love with you! Now tell me, dearest Eliza, how I shall get on with your father?"

Eliza looked at him. "He will be in awe of you. Because you are clever, and, yes, because you are rich. However, since he will shortly be father-in-law to a marquis, he will consider you an inferior son-in-law, so you need not be puffed up with pride!"

"Annie," said Bartholomew. "You may look out of the window, for I am going to kiss your mistress!"

Eliza's senses swam, until he reluctantly freed his lips from hers. She rested her head against his shoulder, then smiled up at him. "So it's to be a Yorkshire wife for you, Mr. Bruton. Who would have thought you'd end up marrying a mere provincial!"

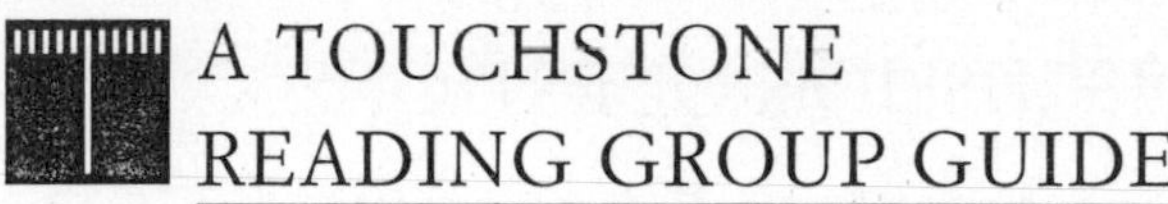

A TOUCHSTONE READING GROUP GUIDE

The Darcy Connection
By Elizabeth Aston

INTRODUCTION

In *The Darcy Connection,* we revisit *Pride and Prejudice*'s Mr. Collins–now a bishop–and his wife, Charlotte, whose two daughters have reached marriageable age. The elder, another Charlotte, is extraordinarily beautiful. Since the Collins inheritance from Longbourn is threatened, the family decides that Charlotte should make a brilliant marriage. With her Darcy connections, she can make the most of a London season and find herself a rich and powerful husband.

Their second daughter, Eliza, is not nearly so beautiful but has charm and a lively intelligence. Too like her godmother, Mrs. Darcy, is Mr. Collins's verdict. He is vexed with what he sees as willfulness, much as he did with Elizabeth Bennet.

Both sisters go to London, where Charlotte's beauty wins her numerous promising suitors, despite her lack of fortune or grand connections other than her Darcy cousins and her wealthy godmother, Lady Grandpoint. But Eliza's witty ways and inclination to interfere in what she considers an unsuitable marriage for her sister infuriate both her family and the suitor–until she herself meets her match and makes a better marriage than her parents could have dreamt of.

DISCUSSION QUESTIONS

1. What is Eliza Collins's first impression of Bartholomew Bruton? What is Bruton's first impression of Eliza? How do their initial "prejudices" turn to affection? Why do you think Bruton realizes his love for Eliza long before she can admit her feelings to herself?

2. Charlotte is like a "marble statue" (page 111), yet she reveals her passionate side when she falls for George Warren. What do you think of Charlotte's character? Is she a good match for Montblaine, the Marble Marquis? Why does Eliza object to the match between Charlotte and Montblaine?

3. What is the difference between Eliza and Anthony's secret engagement, deemed a "boy-and-girl attachment" (page 225), and Eliza's feelings for Bruton? Do you believe that Eliza could fall in and out of love so quickly?

4. Eliza's anonymous sketches of clerical life and London society are a big hit in the Leeds *Gazette* and *London Magazine*. Why is it so risky for Eliza to write these satires? Do you think it is worth the risk? Do you suppose that after her marriage to Bruton, she could possibly reveal herself as the author of the sketches? Why or why not?

5. *The Darcy Connection* features at least two formidable villains: the slick clergyman Mr. Pyke and the dark and dangerous George Warren. Discuss what makes them the villains in the story. Which character do you find more villainous, and why?

6. Eliza escapes Mr. Pyke's blackmail by asking him what is inside the black box he keeps at Bruton's bank. What do you suppose the mysterious black box contains?

7. In the end, how does the "Darcy connection" influence Eliza's social standing? How does it affect her love life? Do you think that such a connection could make or break a marriage in our century? If so, how?

8. Eliza teases her friend Maria for her "melodramatic way of speaking, culled from intensive reading of popular novels whose heroines were greatly admired by Maria" (page 18). Do you think readers are more or less influenced by novels today than they were in the era in which *The Darcy Connection* is set? Do you believe there is a great difference "between the marbled covers of a novel" and "real life," as Eliza asserts (page 23)? Explain your answer.

9. The word *provincial* appears frequently in the novel, from Mr. Bruton's thoughts on Eliza to Eliza's change of heart about marrying a squire. Do you think Bruton meant the term *provincial* as an insult? Eliza tells Bruton at the end, "Who would have thought you'd end up marrying a mere provincial!" (page 287). Is Eliza still a provincial? Why or why not?

10. If you have read Jane Austen's *Pride and Prejudice*, which of Aston's original characters remind you of the characters Austen created two hundred years ago? Which character from *Pride and Prejudice* were you most pleased to revisit in *The Darcy Connection*?

11. How does *The Darcy Connection* compare to other books by Elizabeth Aston?

ENHANCE YOUR BOOK CLUB

1. Eliza writes her satires anonymously, and her publishers know her as "Mrs. Palmer." If you were to write under a pen name, what would it be? Write down your imaginary pseudonym, and have your meeting's host pick each name out of a hat. Can your book club guess whose pen name is whose?

2. Bring a map of England to your book club meeting. Find all the places that Eliza visits on the map: Ripon, Derbyshire, London, and Dover. Also locate on a detailed map of London the areas mentioned in the book: Spitalfields, the Strand, and Covent Garden.

3. Research the history of Spitalfields, the market neighborhood where Eliza and Annie encounter merchants, pickpockets, and Bartholomew Bruton. Compare the novel's description of Spitalfields to what today's visitors see, hear, and buy. You can find pictures and shop descriptions at www.visitspitalfields.com.

AUTHOR QUESTIONS

Q: It is apparent that a great deal of research goes into your novels. What is your favorite source of information on the look, feel, and manners of nineteenth-century England?
A: I like to immerse myself in the literature of the period–novels, essays, letters, memoirs, poetry, even. I also like looking at paintings and art of the time and, of course, clothes and architecture and interiors.

Q: The dialogue in *The Darcy Connection* is sparkling and faithful to its historical setting. How do you re-create the speech patterns of this period? Do you ever find yourself speaking like a Darcy-era character when you're working on a novel?
A: The speech patterns come from reading the literature of the time. They aren't necessarily the same as those a contemporary novelist of that period would use–rather like writing dialects or foreign accents, it's more a matter of suggestion than word-for-word reconstruction.

Q: Comic moments abound in *The Darcy Connection,* from Maria Diggory's wild exaggerations to Charlotte and Eliza's hiding behind the same bush in Montblaine's garden. How do you balance comedy and romance?
A: I enjoy writing comedy, and because my novels are intended to entertain, I want the readers to laugh. And romance without comedy can be very turgid!

Q: "I wish I had been born a man," Eliza says in *The Darcy Connection* (page 79). What are the challenges and rewards of writing about female heroines of the nineteenth century?
A: This is a real problem. It is virtually impossible to look out at the world through the eyes of a nineteenth-century heroine when writing

in the twenty-first century. Women's rights, feminism, and the freedom of modern women, at least in Western democracies, to have an education and a career and to make their own decisions about their lives throw up the stark contrast to how it felt to be a woman in the very patriarchal society of early-nineteenth-century England. So one has to throw away the freedom of movement, the right to education, the cell phone and the car, and imagine oneself into a far narrower world, physically at least, but also emotionally and mentally.

Q: What is one of your favorite places to visit to get inspired to write a Darcy novel?
A: Bath is always a good place to go to remind myself of how Regency England looked. I used to live there and know it well, and it's a city that brings the whole period vividly to life.

Q: When did you first read *Pride and Prejudice*? What was your initial impression of the book? Has it grown in your esteem with further readings?
A: I read *Pride and Prejudice* when I was thirteen, having resisted it until then out of temper that I had been named after a woman in a novel! The more I read it, and I couldn't count the number of times I have read it, the more I am awed by how profound and brilliant a novel it is. I consider it one of the greatest works of world literature.

Q: How would you describe your writing process? Has your level of research and preparation changed as you write more books?
A: I like to plunge into a book, with the main characters and an outline plot in mind, and work very fast and furiously on the first draft. I've done so much research for these books that I feel quite at ease with some aspects, although I always need to do more for each individual book. Then, after the first stage, I research all the points that I then know I need to find out about.

Q: In the novel, Eliza Collins recalls that a governess taught her "that manners smoothed away all difficulties, that knowing how

to behave in any situation was essential" (page 223). How do you navigate manners and morals in your novels? What do you think about these social rules or norms?

A: Manners and morals are two of the hardest things to get right. In some ways I'm lucky, because my parents' lives still had some of the mores of English society of the kind I write about, so I grew up with that. And the much more defined moral structure of that time makes life far easier for a writer than does contemporary, post-modern, nonjudgmental, do-what-you-like society: for example, no divorce, good manners, and consideration for others rather than the much more self-centered attitudes of modern times, a sense of duty, and above all, a complete and absolute sense of "This is right and this is wrong"–at least for one's heroines.

Q: How do you compare your situation as a twenty-first-century novelist with that of a Regency novelist like Jane Austen? What do you see as the greatest challenge female writers faced in the era that you portray in your novels?

A: To be taken seriously as a writer was the hardest thing for a woman novelist of that time. The attitude of society, and of men who were the publishers and the critics and the opinion formers, was so often lofty and patronising. We modern writers have it easy in comparison, although of course there is still a tendency for men to be considered more "important" and significant as writers.

Q: Your fans must be happy to catch up with the Darcy daughters in *The Darcy Connection,* especially Camilla Wytton. Can your readers also expect to revisit Eliza and Bruton in your future work?

A: I hope so! I like to keep up with whatever my characters are up to.